T0285318

.

THE NIGHT FIELD

DONNA GLEE WILLIAMS

THE NIGHT FIELD

Jo Fletcher
BOOKS

First published in Great Britain in 2023 by

Jo Fletcher
BOOKS

Jo Fletcher Books
an imprint of
Quercus Editions Ltd
Carmelite House
50 Victoria Embankment
London EC4Y 0DZ

An Hachette UK company

A CIP catalogue record for this book is available
from the British Library

HB ISBN 978 1 52942 267 2
TPB ISBN 978 1 52942 268 9
Ebook ISBN 978 1 52942 271 9

10 9 8 7 6 5 4 3 2 1

Typeset by CC Book Production
Printed and bound in Great Britain by Clays Ltd, Elcograf S.p.A

Papers used by Jo Fletcher Books are from well-managed forests
and other responsible sources.

For the trees.

THE FARM

Pyn-Poi

Twin posts straddle the broad path. A lintel-beam hangs between them, marked with odd faded symbols that give off the chilly feel of power. A ghost-door? Some kind of gateway?

Not a gateway – nothing behind the posts, nothing on either side. No walls, no fence, nothing for a gate to enter or exit. Nothing but more empty land, flatter than any natural thing.

The boot-men hustle me between the posts and right then the light fades from the sky. Is it only that we crossed over just as the sun went down? I do not think so. There is something dark here, darker than simple night.

I walk on, though. What choice do I have, with my wrists pinioned like a water-hen for the slaughter? These four men that box me in are older than me, bigger than me, and stronger. They have their sticks, and they relish power and pain as if they have never dipped their hands into another's Flow.

So I walk.

It gets darker still, until I can make out a cluster of lights ahead of us. I hear in the men's voices that we are near the end of the journey. I catch the word that means 'dinner'. Wherever we are going, we will be there soon.

Somewhere nearby a fang-foe howls. Others join in. We are being tracked by a hunting pack, and my knife is gone. There is no friendly trunk or vine to climb, no stick to swing, no rock to throw. Those puny rods that hang from the boot-men's belts: They burned like lightning when they landed on my naked legs, but they would be nothing against a pack of hunters – like stalks of grass whipping their fur. And would those men even try to protect me, or would they just throw me to the beasts so that they could get away?

Do not die, Pyn-Poi. Refuse to die in this place. Not until you have finished. Not until it is done.

The rough fabric of this dress they put on me stirs in a puff of night wind that brings me a hint of a smell I recognise: death without decay. My hand twitches up as if to pull my wrap over my nose, but my wrists are bound and my wrap is gone. The feathers are gone. Everything is gone.

I am far, far from the Real and there are no trees here.

The Guard

'Took your time, didn't you?' The Administrator doesn't look up from his desk.

'The men walked steady, sir, and we took no rests, except for lunch. It's a long road—'

'I know exactly how long the road is.' He slaps the pen down and snaps his logbook shut. 'You should have left earlier. New contractees have to be delivered well before the dogs' change-over. The night-hounds'll barely have a chance to give her a good sniff before the day-hounds get back to the kennels. The children like to watch, you know – they don't get much entertainment out here – and we don't want the little ones staying up past their bedtimes, do we?'

'No, sir. Wouldn't want that.' Never argue with an Administrator.

'Well, then, skip the girl over to the kennels double-quick and hand her over. Then get yourself and your men something to eat. Unless you want to stay and watch the fun, of course. You know where the kitchen is?'

'Yes, sir. Been to the Farm before.'

'Of course you have. Well, then. Cook'll take care of you, show you where to sleep. Here's your receipt for the delivery.'

'Thank you, sir. I'll say goodnight to you now, and sorry again about the late hour.'

'Just try leaving before noon next time.'

The Child

At last!

We waited all afternoon for the sounds of the day-hounds baying around the road and, finally, there they were – four town Guards and a funny-looking girl trailing up to the Administration compound. The dogs pushed in tight around them, sometimes running in close enough for one of the men to take a swat at them with his beater. Oooh, the Managers would be mad if they saw that. Nobody gets to hit the dogs but them.

We all ran to get a good place at the fence. Some of the grownups were strolling over, too, pretending this wasn't the most exciting thing to happen in weeks. The Kennel-Managers had already set up some torches – the dogs don't need 'em; they're for us, so we can see. Lain was already rolling the barrel out into the middle of the dog-yard when we got there. I let little Navir squeeze in front of me.

After a long time – they have to check in with the Administrator first, of course – the town Guards brought the new girl up to the fence, snapped her cuffs off, and handed her over to the Kennel-Managers. You could tell she didn't know anything. She stood there looking around, bare legs showing under her clean new burlap work-dress. Just think: she had no idea what was about to happen. That made me shiver a little.

Manager Lain walked the girl into the dog-yard – it was funny to see how she prissed around, trying not to step on the piles of poo in the flickering light. Then the night-hounds caught her scent and things got real noisy. You could hear them throwing themselves against the big old doors of the kennel, crazy to get at this new smell on their land, and snapping at each other when they couldn't. Navir pressed his fingers in his ears and looked up at me like he might cry, but I shouted down at him, pointing: 'Watch now! This will be good.'

Manager Lain pushed the girl down on her knees and yelled at her to get inside the barrel. She didn't go at first, so he kicked her some to make her crawl in through the little hatch. She fit inside easy, no taller than Ritoln. That meant the barrel would roll better when the dogs came out. Sometimes, with the big ones, they have to cram them in hard just to get the hatch to close. Those don't roll around so well. Too heavy. Not as good a show.

While Manager Lain locked the lid down and gave it a tug to check the latch, I watched the shadow of the girl through the old chewed-up wooden slats that leave just enough room for the dogs to push their noses in, but not actually get at the person inside. That would be a waste. Waste is bad. Waste cuts into profits. Letting the dogs tear up a fresh, new tractee would be bad. (But it would be exciting.)

The girl crouched in there on her knees and elbows, rump in the air like a cat. She turned her head this way and that, rubbing at her wrists, shaking her hands every now and then, like she was trying to shake something off her fingertips. Listening, I bet – hearing all that growling and yelping. She twisted around to face the racket of the dogs behind the shuddering wooden doors. This made the barrel roll and toppled her onto her side. Everyone laughed. She scrambled to get onto her knees again, to balance her rocking cage.

Manager Lain stepped out of the dog-yard and slid the bolt of the gate closed behind him. He reached over and ruffled my hair. 'Ready?' he asked and we all shouted 'Yes!'

He nodded at Manager Rethim to tug on the rope. The kennel doors slid aside. A snarling riot of dogs poured into the yard, drowning the girl's scream under their barking. They closed in on the barrel, rolling it from side to side, trying to get at her, pushing their snouts in, gnawing furiously at the old wood. The girl tumbled around like a doll as the rush of dogs shoved the barrel one way and then another. Some of them surged onto the top to dig at her from above, then fell into the rest when the barrel rolled under them.

Navir's hands dropped away from his ears and he was clapping and shouting with the others. I looked up at Manager Lain and he slapped me on the back.

Manager Lain gave us a great show, but finally shouted, 'Enough.' The other Kennel-Managers beat back the hounds with their dog-lashers. It's always over too soon.

Now we had to wait while the night-hounds were herded out to do their jobs. They keep us safe at night, patrolling for any tractees stupid enough to leave their dormitories after dark. But soon, the show would start again. The day-hounds would be coming in for their dinners and they had to learn the new meat's scent, too – even when the sun was up, tractees couldn't be trusted not to wander away from their assigned fields.

But it would be a while yet before they all got in from the Tracts. 'Manager Lain, can we play with her?' I asked. 'Just until the dogs get here?'

'Sure,' he said. 'Why not? Just go along in there and roll her around for a while, stick your own little snouts between the slats and get a whiff of her, why not? Rub yourselves all over that barrel and when the day-hounds get in they'll learn your smell along with hers so that, when we send them hunting, they'll come find YOU.' Navir squealed as Manager Lain lifted him up as if to throw him over the fence into the dog-yard. We all giggled.

After the day-hounds had had their sniff, too, and been put away for the night, Manager Lain let the girl out of the barrel. It was funny to watch her stagger around like she was drunk, trying to get her feet under her after being rolled around for so long. She wasn't so prissy about the dog-piles now, was she?

Supervisor Jagath took her off Lain's hands, with Manager Goban – she's Dekar and Ludi's mother. We tagged along, too, the younger kids circling like a pack of puppies just learning their job, daring each other closer, running in and yapping questions at the girl, then running away again. She didn't even look up. 'What'd you do?' they wanted to know. 'How long is your contract?' 'You kill somebody?' 'This your first time?' Silly question – anybody with eyes could see it was the girl's first time: no mark on her cheek.

The Managers hauled her up the steps to the Barber's porch and dropped her into the big chair that's bolted to the floorboards, then stepped back to let Sakky do his work. The girl was so little and limp that nobody even bothered to strap her in. Manager Goban settled on the steps for a smoke. The other kids and I watched from below, the light from Sakky's brazier making weird upward shadows on everyone's faces. I saw Sakky pick up the long straight razor he uses to shave the tractees so they don't get lice. He turned to the girl and suddenly she went crazy – up out of the chair with something in her hand, maybe the razor, squealing like a goat on slaughter-day.

In a blink, Supervisor Jagath was on her from behind – she's fast for someone so big – her elbow around the girl's neck.

6

Manager Kai had her wrist, roaring, 'Drop it! Drop it!' But the girl wouldn't stop fighting, kicking out at Kai, clawing behind her for Jagath's eyes. I could feel the other children press close around me. This wasn't supposed to happen.

Manager Goban scrambled up the steps, her dog-lasher in her hands, and cracked the girl on the side of her head, hard.

It didn't knock her out, not quite, but it knocked the fight out of her for a minute, long enough for Supervisor Jagath to mash her back down into the barber-chair. Sakky snatched up a couple of straps from the shelf behind the chair and threw them to each of the Managers. Between them, they had the girl down tight in seconds, with the butt of a dog-lasher between her teeth and Supervisor Jagath forcing it back against the top of the barber-chair so that she couldn't move her head while Sakky hacked off her braid and dry-shaved her bald as an egg. Jagath was real mad.

The girl never stopped fighting, though, straining and jerking against the big leather straps and making funny choking, whining sounds against the stick in her mouth. I've never seen anybody get so crazy about being shaved. It's for their own good, they should understand that – not just the lice, you know, but also so they don't have to waste work-time keeping their hair tidy on the Farm.

Sakky cuts my hair. It doesn't hurt at all.

After the shaving was done, Supervisor Jagath kept hold of the girl's head while Sakky pulled the little iron wand out of the brazier, holding it with a leather pad. I started up the steps, but Supervisor Jagath stopped me. 'Sorry,' she said. 'I know I promised, but this one's so wild, we'd better let Sakky handle it. You can do the next one.'

I was disappointed, but I understood. Every tractee's half-moon needs to be crisp and clear so that when the contract is over the circle can be neatly closed with the freedom brand. You have to put it on just right, not sloppy. If someone is bucking or jerking around too much, the mark can get smudged. I probably could have held it steady, but . . .

So Supervisor Jagath held the head and Sakky put the mark on, that little crescent no bigger around than a fat man's thumb, right below the corner of the mouth, the mark that tells all the world that this person's time and life and work belong to the System until the System says otherwise.

And after all that fuss about the haircut, the girl barely squeaked when the glowing metal touched her skin.

Goban

Shooing the kids away – well past their bedtime – we lugged the new tractee down off the porch, dead weight, the tops of her feet dragging the ground, bouncing down one step after another. Jagath's mouth was locked tight, her chin scratched, her eyes narrowed and her big worm eyebrows pulled down in a way that made me keep my mouth shut. This baby bite of fresh meat was going to regret taking a swipe at Guard Mama. Had the little nit been thinking that she could tell the Barber what style to cut her pretty hair? Well, that fat braid of hers belonged to Sakky now, his for selling to the wig-makers back in town, and she'd made Jagath mad on her very first night on the Farm. Big mistake.

Guard Mama snarled, 'Throw some dip on that garbage and dump it in Tract Eleven,' before she stalked off toward the women's houses. We pulled the girl along for a while, then Kai stopped short and growled, 'I am damned well not going to carry this little bitch all the way to Eleven.'

We dropped her, face-first, into the dirt. She lay there moaning, clutching her shaven head. I could see in the bright starlight that Sakky hadn't been any too careful with her after she caused all that trouble; streaks of dark blood dribbled from a handful of razor cuts and smeared her arms and face as she pawed at her scalp.

Kai looked at me, shaking her head – I could tell she was going to have a big bruise on her cheekbone from the scuffle – took careful aim, and planted her boot-toe in the girl's side, right above her hip bone. Nothing too hard, just enough to get her attention. She rolled up into a ball, gasping for breath. Kai grabbed the neck of the work-dress, hauled the girl up onto her knees, and bent down, close to her ear. 'Now you walk,' she said in that soft voice of hers that can scare sun-drunk thugs twice her size back into the picking line. 'You walk.'

The girl walked, arms clenched around her head as if someone were beating her. The night-hounds circled us, baying.

Pyn-Poi

I do not die.

I come to myself again in the dark, with fang-foes circling and two of the boot-women shoving me and pointing at a pale square, like a big tray, on the ground. Smooth-worked slices of wood long dead and lost here in this treeless place. It takes me a long, confused moment to understand: the women want me to stand on the tray. I bend to take off my sandals – respect for the dead – but a hard kick knocks me sprawling onto the ancient wood. My fingers find the grain, stroke it, but do not find even the memory of life there.

The boot-woman with the snake-whisper voice strips the rough dress off me. As she yanks it up over my head, I feel my skull naked and cold in the night air. I finger the hacked stubble. Not a nightmare – the amputation was real. But my tears have gone somewhere else, somewhere very far away. What is there to do now? I get up and let them do their things to me.

And what they do is this: the other one, not the one with the snake-voice, takes the lid off a big bucket, dips a ladle in, and brings out a mounded scoop of something pale and yellowish under the stars. Without warning, she throws it in my face.

I double over coughing, pawing at my face. My eyes burn like red coals in their sockets – I try to shield them while the boot-women throw more of the evil powder and rub it all over me, even in the places strangers should not touch.

But I do not fight them. Not because of their sticks. Not because of the howling things that watch from the shadows. And not, I think, because of the amputation. I stand there and bear their touch because of this: When I gasp at that first face-full of the evil stuff, I smell it and I recognise it and I hate it with the hate you can only feel toward killers of your close kin: Your sister. Your grandmother. Your trees.

The Stink. I breathe in that foulness like a flower, although it makes me choke. The choking does not matter. None of it matters, not the fire in my eyes, or the hard hands on my body or the kicks or the clubs. Not these crazy boot-people who've wandered so far from their Other bodies that they can whoop with joy at another's shaming. Not the fang-foes growling in the dark. Not – and my breath catches in my throat at this – the amputation. Not even that.

None of it matters. The Mothers' feathers are safe with Bazleti, and I . . . I am in the right place.

Finally, I am where I need to be.

The Trees

'I cannot breathe. The air will not come in.'

'I know. It is hard.'

'My leaves are burning. There are no flames, but they burn.'

'And the flying ones, where are they? Who will carry our tomorrow if the flying ones are gone? How will there be fruit without them? How will there be seedlings without fruit? And how can we die without seedlings to come after?'

'Then do not die. We have responsibilities. We must stay alive. Stay alive while she does her work.'

THE REAL

Pyn-Poi

I pound down the path, my lead shrinking with every step. Marak would never stoop to a full-out sprint, but my legs are much shorter and, even without running, she is catching up.

Take cover; maybe she will storm past.

I hook a skinny sapling and skid round it, my palm slipping easy over its smooth young skin, then jump over the muddy runnel beside the trail – leave no footprint! – and land light on the moss. Just like Sook-Sook taught me to do if ever something big and fierce chases me. He will be proud of me when I tell him – if I can find him before Marak finds me.

I hear her shouts, muffled by the trunks and vines, but getting louder – nearer, or maybe just more furious. 'NOW, Pyn-Poi. Or else . . .'

Do not listen. There is always an 'or else'. Just find Sook-Sook. He will protect you. Nothing can hurt you if—

I hunker low, down into the shadows where the branches on the bushes are sparser and there is more room to worm my way toward the mumbling stream. Let me through, child-trees, trees-to-be. Quietly, quietly. Let your little sister through.

A baby green-band hisses a tiny hiss and wiggles off ahead of me, to give me a lesson in how this is done. Flow like the Durma, around this, around that. Do not push, do not fight. Only Flow.

Just then, Marak's sandals thwack clear and loud behind me. She has come around the curve. I drop like a fallen branch. The leaves above me shiver. Shield me, leaves. Shield me, shadows. Hide me, little trees-to-be.

I press my face into the dirt, slow-breathing so my mother will not hear.

And, by some kindness of the trees, she does not. Her footsteps, then her shouts, fade away. I am free.

I huddle under the leaves until the path is silent again. A drop of tree-sweat plinks onto my neck. I wait for ten more breaths and then ten more, just to be sure. Another ten. Another. Then, careful as a peeping ring-tail, I raise my head.

On a thin branch right under my nose, a green wriggler puffs his chest at me, pink as a flower. Three lace-wings chase each other in a beam of morning sun angling in from the break in the foliage along the stream. It is not a very big stream, just one of the many daughters of the Durma that wriggle between the trees, but wide enough to let some sunlight in.

I am not supposed to be anywhere near its banks, not by myself. There will be an 'or else' for that, too, when Marak finds out. But I am not a baby. I know how to take care. I know not to go into the water, not any part of me, not a tiny toe, unless the Flow is stained brown by the rotting leaves of ground-tea, like at our bathing place. I can spot the eyes of a half-sunk big-jaws as well as any grownup, and I can climb trees better than everyone except Sook-Sook. Nothing will catch me, ever.

But which way did Sook-Sook go, upstream or down?

I try to feel for him, like sometimes in the dark I can sense where he is in our house-tree: up in the high branches with Marak in their big hammock or down below by the banked embers of the cook-fire. Today I cannot feel him, not a trace, not anywhere. The Real is just too big.

Think, Pyn-Poi, think. He is starting a bridge today. Where do the People need a new bridge?

Not back by the village, surely – between the house-trees, bridges of all sizes leap across the branching streams like bouncing prong-horns, some down near the water, some way up in the treetops. Sook-Sook has to prune them sometimes, or weave new stems in to grow them stronger, but we do not need a brand-new one there.

So. Away from the village, then. I will have to work my way upstream, up toward the base of the Wall, where the tumbled boulders whip the water into an angry froth.

The footing along the banks that way is rougher than near home. Spray from the flashing water makes moss and green-slick cover everything like a thick, glossy pelt. Before starting across the slippery rocks, I take off my sandals. Sook-Sook always tells me to let my toes grab like a ring-tail's, to let my feet fit the shape I am stepping on. My father never wears sandals at all, not even when we climb the Wall each year. His feet are hard as old stone-wood. If you try to tickle them, he does not even feel it.

Losing my sandals today would get me even more 'or else'. I tie their strings together, flip them over my shoulder, and set off.

Such a relief, poking along all on my own, nobody bossing my every move and telling me things I already know: watch your step. Hold on tight. Tap on that stone before you put your foot there; let the biters know you are coming. Do not put your hand in that crevice; you never know who is at home.

Stick your hand in a hole? Who would *do* that?

It is delicious, being away from people like this, able to concentrate for once, able to listen to the quiet. Behind the rush of the water, you can almost hear the trees thinking, watching me, taking my measure. They are making up their minds about me. I am Sook-

Sook's daughter, of course, and that counts for something. But the trees will have to decide if I get to touch them like my father does.

Being out here with the trees – *so* much better than staying home with Marak and learning whatever I was supposed to learn – yams, I think it was. Something about yams. This, walking with the trees, is fun, every bit of it. Yams are not.

Even more fun when I pull myself up over a tilted table of rock and spot my father's gleaming back. Found you!

Sook-Sook is squatting by some kind of cane frame laid out on a little patch of flat sand. Aiu is with him, sitting on his haunches, alert and watchful while Sook-Sook's attention is occupied. Aiu sees me right away; I wave for him to keep still. Aiu and I have an understanding.

My father is peering at something, a leaf, rubbing it between his fingers. His eyes pinch together over his nose in that look he gets when he worries, or does not understand some tree's new ailment. I could help with that. I am good at chasing his worries away; that is one of my best ways of helping him, he says.

Sook-Sook needs my help a lot, not just with worries. Sometimes to hold the twine for him while he ties up branches so they can rub each other and grow together into the strong ladders and platforms of our house-trees. Not enough hands, he always says – lucky thing I have a daughter. Sometimes I press grafts together for him while he wraps and ties them. I am also pretty good at carrying the shovel and the bag of float-flower seeds when we go to bargain with the leaf-cutters about leaving our fruit-trees alone. Other times, I help him pry up old roots and then keep them out of his way by sitting on the lever-stick while he props them with stones underneath. Those roots, he promises, will turn into the smooth flat steps we follow across the ups and downs of our land. I have ridden on his shoulders up into the rustling green ceiling of the Real more times than I can count, and I earned my very first blisters perched with him up in those high branches, hacking away at new growth that threatened to shade out an important blood-nut tree. Then we came back down again and planted the pruned branches to grow up into another pen for Aunt Saggi's water-hens. So I am not new at helping.

I almost call out to him, but maybe it would be more fun to slip up behind – quiet, quiet! – and startle him. Pay him back for the scary story he told last night, 'The Cutter of Hair and Her Sharp, Sharp Blade'. That was not a good bedtime story. I will show him. I will surprise him, make him jump, and afterward the smile will come and the worried eyebrows will go when he realises it was just me, that I escaped Marak after all. He will be so happy. But first I will make him jump. I can move as quiet as a hunter-cat when I set my mind to it.

But I do not have to use my sneaking skills this time. Not at all. The rumble and splash of the water covers the sounds of my feet scuffling down the rock behind him and then galloping across the mucky sand. Aiu looks up at me. His tail lifts to wag and that is when I pounce – jump straight onto Sook-Sook's back and throw my arms around his bent neck.

I should have said something, maybe, shouted 'SOOK-SOOK!' in one ear and made him jump that way, not by falling on him like a hugging-snake dropping from a tree. That was a mistake.

He shoots to his feet, his knife flashing out, spinning under me so fast that I go flying across the sand and into the water. He drops his blade and, quicker than a wing-flap, he has me by my braid and out of the water before I have time to scream. Before my scalp tears away from my skull. Before the bone-cleaners even know that I have fallen in.

He whips off my dripping wrap, checks me all over for bites and suckers, then gathers me up and lets me cry into his warm, salty neck.

After the tears, though, the scolding:

'What are you doing here . . .?'

'Were you not supposed to . . .?'

'What were you thinking?'

'You are not allowed to . . .'

'You could have been . . .'

'Your mother will . . .'

'Never do that again. Never. Never.'

'Never,' I promise. 'But can I stay? Please? It is just' – I sniffle back the tears in my nose – 'that I have never planted a bridge before, and you do not do it that often. I could not miss it. Marak does not understand. She just wants me to—'

He lays his finger across my lips. 'Keep your respect, little sprout. Marak has a lot on her mind. Important things. Hard and complicated things, and someday, you will—'

'But Sook-Sook, I do not *want* to. I do not want to learn all about planting the yams and balancing the sister-plants and moon-shapes and Permissions and ceremonies—'

'Close your mouth. Who are you? *My* daughter knows better than to speak to her father about women's things.'

I hang my head. Of course I know.

'Do not talk to men about . . .'

'Do what your mother tells you.'

'When you grow up, you will need to . . .'

I know. I have heard it all so often that Sook-Sook could have saved his breath and let me scold myself.

But this is not the time to argue. 'I am sorry,' I whisper. I have to push pretty hard to get the words out.

My eyes crawl across the brown river-sand to Sook-Sook's broad splayed toes, over the bright shell-bead strands that wrap his ankles, up his tree-trunk legs, across the green patterned wrap Marak wove for him last time we were up in rain-quarters, and finally along the scars on his chest. Scars from scraping against rough bark and jagged branches. Scars from a life with trees. Finally, I look him in the eye.

His face is serious, no smile anywhere, but I keep looking and looking until finally, finally, there it is: that first little lip-twitch, that eye-crinkle that tells me I have gotten my way. I can stay. Aiu butts my hand and I scratch his ears. It is going to be a good day.

I walked our tree-bridges all my life, flapping my sandals across the grown-together foot-smoothed bark. I never feared falling into the swirling water below because those great entwined arms of wood along each side – they shield walkers from the edge. The bridges were just a fact of life to me, those high swoops of living wood that weave the clans of the People together across the many-fingered rivers at the base of the Wall, as customary as the ladders and platforms and railings and thatches of our house-trees – invisible, because so well known. I never even thought to ask why the trees gave us the great gift of crossing rivers. I never thought to ask the why of *any* of it. I was very young and things were just . . . as they were. The Real was the Real. Who could imagine anything else, any other way of being?

That day, I did not know I was being taught; I thought Sook-Sook and I were just sneaking away from my mother to play beside the river. I had my father all to myself, that was what mattered: singing story-songs with him while we wrestled bundles of bark and fibre through the tangled thickets along the bank and then rigged them into the big awkward contraption that would, very slowly, invite our bridge.

After a morning of lashing together supports, propping them up, and then connecting them with a long gutter of bark, Sook-Sook called me over to him. 'See here,' he said, laying the slender, ropy dangle of a forever-tree across my palm. I tugged hard on it, making the green above us shiver and dance. A peck-bird flapped away, protesting shrilly. Drips of tree-sweat showered down on my upturned face. I laughed, but my father showed me his serious eyes and said that the dangles on the tree were not playthings. They were its air-roots, living, like my fingers, and breathing, like my lungs. 'We handle them gently, Pyn-Poi.' He stroked the smooth woody cord as if to comfort it, as if I might have hurt it. 'Gently. This one needs a little cradle to carry it across the water. What shape cradle do you think this long, skinny fellow will need?'

'A long, skinny one!' I said, delighted because now I knew what it was for, that long hollow tube of green-tree bark we had split so evenly and anchored across the sloping top edge of our cane structure. I watched my father's careful hands drape the forever-tree dangle so that it ran like water down the bark chute that carried it out toward a giant boulder in the middle of the stream. 'It does not reach!' I thought all the work we had done that morning, all that tying and propping to get the bark trough in place, had gone for nothing.

'Ah, but it will reach, little sprout. Sprouts grow.' He brushed away a nibbler that was whizzing around my head. 'You will see; every day, a bit longer, a bit closer, and soon it will touch the rock. Then we will guide it toward the pocket of dirt you see there caught in that cleft, and it will take root and grab on like a strong fist.'

'But how long will it take?'

'This air-root will kiss stone before another moon comes and goes, I think. Everything grows fast this time of year. That is why we start training right after the rains. And if we do our work well, our baby bridge should have solid roots down by the next Climb.'

The next Climb. An eternity. My face must have fallen, because Sook-Sook laughed and said, 'Training trees is not hurry-work, little twig. You will not walk on this bridge we are starting until you are a grown woman. Then your children will walk on it, too, and your grandchildren and their children after them, all the way down to the sunset of the Real.'

'For true? Or is this a fire-story?'

'For true. You know that big bridge over the Durma? The one we cross on the way to Jer Rugni? They say that bridge was begun over five hundred years ago by people who had big eyes for the future, just like you and me.'

'Our bridge will be like that?'

'Someday. If we do our work well and the trees agree.' He showed me how to gather several dangles into the chute so they could cross the river together and not be lonely.

'Five hundred years, Sook-Sook? We will be Ancestors by then, will we not?'

He held my hands in his to help my fingers knot the reed-weed around the bark tube. 'Yes, Pyn-Poi; in five hundred years you and I will be Ancestors and our kin will cross this bridge when they bring flowers to sing our names at the foot of the Wall. Forever-trees are not like us; their Ancestors do not go to the Plains above. They stay here and bridge yesterday to tomorrow, sending out new stalks and stems from the old, living on living. Living wood never rots or weakens. It does not let go, even when the rains come and try to wash away the Real. That is why we take care not to break or bruise our trees; their health keeps the People whole. When we work with them, what we build is forever. Like them.'

I tucked my father's words away inside me. I never lost them, though I lost much.

The Trees

'The little one is rude. Rude and flighty. Stubborn, too. Will not learn. And she cannot keep still. Up and down, back and forth, all the time. I do not like her at all.' Leaves rustled as a family of ring-tails swarmed through the thick canopy.

'She is young. He was young, too, yesterday. Look at him now.'

'They grow up so quickly.'

'I will miss him when he is gone.'

'She has that nice laugh, though, like waters tumbling over roots. And I think she has big ears for us.'

'But will she ever be ready?'

'She has to be.'

Pyn-Poi

Claw fingers dug into the back of my neck. She had me. 'No,' Marak hissed. 'Today of all days you will *not* run off!'

Today of all days?

She shifted her grip to my shoulder – ow! – and dragged me back along the path toward our house-tree. 'You know perfectly well that Edo and her people are making River Crossing today' – I had forgotten all about that – 'and by tonight the place will be swarming with hungry outclan mouths to feed.'

I shook off her hand and went along, resigned to a spoiled day. 'Why can they not bring their own food?'

'Because we are their hosts, daughter. Because they are our *guests*.' She said this with the flat heavy voice she always uses to tell me something she thinks I should already know.

'But—'

'And because Dohmathi's girl told her mother that she is ready for a husband, and we must show a good hospitality so that Edo will offer—'

'But Biltha is not even a cousin! Why is her husband-getting our problem?'

Marak sighed, one of her loud why-is-my-daughter-so-disappointing sighs. 'Because, Pyn-Poi, Biltha is part of our clan. What is good for the clan is good for the kin, and what is good for the kin, is good for the family, and—'

'I know, I know: what is good for the family is good for the one,' I recited in my best yes-Marak voice. But privately, I wondered if maybe things flowed the other way as well. Is what is good for the one not also good for the family, the kin, the clan, and the People?

'Now make yourself useful, daughter. Scramble up to the top branches there and bring me down some fly-fern to go with supper. And this time do not stuff your bag with old stringy ones. What have I told you about fly-ferns?'

'Not longer than the palm of my hand,' I repeated like a trained parrot. 'Do not pick the ones longer than the palm of my hand.'

'That is right. And your palm does not reach to your elbow.' Marak pulled my arms through the straps of the carry-sack as if I were a string doll, and settled it onto my back with a sharp tug that almost overbalanced me. 'Now go.'

Marak

And, for once, my daughter, do what you are told without flitting off like a crack-wing, day-dreaming and trailing after that father of yours, talking to the trees.

Pyn-Poi

Away from the village, I had my father's full attention. Even now that I was too big to ride on his back, he always climbed close behind me so that we could talk, so that I could ask him all the questions that no one had the time for back at home.

'Sook-Sook, when the stew starts to boil, where do the bubbles come from? How do they get into the pot?'

'Gai-Gai puts them there when you are off playing with Aiu. You have to keep an eye on that grandmother of yours, twiglet. She has mysteries and powers. Watch your foot, now – that vine is rotten.'

I corrected my stance, fists tight around the branch above me. 'But why, Sook-Sook? Why *bubbles*?'

'Oh, because they make the soup jump and wiggle so it does not burn so easily and she does not have to stand there in the smoke stirring it all the time. But the bubbles tickle, so the soup keeps spitting them out. Not like some people I know who *love* to be tickled.'

'Noooooo, Sook-Sook,' I squealed, kicking his hand away as he reached up for my foot. 'I can climb so high you will never catch me.' And I did.

That same year that we planted my first bridge – still a good year, long before the Stink came – the song of the storm-frogs told Marak early that it was time for the People to climb up to rain-quarters. 'Too soon, too soon,' some said, but Marak trusted the frogs and reminded the other kins that the rains were coming earlier each year now, earlier and heavier, too. Some listened to her, some lingered, but our own kin were packed and ready to go when the time came, my mother and her sisters and all the husbands and children, along with enough food to last us until the Real was dry again.

We woke up to a huge breakfast – fresh fish and fruit we would not taste again until after the rains were done – and then slipped our arms into our carry-baskets. My brother Aando helped me get the strap across my forehead just right. 'Helps to lean into the weight as you climb,' he said. I knew that. I was little, but I was not a baby. I had been a baby the year before and had not carried a load, but this year I was big. Strong, too, Sook-Sook always said, from helping him work with the trees – the bridges and the house-trees and the weir-frames and the stair-step paths and benches along the Durma, all of it. But to tell the truth, that year my pack-basket was still very little, smaller even than Gai-Gai's.

We climbed all day, singing goodbye to the old year's cook-fires and gardens and thatches and fish-weirs below us; we would make them new and fresh after the floods swept everything clean. We kept our steps lively by sipping go-strong tea and picking rain-fruit along the steep root stairway that zigged and zagged up the lower face of the Wall – the work of tree-people like my father, but long ago.

Other kins were climbing, too. We heard them singing and laughing around us, weaving their own way up to where they could be safe when the rains came and brought the swollen rivers crashing through our lands. Sometimes, our path crossed theirs and we rested a while with them, all perched there together like crack-wings, looking out through the thinning treetops onto the Real below us. Then we went on.

As the sun slid down toward setting, we began to pass other kins' rain-quarters, some already full of bustle, most still empty and naked, waiting for their people to come up and re-thatch the elegant arches of the storm-trees that stood proud above their nooks and small terraces. Neighbours from our village down in the Real called out friendly greetings as we went by. Later, after the first days of downpour, when things settled down a bit, we would visit back and forth between the rain-quarters, and I would get to hear stories I had never heard, stories from other kins and clans.

But right now, I was tired. My feet were sore, my neck and shoulders hurt from the pack, and my skin was chafed where the straps rubbed me. When I was a baby last year, if I got tired, my father let me perch on top of his pack-basket and carried me until I wanted to walk again. This year, nobody carried me.

We were all tired by the time we reached our little terrace on the Wall, our home until the rivers dropped back to normal. I wanted to drop into my hammock, but Marak said nobody's hammock would be hung until we brought in some dropped wood for the cook-fire.

So, tired and cranky, I went off with my cousins Khaveny and Paji to gather kindling. It was harder to find up here than down below, though it was also drier and burned better. 'And no falling off the Wall,' Marak yelled after us. 'The birds have better things to do.' She turned to chivvy my older cousins into sweeping away last year's thatch, fallen to pieces under our ancient storm-tree. Tomorrow we would start on the new thatching. Even though the stone-flagged terrace angled down and out to tilt the rainwater away from us, and even though the storm-tree itself sheltered under a massive stone overhang, still, when the clouds burst, water would go everywhere. Up in rain-quarters, the linked and overlapping fan-leaves that thatched our living spaces would be even more important than down in the Real. But that first night we slept under nothing more than our storm-tree's leaves and branches.

After the gathering and the sweeping, once our bellies were full and the kin was settling down for the night, my father held my hand while we looked out over the very edge of the terrace, down onto the rippling hills of home. We were about a quarter of the way up the Wall, and the Real below was very big, much bigger than you can know down under the trees. Even with the sun gone down, we could still see, along the curve of the Wall, the gleam of the ribbon-rivers that fell down from the Plains above, where the Ancestors walked. My father told me the river-names one by one, pointing into the twilight, making me say them back to him until he got to the one so close by us that we could hear its rushing fall from where we stood. He did not have to tell me that one.

'That is our river, Sook-Sook. Our Durma.'

'That is right, little sprig. That is where the Durma drops into the Real from the Plains of the Ancestors. And if you look down at the bottom – it is all in shadow right now, but tomorrow you will see – down there, just a little way over from where it falls, that is where we live in ordinary times.'

'Oh, Sook-Sook – it is so little down there! I never knew it was so little. When I am there, it feels *big*.'

'I have a very wise daughter, I think – it takes big eyes to be able to see that something can be both very big and very little at the same time.' Sook-Sook always made me feel smart. 'It is a huge and tiny place, our ordinary-times home. We can see that now, because we have climbed above it. Because these times we are going into, the rain days, these are not ordinary times. This is our in-between time, when we move up to our home between the above and the below, to the place where we can remember Sky.' And he told me again, standing there in the half-light, about how in Those Days long ago, Sky got its feelings hurt when the People forgot all about it, hidden as it was up above the green thatch of the trees. Since that time, Sky sends down stormy tears every year to drive everyone out from under the leaves, up to rain-quarters where we can remember better. 'Now Sky remembers the People,' he said with a great sweep of his hand that gathered in both the starry night and our home below it. 'And the People remember Sky.'

A few days later, after we had refreshed the thatch and settled in, the clouds dropped down like an eyelid closing. Then the rains came.

At first, I was afraid. Thunder boomed and growled, and the water itself was so fierce that it roared. But then I saw my brother and cousins dancing with Gai-Gai in the downpour and my father and mother standing together, soaked, with their arms around each other's waist and their faces tipped up, squinting into the rain. So I stepped out, too, and let Sky's tears plaster my hair to my head and pound my skin till it tingled. I heard Gai-Gai singing then, singing with the rain. Other voices joined in strong, and then we were all together, wet and singing the we-remember song.

The next morning, holding me with one hand and a big fan-leaf over our heads with the other so the rain would not blind us, my father took me to the edge again. Even though trained tree-arms railed off the rim of our terrace, I was not supposed to go down to the edge by myself. But Sook-Sook went with me and let me look right out over the flooded forest and see how the rivers – not ribbons anymore, but great angry torrents – smashed into our land, and exploded up in clouds of fury, wetting our faces under the fan-leaf, like rain from below. We breathed in deeply, taking in the Durma's mist and spray – our river, turned to cloud.

'But our bridge, Sook-Sook! The water will crush it!' Our little bridge's arches were as slender as a prong-horn's leg and could never survive that rage of water.

'Maybe, little sprout.' The drumming of the rain on our fan-leaf almost drowned out his soft voice. 'We will see. If it gets hit by a tumbling boulder ... well, then we will just have to plant a new one, no? Start again. But I have a good feeling about that bridge of ours. Let us wait and see.'

'Is the water mad at the land, Sook-Sook? It looks like it is mad.' Rain streaming off the fan-leaf made little waterfalls around us, but it could not touch me where I stood, my father's hand resting on my shoulder.

'I would not say "mad" exactly. Just very, very strong. Like your mother, when she gets going.'

Good rain days went by, filled with singing and the best kind of work, sitting-around-telling-stories work: etching our clan's fine maps and markings into gourd jugs and bowls. Carving small things, mostly things we needed, but toys and decorations, too. Twisting bark-fibres into cord. Knotting cord into nets for the fish-weirs and the bird-trees. Braiding rope. Weaving wraps and bands.

I never minded *that* kind of work. But always – when the Dry Moon finally, finally came and we got back down off the Wall – as glad as I was to be home again, there was too much of the *other* kind of work: getting the house-tree back just the way Marak wanted it. Working out new Permissions, then planting the new gardens and fish-traps allowed us. Re-setting the tumbled stone of the weirs. Cooking. My mother always wanted me to take this other kind of work very seriously. She was always disappointed.

As I got older, I escaped Marak more often and for longer adventures. When outclan folks called for Sook-Sook to come and see about their trees, I would stalk him, not revealing myself until we had come too far for him to send me back alone. It was a wonderful life, I thought, finding our way up and down the many rivers to plant new bridges or bend new platforms into someone's house-tree. I knew that Marak did not like it, of course. Even after the immediate consequences were finished – the shouting, the extra work – a thorniness grew up between the two of us and between her and Sook-Sook, too. But I was young and stupid about that kind of thing, I guess. I loved walking with my father and seeing him honoured by strangers, and what I loved was the only thing that mattered.

One day I went with him when he was called to talk to a grove of sky-fruit trees that had stopped bearing, threatening a whole village that relied on them for food and trade.

I slipped away, with only the faintest twinge of guilt at abandoning my cousins with our chores. But Paji was much better at pulping the nuts than I was, anyway, and everyone knew that Kimo loved gathering basket-reed. The work would all get done whether I was there or not. And my mother's anger? That would wash away as soon as we came back and Sook-Sook laid his hand on the small of her back. Anger, I thought, was just like dust on a green leaf that rinsed away with the rains.

We would not be gone long, anyway – maybe a half-morning's walking to a troubled grove. We would be back before nightfall.

The Mothers of the outclan village fed us, then showed us to the sky-fruit grove. The trees were old and sturdy, with a good fresh green in their tops. No shelf-mushrooms or wounds on their trunks. No galls that I could see. But also no fruit. Sook-Sook gestured that I should go inquire more deeply.

A little nervous because of all the strangers looking at me, I stepped up to the oldest, wisest tree and settled my mind. I stroked the speckled red trunk, meeting it, learning it as Sook-Sook had taught me, knowing it with my flesh hands first before I dipped my Other hands gently into its Flow.

Then, the worried eyes of the crowd around me were gone. All I knew was the tree. The deep, powerful roots, sipping and sucking at the Flow of First Mother. The fearless, sky-striving trunk. The branches, tussling for air and light like rowdy brothers. The cheerful leaves, recklessly throwing themselves open to the burning sun. And the blossoms . . .?

The blossoms, the sad neglected blossoms. Oh.

I sighed and unwound my Other hands from the tree – slowly, no jerks. 'This tree is well,' I said. 'Healthy. Strong. But the flowers . . . There is something wrong with the flowers.'

The people around us muttered discontentedly. 'She is only a child,' one of the Mothers said. 'What does she know? How can the tree be well, when there is no fruit?'

My father winked at me and put his hands on a well-grown daughter of the oldest tree, muttering the strange, meaningless 'tree-talk' he sometimes used when he wanted to impress people, letting his voice rise and fall like a man in a conversation, leaving pauses for the tree to answer him. People backed away.

His jabbering swelled to a fever pitch and, groaning with effort, he tugged his hands away from the tree. I tried not to grin as he fell to his knees and wiped sweat from his face.

After they had revived him with cane beer, he asked if they had a honey-tender in the village. They did not, but sent a runner for one that lived down the river a ways.

That took a while. We drank more of their beer and ate more of their food until the honey-woman arrived – she was older than Gai-Gai and walked very slowly, leaning on a stick on one side and a grandson on the other.

The old woman listened, her eyes searching in the canopy, while Sook-Sook explained the problem. 'Show me your where your whizz-wings live,' she said.

Then, it was much like before. Everyone trooped after her out to an old hollow feather-tree. The only difference was that, out of respect for the whizz-wings, they gave her plenty of space as she laid her hands on the rough, bird-pecked bark.

From the outside, no different than what my father had done, but I could tell that the old honey-woman was reaching in past the tree itself, into the humming heart of the quiet hive. Too quiet, I realised. Our village's whizz-wings were much louder.

The honey-woman leaned there for a long while. What was it like, I wondered. Would your Other body spread itself through the hive as through one united thing, or break into bits to touch each single whizz-wing? I shook the thought off; such spreading and breaking were too strange, too complicated for me to imagine. I was glad I was a tree-woman instead. Much simpler.

A flurry of honey-suckers broke from the feather-tree's fronds, startling everyone but the old woman. Then, almost like watching someone pull on their wrap, I saw her step back into her flesh body and turn to the crowd. 'This hive is sick,' she announced. 'Something is making the whizz-wings tired. Too tired to bring the fruit.' She looked grim, maybe even frightened.

The Mother who had invited us asked her, 'What do we do?'

My father laid his hand on my shoulder, pulling me away. 'This is honey-business,' he said, 'not tree-business. We should go home now.'

'But Sook-Sook—' I wanted to stay, to hear the honey-woman's answer.

'No, Pyn-Poi. Your mother . . .' He did not have to say more.

When I was eleven, one morning during Drying-Out Days Sook-Sook pulled me away from gathering leaves for the new thatch and led me deep into the muddy-smelling leaves of the brand-new Real.

We climbed high up into the slender-branched tops, way beyond where we could perch comfortably straddled on fat, solid limbs with our ankles locked below us in the usual way. 'Are you holding on tight?'

Did he even need to ask? My toes curled around the tree's smooth skin, my weight pressing the curve of my arch to match the curve of the branch I was standing on, one foot crossing it one way, one crossing it the other, knees a little bent, like he had taught me. Sook-Sook stood on another branch, behind me and a little below. Like him, I gripped the trunk with one hand. 'One hand for the tree,' he always said. 'One hand for the work; one hand for the tree.'

I bounced a little and the trunk – very slim up so high – swayed with my weight.

'Gently, my Pyn-Poi. Gently. Your big old father is too heavy to be standing on such a skinny limb up so close to Sky. Now, be still and look around you,' he said. 'Look closely. Do you see it?'

We had climbed this towering spice-wood because he wanted to show me something, something new and strange in the forest, but all I could take in was the enormous blue above us, bigger than anything down below, and the blazing sunlight that made my eyes shrink into tight squints against my will. 'I cannot see anything, Sook-Sook. The light is too bright up here. It blinds me.'

'Shade your eyes like this,' he said, holding his flat hand to his forehead. 'Look. Tell me what you see.'

The hand-shade *did* help, some. I peered around at the mottled mass of greens and shadows of greens that lay across the Real like a woman's wrap, hiding the skin and bones of her but showing her swells and crevices. It was astonishing, of course, viewed from this high up, but it was not a new thing. I had seen it before, just recently from rain-quarters, but even before that. From the time I was big enough to lock my arms around his neck, Sook-Sook had taken me to every level of the Real, from the roots all the way up to the wind-stirred, blue-sky treetops where the leaf-cover opened and the shape of things could be made out. But what, today, did he want me to notice?

'I see the Real. I see many greens woven together like a blanket, rippling over hills and gullies, more jagged off to the left near the Wall, but smoothing out over toward the right.'

'Yes, off toward the right, that is where the hills flatten out. The edge of the Real. Everything after that is the Swamps. The People do not go there, not even the Lonely Ones. No dry ground. Just big-jaws and bone-cleaners and nibblers. But look out straight in front of you, little twig. Use your eyes.' I looked and looked.

Nothing but the many greens of home.

'I see trees,' I said, turning my head like an owl. 'Glints of rivers between the hills. Some naked places where the rock juts out. Nothing special. Nothing new or different.'

'Nothing?' I think I heard his eyebrow lift. 'Stop looking at things one by one. Let your eyes go blurry,' he said. 'This is important, twiglet. You will need this later. Use your eyes in a new way. Look big. Look at the whole.'

33

Let my eyes go blurry? Look big? The whole what?

But I was eleven years old now, very grown up, well used to Sook-Sook giving me puzzling teaching, and wise in his ways. Sometimes, his muddiest words could take me to the clearest, most interesting understandings. So I tried.

I stared out hard at the hills until my eyes got tired. Then I let go of trying, simply stopped the work of making outlines sharp and bright.

Oh.

The Real went all runny and soft, as if it had just sunk into the waters of the bathing place. Was this what he meant?

I must have sighed, or given some other sign.

'Ah. You have it now, I think,' he said approvingly. 'Now you know: How you see is a choice like any other. This is something you will never forget.'

Scanning slowly from the Wall to the Swamps, I let these new, soft eyes float above the green and—

There it was. There.

My eyes snapped back into sharp-seeing without my willing them to, but now that I had seen it, I could not not-see it: A thing. Green, but wrong – solid, not patchy like branches and leaves. Blobby, as if something under it – trees, maybe? – was covered by a melted coat of slick hive-wax, only green. Small in the larger landscape, the thing must be very big close up. 'What is it, Sook-Sook? I do not understand . . .'

'I do not know for sure, little sapling. I have my suspicions. The thing is growing, swallowing the trees around it. I have to go and see to it.'

'I will go with you,' I announced with all my unshakeable eleven-year-old certainty.

Sook-Sook gave my braid a little tug. 'We will see what your mother has to say.'

34

Sook

The little sprig was up in the house-tree, gathering her things – she had not learned yet that *things* are not what you need for a journey – and I sat waiting on a comfortable root down below. No one had trained this root; it came into the Real on its own with a friendly shape: a flat bowl for your buttocks, smoothed by generations of Marak's kin, with a low swelling behind it to support your back. It faced out toward the kitchen and Gai-Gai usually sat there while she directed the cooking.

Over the years and lifetimes, smoke from the hearth had singed the leaves above it, trimming away foliage until there was an open tunnel to the sky that left a ring of bright sun in the under-tree clearing. Every house-tree has a place like this, a place we sit when we need strong light for fine work, knotting hammocks, for example, or putting a sharp edge on knives. Usually the bright space hummed like a whizz-wing hive, but my wife's mood that day had communicated itself, and people were making themselves scarce. Only old Aiu was there, curled nose to tail by the banked coals of the cook-fire. Age had long ago reduced Aiu's duties to guarding against small kitchen thieves, and his dull hearing muffled his awareness of Marak's anger.

She stood with her back to me, pounding the pulp-nuts, a job she usually left to Pyn-Poi or one of the nieces. Later in the year, the ground here would be hard-packed and neatly swept but, on this day, it had not yet fully dried from the last rains and my wife's feet and ankles were smudged with mud. Her hips bounced a little as she drove the heavy pestle-log down into the cup of the stone-wood stump; you could see the strength of her shoulders as she lifted it into the air. Even after all these years, looking at my wife still made me want to take her out into the trees.

But Marak was angry today. I tried again. 'Something is very wrong out there. I do not know what, but it is spreading. I have to go. I have to see what it is, fix it. This is my work, Marak. I have to go.'

She whirled on me, the pestle-log in her hands heavy as a club. 'Your work? Maybe. Not Pyn-Poi's. You do not have to take her with you. You do not have to take my daughter. Her work is here.'

'But why? The other girls can manage her chores. She is just a little thing, and she loves the trees. She needs to learn—'

Marak huffed out a breath, something between a sigh and a cat spitting. 'She does not need to learn *the trees*, Sook. She needs to learn *this* tree. She needs to learn . . .' Marak cut herself off and I realised that she was talking about women's things. I looked away, up at the treetops, embarrassed.

She started again, her voice quieter. 'Pyn-Poi is my *daughter*, husband. She will grow up, take my place one day, manage the kin and the clan, deal with the neighbours. There are things she must know. She will become me. She will *not* become you.'

'But, wife, every time we try to force her—'

She snorted bitterly. 'She gets more and more headstrong.'

'*Strong*, Marak. Like you. She will make a great Mother someday, if we do not break that strength.' I took a step toward her, laid my hand lightly on her back. 'Imagine the power and wisdom of a clan-Mother who also has big ears for the trees. Our daughter has much space in her heart, my blossom – room for both the trees and the People.'

'But she has no interest in the People, Sook, neither kin nor clan. And she never will, as long as you keep letting her—'

'The girl is still a breastless child. When she is a woman—'

'When she is a woman, she will already need to know what she should have learned in childhood.'

'Give her a little time to grow. Let her learn what she loves for a while. Let me teach her.'

'No,' she said, shrugging off my hand.

I was silent. I did not say what she wanted to hear. I did not say what everyone else said when Marak gave orders.

She smashed the pestle down and down and down again, making the nets and gourds hanging nearby sway with the force of her rage. Tonight's mash would be very smooth, very creamy. She would tell the girls, this, *this*, is the way pulp-nut mash should be prepared. But I would not be there to hear it. I would be away from the house-tree, off toward the sunset place, eating fruit and smoked fish with my daughter.

Pyn-Poi

Hard walking.

Sook-Sook guided us across, instead of along, the long hills and river-carved hollows, so there was a lot of scrambling to do. Also, once we left the Durma far behind, there were few full-grown bridges over the unnamed rivers out there so far from where the People lived. We had to poke up and down the banks looking for fallen logs or vine-braids that could swing us across safely. Sook-Sook said that on the way back we might plant some new bridges.

My father held me tight on these crossings, but he did not have to. I was careful. Everybody had heard the stories about people moving too fast who had set their feet wrong, slipped, and fallen shrieking into the hungry waters. The big-jaws never let you know they are there until it is too late.

It had been a while since we had last crossed water and we were walking now in a flat place different from anywhere my father had ever taken me. Nothing grew here but wild trees, untrained by the People: tall, fat, and wide-spaced trunks, with none of the tightly woven undergrowth that sprang up where the rivers cut the land and let light come down into the Real. No cosy tangle of forever-trees. Green-mossed branches as big as logs had fallen from above, and green ferns of all sizes fluffed out from the bases of the trees. But the overwhelming feeling of this place was brown: brown giants standing in brown dirt, holding up a thatch of green somewhere far, far above our heads.

'Sook-Sook, why is it so quiet here? Where *is* everybody?'

He pointed up to the high canopy. 'All the birds and furry things live up high in the leaves, little sprout, up near the light, so far up that we cannot hear them.'

I took his hand and walked beside him without speaking, tired but too awed by this strange place to want to rest here.

I sensed in front of us a place where the normal dimness darkened. We were walking straight toward it.

Sook-Sook dropped my hand and made the patting gesture he used when there was something with big teeth nearby: Stay here, stay still. I stayed.

He stepped forward, each footfall delicate and precise, like when he was hunting. But his bow still hung from his shoulder – a different kind of danger, then. I looked where his eyes looked and saw a dark strangeness through the tree-trunks. My eyes followed it up and up until my chin was pointing at the sky.

The thing reminded me of the Wall: something solid, sheeting down from the leaf-canopy to the ground. Dull, pale green.

At his signal, I followed Sook-Sook forward, walking where he walked, until I was close enough to see. It was not solid at all. My stomach flapped in my belly like a bird. The thing was a mass of long, string-like leaves, thinner than my little finger. I think I gasped: all one kind of leaf.

Sook

'Sook-Sook ...?' My daughter's voice behind me was frightened. She knew. She was old enough to recognise great wrongness when she saw it.

All one kind of leaf. My gorge rose, like it does when you come on the carcass of an old kill and the cleanup-birds have not gotten there yet but the cleanup-worms have.

Swallowing hard, I gazed up at the mass, trying to understand it, trying to take in the *scope* of it. Huge. It was huge. I stepped nearer. Not even the little air-plants that settle like birds on the trees – not even they had escaped being swallowed by this ... thing.

Finally, I touched it. I thrust my hand right into the very thick of the leaves, tugging the webby vines aside, trying to peer through.

But only more of the same.

Same. Same. Same.

I could not even make out the trunk of the tree under it – of any tree – through the snarl of vine.

All one thing. A killing thing.

Pyn-Poi

Now I do not know what to do.

Sook-Sook and I wormed our way through the wrongness, shoving aside vines, sliding under them, creeping like snakes through the wan tangle of all-one-and-only-one plant, getting our arms and legs snared in loops that would not let go until Sook-Sook cut them with his shiny knife. I had never imagined such sameness could be possible in the living Real. Where were the sister-plants? What had happened to them?

At times, I may have panicked just a little when I lost sight of my father, blinded by the sick, unchanging press of stringy leaves. 'Sook-Sook,' I would squeak. 'Talk to me.'

'Over here, my brave little seedling,' he would answer, and I would follow the sound of his thrashing in the endless, opaque green.

Finally, we reached the trunk of one of the trees that had been swallowed. Sook-Sook used his special knife to hack away a little cave for us in the dark tangle and together we laid our hands on the tree. Gratefully, it allowed our Other hands to fall through its bark and touch its smothering, dying distress.

After, Sook-Sook wiped the tears from my cheek with his thumb. He looked grim. 'Touching this one tree is not enough, not this time, daughter. This time, I have to touch ... bigger. I have to do something that I cannot teach you today.' I opened my mouth to say something – protest, maybe – but the look on his face stopped me.

'But you can help, little twig.' He knows I like to help. 'You can watch over me while I do this thing. I have to' – he paused – 'take a little sleep.' He untied the thong around his waist that held his sheath. He handed it to me and, for the first time in my life, I gripped my father's knife. 'Take it, daughter. Sit with me. Take care of me for a little while.' He lay down on the shreds of the all-one-kind leaves and smiled up at me – a lip-smile only, with serious eyes. He squeezed my hand, and then his lids closed me out.

But that was a long time ago.

It is getting darker now. I do not know what to do. I want my mother. But would even Marak know how to deal with something as wrong as this?

Marak

Keep your mind here, Marak, and off the fact that your daughter is out somewhere idling around with Sook. Keep your mind on the asking. The searching, the asking. This thing you are doing requires every crumb of your attention – heart, mind, and senses, all united. This is respect. This is politeness. This is supplication.

Naked, I move blindly through the black night, setting my feet carefully on the spongy moss, feeling my way, feeling for the subtle call of the rightness, the place where this year's Permission should be asked. I stumble over a root. I never stumble; the tea must be taking effect.

Around me in the dark, I feel the other women like quiet animals moving through the trees with me. Not too close. That, also, is respect. Near enough to protect me and remind me, when the tea takes hold, of what I must do, but not so near as to intrude on the conversation. In union with me. And my Pyn-Poi is not among them. No, do not think of that. Do not distract yourself. Let Sook have her tonight. There is always next year.

Letting my Other body stretch, I reach out to the women around me, the sisters, aunts, nieces, neighbours. I blend their Flows together and draw their support and attention into myself, sharpening the point of my mind even while it spreads out like a bucket of water spilled across the ground. We breathe together, all of us, Other and flesh, pulsing, searching.

And then, there it is, like a glimmer that is not light: the rightness. I turn us toward it, somewhere off to the left, between Elmak's house-tree and the river. My staggering gathers speed and certainty. The women move with me, silently, silently.

Yes. Getting closer. Close now. Here.

Just to be sure, I walk a few steps beyond the spot and feel the confirming decrease in rightness. A little to the left, maybe? A little to the right? No, *this* is the place.

I breathe a sigh of thanks and I sense the women around me do the same. This is a good place. Far enough from the river that the ground will not be too boggy, but right in the middle of our cluster of house-trees. (And not so close to one to make it unfair.)

My body is suddenly very heavy, too heavy to hold up. I am not a tree. I drop to my knees. I am—

I fall on my face.

The sweet smell of dirt and moss and leaf-litter excites me, makes me hungry. I rub my nose in it, my cheeks, wanting it. There is a mewling sound somewhere – a baby? Someone should see to the baby. I nuzzle the ground, sucking down a muddy mix of saliva and dirt. Good. Good.

Yes. This place will give us food.

I press myself into the ground. It loves me. It holds me. It sticks to me, making my eyes gritty, filling my ears, my mouth. So rich. So good.

But then I hear others coming. They are all around me. No. Go away. Leave us alone.

But the others, merciless, press close. Just a little more time, please. Just another moment.

I can feel the legs around me. I hate them. A tight circle around me. Waiting. Wanting.

And then a woman's nagging voice reminding me, 'It is not enough.' A mutter of assent from the others. 'Not enough.'

I cover my ears. 'It *is* enough,' I mumble into the dirt. More than enough. Abundant. Freely given.

A younger voice in the dark: 'But we do not want to search like animals for our food. We do not want to wander like they did in Those Days.' And this time there is a louder clamour: hooting, agreeing, and the sound of digging sticks clacking together.

Go away.

'We want to stay in our village,' someone else says. 'One place, safe, together.'

And then the chant starts. 'Ask Her, ask Her,' they demanded. 'Ask Her.'

But I do not want to ask this thing. I will not. What She already gives us – it *is* enough. I reach out and try to wrap myself around the ground, the whole ground, but my arms are not long enough. Ask Her for more? Why?

The racket of the clashing sticks and stamping feet. Too loud, too loud. She—

And then hands are on my body, wrenching me away from the soil, from Her – away, away, away. Dragging me to my knees. Other hands pry open my fingers. The fistful of dirt I clutch falls away, an unutterable sorrow.

A stick is pressed into my palm. A digging stick. I throw it away, but someone picks it up and forces it into my hand again.

And then they are all silent.

I can feel them around me in the blackness. I hear their breathing, loud, but settling after the noisy chanting. They are waiting for me to do something.

Someone drops onto their knees in front of me. Firm hands clasp my shoulders, shake me hard.

'Mother,' a voice says. Whose? It does not matter. The words must be spoken. The words will be spoken. 'You must ask Her. The People do not want to do as our far-parents did. We do not want to wander the Real always seeking food. We want to stay in one good place, this place. Our place. We want to live in our tall, safe house-trees, put seed into the good ground here, and eat the good food that grows. To do this, we must injure Her. We must put our digging-sticks into Her flesh and open Her. Talk to Her, Mother. Tell Her we will do it tenderly. We will leave room for the sister-plants. Respect will be shown. The net will not be torn. This is what we want. Now, it is for you to ask Her: Does She allow this?'

My eyes sting. Muddy tears. The hands release me with a sharp push that tumbles me back onto the ground.

I crawl away a few feet, but feel the circle of watching women move with me. There is no escape. I grip the digging stick – smoothed by my hands and my mother's – press my lips into the dirt, and breathe the question into the ground.

Pyn-Poi

The night goes on forever.

I sit there, clutching my father's knife as the sickly light fades around us. The little cave in the all-one-kind vines turns into the black belly of some giant creature that has eaten the two of us whole. Without the faint moonlight that usually leaches down through the treetops or the gentle glow of our hearth down below our high-slung hammocks, I am afraid, truly afraid. Not of hunter-cats or stompers or fang-foes or the other normal worries of the Real. What terrifies me is my father's deathly stillness.

As the darkness gathered around us, my father lay unmoving, barely breathing, beside me. People do not sleep like that. I know this. Sleeping people stir, mutter, snort, turn in their hammocks. Not this. Not this lying flat on the ground, hour after hour, nose to the treetops like some cast-off flesh waiting for the cleanup-birds. This is not sleep at all. This is something else, some greater absence. Sook-Sook has gone somewhere, somewhere very Other.

Is he ever coming back?

I long to shake him, to tug at his arm, to yell out, 'Wake up, Sook-Sook! I am scared. I need you.' But I do not. Over and over, I stop myself, hold myself as still as my father. This strange absence is something Sook-Sook chose. It is important. And he asked me to take care of him.

I reach out to lay my hand on his chest, gently, just to check his breathing in the dark, not to interrupt, and I gasp. His skin is cool as a fish. Has he truly died? But no, I can feel the slight, slow rise of his chest. Not dead. But too cold. Far too cold.

I ease down next to him, press myself to his side, drape my arm over his body, and send my own warmth into his vacant flesh.

Marak

I came back to myself slowly. Swaying, swaying. Dizzy. Moving air cooled my skin. I opened gritty eyes, feeling sick and feverish. My mouth tasted of dirt. With great labour, I rolled and spat over the edge of the hammock.

Our big matrimonial hammock. But alone. Where was—? Oh, yes – my man was off somewhere again. I groaned. The Permission-Asking. Harder every year. Soon, Pyn-Poi should take over. But Pyn-Poi had not been there. No, she had been—

'You did well last night, daughter.' Gai-Gai's voice. 'Rest now.'

I turned my head and peered blearily through the woven strands. They had moved our hammock down from the high branches of the house-tree to hang between two low limbs so that I would be able to step out onto solid ground like an old woman. Good.

Thin-slitted, my eyes roved the under-tree clearing in the dim early morning light. Ah, there was my mother – cross-legged on her little mat, Aiu's head on her thigh – scraping strips of basket-tree bark and rocking my hammock with a string tied around her big toe like she did when I was a baby.

'Tell me the story, Gai-Gai.'

'You told it to all of us, last night.'

'But I need it again.'

She nodded and began, 'In Those Days, a certain woman was weaning one of her children, a boy, big and strong but fussy. The woman took some stewed yellow-stick and mashed it between her fingers and placed it on his tongue, but he cried and kicked his legs and spit it out. So she took some red-ball – *all* babies love red-ball – and chewed it up until it was a soft paste and placed it on his tongue, but he cried and kicked and spit it out. He did not like red-ball, either. The woman sighed . . .'

I sighed and closed my eyes, listening to our story and to Gai-Gai's hands drawing bands of bark across smooth stone – whush, whush, whush – over and over until I fell asleep.

I woke up again, more fully this time. I could tell by the lazy, resting voices of the birds that it was afternoon. My belly was uneasy, my bowels still churning from last night's tea.

'I have to go away from the house-tree,' I said like a child.

Gai-Gai grunted, pulled herself to her feet, helped me sit up, and supported me as I found my wobbly balance. With my mother's thin arm around my middle, I stumbled into the privacy of the twine-trunk thicket and squatted.

After, I felt better. I plucked a twig from a tooth-bush, gnawed it until the tip was bristly, and then scrubbed my mouth until my teeth were sweet and slick again.

As we walked slowly together to the bathing place, we passed people on the way: Shispah scraping a hide stretched between two trees, Dohmathi grinding red-stone above a streamlet, Mynno and her daughters, digging-sticks in hand, walking toward the site of the new gardens.

Everyone dipped their head to us. Mynno hissed at her girls to step aside off the path to make way. I nodded as we passed them.

Another year begins.

Well satisfied, I eased my body down into the cool brown water and let it wash away the night.

Pyn-Poi

Sometime after dawn, when the tree-trunks should have been showing themselves if it were not for this unholy cocoon of all-one-kind leaves, Sook-Sook made a sound and rolled over. Tears of relief flooded my eyes. He sat up, rubbed his face, cleared his throat. 'Where is the water-skin?'

I handed it to him. He drank, wolfed down some dry travel-berries, then reached for his knife and bow. 'We have to go. I understand now what this is. I know what to do.'

'Wait, Sook-Sook. Tell me. Where *were* you all night? What *is* this thing?'

He held out the bag of travel-berries for me to take some. 'I will tell you as we walk, sapling. But there is no time to waste – the longer we delay, the more of the Real this poor hungry vine will swallow, and the harder it will be to fix things.'

'But what *is* it? How can it exist like this, covering the trees with masses and masses of all-one-thing, killing the very life that holds it up? It is ... It is ... wrong.' But 'wrong' was not a big enough word for it, for what this plant was. I did not know a word for it. Maybe there *is* no word.

He brushed away a tendril of the stuff that had draped itself around my neck. 'It is a visitor here, Pyn-Poi – a stranger. It does not belong. It is not a member of any kin of this place. That is why it has no sister-plants here. Even more important: That is why nobody eats it.'

'Nobody eats it? How can that be, Sook-Sook?' I could feel my eyes stretch big to take this in. 'Everything has *somebody* that eats

47

it. If not . . . if not, then the Real would fill up with . . .' I fell silent, mouth hanging open – everything *was* filling up with this sick, deranged all-one-kind thing. If it truly had nobody to eat it . . . 'Will it gobble up the whole Real, then?' I asked in a small voice, as if the thing could hear me.

'It will not.' His voice was grim, like a hunter's. 'It will not, my beautiful twig,' and here he tipped up my chin with a brush of his thumb, 'because you and I will take care of this. All we have to do is go and find some eaters for it.'

'But where? Where did it come from?'

'This thing,' he said, 'was sent down on us from the Plains of the Ancestors. I am not sure why. That part is not clear. Are they angry at us up there, or did they drop it by accident? I do not know. But what I do know is that this crazy little vine . . .' Little? '. . . when it is at home, is a harmless and well-behaved member of its clan. It has its own eaters, up there. All we have to do is bring them.'

'But . . .' Up there? How could we bring down something from up above the Wall? Was he thinking of climbing . . .? No. That could not be it. It was not possible. 'But we cannot climb the Wall, Sook-Sook. Not all the way up. Not while we are alive. If this plant's eaters are up there, up where we cannot go, then how—?'

'We will not have to climb, sprout. Or at least, not far. Or at least, I hope not far. You know, anything can be an eater.' I understood this. Starve-beetles could eat your yams. Long-legs could eat the starve-beetles. Sickness, hunter-cats, and bone-cleaners – many things could eat People. The Real was like a great fish-net, woven-together strands of eating and being eaten. My father nodded to himself, already planning. 'One of the main eaters for this vine is something like a whizz-wing, only grey and tiny, no bigger than a nibbler. It nips the vein' – he picked out a strand to show me – 'right here, right where the leaf joins the stem. Then it sucks out the Flow. Too many bites, and the plant dies. And when there are

48

too many of these plants, like there are here' – he lifted his eyes to the tight-woven green sack around us – 'the grey-wings thrive. More grey-wings, less vine. Balance.'

'But how does that help us, if all the grey-wings are up on the Plains of the Ancestors? We need something in the Real.'

'Ah, but they are not *all* of them up there,' he said. 'Some of them live on the Wall – they nest in the storm-trees. They are there. All we have to do is go up and get them.'

'Last night, you did not know, Sook-Sook. How do you know now?'

'Ah. Yes. You may have to learn that someday.'

THE FARM

Pyn-Poi

After the boot-women put their poison on me, we walk again. Not far this time. Not like the day's long walk, but I am tired now, tired like I was when I climbed the Wall, tired so that every step is a problem to think about. Too tired to consider what it means that the Stink is here.

I can hear fang-foes circling us in the dark. When they dash in close, the boot-women strike out with sticks with leather bands at the ends. They make a cracking sound and the beasts yelp in protest and dance away.

With my Other ears, I can hear something else around us, too. Not trees – just small, shrubby things with dull, suffering, sighing voices. What?

The boot-woman in front of me stops short and I nearly run into her. I look up.

Another house-box looms out of the night, a giant one, sitting alone out in this weird flat treeless space. I can make no sense of it, even with the slim curl of moon coming up, just that it is long and low with a few square window-holes. One door gapes into the blackness inside. I shiver in the night chill, then jump when the boot-woman behind me bawls out something I do not understand. A fang-foe yaps somewhere behind us.

Hard hands shove me through the black door. I stumble over rough steps and almost fall, but other hands catch me, steady me, pull me in.

The smell of women all around me, women who have sweated and not gone to water, neither river nor bucket. Voices, cooing and chattering – women's voices. Many women. The moon-star glow of a square hole in the wall. Window. Hands, pulling me, patting me, making me sit on a hard plank shelf. I hit my head sitting down; there is another shelf above. The sounds of baying just outside the walls, hungry and mean.

Water pouring. Someone puts a bowl of water in my hands and I drink like I have never drunk before. Feeling the smooth gourd vessel in my hand, just like in my mother's house-tree – that makes my tears come out.

A wet rag – I jerk away, but then let it be when I realise someone is wiping the fang-foes' shit from my face, my arms, my legs. Taking my stinking sandals away. Washing my feet. Someone sits beside me, shoulder pressed against my shoulder, hip against my hip. Someone takes my hand and squeezes it.

Women all around me. Close. Voices. Questions. Words. All the words I learned in Bazleti's household – gone. Everything gone. I sag against the woman next to me and feel an arm, sharp-boned and wiry, come up around my shoulders.

Alone with strangers, and it is dark.

Naina

The new girl, a youngster with something wrong with her mind, had been seen to and most of the other women had dropped like rag-dolls onto their bunks before the Tract Council could finally settle down to our nightly business. It was late, but somebody has to raise their sights above the details of just getting through each day, has to plan for the long haul, has to make sure there's something in the pot when we come back hungry from the fields. Somebody has to make sure there's a little in our account to buy medicine when Doc says we need it. Somebody has to decide when to plant, when to treat for pests, and when to harvest. Somebody has to lay down the law when fights break out or some starving girl steals from the rice stores. So, as usual, the five of us stayed up after everyone else was sleeping, to take stock of things and make plans for surviving one more day in the System.

No wood for a fire, of course, and the dried dog-droppings and tight-wound bundles of stems we collect are all hoarded for the Tract's cook-fire. Our few precious wax tapers are in Doc's emergency kit.

There wasn't much moon, just enough to catch the glitter of the night-hounds' eyes every now and then when they made a pass at the safe-line. So we sat in the dark, cross-legged there on the hard-packed dirt in front of the bunkhouse, and there wasn't much to tell between us. We could have been five dolls in a matched set, all dressed in the same tattered brown dresses. Even without the System's burlap 'uniforms', anyone would have known us for what we were. Tractees: stringy from hard work on scant rations, faces worn to shoe-leather by the sun, a knuckle's length of hair grown in since our last Hygiene Visit. Some of us had more grey than black on our heads; young Doc had none at all. I guess I was the probably

53

the greyest of the lot. When was the last time I looked in a mirror? Who knows? Probably before Doc was born.

That didn't keep her from speaking up, though, always arguing, always contradicting people. Smart, but more opinions than is good for her, our Doc. 'I'm not sure she's broke-brained at all, Naina, not as such,' she went on.

'Hard to tell, on the first night.' There were nods around the circle at this. 'Everyone's pretty messed up on the first night.'

'But not babbling. Everyone's not *babbling*,' Repjim objected.

'And if they are, at least it's in words. This one isn't making any sense at all.'

'Or maybe just none we can understand,' Doc said.

I took a sip of my tea. Tea. It was a weed, really, left to steep in the sun while we were in the fields. Supposed to be good for you. Tasted like piss, though – and a long contract does teach you exactly what piss tastes like – but Doc said it would keep us from getting sick so much, give us something our bodies needed. And meetings needed tea, some kind of ritual, some kind of civilised thing to remind us – to remind me – that we are not barnyard animals. Even sitting there in the dirt, wearing rags that once I wouldn't have used to clean my shoes, we were *not* animals. 'The girl's talking a different language, you mean?'

'More likely than not. She has a different look to her, too – those broad cheekbones, those golden eyes. That girl's not from around here.'

'But, Doc, how would a foreigner fetch up in this crotch of a place?'

'Good question, Sibba.' How did any of us fetch up here?

'I think she's just broke-brained. We all know what it's like when you first get here. A little bitty town-girl like that, all used to sitting on brocade pillows and eating sweets, well, that kind of girl cracks up easy, especially the first night, what with everybody laughing and clapping and generally jumping for joy while the dogs slaver all over you. She won't last, mark my words, and we'll be stuck—'

'She's not a town-girl—'

'How do you know that?' Sibba hated know-it-alls.

'Doc's right, Sibba,' I said. 'Didn't you notice the shoulders on that girl, the legs? You don't get muscles like that sitting around all day. She may be small, but that child has done some work in her life.'

'Well, that would be a blessing. We could sure use someone who can pick her own weight right from the beginning. The rains seem to be coming earlier every year; we can't afford to fall behind in the harvest. We've got to finish the field by the river tomorrow or else ...'

The conversation drifted off toward how to squeeze enough fibre out of the Tract's exhausted fields before the rains came, so we could afford seed, fertilisers, and bug-killers, *and* keep the Guards paid off after Administration took out our rents and the System's profits. Those always came out first.

I heard myself sigh.

It wasn't a sigh about anything in particular, just another day done. Another day of Being Naina. One more day on Tract Eleven.

The dark was quiet around me now, just the rustle of bony bodies trying to fit themselves together for one more night on the hard wooden bunks. A few low mutters. Someone telling someone else to move over.

Time to sleep. One more night.

I stooped and slid into the place that went with my position – outer sleeper on the bottom bunk nearest the door – and closed my eyes, then opened them again.

I didn't often think about my own stolen life. That was all too long ago, too far gone to seem like more than a dream or a fairy-story. That was another person. A younger person. A stupid person.

But when a new girl showed up, it always rang old bells.

Put it out of your mind, I told myself. Nobody died today. Everybody ate. The bugs didn't come.

But still, I wondered about her, the strange-eyed new girl. Where had she come from? What kind of mess had gotten her all tangled up in the System? How had she earned herself a place on the Farm?

THE REAL

Pyn-Poi

A few months after Sook-Sook brought the grey-wings down and saved the Real, I was twelve and Marak got tired of being married to a tree-man.

My father seemed surprised. For a man with such big eyes for trees, he was a little blind about other things.

He looked perplexed, but gave Marak back her strands of bright coloured shell-beads without arguing. His ankles looked pale and strange without them. Now he would have to go back to his mother's kin, and who would finish teaching me? The trees my father had planted to keep our riverbank from washing away, back before I was born, and the bridges we had started together when I was a child – who would take care of them now?

'The trees can take care of themselves,' Marak snapped, tired of my whining. 'And anyway, the wandering tree-keepers will see to them on their own schedule, just like they did before your father ever came here.'

Wandering tree-keepers! Strangers touching *our* trees' roots and branches? Unthinkable. I stormed off to find my father.

'But Sook-Sook, who is going to take care of our trees?' Even to me, I sounded like a baby.

'You will, my beautiful sapling.'

I kicked my dangling heels back and forth under the branch where I perched just above my parents' platform. 'Make her change her mind. You know you can.' But my father was packing. He had brought very little with him into the marriage and he was taking very little away, just his tools and some clothes that he was wrapping up in his travel-hammock. His unstrung bow hung from a knob of bark, a bow he used too rarely, according to Marak, because he always had his nose in the treetops and not on the game-trails, where a real man would be finding meat so that his wife did not have to spend the kin's wealth trading for food.

'You know your mother,' he said and made that funny little shrug of his. 'When she decides something . . . She has the gift of stubbornness. You are a lot like her.'

I turned my back on him, slid down the ladder, and ran out into the trees. I was not at all, in any way, the least bit like my mother.

The Trees

'There is only one of them now.'

'I thought there were two.'

'There *were* two. Now there is only one.'

'Are you sure? I could have sworn that there were—'

'Yes, yes – there were two; the older one went away. They do that. That leaves the one. Remember, they are not like us; sometimes they become fewer. Look, there she is, down by your roots.'

'Are you sure that is her? I thought she was smaller.'

'She was a sprout. She grew.'

'Really? That fast? It is so hard to keep track. What happened to the other one? Did the birds take him already?'

'No. He moved to another place. They do that sometimes.'

'Maybe he will come back. He had good hands.'
'So does she.'

Pyn-Poi

Having Marak marry again was like a drought and a flood together.
The good thing was that soon a new baby was growing inside her
and it *could* be a girl. Why not? Then I would no longer be her only
daughter, stuck with turning into a Mother when Marak got too
old to lead: looking after the kin and the clan, speaking with First
Mother during ceremonies, dealing with the other Mothers all year
round, organising the River-Crossings and marriages, all of it. Also,
I was getting old enough to think about my own marriage, and oh,
the trouble it would save if I were not the heir of a powerful clan-
Mother! As Marak's pregnancy swelled, I catered to her the best I
could, bringing her feminine foods and thinking girl-thoughts at
her belly all the time.

The bad thing about the marriage was having a new man stealing
Sook-Sook's place. I may have been a little surly to Peng. To make
matters worse, he seemed to want to act a father to me, always
asking if there was anything wrong, imparting wise sayings, and
trying to tell me stories but not getting them right. (He was a very
bad storyteller, though a good hunter, according to my brother.) He
told me I could call him Peng-Peng. I got out of it by never saying
his name at all. He was always spattering questions on me about
how I spent my days.

The way I spent my days was with the trees. I not only cared
for the delicate young spans across our river and the roots that
buttressed our riverbank, but also trimmed and tended the older
bridges as well. I started some humpy loops beside our paths that I
hoped would become benches someday, and poulticed small wounds

in the bark of both trained and wild trees to keep the little eaters from getting in.

I filled many hours clambering through the tangled treetops, breathing in their exhalations, learning how the smell of them changed across the seasons. Listening to their branches move in the wind and under the weight of the animals that lived in them. Running my hands over their skin, and my Other hands deep inside them to where the mysteries were. Savouring the flicker of the forever-trees between oneness and many-ness as they worked together with their kins, clans, and outclan sister-plants. Following their slow shaping from cord-like dangles to vine-like stems that grew into the mighty trunks and limbs of their close-woven, complicated groves. Sometimes, after a day with the trees, it was almost as if I could overhear one speaking to another. I listened. I learned. Even without Sook-Sook. And learning from trees is not hurry-work.

Marak was not pleased with me. 'Who will marry a girl who does nothing in the garden and brings home neither fish nor fruit? Who will marry a girl who gives all her caresses to trees? Who will marry a girl . . .?'

The Trees

'Do you think she is lonely? I mean, all by herself like that, with just the one trunk?'

Pyn-Poi

Because of my little-sister-to-come, that year we left for rain-quarters even before the storm-frogs told us to. Marak balked at the idea, but Gai-Gai insisted, so we took our time and overnighted on an empty terrace. It felt odd, sleeping in a place that was not our place, but the climb was gentler in two stages like that, not just for my baby-round mother but for all of us; the harder, longer rains in recent years meant we had to carry heavier food-packs up the Wall to see us through. And my grandmother also carried the heaviness of her years.

The next day, we finished the trip by mid-afternoon, in plenty of time to start settling in before night fell. While the little cousins got started on laying in dropped wood for the fire, the big cousins swept out the mess of old thatch, fallen leaves, abandoned nests, and animal-litter. We launched our sweepings over the edge with a shout and watched them all flutter away into the leafy Real below us. I let my eyes rove up across the green-and-stone mottled Wall, saying over the names of the waterfalls the way my father taught me: Aguach, Gaajad, Laku, Daduma like a narrow thread, Mardid like a broad curtain, Mardid's near neighbour Ringgi, and our beloved Durma, whose rumbling falls we could hear from where we stood.

Because we had come up early, that year the settling-in chores were relaxed, even placid. Of course, Peng was new and had to be shown our kin's particular way of thatching, of making our food-stores safe from little eaters, and of stacking firewood, but he was new-married to a clan-Mother with a baby on the way, so he was easy-going about being teased and bossed around a little. Sometimes, in the general good mood on the terrace, I forgot to be sulky to him. I still avoided using his name, though.

When the rains finally burst, it felt funny to watch Peng with his arm around Marak's pregnant waist. They leaned together and lifted their faces up into the rain. Then we were all dancing and singing, and things felt right again.

That night, the Stink came.

Later, we knew it came from the Durma, but that first night, we did not understand. We woke up to a bad smell that clawed at the back of your nose where it meets your throat, so that you could not tell if you were breathing it or drinking it. It brought tears, not like sorrow or joy does, but like getting a thousand grains of the tiniest sand in your eyes and not being able to rub them out. It did not smell like anything in the Real but, if I had to say it was like something, the closest I could come would be a nasty tea Marak gave me once when I was little and my lungs got stuck together. It was not that smell, but it was that *sort* of smell.

We covered our faces with our hands, with leaves, with our wraps and huddled around my mother at the very back of the terrace, almost in the hearth. Even *she* did not know what to do, and this frightened us beyond questions, beyond whining, beyond anything except clutching each other and taking the tiniest sips of air, trying not to let the badness down into our chests, but then we would cough and the burn would go all the way to our core, jerking out more and more coughing as the night wore on. Would we cough ourselves right out of our bodies?

The bad smell went away around dawn, as mysteriously as it had come, leaving the Wall silent in a way that made my flesh crawl. The steady, high-pitched chorus of hoppers and nibblers and peepers, the low drumbeats of croakers, the songs of birds and the rustle of beasts – all gone.

Three days later, my mother's belly wrung out my little sister, small and perfect and dead.

After the Stink, the leaves on the Wall browned and curled up. Berries that were hanging tasted poisonous and no more came because the flowers withered and whizz-wings died. For the first time in my life, I knew long-time hunger as Peng and my brother and uncles failed and failed to bring us meat. The only thing any good on the Wall were the starch-roots. We dug them up too early, when they were still small and bitter, but we could eat them if we soaked them first and threw the water away. My mother, pale and grim, stretched out the nuts and smoked fish we had carried up from below to supplement the bounty we expected from the Wall. People from other kins wandered in through the rains to ask us for food-help, but Marak said no, she had to take care of her own.

Sprout by sprout through that long hungry season, the green came back to the Wall, as if the nightmare was over.

When the rains died away to nothing more than a few brief afternoon downpours, we shrugged on our pack-baskets (now empty of food, but carrying the cord we had plied and the fishnets we had knotted during the rainy weather), and started back down the Wall. Everyone we met on the road looked skinny and haggard; it startled me to think I must look the same to them, with my ribs poking out where they did not use to show.

When we got back down, everything was the way it was supposed to be – all soggy and covered with mud – except that a ghost of the bad smell lingered. Fish had died and been seined out of the flood by the tree branches. They rotted there for a long time. The cleanup-birds would not eat them.

Our young bridge was still there, strong enough to hold my weight if I crossed it gently. But the shiny, leathery leaves of the forever-trees around it were tipped with bloody brown.

The Trees

'I am afraid.'

'Afraid.'

Afraid, afraid, afraid. Every leaf, every rootlet, every bloom: Afraid.

Pyn-Poi

The Stink came back every year after that, right at the beginning of the rains, and stayed longer and longer. Sometimes it fell on us at night, sometimes in the day – always right around the time when the rivers first swelled and pounded themselves into clouds of fine spray on the rocks at the base of the Wall.

After that second year, the coming of the rains stopped being a time of excitement and celebration. We dreaded it now, like some invisible hunter-cat that would stalk in among us and snatch our weak ones and elders away. The Stink took Biang's great-grandfather the year after it killed my baby sister, and it gave my cousin Sim a wheezing cough that never left him, even when dry season came. So many babies were lost that women stopped welcoming their husbands a few months after the rains, for fear of losing a belly-child when the badness came again. But even breast-babies, timed for the safety of dry season, sometimes died when that smell came down from above. Sickness and change dogged us. The fish-people and the honey-people despaired. The Mothers met and met again, sometimes for thinking and talking that went nowhere and sometimes for ceremonies that went up on smoke into the night.

The third year, Marak made us stagger up to rain-quarters under back-bending loads, food enough to see us through the season because we could no longer count on the Wall to feed us. That year, we did not dance and sing when the first clouds broke open; we thatched the arches of the storm-tree as tight as a basket and plugged up kinks to try to keep the Stink out, but still it found us.

Some said that Sky was angry with us.

No, said others, the Stink comes with the mists from the waterfalls. The rivers. We must have offended the rivers.

64

It is the Ancestors, others claimed; it comes down from the Plains above.

That third year, it took Gai-Gai.

Her death was a gasping and horrible thing. The hacking cough that seized her as she clutched her wrap over her nose against the Stink – that cough got worse instead of better as the air on the Wall slowly cleared. Deep, strangling spasms made her hammock jump, even after the smell had finally passed.

All those long days and nights, her daughters took turns sitting by her. Offering her food. Begging her to drink. Thumping her back when she choked. Turning her from side to side in her low hammock. Keeping a small fire going to warm her. Holding a big fan-leaf over her to keep the drips off when the wind blew the wrong way.

My mother mixed some medicine, go-strong leaves steeped with silver-bark until the tea was nearly black. Kneeling, she lifted her mother's head and offered the brew, first in a cup, then in a spoon, and finally in a hollow reed that let it fall, drop by drop, into Gai-Gai's slack, dry mouth.

Marak was forceful at first, then cajoling, then desperate. 'Please try, Gai-Gai. Please. Just a little. Just a sip. A drop. Now, swallow. Swallow . . .'

But Gai-Gai was too weak to swallow, too intent on breathing. She choked on the tea, splattering the dark bitterness onto her hammock, staining the faded strands.

Finally, late at night, Marak set the clay pot down beside her on the smooth stone floor under the storm-tree. 'Go rest,' she told Dokha and Saggi. 'I will sit with her a while.'

I bent to pick up the little pot, to clear it away before someone tripped over it in the dark. As I reached for it, Marak's hand closed over my wrist, stopping me, then opened again and pulled away. Her face turned up toward mine, and she nodded.

I took it away, the tea for making you strong. I carried it down our terrace in the pounding rain and threw it over the edge. Then I went back, easing through the storm-trees' arches, trying not to wake anyone. I wrung out my wrap and settled on the stone floor beside my mother. She was holding Gai-Gai's hand and rocking the hammock very gently. She did not look at me, but she did not send me away, either.

The coughs grew weaker, the wheezing battle for air more intense. My grandmother's eyes were not peaceful. This was not an easy passage. The hunger for air must be a terrible thing, to judge from those wide, staring eyes. That terror. This was not the death a beloved Mother deserved.

I must have dozed, because at some point it came to me that Marak's hand was clasping mine and I did not remember how it got there. One hand holding her mother, one hand holding me. I did not move.

After a long time of silence, except for those rasping gasps, Marak told me to get the others.

I went to each hammock and woke them all one by one, a hand on a back, a whisper in an ear, a tap on a shoulder. 'Marak says to come.' In the dark, I could hear my mother's voice begin to hum.

When I came back to Gai-Gai's hammock, now ringed by shadowy faces and shuffling, uneasy feet, Marak was singing, quietly, under her breath, like you would sing the last round of a lullaby when the baby's eyelids are already fluttering closed.

My aunts stepped nearer and joined the soft farewell, sister-voices so like my mother's in tone and texture that they became one voice. And then all of us were singing, goodbye, goodbye, until suddenly, with a sharp slice of her hand, Marak cut us off.

She leaned in, bent over her mother, brushed away strands of hair from her ear, and said, 'Tell the Ancestors that Marak says, *This must stop.*'

After that day, it became a part of the People's way of death to ask every departing person to carry a message. Intervene on our behalf. Demand that the Ancestors stop sending poison down into the Real.

The Trees

'Do something.'
'Do something!'

Pyn-Poi

Another anxious year went by.

When the Dry Moon finally brought us back down from the Wall, I found the trees more sick and brown, even the forever-trees. On that last return, their branches were half-naked, their leaves on the ground, mashed in the muck like the foliage of ordinary trees. This was unheard of; forever-trees *always* changed gradually over the year, one leaf dropping here, another there, replaced by fresh growth, but never all at once. I picked one up and rubbed the mud off it with my thumb. The tough, smooth surface was the colour of blood-stone. I wanted my father so badly then that my heart hurt in my chest. But I did not know where he was. He had taken up the work of a wandering tree-keeper and only dropped back into my life unexpectedly every few months, to see, he said, how things were growing.

Angrily, I did his work. I comforted the trees as best I could, awkward and uncertain without my father's questions to guide my attention and his stories to guide my thinking, without his Other

67

hands to guide my touch and his ears to help me hear and understand. But I could still go to the trees. I could stand with them. Even when you cannot make things better, there is a kind of rightness in bearing witness, in accompanying suffering. That much, at least, I could do.

Marak was tense all the time, preoccupied with the many strands of our unravelling life: The catches from the weirs were declining. Our whiz-wings were ailing and the few fruit that set were marred with spots and stains. Our hunters had to travel further and further to bring back game. Our water-hens' eggs were weak and brittle, sometimes crushed in the nest by their own mother's weight.

Marak took the dream-tea over and over again until she was gaunt with it, but her dreams were either mute or filled with stone and spiders and images so strange that they gave no guidance.

Because I was her daughter, I did not actually hear the murmuring against her, but when I walked with her to the bathing place, I could see how people's eyes slid away. The Stink was not my mother's fault and no one was stupid enough to think so. But not knowing what to do – they blamed her for that.

The gathering catastrophe kept Marak's attention off her disappointing daughter. She more or less gave up on me, I think. I spent all my days with the trees.

Even though the times were dark and strange, some things did stay the same. I was still the only daughter of a powerful clan-Mother; I should have known it would happen soon. I was sixteen.

I had known Kumne all my life. He was an outclan boy from the far side of the Ringgi. When we were little, we played together every year when our clan went to visit his mother's people during River-Crossing for trade and marriage-making. He was a good climber – almost as good as me – and we chased each other through the high branches like ring-tails, leaving the others far behind us. Later, when we were a bit older and his life filled up with boy-things and dignity, he ignored me. That hurt my feelings for a while but, a few years later, I became interesting again and we went out into the trees together, happily playing with each other's parts, though never enough to invite a baby.

I liked Kumne. I really did. My heart swelled each year when I saw him grinning at me from the branches above the path as my people filed in over the big gnarled Ringgi-bridge. He was always good company, tall and well-muscled, a witty storyteller, and said to be a good hunter. I should have known what was coming. It was time. But still, I was shocked when Marak told me that Kumne's kin had sent a message.

At first, I did not know what she was talking about. A message? Now? The River-Crossing had just happened; the next was almost a year away.

And then I understood.

I stood there, feeling my mother's canny eyes on my face. My mouth seemed to be hanging open; I shut it.

'He is a strong boy, this Kumne,' she added in an approving voice. 'Smart, too, they say.'

I nodded, licked my lips. Kumne? Now?

'But—'

'Hush,' she said. 'It is a strong kin. He will bring us good blood.'

Now? With the Stink, and people getting sick, even in the middle of the dry season, and the fish going away? Now, with the trees screaming in my Other ears? *Now?*

How could I even think about marriage? The trees were demanding ... well, something, some kind of action. Something had to be done. Somebody would have to do it.

Marak said I would learn to love Kumne, but I knew that already. I knew that I could love him if I shared his hammock – if I shared his hammock and skinned the meat he killed and finally, finally learned to cook. Kumne, with his big, watchful eyes – he would be easy to love. Love was not the problem.

The trees were talking to me every day now and, in a different way, so was the Stink. Something had to be done. Something was being demanded. I did not know what, exactly, and how would I ever know if Kumne came into our house-tree and filled my ears with husband-talk and my belly with babies?

Babies. The very idea of that made me catch my breath, made me hear again the wailing as we laid my little sister out for the cleanup-birds.

No.

No babies.

Even when it was not upon us, the Stink was lying in wait, ready to snatch our little ones. For months at a time, husbands were sleeping out in the wild trees, away from their wives, to keep from inviting babies at the wrong time of the year. Something had to be done about this.

How could I marry now?

How could I not? Marak demanded. The kin must go on. Bad times come and go, always: Sicknesses. Wars. Hungers. Killing storms. Out-of-season rains that flood the land, wash away the gardens, carry people off. These things happen, but the kin must go on and I was her daughter. It was my job . . .

Sometimes, I ran away from these conversations, just left the house-tree and climbed. I wanted my father. He would know what to do. And, strangely, I wanted Kumne. If we could talk, he would listen. He would ask questions. He would understand.

But Kumne was far away, by the banks of the Ringgi, waiting for our answer. And my father was off who-knows-where, seeing to unknown trees. There was no one to listen to me. So I listened to myself.

I told Marak no. No. I would not marry Kumne. Instead, I would . . . What?

Marak

Stubborn. Head harder than stone-wood.

I explained it to the girl, over and over, in words a ring-tail could understand: This is a *good* thing. A fine young man wants you. He will hang his hammock in our house-tree and soon you will have a daughter of your own. Our kin will grow.

Why can she not see this?

Is she just trying to hurt me? To spite me, maybe, for sending her father away? She was always Sook's girl, not mine. But this? I would never have thought her this selfish, this irresponsible.

She knows that I have no other daughters of the flesh, not since her little sister. I turn to Peng every night, tireless as a young girl, but no more babies answer our invitation. Years. No babies. No daughters. Pyn-Poi is my only – our only – hope for tomorrow. How can she think of saying no?

If she is unwilling, what are we supposed to do? I have to make her understand. Our kin needs this, for there to be a daughter, not just my daughter, but also my daughter's daughter, and her daughter after that, twining down in one unbroken cord from the First Mother to the Last. Yes, the Stink is real and vicious and something has to be done. But what *can* be done? Stink or no Stink, the kin must continue, or there is nothing.

The girl is not stupid, no matter how she acts sometimes. She *knows* it will be her job to manage the family, the kin, and the clan. She *knows* Kumne would be a good partner in this, but every time I mention his name, she just stands there looking over my shoulders and muttering about the Stink and the trees.

It is not the boy she objects to. She admits that she likes him well enough. And who would not, a big strong boy like that, and not even done with his growing.

71

But her mind is filled with the trees – the trees sick, the trees dying, the trees whispering in her ears – nothing but the trees.

'So tell me, little tree-woman: What are the trees saying to you? What do they want from you? From us? What will make things better?'

'I do not know,' she says, real misery on her face. 'I do not know *yet*. But something. I have to listen. I have to wait. I have to . . . not become a wife.'

As if refusing Kumne will somehow help things, as if it will make the Stink go away. This is Sook's fault.

Or my fault, maybe. I should never have allowed her to run about so much with her father. I should have held her closer, made her learn her work and the love of her work. I failed her. And now she says she will not marry. I failed them all. My fault.

If only the little one had lived. But the Stink . . .

And now I have only one girl. And I am getting old.

Oh, my daughter, tomorrow comes sooner than you can imagine. You are our tomorrow.

Pyn-Poi

Marak pushed me hard. I must have led the boy on, she said, and clans had gone to war over less. Kumne's mother would never welcome us back now. We would have to find another place to go for River-Crossing, but who would ever want us if her daughter showed herself to be a careless, selfish, disobedient shame to the clan?

'A shame to the clan' – I heard those words a lot, those and many others, but I stood firm and in the end they did not force me, not with actual force. After all was said and done, Marak sent a large blood-stone as a present to Kumne's mother and I remained an unmarried daughter, and opened my ears wider than they had ever opened before.

The Trees

'You must stop it.'
   'Go to where it comes from and stop it.'
   'Go upstream. Go upstream and stop it.'
   'Go up!'
   'Go,' we shouted as loud as we could. 'UP!'

Pyn-Poi

Up.

I stared balefully at the Wall from the highest perch in our house-tree, my eyes climbing from the rippled green of its base, up past its naked shoulders, all the way to the jagged edge where stone meets sky and the Plains of the Ancestors begin.

Up.

The Trees

'But who will take care of us if she goes?'
   'She will.'

Pyn-Poi

'But *why* do you not want me to go?'

73

I had travelled a long way to find my father and get his blessing on this mad journey I was contemplating. I had crossed the Ringgi and the Mardid to his mother's house-tree. I had braved the awkward and time-consuming courtesies of visiting his kin to learn where to look for him. I had tracked him for days out among wild trees that did not know me. Now here I was, and things were not going as I had planned.

These days, Sook-Sook slept on the ground, not up in the high, safe branches. (His joints had gotten painful and knobby since the coming of the Stink, and climbing was hard for him now.) The mosses around his little fire were soft enough and I had slept on the ground before but, still, it made me uneasy.

'This thing you are thinking of – it is wrong. It is crazy. That place belongs to the Ancestors, Pyn-Poi. Going there without being taken by the birds . . . You will make them angry, maybe start a war.'

'But, Sook-Sook, they have started one already. Are they not sending down death on us every time the rains come? Are the People not dying just as surely as if they had been pierced by arrows? And it is not just the People, Sook-Sook. Can you not see the brown leaves, feel the choking of the Flow, hear the wailing fear in every rooted thing? How can you not—'

'I hear them, daughter,' he said, his voice heavy and hopeless. 'Of course I do. Every day, I see, I touch, I listen. Our trees are sick; there is no question. That is why they need us beside them – I say *us* because, no matter what your mother thinks or hopes or wants, you are a tree-woman.' *Tree-woman.* He had never called me that before, never actually spoken those words. 'It is our work to take care of our trees, to comfort them, even if this is the End. Especially if this is the End. They need you here.'

'But there is nothing I can *do* here. Can you not see, Sook-Sook? Unless we stop what is killing them, all we can do is watch them die.'

'Do not speak disrespectfully of watching. When your grandmother was dying, did you abandon her to do the hard work alone?'

We had not, of course. Her daughters had hovered near, and the whole kin around them, singing encouragement.

'Pyn-Poi, Gai-Gai was a great clan-Mother, revered and beloved across the rivers. Would her people leave her alone in the final work of her life?'

'It is not the same thing at all, Sook-Sook.' I was getting a little angry at his obtuseness. 'I do not *want* our trees to die.'

'You did not want Gai-Gai to die, either.'

'I know, I know. But I did not know what to do to stop it. If I had known . . .'

'And you think you know what to do about this—'

'No. Of course not. Not exactly. But I know which direction the death comes from. I know where I must go to meet the death-senders. I will know what to do, what to say, how to bargain with them, when I meet them face to face.'

'The Ancestors?'

'The Ancestors.'

He was silent for a while.

'Then Marak should send your brother,' he finally said. 'If some-one must go, it should be Aando. He is older. He is stronger. He can protect himself. Also, he is more diplomatic than you.'

'But . . .' Round and round we went. Aando had a wife now, and responsibilities to his wife's kin.

But I had responsibilities, too, Sook insisted – I was a tree-woman. It was because I was a tree-woman that I had to go.

A tree-*woman*, he repeated heavily, a weaponless woman who might be snatched from the Wall by a rapacious Lonely One, or eaten up by a ravening Ancestor, to say nothing of honest hungry animals.

I would take a stick, I said. A big stick.

But, but, but . . .

The next morning, Sook was gone. I left my father's camp unblessed.

Sook

I lift the wriggling baby, still bloody from birth, and look into those wide, wondering eyes. I see her see me for the first time, see her know me, see the exact moment when she consents to be my daughter. What I see hits my heart like a bolt of fire from the sky, splitting me open and setting me alight with something fiercer than any burning. My eyes seek Marak's and I see that she too is on fire with this thing.

With one hand cupping the small buttocks and one hand under her shoulders, fingers spread to steady her head, I raise my child high. 'This is the Real, my daughter,' I breathe. 'It is yours. I give it to you.'

I turn slowly, showing her the waiting People crowding around and the trees leaning in to see her. I hear the crooning welcome rise from the throats of neighbours and kin, hear the rustle of the leaves greeting her, and just then my daughter's own voice, ragged and untried, peals out in a strong, loud cry.

'Shout, my daughter!' I laugh, showing her toward the morning sun and toward the evening sun, toward the Swamps and the Wall that bound the land. 'Yell out your name! Tell the Real that Pyn-Poi is here at last!'

In this dream, the baby's slick, froggy thighs kick and struggle against my fingers. I grip her more tightly, trying to keep her from falling, but somehow she turns into a feathered thing, flapping wildly to take flight. No. I have to hold you, keep you safe. I am your—

But the wings break free and spread, enormous in their strength, beating down against the air, breaking skyward through the branches, raining twigs and leaves down on my head, and then, with a shuddering cry, gone up and lost into the sky.

Pyn-Poi

Nothing I had ever seen or done scared me as badly as going to Marak to tell her that I, her only daughter, not only would not marry, but also would leave the kin to climb the Wall we do not climb, *all* the way up, to have a talk with the Ancestors.

Marak listened to me with grim fury, her jaw tight and fire in her eyes. I had felt the sting of her anger many times over the years, mostly about small things: running away from chores, missteps at the hearth, lapses in correct behaviour. Something as big as this – would she skin me and cook me?

But when the pot finally boiled over, it turned out that it was not *me* at all that she raged at – it was at those crazy, cruel, heartless, ungrateful, murdering Ancestors. In fact, she approved so whole-heartedly of my plan that I had to talk her out of coming with me to give those Ancestors of ours a proper tongue-lashing for the goings-on of the last four years. And, as for my responsibilities as her heir, what was the point in having an heir if babies could not get born? Without babies—

Go. I should go. By all means. Go with *her* blessing at least, and with the blessing of all the Mothers, if she had her way.

And of course she had her way. Within days, she had called the clan-Mothers together and they each gave me their feathers to carry up to the Plains to demand an accounting in the name of them all. Also, by a long, slippery line of step-stone logic and favours, she arranged to adopt Pariat, the wife of my brother Aando, who was a little older than I and much more sensible. Pariat got along well with Marak and would grow into a fine Mother of the clan. It would be odd to have Aando back in our house-tree – but then I would not be there to notice.

And one more thing. This touched my heart more than you can

77

understand and I knew my mother was behind it: The Mothers found a way that I might be given the attributes of a woman in a ceremony separate from marriage. I had not known this was possible, but none of them could say no to Marak.

So, the day before I left, I received my adulthood from my mother's hands with all our village singing around me and the rustling of the watching trees. I wished Sook-Sook was there to see.

Marak

All those years when Pyn-Poi was dashing around in the trees, chasing after her father, working hard on every little thing except what she was supposed to, I tried to hold her. I clutched her hard, too hard, trying to force her, to shape her, like someone carving a pretty doll out of a fallen branch. I was wrong.

My child was not a block of wood. She was a living tree, pushing up through everything that came between her and the sun. I was one of those things, and she shouldered past me like any young creature must.

But maybe it is not too late. Or, maybe too late in some ways, but not in others. Nothing will bring back the years I lost, the years I tried to make her into something she was not. Years I could have . . .

But now. Now is all we have. And in this blighted, terrible Now, when all our stories seem to be ending, I reclaim my place. I reclaim being my daughter's mother. I will bless her, my girl, my only, with all the blessings that Flow down through me from my mother, and her mother, and all the Mothers chaining back to the Beginning.

Pyn-Poi is going. Nothing can stop that. But she goes with my blessing, and so I have not lost her.

Pyn-Poi

The night before the climb, it took me a long time to realise that I was afraid. I could not sleep, but I thought it was because the nibblers were buzzing more loudly than usual, or maybe it was because the air pressed around me too closely, like it does sometimes under the trees, with a kind of hot heaviness that made my sweat sticky and sent sleep over the bridge and far away.

I knew I should rest. I needed to be strong for tomorrow. But my hammock-strings pressed hard into my skin and the snoring of the household taunted me. *They* were sleeping fine, helped by the fruit-beer from my adulthood feast. *They* were not the ones who would climb up right out of the Real as soon as dawn touched the leaves. They would stay here, in their right places. Even under attack by the evil Stink, held by branches of kinship as sturdy as the ancient house-tree itself, they would still be here, together.

But someone would not be. Someone would be ant-crawling up the stony Wall, the bridge between the living and the Ancestors.

That is when I began to understand that I was afraid.

This feeling that clogged my chest and backed up into my throat like stagnant water – it was fear. Nothing but fear.

I was a good climber, strong. Not bulging strong in the arms like Peng and Aando, but smooth-strong all over, like a prong-horn or a hunter-cat. I had been up and down trees all my life, on my own since I could walk and on Sook-Sook's back before that. But this thing tomorrow, climbing the Wall we do not climb, was different from climbing trees. No branches. No vines. And up there, I would be alone in a new way.

I had been alone before, of course. It takes a lot of solitude to learn to listen to trees. But this? Climbing away from my kin, from the People, away from the Real itself? No friendly branches to offer me a second chance if my foot slipped. No one to help me hobble home, like that time when I had hurt my ankle in a tumble. No mother to mend my hurts. Alone, alone, alone.

A person always climbs alone, really. But where I was going, no one would find me if I fell.

I asked my kin not to sing me off or give me goodbye gifts to weigh me down on the climb, but I could not keep them from getting up before dawn with me and swarming around while I got ready. It was too much. I escaped and came down to bathe in the Durma one last time before my journey.

I have never been to the bathing place this early before. I have never been here alone. The emptiness is eerie – no children splashing, no one joking around as they scrub off the scents and stains of the day. The rock where we sit to braid up our hair after washing is vacant and shadowed. The sun is not yet above the trees, though dawn's early dimness is clearing moment by moment.

Out over the water, the canopy of leaves breaks open to the sky and a wedge of the Wall looms. I step down the looping roots into the coolness. The water is dark and clear; no feet have stirred the mud on the bottom. I wade out, pushing through the float-flowers. A little shiver dances up my skin. How could I ever have taken all this for granted?

I take a breath and bend my knees, kneeling into the stillness. Mother Durma closes over my head, shutting out the chittering sounds of dawn: the dawn-frogs and hoppers and the sleepy, waking birds. How long will it be before I come to this water again?

I open my eyes.

Off to my right I see the dim, reaching stalks of float-flowers and reeds. Off to my left, darkness and deep water. The Flow tugs at me. My hair drifts around, questing.

If I do not lift my head, if I do not come back up to the surface, this moment will never end. I will never leave. Everything will last forever.

But then I need to breathe.

I lift my face into the air.

THE FARM

Lakka

Well, dammit.

Naina's gone and roped me into wet-nursing this brand new girl who showed up on our doorstep not even able to talk – an infant, really, in every way that matters, and now *I'm* the one who's supposed to keep the dogs off her, and the Guards, and keep her from poaching her brains in the sun or turning into a snack for the crocodiles by the river. Great. Just great.

Why me? Maja's so much better at this kind of thing. Maybe I could—

No, Naina would flay me if she thought I was trying to get out of doing my share. *Sure* the new ones have to be looked after, but this girl – she doesn't even understand words.

Well, a few, maybe. When I pointed at the pump and said, 'Water,' her head came up quick and there was a sort of glint of understanding in her eyes. But then she just stood there, staring at the thing like she'd never seen a pump in her life. She touched her fingers to the drops still hanging from the lip of the rusty old spout, but I had to show her how to work the handle to get the flow going into the trough.

I wondered if she was from some kind of wealthy family, maybe, a little rich brat who'd never had to pump her own water before. But no – look at her hands, her fingernails. And she looks strong, not like that last one that Shano couldn't even keep alive for a month, always whining and falling behind and wasting her breath on crying instead of working, silly mouse. This one's at least done *some* kind of work, sometime, somewhere. Wish I knew what, though.

And I wish I knew how I'm supposed to keep her alive.

Pyn-Poi

Dreams of Long-Legs. Dreams of Silk-Moth. Soft insect voices talking about fibres and threads and roots and hairs. Strands that connect. Vines. Webs. Something about things growing back.

I knew they were talking about me, arguing fiercely, but they were using the language of the Ancestors. 'Talk in words I can understand,' I demanded. 'Talk to me!'

'Shhh,' they said and began to wrap me in their filaments. 'Shhh.' I thrashed and fought as they bound my legs together and my arms tight to my body. Each strand was thin as a single hair, but I could not break them. If I could not get free, Long-Legs would hang me from her web like she does, and eat me when the time was right.

But it was also possible that they were wrapping me like Silk-Moth's cocoon so that I could grow wings.

'Shhh. Shhh. Shhh.' I could feel the insect-breath of their crooning as, strand by strand, they wrapped me tight until I could not fight, could not move, could not breathe.

Then I could no longer hold my form.

I began to dissolve. I had no mouth to scream.

I woke up in a panic, buried, tangled in tree-roots, flailing to get free. 'Shhh, now.' A rough voice in my ear. The screaming darkness faded.

I was lying on my side on hard flat wood, dead so long ago that it did not even remember what kind of tree it had been. Someone's foot under my chin. The burn on my cheek pulsing fire. An arm draped across my shoulder, gripping me. 'Shhh. Shhh. Shhh.' The breath raked my shaven scalp – the amputation had been no dream. A hand patted my back, like you would pat a fretful baby to make it sleep.

And then something that I had heard Bazleti say on her many visits to the buried box: 'It's okay. You're okay. Everything will be okay.' I wished I knew what the words meant.

A thousand cries filled the darkness, each one soft and wispy, but together they were deafening. I covered my ears, but these were not flesh voices and there was no escape. I tried to hear what they were saying, to pick one lament from the many and give it the relief of being heard, but that was like trying to tease out one drop from a river. Drowning in grief, I tried to get away then, tried to send myself far, but the roaring moaning went on forever in all directions as far as my feet could run, as far as my wings could carry me.

This is not *my* despair, I told myself, not mine, not mine, not mine, but I could not escape.

An ear-splitting whistle dragged me up from sleep. The arm over my shoulder pulled away, the feet in my face kicked. Just as I heaved myself up on one elbow to see what was making that terrible sound, the shrillness stopped.

Pale morning light let me see that this bed-shelf was packed with women, some with their heads at one end, some at the other. Bare, dirty legs dangled from the shelf above us, then jumped down. Women's voices came to life all around me like the dawn chorus of birds around my kin's house-tree. I rolled out of the bunk with the others. 'Morning,' someone said. A word I could understand.

Lakka

At first, I thought what everybody else thought: This new girl was crazy, or maybe one of those people who come into the world wrong and never get right. She looked peculiar, for one thing, with strange pale eyes the colour of watered-down beer. And the thing about not being able to talk.

Well, it wasn't *exactly* true that she couldn't talk, I guess. She babbled hopefully at everyone she met and seemed disappointed when we didn't understand. She did have a few words, but she said them funny, with an odd, irritating lift that always made her sound like she was asking a question. Also, for some reason, she could never get the 'b' sound right – even later, years into her contract, she still had trouble with it.

She knew the words for bunk and window and water from the first day. Also 'thank you'. She was annoying about always saying 'thank you' for any little thing you did for her: When you scooted over to make room on the bunk. When you gave her a hand in the fields. When you taught her some little thing about getting along on the Tract. Always 'thank you'. It made her stick out even more than her looks; tractees aren't a real polite bunch as a rule.

I'm not sure why Naina put me in charge of her. I was still fairly new myself and still all chewed up with fury at being sent to the Farm. My life had been ripped away from me on a ten-year contract. I would never get it back.

But angry or not, I'd been there long enough to learn that you didn't argue with Naina. On Tract Eleven, her word was law. More than law, her word was *food*. Naina handled the Tract accounts, which meant she handled everything: renting our tools, buying our seed, 'selling' our crop back to Administration. And she controlled the rations. If the bossy old bitch wanted me to babysit the new idiot child, then that child would be babysat. I might be a felon, but I wasn't stupid.

Sibba

Breakfast time. The line shuffled forward. I nodded my approval as Lakka shoved the new girl into place behind Lucha.

'Morning, Sibba,' Lakka said, when they got to the front of the line. 'This is . . . uh, the new girl.'

'Morning, New Girl.' It was my turn that day, pot-watching for the Tract Council, keeping an eye on the ladle, seeing that favours didn't get paid off with extra and grudges didn't get paid back by light skims off the watery top. Someone had to make sure that everyone got their fair share of not enough.

And there was *never* enough, even in the good seasons when the rains came right and the bugs held off. Then, when our harvest-bags bulged with the fat white bolls of fibre, the Weighmaster would suddenly tell the Council that, oh, too bad, the prices have gone down. And there was nothing we could do but smile respectfully and grit our teeth against the words that wanted to be said, because that price could go down even further if you argued – the Weighmaster had a temper. So it didn't really matter – good year or bad, we were always hungry.

Cook-Mama's crew did their best. The rat-chewed rice we got from the Dispensary on credit against the harvest, they filled out sometimes with snatches of things that grew along the lanes between the fields, whenever the Guards let us grab them on the run back in the evening. Who knew that weeds could be good for you? Those round red berries that sprang up at the ends of the rows – Doc said that they could keep you from getting bloody gums and losing your teeth. They gave a hot, peppery bite to the morning mush, too. And the bulbs of onion-breath, from when we weeded the fields – those gave another taste to the killingly monotonous rice. And the leaves of that vine that we had to keep back from climbing the fibre stems and pulling down the plants – those had something to them, too. Slimy when you cooked them, though, and no flavour at all. Any one of us would have cheerfully killed for a packet of salt.

And everyone was always starved for meat. Always. We dreamed of meat, asleep and awake – roasting, sizzling, dripping, bloody meat. Memories of meat tortured us, but were impossible to turn away from. The Tract Council bought a few beans for Cook-Mama to dole out into the daily mush, but beans were like gold at the Dispensary, and there was never enough in our account to buy what it would take to staunch our yearning for meat and grease.

The gourd-seeds were our home-grown treasure. A long time ago, someone traded for or smuggled in the seed of the vines that still snake around the back of the bunkhouse in the dry season. These gave us huge gourds that were no good for eating but yielded fat, oily seeds for the pot. Not enough, though. Never enough. The Council offered prizes – an extra quarter-ladle of morning mush – for anyone who brought in a bird or a rat. When the grasshoppers came, we ate them raw in the fields.

Pyn-Poi

Too much, too fast, too strange.

That first morning, my eyes were too stunned and bewildered to take in my new place. Someone dragged me to a line of bony women with obscene bare skulls. Someone told me to stay. I stayed. I walked forward when someone nudged me. Stopped when the person in front of me stopped. Walked when they walked. The smell of food.

I touched my cheek cautiously. Someone had smeared a sticky salve on it, but the place where the boot-women had wounded me with fire still burned as if the hot stick was even now digging into my skin. Sick greyness washed over me as I remembered the smell of my own flesh cooking. I jerked away from the memory, back to the now.

Standing in the line of brown-clad waiting women, I struggled to wake up, to bring my two bodies together, to be in the place I was in. I looked around me, taking in the naked heads, the backs, the scratched and scarred legs, the gourd bowls held ready. Then my eyes opened past the women to the land around me, the no-hill, no-tree place with the too-big sky. And then I finally *saw*.

In front of me and on either side, for as far as my eye could travel: An endless stretch of land with only one kind of plant covering it. One plant. Only one.

My stomach twisted and I dropped to my knees, retching.

Later, I could see how crazy I must have seemed to them that first morning, babbling and sobbing and pointing at the tortured fields. This perversion, it was normal to them. They could not hear the thousand thousand cries.

But can you see how crazy *they* seemed to me, standing there calmly in line or sitting in the dirt eating their morning rice, in the face of an indecency so great that not even the darkest nightmare-stories of the People speak of it? As if rape and mutilation were an everyday thing: common, accepted.

And there was no one to share the horror. I pointed and wailed, and the women looked at me sympathetically and went on with their eating. A woman with an ugly gnarled jawbone pushed me back into line. People made hushing noises. 'Food,' they said. 'Breakfast.' As if they were altogether blind. As if I had come to some nightmare place where only *my* eyes could see.

Food, they said, and someone handed me a gourd bowl of grey rice slurry.

But, I said. Look, I said.

Food, they said. Food.

I lowered my eyes and ate.

Lining up. Being counted. That was the ritual of the place. Where my clan had our own special ways of going to water, of drawing the morning blessing on the house-tree's bark, of asking Permissions, of thanking our food, these people had lines. Whistles and lines.

The line-witches could make counting happen at any time, night or day. Three shrieking peals and we would drop whatever we were doing – eating, hoeing, pissing, it didn't matter – and sprint to our places in front of them, racing not to be the last one in line, the one who would get the attention.

All those lines blur into one: At the sleeping-box – the bunkhouse – women with naked skulls rubbing their eyes, shielding them against the low morning sun while boot-women paced behind us. At the edge of those endless obscene fields, before work, standing with hoes in our hands, rooted in place like the plants themselves. Stopped along the road on our way back to the bunkhouse in the evening, hungry, exhausted but not allowed to move until the count came out right. In the middle of our evening meal, my precious gourd bowl shoved quick behind the corner-post of the bunkhouse with prayers that no one would take my food or kick it over in the rush. Or just before the boot-women left us there, with the night-hounds prowling the fields around us.

That first morning, someone pushed me into my place, women on either side of me, women in front of me, five lines of them. I was in the sixth line, behind all the others. So many women. There seemed to be hundreds of them. Hundreds of us. A village of the amputated, all bald and scarred. Later I learned there were only sixty-three. The number rose and fell over the years but, when I first came, that was the number the line-witches counted toward. I was Sixty-Three.

Over time, I learned my number-words that way, as the well-fed counting Guard walked behind us, rapping each shoulder with her stick as she called out the tally.

Those lines were where I first learned to wait. There were always delays: confusion over the count, disputes with the Council, someone skipped, someone left back at the bunkhouse because they were dying. Sometimes the Guards made us stand in line and wait as a punishment. Sometimes, just because they could. Maybe they didn't want to hurry back; maybe there was more work waiting for them at Administration. Maybe they just liked to see us standing there, sweating. You don't always know why you are waiting or what you are waiting for.

Lakka

There really wasn't a title for what Naina was. I guess you could have called her the senior member of the Tract Council, but really Repjim was older than Naina and Shano had served longer on her contract.

But Naina ran Eleven. Administration called her our 'Motivator', but 'motivating' was a pale, weak word for what Naina did. The Managers called her Tract-Mama.

You could think of her as the chief of the Tract, the head of the body, the mother of the family, or the boss of the business. To us, she was just Naina, but I think that, once, she'd had a whole string of other names, fancy ones. Things can change, even for people with fancy names.

You could tell by Naina's way of talking that she'd been somebody once. People said that she and Sibba had had some trouble at the beginning because of it. Sibba never cared much for upper-crusty bitches who thought they knew stuff, but the two of them had sorted it out. Nobody'd gotten hurt and now Sibba was Naina's right arm.

The day after the new girl came, Naina was talking with the three Managers who'd just ridden up, trying to find out why they'd come out with a pack of night-hounds in the morning. Inspections and counts – sure, those were normal, those were to be expected. Night-hounds, during the day, were not. 'But, Manager Goban, you understand that dealing with the dogs slows down the picking,' she said mildly. 'You want us to get the harvest in, don't you, before—'

'We'll keep 'em off you,' Goban said, heaving herself back up onto her big grey riding mule, 'more or less. The new girl misbehaved last night and Guard-Mama wants to make a point.' The bitch wheeled her mule around to face the count-line and let loose with that bellow of hers that could cut across a whole field. 'Collective consequences, girls. We'll be keeping you company today, giving the night-hounds a chance to sharpen up, develop a taste for meat on the hoof. Just keep the line together, fast and tight, and nobody'll get hurt. Much. Oh, and Guard-Mama sends her love and wants you to know that today – and tomorrow, and the next day, too, until she tells us to stop – is all courtesy of our new little missy. Sixty-Three made a fuss at the Barber's last night, and so . . .'

Baleful glares. Angry muttering. Did the Managers really believe all that anger was directed at the new kid?

'We don't like it any more than you do,' Goban went on, 'broiling our brains all day, not a cloud in sight. But this is what happens when somebody misbehaves. Everybody suffers. So just keep it tight out there and let's get this new girl broke in good and proper. Then you can relax and go back to your nice friendly day-hounds. Now – MOVE OUT!'

'Move out!' the other Managers bawled, cracking their dog-lashers. 'MOVE OUT!'

Pyn-Poi

Things moved too fast for me that day, like being tumbled in a river swollen with rain – no way to get a grasp on anything, to get my feet down on solid ground, to take a breath, to think what things might mean: The cursed land. The endless low, tormented brush. The thousand thousand cries. The shaven, skeletal women around me. The huge beasts, like something out of a fire-story, that the three boot-women climbed up on after the counting and the yelling were done.

Some bald person put my gourd bowl back into my hands, squeezed my fist around its rim, and said something urgent about it. Someone else spun me around and gave me a shove. Everyone started to run and I ran with them, clutching the bowl, not knowing why we ran, not knowing the why of *anything*.

We ran in a clump, tight together like a flock of water-hens. We ran at the speed of the slowest, urged on by the boot-women towering above on their monsters, one in front of us and the other two behind, occasionally shouting out a word or cracking a lash at laggers or at fang-foes that circled in too close.

I settled into the run. Feet, some bare, some sandalled, pounded the dead, sandy ground around me. Legs pumped under ragged brown dresses. Deep, heavy panting all around. Sun-scorched skin, poxy with lumps and bumps. Stringy muscle. Scars – not just the cheek scars, but also jagged lines of mauling on arms and legs, old and dull or new and gleaming. Work of the fang-foes?

I saw two strong runners slow and jostle toward the back. I looked over my shoulder as they paced an older woman, wrinkled as a shrivelled berry, who was beginning to fall behind. Each wrapped one arm around her waist and scooped her up, speeding her back into the centre of the tight-pressed mass.

I stumbled then and turned my eyes back to the front and ran with the rest.

The Trees

'Her feet are back in the dirt now.'

'At last.' Rustling, nodding. 'Good. Good.'

'But we should have taught her better how to listen to the small ones, maybe. They are all around her now, but so many voices, all at once – it confuses her.'

'She is her father's daughter. She will learn.'

'But is it too late?'

'She recognised the death-stink. She knows where it comes from now. She knows she is where she needs to be. Nothing is too late.'

Pyn-Poi

A whistle shrilled out from one of the boot-women and everyone jostled to a stop. One of the bald women tugged me into place beside her and held me there, my arm in a snare-tight grip. We made a line again, this one spaced out along the bizarre, agonised land. A chance to catch our breath. I tore my eyes away from the panting fang-foes and looked around me. What I saw was hard to look at: More straight lines, row on row, of this one starved and lonely plant, a low bush bearing some kind of cloud-white fruit. One plant only, everywhere, reaching out to the edge of the sky.

So much wrongness here. The place was soaked in it. I bent down, picked up a handful of the crumbly soil, crushed the clods in my hand, and sniffed it. Tears came to my eyes: Nothing rotting. Nothing crawling. Dead.

Why would someone do this thing? Because – there was no question in my mind – this killing, this torture had been *done*. There was nothing natural about this, nothing accidental. Not like a fire or a monster wind. Things like this did not just *happen* to a place. Someone had deliberately stripped the land of life then replanted it in this sick way. But what madness or malice would do such a thing? How did the scraggly bushes even survive such loneliness, without the press of sister-plants to lift and sustain them, without crawlers in the soil, without fliers in the air?

I had heard fire-stories about great killings, annihilations of one kin by another, even whole clans. Could this be something done to the land of some vanquished enemy, to rub out any trace of their life and memory? To make extinction permanent?

But the land was innocent. The land is always innocent. These boot-people, they were sick. They had forgotten how to step out of themselves, forgotten so long ago that they had lost the knowledge of what it was like to be Other. Yes, I thought, standing there in the sun while the loud line-witch stalked closer to me, any depravity would be possible to such people, even this – torturing the very soil itself.

Two of the boot-women were afoot now, holding their big riding-animals by thin strings. One of them, the little one, had, with nothing but her voice, made the fang-foes gather around her. Away from us. She kept talking to them and moving among them, though their eyes were all turned our way, straining. The other boot-woman, the loud one, was pacing her beast along our line, throwing down heavy spans of brown fabric as she passed each person.

When she came to me, I shied back, away from the huge monster. The rider made a sound – a laugh or a growl? – and turned the animal closer.

I heard the women around me hissing, caught words I knew from Bazleti: 'Still! Be still!' So, trembling, I made myself not jerk away while the boot-woman brought the giant thing right up to me, the big crushing hooves stepping close, the big snout nosing into my soft neck, right where one hard bite can break a person's Flow forever. I could feel its breath on my skin. The boot-woman said something, I think taunting me. Her animal nuzzled and whuffed at my neck.

Suddenly I realised that even if the boot-woman who rode it was broken, the animal was not. It was just *curious*. Only curious. I let it taste me, turning my chin to it, then reached up to rub its nose. Its eyes were enormous, intelligent, sympathetic.

The boot-woman twitched the strings, pulling the animal's head from me. She threw down a pile of brown cloth at my feet, the same rough cloth as the dress I was wearing. I picked it up. It was a bag.

The work that first day was picking fibre. The work was always fibre, but it was not always picking.

Sometimes it was beating at the Mother as if you hated her, stabbing her, chopping at her with a heavy mattock to break up clods dry as shards of pottery – no Permission ever asked or granted. Sometimes it was attacking any sister-plants that had the courage to show their faces, hoeing violently between the rows, scything the ditches that ran beside the fields. Sometimes it was planting, that back-breaking stoop to poke the black seeds into the Mother in lines as straight as a dart-tube. Later, it would be thinning out the seedlings to get those perfectly spaced stripes of plants we could walk between at picking time. Then there was feeding them, with those heavy blue gourd-boxes of stinky grow-big tea sloshing on our backs with little pipes, like snakes, that we dripped at the feet of the plants. And there was poisoning, too. I did not know about that yet. Not until later.

That first day, it was picking.

We streamed out across one end of the field into a single line, each of us standing in the thin path between rows of the white-fluff bushes. I dragged the long bag behind me, wearing my food-bowl like the others did, tied on my bereft scalp as a shield against the merciless sun.

Shouting incomprehensibly, the boot-women dragged me from a place in the middle of the line and put me at one end. The girl next to me came with me. She tried to take the place at the very end, but they yelled at her, so she stepped into the row just inside mine. Muttering, the others tightened up the line, stepping into the places we had just vacated. The whistle blew. We started across the field, the Boot-women grinning in a way I did not understand.

I watched the girl next to me and tried to do what she did: tug the soft puffs of fibre from the shell-like pods without shredding my skin on the bristly stems and sharp leaves. My hands were tender from too long without work; bright drops of red soon stained the fistfuls of white fibre I crammed into my bag. Everyone was faster than I.

And then I learned why the Boot-women were grinning.

I learned about *dogs*.

The *dogs* were the reason that it took so few boot-people to guard us on the Farm. Those dusty grey and brown and mottled fang-foes haunted the fields around us always, prowling through the scruffy plants while we worked, howling through our nights, circling us, awake or dreaming.

That first morning, I learned that the tract-women must keep together, as close as we could get to each other, like any animal family must when a predator is near. But whoever was at the end of the line was unprotected.

The dogs circled us like silent cleanup-birds above dead food, leaping in as they trotted around the line and snapping at my heels. Heart pounding like a too-fast drum, I thought about the jagged scars some of the women bore on their legs and tried to keep my eyes and ears open, whirling with the bag, flapping it in the dogs' faces to drive them off while I poured myself into snatching the white balls off the drying, dying plants.

Fending off the snarling animals, I began to fall behind. The girl in the next row over began to help me, to reach through from her row and pluck the white bolls from my side as well as hers, but still I was too slow.

The widening gap between me and the others drew the dogs even more. Too many of them. I would stave off a lunge from one beast and another would dart in and snap at me from the other side. Their jaws made a sharp, wet sound as they cracked together.

Too many, too fast. I could not keep them off. Would today be the day my story ended?

One of the boot-women trotted over, leaped down and pulled me backward, out of the line, jabbering angrily at me and pointing at the white balls I had left on the plants in my hurry to keep up with the others. She stood over me while I picked one plant clean, then the next, and the next, as the line of pickers pulled away from me.

When she saw that I was getting all of the fibre bundles off the plants, she barked words at me and then heaved herself back up on her animal. She watched from above for a while, then trotted back to her fellows, leaving me alone, far from the rest of the pickers.

So. I was supposed to strip the plants completely. But I had to get back to the rest of the group. The dogs ...

I spun to ward off a speckled, snarling brown mass of fur, but felt other teeth close on the tendon behind my heel. I kicked back hard, right into the jaw of the one behind me, and it fled with a yowl. The pack closed in, silent and intent now that I was away from the safety of the group. I flailed the bag around me. Help – a weapon. A stick. A rock. Anything ...

One of the boot-women looked over, saw the commotion, and pointed it out to the others, casually, like someone would point out a fancy bird on a branch. Grins and laughter. Were they going to watch me be torn to pieces in front of them?

Shouts from the line of pickers. I looked up. They were waving their arms, gesturing, yelling, but I did not understand. The girl one row over from me caught my eye. I saw her bend as if to pick up something from the ground and then mime throwing it, under-handed. She pointed at the nearest hound, a big splotchy beast, every colour that a fang-foe can be.

I understood her. I snatched up a handful of the dead soil from the ground and, as the dog rushed in at me, I threw it – low, so the boot-women would not see – right into its face. It angled off, sneezing and shaking its head, and did not come at me again.

That day, I learned to negotiate with the dogs, and to pick fibre, pick as if my life depended on it, pick as if nothing else mattered, pick with no other thought than 'faster, faster, faster'. That is the way with fibre. It is never satisfied.

I also learned that, on the Tract, we could save each other. That day, it was that girl picking fibre beside me. She saved me from those tearing teeth. Her name was Lakka.

Lakka

After the new girl's first day in the fields – which she nearly didn't survive, because the Managers brought in night-hounds to harass us – Chombly tried to have a go at her. Can't blame her for trying, I suppose, but . . .

It was dinner time. I was sitting with Korva, as usual, leaning against the wall of the bunkhouse in our regular place, chewing and chatting. Not that much to say, of course – nothing really happens on the Tract, but you have to talk. At least I do. Sixty-Three, not so much for conversation, was on my other side. Glued to me, just like Naina wanted, practically passed out from the day's work. We were all dead-tired – we lived that way – but Sixty-Three, Binpoy, wasn't used to things yet. Her eyes closed and her head drooped over her bowl of rice. Too tired to eat, I guess – not something you see on the Tract that often.

Korva glanced across me and pointed, with chin, eyes, and jerk of her head. I turned and saw fingers in Binpoy's bowl. Not Binpoy's fingers. Well. Had to put a stop to that.

By the time Sibba and Naina and their little helpers had elbowed their way through the knot of shouting women, it was over. Taken care of. And everyone agreed that nothing was going on, not a thing. Chombly had taken a little tumble, that was all, and bashed her face against the corner-post of the building, but she was okay. No, no problem here, Chombly agreed, sullen but silent.

Doc looked her over. Nothing but a bloody nose, she said. Naina glared but let it be. Anyone else wants to mess with my girl, they know what they'll get.

Naina

'Our new girl, Number Sixty-Three – anybody found out her name yet?' In the dark, heads shook around the circle. I swatted at something biting my neck and took another sip of piss-tea. 'She could have gotten herself pretty chewed up today.'

'She could have gotten herself killed today,' Sibba said. 'She started out on the bad side of Guard-Mama, and now Goban's crew's pegged her for a troublemaker.'

'That child has got to learn to talk, or if not talk, at least to listen. At least to understand enough that she doesn't get herself killed and leave the Tract short-handed and dangling for her share. Please ask Lakka to see to it as soon as possible. Tell her to get some help if she needs it – don't we have some schoolteachers in the group?'

'Isavuay. Wasn't she a—'

'She taught dancing.'

'Oh. Well, Marneta then. She worked in a bookstore.'

'A newsstand.'

'So she can read.'

I cut off the conversation with a chop of my hand. 'Sixty-Three doesn't have to be able to read. She has to be able to understand enough to stand still when she's told, run when she needs to run, and to pick the damned plants clean. And somebody please find out the girl's name.'

'Now, what's this feud going on between Sanni and Muctan?'

Lakka

About some things, Binpoy and I never really understood each other. Even later, when we were tract-sisters and she'd learned the language and could talk just about as well as any of us (except Doc, of course), she could never really grasp what I'd done to wind up on the Farm. The whole idea of inheriting land – she really couldn't swallow that at all. And inheriting something, anything, from a husband? That bewildered her, too. And being locked up for something you didn't do.

That things could be so different somewhere, somewhere real – crazy talk.

Once we got to know each other, Binpoy told me that, where she came from, if you got punished, *everybody* knew what you'd done – it couldn't happen on the word of a pack of greedy in-laws who'd never liked you in the first place and just wanted your dead husband's land back in the family. It wasn't even a big parcel, just enough to feed us and the children we were supposed to have someday. Nothing, really. I should have let it go. But I was stubborn.

And then I was on the Farm.

Binpoy insisted that could never happen where she grew up. She claimed there was nothing like the Farm there – a lying, wishful dream. So where was it, this place she came from? She closed her eyes for a moment, like she was looking inside herself for something – directions, a memory, something – and then opened them again and pointed off to the east. 'That way, I think. Where the river goes.'

Where the river went? That was crazy. (A lot about Binpoy sounded crazy in the early days.)

I never had much schooling – you don't need it to be a farmer's wife – but everyone knew that to the east of the Farm, the land falls off into a narrow belt of jungle at the base of the Mine. Nobody lives there except those hungry cannibal-monsters your mother would threaten you with when you were bad. 'Behave now, or I'll throw you off the Edge and the Wildmen will eat you and suck your bones.' Could Binpoy really be—?

There wasn't enough flesh on any of us to interest a cannibal and nobody on the Tract really cared that much about your story from before, but over the months and years I came to understand that Binpoy was from somewhere very far away, somewhere really, really different.

Pyn-Poi

How many days went by like that first one, with the hounds after us every moment in the fields? I thought it was always like that – I did not understand until later that this was special treatment, aimed at me, punishing all of us because I had tried to protect myself against the attacker with the blade on that first night. It was supposed to teach me a lesson, and it did.

I learned that we took care of each other, we women of Tract Eleven. Mostly, those first days, it was Lakka – I did not know her name then, but she took care of me, helped me with my row when the Managers were not looking, shared the water in the gourd strung over her shoulder, hissed at the others to make them slow down when I began to fall behind, gave the dogs a face-full of sand when they came too near, and showed me her tricks to be swift: Pick steadily, with a plan, from the top of the plant to the bottom, not with random moves here and there. When you can, pull off more than one boll at a grab. Do not put each boll in the bag, one after another, as you pick them – that wastes time. Grab as many as your hands will hold, then cram them down into the bag, fast, then reach for more. Keep your eyes moving a little ahead of your fingers. Tiny savings of time, just moments, half-moments, but they added up and, with Lakka's help, I learned to keep pace with the others.

As I got faster and began to be able to spare a little attention to notice the people around me, I learned another thing, too: that I was strong. The women I worked and slept beside were tough and sinewy like well-tanned leather, but they were not healthy. I saw signs of curses everywhere. Half of one woman's face – her cheek from ear to nose – was marred by a splash of raw pinkness that ran down her neck and under her dress, livid against her sun-stained skin, like a scar but smooth. A number of the women carried these patches of unwholesome paleness. Others bore crops of pebbly lumps or strange swellings like birds' eggs, under their skin. Many were covered by scabby rashes or slashed with scars. More eyes than was right, even young eyes, were clouded over by a white cast like a mist on a moonlit night.

Had they always been like this? Perhaps their people sent the cursed to this place to punish them? But punish them for what? For their curses? Then why was I here, with all the smooth strength the Mother had given me? Or were these afflictions something that had struck them only after coming to this place, with its too-much work, too-little food, and too-close living? Would I become like them, old young, chewed up by illness?

There was a healer among them – among us – not a very good one, I thought, or at least not a very successful one. At night, coughs echoed through the wooden box we lived in, coughs and restless turnings and mutterings from the hard, tight-packed bed-shelves. I heard this and was afraid, and was right to be afraid. There was much sickness in the closed-in air – deaths, too: bodies that had to be turned over to the boot-women when they came so that the count would come out right.

The first death I saw on the Tract was Bian, a still, skeletal presence with wounded breasts, open and raw as if they had been gnawed off. We took turns fanning her at night so that the flies would not land on the raw meat of her. I do not know if someone stayed behind during the day to do this. Probably not; the fibre needed us all in the fields.

The healer – Doc – did her best with water and wads of fibre to keep Bian's wounds clean but, still, they smelled. I tried to understand from Lakka what had injured Bian so viciously. Had the fang-foes gotten at her? With my hands, I mimed teeth biting, fingers chewing on invisible flesh. 'Dogs?' I asked. 'Bite?'

No, Lakka told me. Not the hounds. As best I could understand her words, she said that Bian's wounds were from the inside. Something to do with the lumps.

Toward the end, Bian was moved to an empty bed-shelf in the back to give her room to die. She was very quiet about it. Mostly they all were, the ones who dropped their flesh bodies and escaped that place.

I never learned its name, but there was a river – what else could you call it? – though its waters were brown and opaque and far, far wider than the lively Durma or her sisters. Its Flow was tired and sluggish like a fat snake that has just eaten, but still, seeing it that first time made my heart sing.

Rivers meant certain things to me: Water to drink. Bathing places we kept free from big-jaws and bone-cleaners by training ground-tea to grow on the banks. Cool dips in the evening to rinse away the sweet body smells that would sour if we did not start them fresh each morning. Float-flowers and mat-reeds cupped in the bends of the Flow. And, most of all, food: Shining fish, fat water-snakes, river-clams, coil-clams, reed-roots. Singed in the cook-fire, baked in the ashes, boiled in the stew, or smoked and saved for travel. Wonderful, wonderful food.

The day we picked fibre bolls in that field near the river, I was so hungry for flesh-food that I could actually feel the fish swimming by us: twitching fins and streaming gills invisible in the opaque water, but so near.

But this river without a name was another kind of river altogether, as wrong and tortured as the monstrous fibre-garden beside it. Flat, shadeless, smelling of mud and rot – and out of reach, because the hounds would not let us come close enough even to wet our feet.

The only kinship that river had to our rivers at home was the mat-reed fringing the edge and the big-jaws lying there, half-hidden, watching us.

After that first day in the field near the river, I dreamed of home. I dreamed of my mother, my father, my brother. Peng, Gai-Gai, the cousins, the aunts. I dreamed of tender water-snake threaded on skewers and roasted over a fire of spice-wood branches dropped from above for our delight. I dreamed I was feeding bits of the smoky meat to my little sister, now grown into a fat and sturdy child, although she was dead.

Back in the Real, we had fibre, too – little sturdy shrubs that tussled for light and life with their sister-plants near the rivers. They gave the People their compact little bundles of fluff to twirl into cord – nothing at all like the bloated, ghost-white handfuls we plucked from the endless fields.

The bolls of the sick, twisted plants on the Farm were swollen things, big as a child's fist. At the bottom of the fist, a clawed, five-pointed star divided the boll into separate clots of moon-white fuzz, each about as big as the end of my thumb. Picking, we grabbed the base to snap the boll off the dry stem. (My palms, my fingers went raw, then bloody, then finally rock-hard like everyone else's.)

We kept some of the fibre from our picking, not much, to twist, between our fingers into coarse thread that could, with a bit of holed stalk, stitch up tears in the tattered brown bags we wore. We would do this at night, waiting for our supper, sitting under the eaves, leaning against the wall of the bunkhouse in the fading light. Twisted a little fatter, the fibre would make a strong white cord that we could use to tie our gourd-helmets onto our heads and finger-weave into belts and bands to hold our water-gourds as we worked. Some of these were lovely things, with intricate white-on-white patterns that turned grey in the dirt. Some people made net-bags or little hammocks to drape across the sleeping-shelf over their heads. There was nothing to carry in these bags, though, and no possessions to store in the hammocks. It was the making that mattered. Even in a place like that, people have to make things.

When I was young, my life was fed by women. My mother. Gai-Gai. My aunts. The Mothers that I thought were all the Mothers, before I understood how big things are.

Then, when I came to this place to meet the Ancestors, I was fed by more women: Bazleti, Khukmama, and all the sacred sex-witches who took care of me when I was nearly dead.

Then, I was boxed up and sent to the Farm: More women. Only women, at least on our Tract, which was our world. There were other Tracts, I learned, other bunkhouses, other women, and men, too, sweating in the sun, more people and more land than my mind could hold at that time, all to serve one master: fibre.

We were fibre's slave, tending its needs, guessing at its wants, watching it always for signs of unhappiness: the tell-tale curl of a leaf, the brown spot that meant disaster, the fiery orange beetle, the wounded boll, the ominous cocoon.

I knew none of that when I came to those women, the women of Tract Eleven, and had no way of finding out, no way of asking what had cursed the land. Because that was the only way I could understand what had happened here – a curse, something like out of the stories we told around the fire at home. Some evil had befallen this place and uprooted the hale and natural thicket of life, leaving everything sick, crazy, and obscene. The violent monthly amputation of our fecund hair, the brutality of the boot-women, the forced-growing of sad lonely creatures that did not even look like the fibre-plants back in the Real.

Sickness. It was all sickness. And somehow these people's sickness was washing over into the Real with the Stink, the killing Stink that smell-echoed the curse-powder the boot-women had thrown on me the first night. What was it? What part did that loathsome yellow powder play in the story of this poisoned land?

Questions. I had no way of asking questions. I needed words, their words.

I was as hungry for words as I was for food. Not really – working from sunup to sundown on an empty belly, this is a curse, too – a heavy one. (I often dreamed of Gai-Gai's big pot, overflowing with greasy fish-stew, and a pile of hot rounds beside it.) But my word-hunger was very strong, and not just because of the feathers that I carried, or rather that Bazleti now held for me, but also because I was lonely. People were talking, arguing, gesturing all around me, and I might as well have been back in that underground box again. Without words, I was like one of the Lonely Ones, haunting the edges of life but unable to join it.

Once again, women fed me. Patiently, and sometimes not so patiently, words were offered to me over bowls of watery rice soup, whispered to me while we stood in line, shouted at me across a field, 'A dog!' A Manager A cloud. The moon.

Words make a person strong. Able to ask questions. Able to say 'No'.

My life, that first season on the Farm, would make a terrible story, not the kind of thing you would want to sit around the fire and listen to. But it was more terrible to live it. The Farm ground into me like a stone. It made my hands hard, and my muscles. It made *me* hard.

On the Wall, I had known that either I would get to the top, or I would die. One way or another, the ordeal would be over. But the agony of the Farm was that it did not end: day in, day out, whistles, lines, running, working. One day the same as the next. No tomorrow. Even the food we ate and the water we drank were tools of torture: enough rice to keep us on our feet for another day, and enough water, too, drawn up into a wooden box by hand-pumping from a hole in the ground. The rivery Real I had come from had no need of wells or pumps, and this notion of pulling up water from the Mother's secret places was new to me and a little shocking. As was the kind of work we did here.

I was a stranger to labour carried on for so long that it becomes a torment to the body – shoulders, arms, back, all burning as if with flames. Skin worn to blisters, then weeping sores, then bloody meat. The People never even conceived of this way of working – not in our darkest fire-stories and certainly not in our lives. A while of tending the garden, then a while of climbing for fruit, then a while of braiding a mat – hard work, maybe, but not a daily ordeal that tries your very will to live. The Farm taught me about that kind of work. Pain that did not end. I learned that it would not kill me.

Field-work is hard and painful, but it makes a boring story. Language-learning, too, even if it is the vine that connects all things.

Lakka never let me rest from that work, either. She was always beside me in the fields, teaching me, testing me, nagging me. She forced me to learn the words to the songs we sang to make the work pulse. She would not let the kitchen people give me my food until I had asked for it properly, by name. As she gave me more and more words, she also made me learn how to put them together right. 'You, hoe here' is different from 'You, here's a hoe', and I had to learn this, too. Even in our crowded bed at night, she reviewed what I had learned that day so that I would go to sleep with the teaching in my ears. Sometimes I got sick of Lakka, sick of words, sick of learning, but her Flow never faltered and there was enough of me to be grateful for it. Usually. Painful work may not kill you, but loneliness can, and it was the words she taught me that eventually let me join in conversation and clanship with the women around me.

Without Lakka, I would have been one of the many who die quick on the Farm. My feathers would have rotted on some shelf in the Happy Palace and Khukmama's broom would have swept their dust away.

Many days, I had no thoughts at all. Not about home and what was going on there, not about who might be dead by now and which of our injured trees had tipped over that edge from which there was no return. Not about the Mothers' feathers. I had lost them; I lost myself, too. And then, when I remembered again, I'd feel sick and ashamed, berating myself for forgetting.

Stay alive.

Get up when the whistle shrieks, gobble down as much as the

Pot-Mama gives you, run when you're told to run, pick where you're told to pick.

Stay close to the others.

Avoid the dogs.

Don't let your eyes touch a Manager's.

The work was eating me alive. It did not just take all my strength – it took all my thought, my care, my attention. Labour and nagging terror – of the life-sucking lumps, of the bugs that would eat the bolls, of the rains that would fall too early, of the crop that would fail – squeezed the Tract like the coils of a hugging-snake, and I was caught along with the others.

Lakka made me understand that if I could simply survive and outlast this deathly 'contract' curse, I would be released from the Farm. They would scar me again, closing the System's circle, and give me a new dress and shoes, and I would walk out the ghost-gate. Every day puts you closer; this is what tractees lived for.

Stay alive.

Don't think.

Pluck one more boll, cram one more handful into the bag.

One more handful.

One more bag.

One more day.

Endure.

I stopped considering the People. They didn't exist anymore, and the Real was just a far-off fire-story. A cradle-song.

But at night, on the hard bunk, Marak would come to me in dream or memory. It was always night-time, sitting around the women's fire, and she would be telling the story of the First Permission – the baby who would only eat moon-root and the friendly bird that taught First Planter how to make more grow by putting seeds into the ground. Asking First Mother if she would allow this. Making the promises that went with the request: to be tender with the sister-plants, gentle with the dirt, and generous with all eaters.

But always, before the Permission was granted, my mother would look around the circle and see that I was not there. 'Lazy girl,' she would say, shaking her head like she always had over my failings. 'Always running away from her work.'

When my amputation was just beginning to heal and a thin fleece of new hair was trying to cover my skull's nakedness, a different kind of day happened. The same shrill whistle woke us, the same lines and counts bedevilled our morning, but no bags or tools were dealt out. We simply ran, chased by the mules and the boot-women on them, with lashers snapping cries out of the runners at the back.

Lakka trotted by my side, as always, badgering me: keep up, stay in the middle, don't attract attention. This run was a lot longer than our usual dash out to our fields around the bunkhouse. With the bobbing heads crowding around me, it was hard to see much, but all that long, long way, there was nothing but flat, one-plant-only fields and once, a box very far out toward the sky that might have been another bunkhouse made tiny by distance.

A nightmare world.

Finally, up ahead I saw more box-houses, a cluster. A big pen . . .

I recognised it.

The barrel. The fang-foes. The amputation. The scarring-stick.

No. I couldn't. Not again. No. Please.

But I was just one small leaf dropped into this river of running women and I couldn't fight the Flow.

As the herd of us careened into an open corral between the buildings, we passed a group of children playing, healthy and strangely fat to my new tractee eyes. One of them looked up incuriously and his glance followed us for a few moments before he turned back to their game.

That glance terrified me. Those eyes were not empty, were not dull, were not blind. No, not blind at all – that child saw our dusty, bony, panting bodies as clearly as I saw him.

But the boy didn't see *us* as you see a person, or a tree, or a dog. Something vital was invisible to him. We were things, just things. Like dust. Like shovels. Like shit that you bury in the dirt. Not selves, not Other – just things.

If eyes like that look at you too long, do you finally, finally turn into a *thing*? Does your Other body dry up like these fields? Does it blow away on the wind?

That was on my first 'Hygiene Visit' to Administration. There were many others, always just as our hair was beginning to heal from the last cutting – about once a month, except during harvest. (And when the sickness came. But that was later.) The thing with the dogs and the barrel never happened again. The branding – that would only happen again when the System was ready to let us go. But the severing of the hair – every visit. Over time, I became resigned to the monthly amputations and was able to bear them without being strapped down, so they stopped beating me.

It was on one of these Hygiene Visits that I became family with Lakka and Pino and Korva.

Back in the Real, friendship was woven by doing things together, but on the Tract there was nothing we did *not* do together – working, eating, shitting, sleeping – in each other's faces every hour of the day. Our very lives depended on togetherness, because of the dogs. So how did the four of us become special to each other – sisters, really, a little kin of our own within the larger clan? It was a sort of magic, I suppose, the alchemy of substances being placed in a pot side by side, separate until some furious fire melts them and they run together.

We were in the Thought Hygiene Room, kneeling side by side while we waited our turns for the Barber's chair, the poison powder against body-bugs, and the Doctor that felt between our legs and looked at our teeth. (We did our best, scrubbing our teeth every day with twigs from the tooth-bush, but sometimes they went bad and the Doctor yanked them out.)

We were being chanted over, as usual – words from the System's *Principles of Productivity*. But today we had a new Hygienist, fresh and eager. So, instead of letting us drowse there while the spells filled our ears, she would murmur the incantations for a time, pacing between our rows, fingering square white power-leaves all bundled into a packet, and then pounce on one of us, demanding that we parrot back her words. If we got them wrong, she would drop a blow onto our shoulders with her dog-lasher.

This meant that we had to actually listen to the words she pulled from the leaves, and by now I had learned enough to understand a bit – Lakka's language teaching wasn't always a blessing.

That day, something in the chant struck me funny – about how good women should keep themselves always clean, always tidy and sweet-smelling and nicely dressed, always ready for the attentions of their good men. The sing-song push of the woman's voice as she strode up and down between our dusty, stinking, sore-speckled bodies – just at that moment, I caught Pino's eye and all was lost.

Laughter jumped like flames from one to the other of us, and then there was no stopping it. All four of us in that back row went up like dry oil-wood in a fire. Even in a place like the Farm, people have to laugh and, that day, we did.

They beat us for it, of course. The four of us were bruised and sore for days, hobbling around like old women, but I think none of us would have counted that a bad price for the laugh and the sisterhood that was born that morning.

We walked past a black box every time we went to Administration, keeping our distance. It hung in the courtyard between the Barber's porch and the Thought Hygiene Room. It smelled bad. Flies buzzed over the foulings below it. Sometimes little sounds came out through its wooden sides.

We walked fast around it.

Sometimes, on our runs to or from Administration, we passed groups of shaven, brown-clad men working in the fields. They did not lift their eyes to us as women and we did not look at them as men.

Other than the Hygiene Visits, one day bled into the next like unset dye. Pain is pain, whether it is in your shoulders from the reaching, your back from the bending, or your palms from the blisters. The pain of the labour was maybe the biggest thing in our lives on the Tract, but it wasn't the only thing.

What we lived for was food: Lifting the rough edge of a gourd to our lips, tilting our heads back, guzzling down our thin, tasteless breakfast soup, and feeling – just briefly – the illusion of our water-plumped stomachs being full. The smell of our evening mush steaming over the fetid dog-dung fire. Scooping it out of our bowls with sticky fingers, then sadly licking those fingers clean. Eating was what we lived for, though the joy of it was always crushed by the fact of not enough. Never enough.

There wasn't much else. Dancing – our limbs were too heavy to dance. Sex – our heart-fires were too burned down by work and sun and illness for sex, though we did take some dull animal comfort from cuddling with our tract-sisters in our bunks at night.

The only pleasure we had that wasn't stained by scarcity and didn't depend on our tired bodies' strength was through our voices: storytelling. At night, work done and supper eaten, while our bellies were as full as they would ever get, women would talk and I would listen.

Sitting there, leaning against the walls of the bunkhouse with my friends, I often heard a word I didn't understand. It came up a lot in the stories about how this person or that came to be on the Tract: the System. I tried to guess at the meaning of the word and also of the sly, respectful hatred with which it was spoken.

Late one night, after the talking broke up, while everyone was crawling into their bunks, I asked Lakka what kind of being this System was, but she had a hard time explaining. 'Not a person like you and me, you know, but long fingers in everything,' Lakka said. 'Eyes everywhere. *So* many eyes. And always hungry. Sucks everyone in, chews 'em up, spits 'em out. Owns everything, runs everything.' She touched the little scar on her cheek, then touched mine. 'Owns me. Owns you.'

The System. The opposite of Mother.

People got sick. People died, or ended their own stories. Fought. Were punished – and not just by the Managers – punished in ways that shocked me. Marak's discipline was soft compared to what the Tract-Mothers did to women who stole food, or hurt people, or defied Naina.

This is how I came to understand the beatings, the starvings, and, worst of all, the lock-outs: the fibre was all that mattered. That white fluff was the only thing that could earn us rice, beans, medicine – life. To get food, we had to give the Weighmaster fibre. And – it took me a long time to understand this – we each owed 'rent' to the System for the privilege of working the Farm's soil. That came out of our account *before* any of our credit was turned to food.

Everyone had to work, whether they wanted to or not, to force the sick, sad plants to yield up the harvest. The clan, the Tract, had to survive. Harsh discipline was nothing next to this bigger thing.

Back in the Real, if you could not or would not do right, the Mothers would send you away. We thought this was a terrible thing, becoming a Lonely One, a punishment worse than death. But the trees would still feed you, even if you had done great wrong. Even if you were broken. Now, in this new place, I realised that being cast out was not so terrible. Nothing like being part of a village you can't walk away from when they ask you to do something that you cannot do.

My people had never imagined a world where you couldn't just take up all the possessions you could carry and go. On the Farm, on the Tract, there was no escape. If bad blood stirred up between women, they still had to work together. If the Tract-Mothers said to do something and you thought it was wrong, the dogs and the Managers and the scar on your cheek and the endless dry, brushy emptiness that walled us in on every side forced you to stay and be a part of the wrongness.

By comparison, being a Lonely One would have been soft and easy. It would have been a gift.

Why did this System of theirs hate us so?

The women on the Tract were like heroes in the ancient fire-stories. Smart. Brave enough to survive ordeals tougher than what witches go through to come into their powers. Then strong enough to get up the next morning and do it again.

But there on Tract Eleven, we never came through into anything and the ordeal was never done.

The first time the cutter-bugs came, I had already lived through one harvest, one monsoon – terrifying, because we had no rain-quarters to escape to – and one planting. I had learned a lot of the speaking of the place, so I understood quickly that something terrible had happened that day when Chinka found the first of the fire-orange, shield-shaped beetles. A spasm of urgency gripped the line as we dropped all efforts at weeding and turned to picking the bugs off the plants. We picked and picked, fast but careful, like little ring-tails grooming a boss ring-tail to win its favour. We picked as if those black-speckled orange eaters were a precious fruit – they were pretty things, if you could look at them without seeing the chopped-up mess they made of the young leaves. We picked until it was too dark to see them anymore, then trudged back to the bunkhouse.

'No harvest,' I heard the mutter around me. 'Contract extensions.'

'We'll starve,' I heard.

'They'll punish us, beat us all, if it jumps to the next Tract,' I heard. 'They'll take our pump-handle, let us die.'

'Where did the damned things come from? We were doing alright – why now? Why did they have to come now?'

Why did they have to come? What did these people expect? A planting without birds or leather-wings, unguarded by any frog-kin, untended by spiders, laid out like a feast with only one kind of plant from this edge of the sky to that one? Why *wouldn't* its eaters come?

Next morning – even more of them. The plants lit up with an orange blaze, not just in the field where they had started but in the next field, too. We fought them, crushing their bodies between our fingernails and dropping them on the ground until thin orange rivers ran up and down the rows between the tattered plants, crunching under our feet.

'Somebody has to *do* something.'

And that night, after the count-line, Naina spoke to the Managers.

After a long, vague night away in dreams that abandoned me on waking, I stumbled out to breakfast to find an oxcart rolled up in front of the bunkhouse, loaded with a mountain of big, square yellow gourds, brighter than star-flowers. The idea of these was familiar to me – they were very like the blue ones from which we trickled out grow-big teas to feed the baby plants. At the very back of the cart stood a huge black barrel with word-markings on it, strange ones – none of the ones I'd learned from Lakka's schooling with the charred stems on a patch of smooth wall-board.

We finished the count-line fast that day – even the Managers seemed to have caught the urgency of the crisis – and then Sibba shouted, 'Grab a tank, girls!'

Lakka helped me strap the thing onto my back. Like the blue

ones, this was – when it was empty – much lighter than it looked, with a long, narrow neck, flexible as a water-hen's. I was supposed to hold this in my hand but, instead of keeping a thumb over the neck-hole to dribble out the contents, Lakka showed me how to work a sort of stopcock at the end of it. 'Spray,' she said. I didn't know what 'spray' meant.

Then she strapped one on her back, too, and guided me into the line at the well. 'It has to be mixed with water,' she said.

'Mixed with water?' I echoed with the shrug that had become our signal when I didn't understand.

'The bug-killer.'

And, when I heard the word, even before I smelled the smell, I felt a sick shaking in my chest.

'No,' I said.

The brighter-than-flowers yellow container now hung hard from the straps digging into my collarbone. In the jostle around the well, I'd filled it up, like the others. Like the others, I'd stood in line for the black barrel, stepping forward one place at a time until I could smell it. I knew that smell. The reek of death. I began to tremble under the weight on my back and the questions in my head.

Like the others, I let Sibba ladle the poison powder into the shell on my back and felt the same pounding as she rammed shut the cap that closed it in.

Then, with the others, I walked, harassed by the Managers' shouts and lashes because we were slow now under the sloshing heaviness that dragged us down.

All this I had done, shaking, sick, wanting to turn away like you want to turn away from a dead body the cleanup-birds haven't fin-ished with yet. But I could not turn away. That evil smell was like the paw-print of an animal that you must track or it will kill you in your sleep. I had to follow it, wherever it led.

But when we got to the field and Lakka pointed me down the row and squeezed her finger on the stopcock to show me how to send the stinking death-juice spattering onto the ravaged leaves, I could not do it. The hard straps scraped my arms as I slid the yellow gourd onto the ground. 'No.'

Lakka made the little shrug, my shrug, the one I used when I didn't understand. 'No,' I said again. 'No.'

'You have to, Binpoy,' she said. 'We all have to. No choice about it. I know it smells like sick-dog shit, but the cutter-bugs ... This'll kill the little bastards. It's a bug-killer.' She said that last slow and loud, like you might speak to a deaf person.

'What's the hold-up there?' someone yelled. 'Hurry along – these critters won't kill themselves.'

Lakka bent over as if to take up the load I'd dropped, but the weight on her own back almost overbalanced her. She caught herself, straightened, and said, 'Come on, little sister. Pick it up now. Put it on. Let's get it done.'

'No,' I said, backing away from the killer that doesn't just kill bugs. All across the field, brown-clad women ridden by unnatural yellow monsters were slogging up the rows of tattered knee-high plants, spewing poison out so that the stench of it clawed the air. Some of them had the neck of their dresses pulled up and over their noses. I thought of my kin, huddled at the back of our rain-quarters, trying not to breathe. 'No.'

'What's going on there, Lakka?' Sibba bellowed across the field. Lakka waved her off and grabbed my wrist, pulling me back toward the indecent yellow, yellow like nothing in the Real.

'No,' I said again. No. No. No.

'Binpoy. Listen to me. This is something we do when the bugs come. We have to, or they'll eat the plants. You understand? No plants, no harvest. No fibre. Nothing to take to the Weighmaster. Nothing in our account to buy food. No food, you understand?' I nodded. 'No *food*. People starve, start to die. Or we "borrow", just to keep eating. You know what "borrowing" means, Binpoy? It means extending our contracts. Yours. Mine. Everyone's. More time. More time in this hellhole. More of our lives wasted. But don't worry about it; see – our Council is smart. They keep back some credit, when we have it, just so we can get bug-killer when we need it. To save the crop. To save *us*. We'll be okay. Now you just be a good girl and put that back on and—'

'No,' I said carefully. 'This kills.'

'That's right,' she said. 'It kills bugs. It's a bug-killer. They make it just for—'

'No,' I insisted. 'Not just bugs this kills. Look.' I snatched up a handful of the pale, dusty field. 'Look at the dirt. The dirt – dead. This kills dirt.' I waved up at the empty sky. 'No birds. Kills birds. No . . .' I didn't know the words for peepers or wrigglers or any of the spider-kin or the little creatures that should grow in the puddles after the rains. None of these were part of the world Lakka had taught me. I made a vague wiggling movement with my hands. 'It kills little things. Kills all, Lakka. Kills trees. Kills People. Kills *life*.'

They could not make me do it.

Some of the Mothers came over – Sibba, Shano, Doc – and yelled at me a while, one at a time and all together. Then they called some of the strong ones to come and force me, angrier now because this pulled more workers back from the line. Chirun lifted the yellow pack up to my shoulders while Nepaka held me hard by the nose and one ear. Someone dragged my arms through the straps, but when they had me loaded again, I just dropped onto my knees in the dead dirt.

Lakka squatted in front of me, almost crying, trying to explain what she'd already explained, refusing to listen to me, or maybe not understanding my feeble baby words. But then she looked up and her word-stream stopped. Naina, the clan-Mother, had come.

Naina looked more ancient than any woman can be and still live, but the Tract never bent her or made her weak. It just gnawed away at her until there was nothing left but hardness and black eyes with points like arrows. If she thought of me at all, she thought that I was strange and that I didn't understand her and that I was just another tool in her hand. She was wrong, though. I was my own tool.

'What's the problem here?' she rumbled in that soft voice of hers that sliced like a stone shard.

'Binpoy won't work today, Naina. She won't put on the sprayer. Something about the smell, I think.'

'She ever show herself prissy before? Lazy? Work-shy?'

'No, Naina. Never. Binpoy's always been a good girl, hard at it with the rest of us. Willing and strong, too. I don't know what got into her this morning.'

Naina stepped toward me slowly, almost ambling. No rush.

Stiffen your back, Pyn-Poi. Refuse to be small.

She towered over me there kneeling in the dead dirt with my arms tangled in the straps of the killing thing. From nowhere, a memory of a young snuffle-pig at the end of a chase – cornered, panting – taking a stand in front of a fang-foe. Caught – no more running, no more trying to hide.

'I understand you don't want to work today,' she said.

'No, Naina. I never say that. I work – you know I work. Anyone says different – they . . .' I didn't know the word for 'lie'.

'Then . . .?' and she eyed the yellow thing riding my back.

'I work. I do anything. But not this. This thing . . . It kills.' I also didn't know the word for 'poison'. 'Naina. People get sick. The lumps, Naina. People get skinny, turn to bone. People die, long and slow. This kills, Naina.' I thumped the yellow thing behind me like a drum. 'And not just us . . .'

I snapped my jaws tight. Do not mention the others. *They* wouldn't mean anything to Naina. Not her clan. No, all that matters is the one thing she lets herself care about: that the harvest comes in and her own clan – Tract Eleven – doesn't starve. A very simple world. But—

Naina looked down at me with those strange, not-kind, not-cruel eyes, wrinkled her nose, and said, 'Well, the stuff does stink like a seven-day fish, doesn't it, girl? But the spraying has to be done. You see the bugs, don't you? They are eating our fibre. Eating our *food*, Binpoy; without the crop, the Tract doesn't eat. But this stinky stuff will kill them. Has to be done. And if it has to be done, then we do it. So you just pull yourself together and get back into line and we'll say no more about this little tantrum of yours. Go on, now.'

And maybe it was her eyes that made me try to explain, to tell about the Stink, and the dying, and the Real world below the Wall, but I didn't have enough words maybe, or maybe I had too many, because then I was sprawled on the ground, my cheek stinging from Naina's palm, rock-hard from years of fieldwork.

The heavy sprayer lay beside me, the twisted straps a stranglehold.

I blinked up at her through the tears that jumped into my eyes at the force of the blow.

'This is not a choice, girl.' Her voice was still soft, no anger, no malice. I rubbed my cheek. 'We won't be wasting time here. There's a job at hand and you'll do your part or there will be consequences, you understand? You can tell all the stories you want, but tell them walking. Tell them spraying. Now, get on your feet and get to work.'

I said no.

And she said there were consequences for not working.

I said no.

And she said that if you didn't work, you didn't get to use up food and water and bed-space – that these things were only for tractees that did their part.

I tried to make her understand that I would do any work – weeding, clearing the flood-ditches, keeping sick Ena's bottom clean – anything, but not the poison.

And she said calmly, in her cool-breeze voice, that if everyone got to pick only the work they wanted, then the Tract would die for sure and that it was her job to keep people alive, so I would sleep out with the night-hounds and I wouldn't be eating or drinking until I worked like the rest of them. 'Water, food – it belongs to the Tract. We pay for it. We *work* for it.'

I felt her dry fingers at my neck, plucking up the fibre band that held my water-gourd. Without thinking, I clutched her hand to stop her taking it. Chirun stepped forward then, but Naina said, 'None of that, now,' and gently – no anger – pried loose my fingers, lifted the water-gourd from around my neck, pulled out the stopper, and emptied it on the ground in front of me. 'Chirun, Sibba, please let the others know that Binpoy is locked out.'

Lakka, muddy tears streaking her face, yelled at me some more and shook my shoulders hard, but Naina told her to get back into line and they left me there, kneeling in the dirt.

Everyone turned away, walking heavily into the field under their loads of poison. Even the dogs didn't come near me.

I had a strange moment then: Even though I *knew* how those straps would grate my skin raw, how they would bite deep into my shoulders, how the weight of the yellow gourd would crush down my spine, my knees, my ankles, how it would drive my feet down into the sandy soil between the rows and make it hard to walk, even though I knew all these things and *also* that the poison tea was deadly, still, at that moment, all I wanted in the world was to be out there in the line with the others, doing my part, helping, defending the crop that would feed us all, that would keep us alive. I wanted to be part of the work.

I almost joined them then. I came close.

But as they sprayed, the Stink rolled off the field, covering us all like a shared shroud.

I slipped my arms out of the straps and clambered to my feet.

Then I didn't know what to do.

I don't mean about the poison or the People I'd abandoned, except in my dreams, or the feathers that Bazleti kept for me. I mean that I didn't know what to do right *then*. I'd never been in the fields without work, without direction, someone telling me, 'weed there', 'hoe there'. What was I supposed to do now? I couldn't walk back to the bunkhouse; the day-hounds had already taken notice that one of us was separated from the group. They were gathering, circling, baying that sharp squealing howl they used to tell each other that a tractee was outside the safe-line and alone – fair prey.

I *had* to stay with the others.

I started across the field, deeper into the Stink, and the dogs pulled back. Ah, vicious but not fools, they couldn't bear the smell, either.

I followed the line of sprayers, like yellow beetles toiling across the ground, splashing the plants with death that dripped down off the leaves and soaked into the dirt under our feet. I stayed close enough to them that the dogs wouldn't pull me down, but none of the others looked at me. No one spoke. Not to me.

When the Managers came by and whistled for the count, everyone came running, awkward under the yellow loads. They let me take my place in line, but none of the usual under-the-breath conversation while we waited included me. No one met my eyes. Even Lakka looked away. I learned what it is like to be a ghost, a thirsty ghost grilling in the sun while everyone around me used the time in the count-line to suck on their water-gourds.

A ghost I was until we trotted back to the bunkhouse that evening. I trailed behind the others, dizzy and weak, my tongue as dry as my skin, my eyes raw from dryness. As I dropped back, away from the group, the Managers' lashes landed over and over again on my shoulders, but I couldn't make my legs move faster.

They beat me until I fell, then made the others wait while they beat me until I got up again. None of the tract-women helped me, no sister's arm wrapped around my waist to steady me and pull me along. I staggered on behind the rest, then fell again and lay face in the sand, gasping for breath.

But . . . No one was shouting at me. No stripes of pain were landing on my back. What—?

I lifted my head and looked around hazily. The Managers. The mules. Everyone backing away, leaving an empty space.

Baying. Barking. Snarling—

The dogs.

They were going to let the dogs have me.

A wave of panic flooded me like a monsoon river, lifting me to my knees, launching me like a loosed arrow toward the herd of watching women.

I shouldered my way into the group, reaching for support, for help. Lakka . . . ?

Lakka was nowhere in sight. Hard elbows knocked my hands away. No help, then, except the terror of those snapping jaws that poured through me like go-strong tea and kept my feet moving.

When that stumbling, staggering death-run finally came to an end, I dragged myself to the bunkhouse wall, to throw myself down in its shade and catch my breath. Then I was, for a moment, not a ghost: Chirun shoved me back, away from the eaves. 'Shade's for tractees that work,' she growled.

Shano and Sibba kicked me away from the water-trough.

The sweet steam from the night's rice mash made hunger a more piercing thing than I'd ever known, even during those bad days on the Wall, but I didn't try to line up for the pot; I'd seen lock-outs before.

Angry that I had not shared the evil spraying, some of the women waved gourds full of food my way, brandishing the aroma like a weapon and laughing when my belly rumbled. Chombly spat a mouthful of water at my feet and laughed. Grenda emptied a gourd of water over her head and stood in front of me dripping and grinning. But most of the women just looked away from me while they ate, eyes searching the horizon beyond the bunkhouse for something else, anything, to occupy their attention.

At dusk, Naina unhooked the pump-handle from the well and drained the trough. I watched the water disappear, sucked away into the parched dirt.

That night was a bad time of thirst and the night-hounds watching from just yards away, no wall between us, their glittering eyes on me as they padded up and down the invisible line that something forbids them to cross. I had become a Lonely One.

Lying in the dirt outside the bunkhouse door, I thought, yes, maybe I *am* like Marak. I am right and I am strong and I am not afraid to drop my flesh body for the People. I will not add my labour to the spreading of the Stink. My hands will be clean; they will not reek of killing. If the Real is to be poisoned, it will be without any help from me.

That's what I thought. That's what I was ready to do. Dying would be no big thing. Just thirst and drying up. A little torture, a little time, and then the birds could carry me where I needed to go.

But, that night, the trees came back.

It had been so long. I had thought, the few times that I thought of them at all, that they could not reach me in this deathly place, but here they were again. With me. Branches sighing and rustling around me, twigs stroking me, green and brown and shady, cool and sheltering, cushiony with moss even as the gritty ground pressed hard into my bony hip.

Maybe I deceived myself. Maybe I was no different from any other person forced by hunger or fear to pick up a yellow tank and slop death across the land. Maybe thirst and hunger drove me to fever-dreams that told me what I wanted to hear, what I needed to hear to stay alive. The Other world is subtle and wishes can be tricky things. The will to live . . .? Who could know anything for certain?

But what happened was this. I heard the trees tell me that one field, one tank of poison – these were not big things, just little leaves on a mighty tree. Keeping my two hands clean was a little thing. The big thing was to keep myself alive, to understand, to travel down the Flow to the root of things. 'Do you mean . . .?' I asked. 'Do you mean . . .?'

And they answered, 'Yes.'

Maybe it was a lying delirium, but I obeyed. I was thirsty and I obeyed.

When the wake-up whistle called the tract-women to come out to eat and drink and face the next day of poisoning the land, I stood before Naina, making my eyes meet hers, and croaked out that I would obey. I would spray.

Naina

Well, that went quick. Frankly, I was a little surprised.

I expected more fuss from the wild-child, storming the breakfast line, maybe, or attacking the well in the morning. They do that sometimes, the hard-headed ones. We take the handle off the well so they can't cheat the lock-out, and thirst makes them a little crazy after the first night.

Usually, it takes a couple of days for them to settle down. Then they cry and beg and clutch my knees and kiss my feet. They'll never do it again, they say. They'll be good, only give them water.

The scenes are tiresome, but discipline keeps us alive and lock-outs are a lesson for everyone, not just the offender, so I let miscreants grovel a while before I let them back into the good graces of Tract.

But that Binpoy . . .? Never what you expect.

That morning, after just one night, she walked up to me, straight-backed and fierce-eyed. I could feel Big Nepaka stiffening to protect me, but the little wild one didn't make any move to attack. She just stood there, about three paces in front of me, waiting. People stopped eating, stopped talking.

I nodded to her and the girl tipped her head to me, like some big Contract-Manager acknowledging a subordinate. 'I will spray,' she said.

Ragged, early morning voices cheered, people clapped, and Cook-Mama scrambled to get Binpoy a bowl of breakfast soup. Everyone is always relieved when a lock-out is finished.

But the whole thing felt odd to me. That girl didn't break like others do. She didn't give up. Something changed her mind.

Pyn-Poi

They gave me water.
   They gave me food.
   They gave me a tank full of poison, and I sprayed.

THE WALL

Pyn-Poi

On that last morning with my people, when I got back from the bathing place I found my aunts had laid out a breakfast feast worthy of a wedding. (Or maybe a funeral.) A big pot of boiled nut-meal, flavoured with spice-bark and sweet-cane. Grilled fish. Piles of every fruit we could still find in the Real. Steaming cups of go-strong tea. I was not hungry – leather-wings seemed to have gotten into my belly and were flapping to get free – but I ate. Not just to fuel my body for the climb, but because this would be my last meal with my kin, until . . .

Until the job was done.

So I sat on our big eating mat and let my kin cater to me like to a bride. My mother banded my hair in a woman's head-wrap for the first time, a beautiful blue cloth that she herself had woven and pattern-dyed. My brother and aunts and cousins took turns putting bites of fruit into my mouth, as if I were a baby bird. All this took a long time, but maybe there was no hurry: The first part of the climb would be up the well-known path to rain-quarters, along the falls of the Durma, mostly following old root steps trained by tree-people long ago.

When I was as full as a gather-sack, I stood up to go. My body seemed very heavy. Everyone fell silent around me while I shrugged into the small hunters' pack Aando had given me for the climb.

I picked up my walking stick. My mother rose from her place and took my other hand. We walked out side by side from under our house-tree, our whole kin following behind us.

As we neared the worn and mossy steps that led up to rain-quarters, I saw the crowd, clan and outclan, standing quietly under the trees around the base of the Wall, nearby but not too close, watching but not intruding.

My mother blessed me then, her hands on my shoulders squeezing tight, almost shaking me with the fierceness of her blessing. And I blessed her, too, and my kin, clan, and People, and the watching trees as well. Then I turned my back on them and started up the Wall.

I had asked them not to sing to me, because I was afraid that the words of the goodbye song would crumple me into a weeping heap, never to rise again. And they did as I had asked. They did not sing.

What they did was hum, very quietly, under their breath, and the wordless tune of the People's farewell rose with me as I began to climb.

It felt wrong – odd and beyond odd – to be climbing those steps in the middle of the dry season and without my kin. But my time of aloneness had not started yet – as my head rose level with that stone balcony above the first pitch of stairs, a man's gruff voice shocked my ears. I clutched a root-grip and kept myself from tumbling backward. Someone on the path? Here? Those stories about jealous Ancestors, come down to eat the living, flashed like lightning across my mind.

But I knew that voice, and those feet on the ledge. I recognised those legs, even without my mother's shell-beads around the ankles.

He had come.

A strong hand reached down to haul me up.

'Oh, Sook-Sook! You scared me – for a moment there, I thought you were an Ancestor!'

'Not yet.' He pulled me to him. There is a way a daughter can only feel wrapped in her father's arms, and I let my startled heart calm itself there in his embrace. But that moment of all-is-right could not last. He let me go, and shouldered his bow. 'My Pyn-Poi was a wise child and has not lost her wisdom with her growing. Only fools and infants would fail to fear, up on the Wall out of season, when the rain-shelters are deserted. The path is stalked by hunter-cats and Lonely Ones. Even birds – winged hunters can snap your neck, knock you off the path to eat your broken body. Better not to walk alone, not until you have to. Your old Sook will hobble along with you as far as these crotchety legs can carry me.'

The Trees

'She has gone.'

'Where?'

'Up. Where she needs to go.'

'Ah, up. Like us. Up. She is getting taller.'

'Yes. Like us. But different. Up – and away. Send out a root in her direction. She should not be alone.'

Pyn-Poi

We climbed slowly. My father limped now, and leaned heavily on his stick. Often I had to wait for him, making a show of hunting for roots beside the track. But there was no particular hurry to the day. One step at a time. Tonight, our kin's rain-quarters. Tomorrow, the next thing.

I was glad that my alone-time had not yet come, though my father had become a very silent man over the years. Walking with him was not much of a matter of words. I wished he *would* give me words, stories like he used to tell, something to explain everything I did not know about the Ancestors and why they might send down the evil Stink to poison their own children and the place that had been their place when they walked in their flesh bodies among the living. But even in the old days, stories had been only one of his ways of teaching.

I remembered, as a child, following his eyes with my eyes, so that I could see what brought him to a sudden watchfulness: The flip of a hunter-cat's tail on the bough above us, suggesting that we go find another tree while it took its noon rest. I remembered him pressing my palms to the skin of a tree, guiding my Other hands in so that I could feel the thrill of life that was the honey-hive hidden at its heart. Sometimes he would cup his hands around his ear and turn his head from side to side until he caught the wisp of sound he was listening for, and I would do the same, and hear what he heard. He would scratch the underside of a twig and sniff at it, and I learned to do the same to tell if its Flow was thriving.

That was the way I had always learned from my Sook-Sook, sending my attention scampering off after his like a yapper pup following its mother. But on this day, my father walked behind me. I knew my back was guarded by his hunting bow and his watchful eyes. But I walked in front now and the direction of my attention was my own.

We climbed mostly over old root-crafted steps, stacked coils of mossy living wood like mighty hugging-snakes gripping the Wall, each with a gather of soil or a flagstone caught behind it, a flat place where climbers could plant their feet. This low on the Wall, the path was still shady and green, with ambitious trees clinging to the stone above and below us. Except for the steepness of the way, I could pretend to myself that I was home. But I was not. I was on my way to another place.

My father fell behind, and I gave some thought to what it must be costing a man with painful knees to make this climb with me. I was just getting ready to tell him that he had done enough and he should go home now when, like a creeping chill, I became aware that hungry eyes were watching me. I whirled, scanning the craggy trees for a predator, and saw that my father had an arrow nocked and ready, his eyes locked on a man, naked and grinning, just upslope from us. The man's eyes were the kind that make you want to pull your wrap closer around you, to cover yourself, to hide your body like a treasure from a thief. My hand tightened on my stick.

'Sook-Sook . . .?'

'Just keep walking, Pyn-Poi,' he said, and I did.

The grinning Lonely One was the only person we passed that day.

Just as the sun was beginning to drop behind the rim of the Wall, my father shot a large rock-hen – slate-grey, fat, and beautiful. We thanked it together and he tucked its legs into his belt, where it dangled until we got to our kin's rain-quarters.

So strange, coming into that place without Marak there pealing out orders, organising us, turning chaos into home. Without her, without any of them, the stone terrace looked haunted. The live-again fern that, during the rains, furred the branches of the storm-tree in green, was all dried and brown now. The thatch was ragged in places, though not completely fallen in, and a pair of crook-necks had nested where they should not have. Well, we would leave them for Marak to deal with; Sook-Sook and I did not mind sharing.

Without laying down his bow or quiver, my father led us in through the drooping arches to the great central trunk of the storm-tree. I heard him say something to it, a greeting – I did not catch his words. He placed his hands on either side of the bole and then pressed his cheek to the rough bark. I understood then, a little, how it might have been hard for a woman to stay married to a man whose tenderness flowed to trees.

Before it occurred to me that it might be wrong to stare, he opened his eyes and beckoned me closer. 'Feel it,' he said, taking my hand and laying it against the tree, under his own. 'Touch it. This tree is suffering less.' What did he mean? Less than what?

Obediently, I closed my eyes and put my attention to my Other hands, felt their form and then freed them from my flesh hands: how different they were, finger by finger, distinct, and able to go where flesh could not take me, able to touch where flesh could not touch. When I had gotten them clear, I let them reach inward, sinking down past the surface, in through the bark, into the living skin of the tree, where the throbbing Flow stroked my Other fingertips, humming with life. The touch-sound startled my eyes open, and my hands were flesh again, resting only on the outer shell of things.

'This one is suffering *so* much less than the trees below, Sook-Sook! It is hardly sick at all.' And, indeed, the leaves were untainted, though a little dusty, and there was no scatter below the branches. 'Why? Why should a tree up so high feel the poison less?'

He shrugged. 'A question for the Ancestors, maybe.'

A question for the Ancestors, indeed.

My aunts had filled my small pack with food, light to carry but dense with power – nuts, sweets, smoked meat. I held out a bag of fruit-sugar lumps to Sook-Sook, but he said I should save it, so I cleaned and gutted the rock-hen while he gathered fallen branches. He did not build the fire in our usual hearth, back under the storm-tree. This night, this odd dry night in our rain-place, Sook-Sook built our cook-fire out in the open, under the flecks of light that hung like unmoving spark-flies in the night sky.

I hacked the rock-hen into small pieces so it would cook quickly – we were both hungry from the climb – and threaded it onto skewers of green spice-wood from the bush that grew by the edge, alternating the meat between some starch-roots that I had poked up along the path, pressing them close so that the grease from the bird would baste the root. Then we waited, turning the skewers, swallowing down the hunger that the good smell woke, making sure the sticks did not burn through and tumble our dinner into the coals.

Ever since I was a tiny child, one of the things that had always excited me about being in rain-quarters was the Flow of the air up here, so like a river-stream – playing with my hair, fingering the edges of my wrap like a flirting boy. So alive. So different from the still, close thing that swathed us down under the trees. Down below, we mostly knew the wind as moving branches, dancing shadows, and the restlessness of leaves. Up here, we knew the wind on our own skin, cooling the sweat from the long climb and snatching away the smoke from our cook-fire.

My father leaned forward with a stick, to poke up the fire where it was falling asleep. 'Have to remind things to do their job sometimes,' he said.

He settled back against his leaning rock and we were quiet for a while. I was too big to crawl into his lap like I used to, too grown-up to slide in under his arm and lean against his chest. But . . .

'Tell me a story, Sook-Sook? Something long and complicated, like you used to? With a good ending? A happy ending?'

So, while we sat there on my last night not-alone, enjoying the teasing wind and the smell of our dinner roasting, my father told me again the about the spark-flies that fell in love beyond reason with the shining round face that came peeping, some nights, between the branches. They were so smitten that, against all advice, they flew up through the branches to woo the moon, pushing higher and higher until they had gone so high that the air became thick and cold and they could no longer move their wings and the sky's dark amber trapped them there, glittering prisoners until the end of time.

I gazed up at the stars. 'I do not think that is a happy ending,' I said.

'No? To be joined with your love for all the ages, until the Real is drowned and the moon goes dark? Look, here she comes now to walk among them . . .'

And sure enough, a cool glow on the distant edge of things was just then giving birth to the rim of the moon, crowning like a baby's head.

We ate our rock-hen and watched the moon rise.

I opened my eyes, chilly in the cool night-breeze. The fire was nothing but coals, and I had edged closer to them in my sleep. The birds and peepers had dropped out of the night-chorus; other than the high steady shiver of hopper-song and the rustle of leaves, it was quiet here, quieter than any place I had ever been in the Real. The moon was gone.

Across from me, Sook-Sook's place was empty. Wakefulness flooded my body. I sat up, looked around.

There he was, a shadow against the starry sky, left hand on the root railing at the edge of the terrace, right hand on his bow. He was still an erect man; the years had hobbled his knees, but they had not bent his spine. I got up and went to join him.

He made a space for me there at the rail and dropped his arm over my shoulder. We looked out together over the rolling blackness below us marked by star-glints where rivers showed through the trees.

But what pulled my eyes was the Wall itself, curving out on either hand. The now-black greenery covered it like a ragged pelt below us. Above us, this covering got sparse and speckled as my eyes rose higher, until the pale bald stone of the Wall stood like naked bone in the night, rising, rising above us until it reached the line where the sky began. Above that, only the spark-fly stars.

The face of the Wall was streaked by the dark tear-tracks of the seven rivers. Sook-Sook had me tell him their names again, and I recited them, pointing to each like when I was a child, ending, as always, with our own.

'Work your way up as close to Mother Durma as you can. She will take care of you,' he said, leaning out a bit to see, off to our right, her gleaming fall, all the way down into the Real. 'Up high, you will need her for drinking water. On the lower Wall, you will find many springs and streamlets – in the daylight, you can see fine stripes of wetness from here if you look close enough. Watch for patches of green; where there is green, there is water. But up high, it will be hard and hot, with no trees to shelter you from the bully sun. You will have to drink a lot to keep you strong. Get near the Durma and look for little streams and trickles that break away from the main falls – fill your water-skin from those. But be careful when you come near water. Wet rock can—'

'—set you on your rear end faster than a nibbler's blink. I know. I will watch where I set my feet. But . . .' – I sucked in a deep breath and tried to make my voice steady – 'But . . . if I do fall, Sook-Sook . . .

If I fall and there is nobody there to . . .' My throat closed on the words, but my father could still hear them.

'Listen to me, Pyn-Poi, little bud, little blossom. You will not fall. The Mothers' feathers you carry – they will carry you, up over the edge, and into that place where the Stink comes from and where it can be stopped. Because you are right. It *has* to be stopped. Otherwise, everything is finished, everything is done. You will not fall, daughter, because you cannot fall. But, if I am wrong and your feathers fail you, and time is truly closing its jaws on us all, still, do not be afraid. You will never be alone. If you should fall, the feathered ones will find you, wherever you are, and be your brothers, the crook-necks and black-beaks and cleanup-birds and all their kin. They will set your Other body free and take you where you need to go.'

He blessed me then, gently, his hands light on my shoulders. I looked down and thought I saw, maybe, the dim glows that were the fires of the People, diffused by the cover of the trees.

In the morning, he was gone.

No crying.

Sook-Sook hated goodbyes. I knew this. I knew it from the way he had left Marak's house-tree when I was a child and I knew it from all our small partings since. But this – this was different. He could have at least stayed and breakfasted with me, maybe gone with me just a little farther up the Wall. Just a *little* farther.

I knew I was being selfish. Walking pained him and steep climbing – well, I did not want to think about that. I remembered the leering man we had passed on the way up, and how safe I had felt knowing Sook-Sook walked behind me with an arrow on his string.

But surely, up this high, the risk of meeting broken people was past? At this season, Lonely Ones would be squatting in the lower rain-quarters, from which they could easily slip down and poach fruit and meat from the People's lands. Surely that danger, at least, was behind me. Unless someone had followed me up, I thought uneasily, maybe someone hungry for a different kind of game.

I shook off the thought and scrubbed the prickles from my eyes. I could out-climb any half-starved Lonely One, could I not?

Yes, I could. But only if I got started.

I turned to the fire and rooted through the embers for the starch-roots I had buried to bake through the night, rolling them aside to cool while I poked up the fire. The dawn air was chilly. I would soon climb up past where flat space and friendly bits of dropped wood would allow the luxury of a morning fire.

When the roots were cool enough, I moved over to Sook-Sook's leaning rock and ate two of them while I watched the sun come up over green hills dappled by puddles of milky cloud.

Sunrise is something the People rarely see. Mostly, when we are up in rain-quarters, clouds veil the sky as thickly as the treetops do down below. But sometimes, down in the Real, when I had stayed the night in the top of a tree that stood proud above its neighbours, I had been a witness to this coming, brighter than any fire, this rim that raised itself as smoothly as the eye of a big-jaws breaking the surface of a pool.

I watched it now and slowly chewed the life from the dry, fluffy starch-roots.

I gathered my things to go and found that my father had left me some gifts.

Beside my pack, on a woven mat, a bulging bark packet and a knife rested. I caught my breath – he had given me his knife. Me – a girl. Me – not of his father's clan, which had handed down this gleaming blade since Those Days.

Me.

I blinked, uneasy, but my father was gone, long gone down the laddered path. There was no one to argue with.

My hand felt weak as I reached to pick it up but, when I touched it, my fingers came alive, curling around the leather-wrapped hilt and pulling it from its fine wickerwork sheath. It was heavy to hold and shone strangely in the low-angled morning light.

I had grown up around this knife; unlike others that needed to be replaced often, it had been at my father's belt as long as I could remember. More slender than any chipped stone, this blade never shattered. Sharper than any worked bone, it never splintered. My father looked down with scorn on people who pruned when they could persuade but, when he needed to chop, upstart thickets of cane and strangler-vine fell before him like soft twigs. Because of this knife. And now it was mine.

I slipped it back into its wicker sheath, tied the band around my waist, and slid it behind me so it would not scrape the ladder-roots when the way was steep. Then I took up the packet.

I unwound the string that held it closed, looked in, and sniffed the leathery wad I found there. Go-strong. I grinned and blessed my father, wherever he was. Yes; I would go strong.

The basketwork mat under his gifts finally caught my eye. It was reed-woven, very plain, about as long as my double arm-span, and folded long-ways down the middle. When I tried to open it out, I found that one end was stitched together so that it unfolded into a beak-like hood, with strings to tie it under my chin – a rain-shield like we wear when we have to be outside during hard downpours. And I understood: Even though it would be long months until the next rains, this third gift could also protect me, up above the trees, against the blows of the sun.

Sook

I am getting old.

I never thought it would happen to me. My father stayed young until the day he died. Is the Stink-sickness stiffening my limbs? The same thing that is sickening the trees is sickening the People – could that badness have gotten into my joints, like sand, so that when I move I grind myself down?

Pyn-Poi is taller than I am. How did that happen? And so strong. And now she is gone. Up. To where the Stink comes from.

I did not want her to go, but maybe it is a good thing. Not that the Ancestors will listen to her – they only listen to the dead. But, still, it is good that she goes. Good that she tries.

When I looked into my daughter's eyes on our last Climb together, I saw that they were on fire with purpose and hope.

Purpose and hope. What more could I want for my child? All of us must die. (Once, I would have added, 'except for the trees'.) But I do not want my daughter to die without that blazing fire warming her, lifting her, lighting her up. No, this is better, I am sure.

Let her try the killing climb. Better that than sitting here like me, day after day, feeling everything wither and twist.

Pyn-Poi is her mother's daughter. And Marak was always happier when there was something – or someone – to push against.

This will be my Pyn-Poi's thing to push against. And if she falls, may the cleanup-birds come quickly and carry her where she needs to go.

Pyn-Poi

My first day alone.

I held my big water-skin under the thin stream off to the side of

145

our terrace, filled it until it bulged, then pressed the wooden stopper down deep into its throat and checked it carefully to make sure it was well sealed. My few things, along with the packet of go-strong leaf and the mat, tightly rolled, went into Aando's pack. I re-wrapped my head, with the Mothers' feathers tucked safely into a fold of the cloth, then blessed our storm-tree and set off.

The trail, at first, looked no different from yesterday. Except now I was alone. Not backed up by my father's sharp eyes, now *my* eyes needed to look in all directions at once. I needed to watch for snakes – I tapped along with my walking stick to warn them I was coming. (Sook-Sook always said that bad things with snakes only happen when you surprise them.) Watch for hunter-cats – and listen for that tell-tale silence of the chorus when they come near. Watch for stones that would trip me up and throw me down. Roots, too – the trees this high were less well-trained than those down below. Watch the sky for feather-foes where there was no cover of trees to keep them from diving on me and spearing my spine to turn me into a helpless meal.

These open stretches came more often throughout the day as I climbed the towering stairs and steep paths, the trees growing ever sparser and smaller. Not younger, though – even trees no taller than I were weathered and bony with age. My Other hands itched to stop and settle into those ancient dwarves, to stroke their Flow and learn about their ways in this steep, stony place, but I held myself to my purpose and walked on, hacking my way through thorny bramble-thickets that overran the path in places, stepping carefully over wild roots that followed their own plan up here, working my way always roughly along the falls of the Durma. The springs that broke from the stone of the lower Wall were becoming rarer now and, without river-water, I would soon dry up like a fish on a smoking rack.

As I walked, I wondered about what was in front of me. If – no – *when* I made it to the top and set my feet on the Plains above, I would meet the Ancestors. Would my little sister be there? Would someone have given her a name? Would she still be a baby, walking around on those baby legs like an adult, only smaller? Or would some kind Ancestor, maybe a woman who died in childbirth, love her and see to her needs? Would she even have needs, being an Ancestor now? Maybe Gai-Gai would have found her and would be taking care of her like she took care of me.

The upward path grew less like a stair and more like a ladder as the afternoon sun pounded down. I pulled out the rolled mat from my pack, settled it over my head, tied its strings under my chin, and sent a breath of thanks down toward my father for this gift of shade up here where no trees grow.

My mind wandered to the cool shadows of my home – the great house-tree, *our* house-tree – tucked in between jagged folds of land on either side, with the voices of my kin swarming like birds in its green. The clatter of pots from the fire-bench. A speck of sunlight dancing back and forth on the moss in front of me, and me, a small child, chasing it, tickling it with my toes.

When I was little, I thought those rare, glowing visitors from above were tiny animals that I could collect, maybe, like the water-hens Aunt Saggi kept in pens for their eggs. But Sook-Sook explained to me that those teasing dots of light were actually drops of sun that the Ancestors sprinkle on their kin from the Plains above. They spatter down through the leaves and branches onto the ground, blessing it with brightness. 'You can chase them,' he told me, 'but you can never catch them.' I did chase them, but it was not until I climbed up above the green that I really understood what the word 'sun' could mean.

Raw naked stone.

I had looked up at it all my life, that pale grey of the Wall, indecently bald where the green frayed away to nothing. But I had never imagined what it would *feel* like up in this world without trees, this chopping block for the slicing sun.

Climbing up this scratch of a track was nothing like walking the green paths of my People, with their ancient steps, rails, and handholds shaped from the smooth living curves of roots and tree-arms. Up this high, no turnings or crossings. No rain-quarters. Too far for the People to climb. Too few terraces. No storm-trees for shelter. The only sign of life up here was an occasional spatter of dry pellets from prong-horns or their near kin. Everything was sharp-edged and cutting, hot, and quiet as death.

I had been wrapped since birth in the Real's woven song: whole clans of beings – frogs, hoppers, birds, and the trees themselves – chattering about the daily business of their lives. My empty ears could not help but reach out for that chorus, but on the Wall there was just the wind and, every now and then, the cry of a single bird or the whir of one lonely hopper.

The hooded mat my father had given me fended off the sun's direct blows, but nothing protected me from the oven-heat that bounced back from the baking rock and sucked away my juices. My feet were tough and protected by sturdy reed sandals, but this was like walking across a griddle. No, a griddle is nice and smooth. This was like walking across a bed of fiery coals covered by a midden of jagged, broken shards.

Water. I needed to find water. Soon. The path had taken a switchback away from the falls of the Durma and I had not passed a spring or a trickle since yesterday. I made myself chew some flakes of smoked fish for strength, but the food was ash on my parched tongue.

My mouth hurt from dryness, but my water-skin had grown too

light and I took only sips. I clambered out onto a shoulder of stone to scan the Wall for wetness.

Nothing. No hint of green anywhere. No smell of life. Nothing that flowed or seeped or dripped. But—

Movement. Close. On the trail just behind me. I flattened to the rock and let my heart catch up.

Slowly, slowly – quickness catches the eye – I lifted my head just enough to see—

It was a man. Coming this way.

The Lonely One we had met on the lower slopes?

No, not the same. Rangy and haggard like the one Sook-Sook had scared off, but not the same one. This one was draped in pale ragged skins, nothing like the bright weavings worn by the People. Was that a knife, or maybe a club, hanging from his waist? And that dark tail of rope hanging from the skin over his shoulder – what was that?

I studied it, squinting to squeeze out every bit of sight in my eyes, and—

Not rope – a braid. A woman's braid.

A woman's *skin*.

Fear gave me wings. I forgot heat, forgot thirst, forgot everything except putting distance between me and the eater behind me: Push each stride further, faster – still careful, but faster, faster.

After a steep scramble, the path switchbacked toward the Durma again. The footing turned rougher, angling sharply with the slope of the Wall – hard on tired ankles. Keep moving, though – walking easier now with the air cooling after the sun dropped behind the rim of the Wall. Have to get away. Have to get to water.

But shadows climbed out from the rocks. The sun was going, leaving me alone on this wall of rock with a hungry Lonely One behind me. I pushed on until a stumble in the dark was as likely to kill me as he was, then stopped.

A terrible place to pass the night – very narrow, with a forever-drop to one side, and a sheer stone face on the other – but I settled, ate some of the nut-meats my mother had sent with me, fat and sweet ones, but I craved juicy, thirst-quenching fruit. My pack was light now. It took a lot of provender to fuel such a steep climb. I would have to be more careful of my food tomorrow.

The cooling air comforted me at first but, as fire-hot as the Wall was during the day, it was also bone-chilling cold as soon as the night fell. I had picked up a few sticks for a fire under the last patch of trees, but I did not dare light them now.

I thought I would watch all night and listen for steps on the path behind me, but I fell into a fitful sleep sitting up, my back against the Wall, my arms wrapped around my knees, and my toes hanging out into the starry abyss.

That night, the trees came to me on great striding legs I could not see. They surrounded me, all their kins and clans jostling together, tangling their branches, rustling with concern. One of them, an old, many-buttressed forever-tree, shaggy with fern and moss, leaned in and pressed a branch against my breast. It was uncomfortable, like an elbow pushing into my ribs, and I wriggled to back away but it had me pinned against the rock and I could not move.

With horror, I felt the branch slide into me – through my skin and into my chest. I struggled, but the leaves murmured something, and then I understood.

I looked down and saw that, where the branch went into my chest, there was no blood, no wound. The wood simply plunged through the surface of my skin. It was the tree's Other branch, sinking into me, deeper every moment, through my muscle, through my ribs. I stopped struggling and let myself be known. The Other, limber as a young vine, wrapped itself like a fist around my heart, not tight, not squeezing me in any way, just holding my heart and feeling the Flow of me. Understanding that this was only fair – I touch them; they touch me – I relaxed into the strange sensation. I felt it feeling me, and I felt wonder – the tree's wonder and my own.

After many days of drinking me in, the tree released my heart and withdrew. As it pulled out of my chest, I gasped in bereavement. My sight came back and, with it, tears – agony to be separate again, separate and alone.

The tree patted me awkwardly (this was with its wooden branches, not its Other), shook its leaves, and turned away.

'Wait!' I wailed. 'What do you mean?' The gathered trees all turned their backs and filed sombrely down the hill, leaving me alone. I struggled to follow them, thrashing with my arms, but my legs were locked deep in the stone and I could not get free. 'Wait!'

Panic woke me. I scrubbed at my eyes, looked around, tried to get my bearings in this world again.

Off down the trail behind me, a cold glow stained the darkness against the Wall. The Lonely One's fire.

I waited, shivering in the night, until the dawn touched the Wall and I could walk again.

The prong-horn rack I was on ended abruptly, rubbed out by a raw swath of tumbled stone that must have slid down from above. I let myself take a swallow of water, fumbling with the cap. Only a sip, I told myself, but then I could not stop, and left just a little, maybe two swallows, at the bottom of the water-skin.

I began to climb in earnest then, laying aside my walking stick so that I could have both hands to ant-crawl over the rubble, trying not to stray from the level of the path, to come across to the other side where the way *must* continue. Up and toward water.

I was falling before I knew I had been hit.

Rocks raked my shins, my belly, my breasts as I slithered down the treacherous slope, thrashing to dig in, to grasp anything at all that would slow my slide.

It was not until I came to a bone-jarring stop on a tilted ledge that I realised I had heard the hunting shriek of a knife-beak and felt the breath of its wings an instant before it struck me.

And it was not until then that I saw I was bleeding.

I sat up, swaying and light-headed, and fumbled under my chin for the ties of my father's sun-shield. It was not until I got it off me and saw where the knife-beak had driven through the tight-woven reeds into the meat of my right shoulder that I began to feel the pain.

I craned my neck to look – the wound was just visible through the slashed bloody fabric on my back: torn skin over something that looked like a cut of prong-horn before you roast it. I retched at the sight, but my stomach was too empty to vomit.

I pulled the back of my wrap around to see how much blood I had leaked. A lot, but not the flood you would get from a pulsing wound. Good. One thing at least was good. But I could not afford to lose any more. Not up this high. Not alone, with a near-empty water-skin, precious little food, and a hungry eater on my trail. I remembered my mother's words, spoken over so many of our childhood injuries: 'The Flow must stay in,' she would say, holding one or the other of us down while her powerful hands kept pressure on a seeping wound. 'First, before all things, the Flow must stay in.'

I tried to press on the damage with my left hand, but I could just barely reach the place and the angle was wrong for the kind of heavy, steady force needed, so I balled up a handful of my wrap and packed it onto the wound as best I could, then leaned into a bulge of stone to hold it in place, gasping at the pain as I pushed back against the rock. My mother's hands, I thought vaguely. My Mother's hands, tamping the Flow back into me, like the time I had fallen out of the night-tree and gashed my leg on that broken branch on the way down. The Flow must stay in. My sight greyed out around the edges.

From grey to grey.

I came back to myself, face pressed to stone, eyes filled with grey, a grey that flew apart into splotches of dark and light as my eyes remembered how to see. A pale, milky green – lichen. Brown and orange flecks and streaks of a deeper colour, like blood-stone.

My blood.

I had fallen. I was hurt. I jerked my head up. The Lonely One—

But no – he had been on the trail, now somewhere high above me. Brother Knife-Beak might have killed me, but he had saved me, too, dropped me fast and hard, away from the path and the Lonely One.

Pain had awakened me, tumbled sideways there against the stone, but it was thirst that dragged me up, thirst and those dark forms circling above in the blazing sun that had somehow jumped to morning again. Winged shadows danced around me, slid across my skin – the cleanup-birds that Sook-Sook promised would see to my flesh if I died far from my kin.

'Too soon,' I croaked up at the hungry ones. 'Not dead!' To show them their mistake, I pushed myself toward sitting and the flare of pain in my right shoulder made me dip toward the grey place again. Left arm, fool – use your *left* arm. I held the world tight – do not faint; not now! – and waved away the birds. 'Not dead,' I insisted. 'Go away. I will call you when I need you.' The circling black shapes peeled away.

I looked around me on the bleak stone shelf, not dead.

Water. I wanted water more than anything else in the world, more than I had ever wanted anything, more than it is possible to want. Water.

My slide had dumped me onto a ledge that I once would have described as narrow, but long hours on the precarious, nearly invisible prong-horn track above had changed the meaning of that word. Now this slanting stone porch seemed wide, smooth and generous – a broad-shouldered man could walk here without having to turn and sidle along with his face to the rock. This wonder of a path tilted sharply upward to my right. This was good – although the fall may have saved me from being eaten, I hated to think how much of my hard-won height I had lost. The knife-beak had knocked me so cleanly from the trail – would the Lonely One be able to track me down that streak of rubble? Surely not, not unless the man had the nose of a fang-foe and could climb like a ring-tail.

As I gaped dizzily out over the edge, it seemed to me that I now sat a little over halfway, though not nearly three-quarters of the way to the upper rim where the Ancestors' world began. So much ground lost in one quick flash. I pushed despair away.

Because of the curve of the Wall, I could see three of the falling rivers far off to my right. The Durma was hidden from my sight, though I knew it had to be near. I needed it to be near. Without water . . .

Water. Where was my water-skin? I had left some swallows in the bottom of it, not much, but some. Where?

I saw my pack, not too far away on the same ledge, and crawled toward it. One shoulder band had broken in the fall and, worse, some greedy animal had torn into it. I pawed the bottom for crumbs, then tipped it and shook it. My fire-stone rattled out, along with Sook-Sook's packet of go-strong leaf, but nothing was left of the smoked fish and nuts that I had been hoarding.

Well.

But hunger was not the killer here; thirst was.

Where was my water?

I drew my legs under me to stand, but as I leaned forward, away from the rock that supported me, the move tore at my shoulder. An arrow of pain reminded me – do not let that wound open again. Do not lose more Flow to the Wall.

I pulled myself up, as slow as Gai-Gai on a bad morning, and found that not all the blood was from the knife-beak's stab. A cut under my chin had dribbled a long brown stain down my chest. Deep scrapes and gashes on my arms and legs were scabbing fast in the dry air. A hard swelling on my forehead was tender to the touch, but not leaking; my head-wrap had given my skull some protection. My belly and chest were bruised but not punctured.

Another small good thing: My father's knife was still at my side. But the water?

My legs were so weak that I thought better of walking and dropped again to my battered knees. I struggled into the sun-shield. It had probably saved my life by confusing the knife-beak about where my neck was, but the real reason I put it back on was to shade my feverish eyes. With my pack dragging from my left shoulder, I crawled along the stone sill like a baby. I had to find either the water-skin or the Durma soon, or call the brother cleanup-birds and let them take me where I needed to go.

I never found the water-skin. Maybe it fell back into the Real. Maybe it came down on the ledge to the left of where I landed. Maybe I should have turned back and searched in the other direction. But that would have been the wrong direction, away from Mother Durma, and down. My thoughts were cloudy like a river muddied by shuffling feet.

Up. Toward water. Keep moving.

I passed a fiery night, drugged by fever and the light-headedness that comes with a drying body. My sleep was disturbed by pain and chills and a loud, fierce discussion between the birds and the trees. I could not make out what had stirred them up, just that it was very serious. I wished they would be quiet so I could sleep.

Waking was even stranger. My Other body – not just my hands, but all of it – rose from the stone shelf on which I lay. I felt uneasy – was this allowed? – but luckily Marak was not around to see me playing outside like this. I sailed up into the air, a little queasy from the height, and hovered above myself.

There below me was my flesh, huddled into the Wall, pressed as far as it could get from the edge. It looked so battered there, so forlorn, that a flood of pity brought tears to my Other eyes. I stopped myself from rushing back – I should not waste this chance to take stock of where I was.

I turned my attention in the direction of the Durma. Ah, there it was – very near, just around that bulge of rock. Just a little farther, I told my flesh body, poor thing. Just a little more.

I saw that this smooth stone path was about two-thirds of the way up the Wall. It ran on from where my body lay, straight up to a perch that overlooked the Durma falls, and then on from there as a faint trail of handholds up the rock – a sort of ladder.

As I drifted higher to get a better sense of what was still before me, I looked back and saw that cleanup-birds had landed on the shelf and were strutting around something that was mine. They were big, too big for what I had to do. I took one last quick glance at the path – the shelf, the stone ladder, the switchbacks above – and dove for my flesh body.

'Not yet!' I shouted, or tried to – my voice came out like the cracked caw of one of their own.

'No,' they squawked back. 'Now.'

I scrabbled for a handful of gravel and heaved it at them. 'Not yet!'

Disgruntled, the massive birds lifted noisily away from me and swooped off to find less argumentative food.

Good – as weak as I was, I was not sure I could bring down a cleanup-bird.

I lay very still and waited for the black-beaks.

I did not wait long.

A pair of them settled onto the rock not far from me. They must have been following behind the cleanup-birds, to see what good thing their higher-flying brothers might find for breakfast.

They hopped in nearer and dodged away, testing me, their raucous squawking louder now. They moved faster than the heavy-bodied cleanup-birds – could I match their quickness?

I held myself still as a dead thing.

They bounced closer and hopped away. I stifled a shout and almost jerked when the smaller one gave my forearm a hard, twisting nip with its heavy beak. As if from far away, I noticed how loose my skin was where the bird pinched me, like an old woman's, or a withered fruit.

The bird came for me again, jumping toward my face.

I grabbed.

My body did not fail me. My fist clenched around the black-beaked head and gave one sharp shake, breaking the bird's neck. I thanked it as I felt the wind of its Other wings lifting into the sky. Or maybe that was its flesh wings, each as long as my arm, flailing at me with the fury of a body that does not want to die.

When the bruising wings hung still, I cut off the bird's head with one strong draw of my father's blade and popped the spurting neck into my mouth before anything could be wasted. The shaggy neck-feathers rasped at my sun-burned lips but no breast-baby ever sucked milk more eagerly than I sucked the warm, sticky Flow from Brother Black-Beak.

After I drank the black-beak's life, I was left with its flesh. No time to pluck it or skin it. Now, while I was strong with its Flow, was the time to walk. But good meat could not be wasted. I would carry it with me. Once I was safely by the Durma's water, or when it got too dark to keep going, I would eat.

When I opened my pack to tuck it away, my eyes fell on my father's other gift, the packet of go-strong leaf. If only I had some water – no one ever needed go-strong tea more than I did right now. I untied the thong that held it closed and fingered the brown clump, wondering. Even the herb's odd musky scent seemed to strengthen me. Or maybe that was the black-beak's Flow beginning to make itself at home?

I had no water, but I needed the go-strong badly. Even with the help of the black-beak, I was dry and light-headed – feverish, I thought. Weak as a newborn. I had never heard of anyone eating the pure leaf. But neither had I ever heard that it was poison, or harmful in any way.

Maybe just a little. A taste. Just to see.

The Durma was not far. I knew that now. I could have water soon, real water, but only if I could keep putting one foot in front of another. Just a little farther.

I tore off a piece of the leathery leaf, folded it into my mouth, and chewed.

The herb's first bitterness on the tongue roiled into a biting astringency that made my mouth draw up like tanning leather. I kept chewing.

My tongue and lips began to tingle and then to burn as if I had bitten into a fire-pepper. Then I felt the go-strong rush through me with a whoosh like a wind. That wind blew my heart big, so that I could feel it heaving against my breastbone like caged wings. Or was that the black-beak? Was it trying to break free of me? Or was it straining its wings to carry me up the Wall?

I contemplated the question for what seemed, inside me, like a long time but was, in the world under the sun, no more than the space between two crushes of my jaw as I ground the bitter leaf between my teeth. Time changed its Flow so that I could consider each tiny fraction of each breath, each thought, each move.

The world went bright with light and sound and smell again. Things were no longer hazed with grey shadow. The early morning sun honed the outlines between objects like sharpened blades, as if everything had become more distinctly itself, unblurred. The rustling air seemed to be speaking words just at the threshold of my hearing. The musk of the dead black-beak was overpowering. Even raw and still warm from life, the smell of its meat made my belly rumble.

Later. I would eat it later.

Right now, I had to walk.

Water.

Walking seemed easy again. The pain of my wound was still there, and the burn of weariness in my legs, and the thirst – one black-beak's blood did not count for much against the pounding sun as it rose. But these things all seemed very far away now, like a distant cook-fire seen through a break in the leaves. I was not numb; I knew that I was tired and hurt and thirsty, but those things did not have much to do with my walking – one step, then another – on my plodding way to the Durma. Time became strange, then wispy like smoke, then vanished altogether.

Finally, after years or seconds of walking, I heard it: the low hissing rumble of a great river leaping down into the Real. Soon I felt it, too, as if the water sang through the Wall itself and up into the soles of my feet. I held myself back from running – the path was smooth here, but narrow. Don't fall, Pyn-Poi. Not after coming this far.

I kept to my steady pace until I stepped around the last swell of stone and the sound jumped up to a sudden roar. Cool swirls of smoky steam wrapped me round and I lifted my face to them, closing my eyes to relish the fine sprinkle of spray on my cheeks. I licked my lips – water. I had made it to water.

I opened my eyes. The small hairs of my arms were silvered with tiny drops. I lapped them up like a grooming fur-friend

I took a step toward the waterfall and my story almost ended there. What I set my foot on was no longer the dry, gritty rock I had been walking since I left the trees below. This stone had been wet with spray since the Durma first jumped down from the Plains of the Ancestors, back in Those Days. It was as slick as any step-stone down in the mossy green Real below and my foot flew out from under me.

In the strange altered rhythm that still lingered from the go-strong leaf, I had plenty of time to watch myself falling forward, the path's lip coming up to meet me, the sky's mouth opening below to swallow me. Plenty of time to see how I should twist my shoulders to roll my body inward, away from the edge, toward the Wall. Time also to scan the ground in front of me and find the knob of rock I should grasp to anchor myself against sliding.

And then there I was, still, my face mashed against wetness, my left hand clawed around stone, my right shoulder and hip hard against the Wall. I took a slow breath, and then another. Slowly then. Slowly.

I raised my head.

This was a very different river from the cool gracious Flow where I had bathed before starting out, what, was it just four days ago? Or was it five?

This Durma fell hard and raged at its falling, growling as if it was angry at having to leap out of the world of the Ancestors. It poured whitely down a narrow cleft in the Wall that looked like it had been sliced out by a giant's knife on purpose to channel the Mother of All Flow. Clouds billowed up out of the fissure, almost hiding the water from sight.

My heart fell. That stone funnel – it kept the Durma gathered in one massive torrent deep in the cut – I could not reach it. The small wandering rivulets that I had counted on to let me drink – there were none. Here, within sight of the Durma, water was as far away as ever.

I had come so far, with the promise of Durma-water dangling in

front of me like a moon-root in front of a snuffle-pig. And now here
I was, and there *it* was, and there was no way to drink.

But there had to be a way, something I was not seeing. There
had to be.

Warily, keeping to my hands and knees on the slick rock, I crept
forward along the platform that overlooked the falls.

Green! – so good to see green again, the rock-slime itself and the
band of moss above it. And there! – a hedge of tiny trees that looked
like toys for doll-play, knuckled into a seam in the stone. And there! –
a lace-wing, one lonely lace-wing, prancing in the eddies of mist.

I paused to watch it, licking the dew off my forearms again. As
my eyes rose to follow its bright wings, I noticed behind it an odd
pattern of small rough rectangles, a double line of them running up
the rock face, parallel to the falls, beginning where the path ended
in a sharp fall-off at the Durma's crevice.

The way up.

I had seen this thing when my Other body flew above the Wall.
The ladder.

I examined the chisel-marks around the neat, boxy toe-holds in the
rock, each broader than my fist. Carved by hands and tools. But
whose? And when? The slots were not raw and new, but they were
not ancient, either, not worn smooth by weather or passing feet. In
fact, each depression had a slight rim at the bottom, a lip that held
my fingers secure when I tested myself on the lowest handholds.

Someone had travelled this path before me and cared enough to
peck out these steps for easy climbing.

In fact, now that I stopped to think about it, the path that caught
me when the knife-beak knocked me off the rock, the path I had
been walking ever since, seemed all along too flat and smooth to

be a natural sill of rock. Had that been smoothed by someone's work as well?

The ladder, the path – could Lonely Ones have built them? Could the broken, dangerous cast-offs of the People, the ones who had let their Other bodies wander too far and get lost – could *they* have climbed this high and done such work?

No, that could not be. This neat path, the tidy, sculpted hand-holds – these were big things, the fruit of many people planning and working together for a long time. Maybe years. Lonely Ones were alone because they *could not* harness themselves to living and working with their kin, for the wellbeing of something larger than themselves. They were solitary, driven out one at a time because they had done things that pushed past their clan's willingness to make a place for them – killing or raping or some other obscenity against the Real. Lonely Ones would never have the health of mind to join into a great work like this. But – my breath caught – would the Ancestors?

It was said that the Ancestors sometimes came down to walk among the trees again and tend to their own mysterious plans and purposes. People – whole families, even – sometimes disappeared without a trace; it was said that a jealous Ancestor, hungry for life, had eaten them up. When a special treasure came to a kin – a new honey-hive found, or twins safely birthed – it was sometimes called a gift from the Ancestors. Could this be the path they used for their comings and goings?

But did it matter, Ancestors from above or secret stone-workers from below? In spite of everything, the Mothers' feathers were still safe in my head-wrap. The ladder led upward. My way led upward. I tipped my head back, and shaded my eyes, trying to see how high the slots ran, but not far above me the stone face leaned back from the path and I could not see the end of them.

I licked the glistening leaves of the tiny trees and sucked up a little water that had pooled in a dimple in the rock. Not enough. Not nearly enough. But it soothed my throat and gave me courage.

People had come this way before. I was not the first. The Durma was near and there would be a place – there had to be – where she would share her water with me.

I opened my father's gift, tore off a shred of go-strong leaf, much smaller than before, and cautiously began to chew.

Any single step on a ladder is easy.

You simply step up with one foot, swing your weight onto it, straighten that leg, shift your hands, and step up with the other foot. Easy.

Then you do it again.

Again and again and again.

But the problem it is that, once you have started, you cannot rest until you get to the end. You can pause for a moment, maybe, to catch your breath, but your legs are still carrying your weight and the muscles of your arms are still fiery with the burn of holding you.

You can never let go, never really *stop*. You can only push on and on until you get to the very top. You keep climbing, or you turn back. For me, that choice had been made days ago. Maybe years ago, when the killing Stink first settled on the Real.

I carried the feathers for the People.

Up.

I raised my right foot, scrabbled for the next slot, jammed my toe into it, and heaved myself up, the pain in my torn shoulder adding my grunt to the rumble of the Durma falls.

Then I did it again.

Again and again and again.

Was there any end to this climb? Was the rim up there just a fire-story, just a dream? Would I drag myself up forever, or until I fell? It was all the same. A Wall without a top. A waterfall without a source. A climb without an end.

One more step up. Just one more. That is all. Do not think past that. Just this one more thing. Just—

I reached for the next handhold and clawed open air.

The shock of it cleared my mind-cloud like a sudden wind.

The top. I had come to the top.

I groped over the edge and found the next notch cut into the table-flatness above my head. I grabbed it, scraping my wrist against the rough stone edge.

Straighten your knee. Just a little bit more. Up with the other hand.

And there it was, the next slot. I heaved. Stepped. Heaved. Stepped. And then I was lying on level ground under a sky so blue, so bright, so painfully beautiful that I had to roll away from it.

I found myself on a small stone balcony overlooking the falls of the Durma, railed in, not by the twining arms of trees but by rocks piled and interlocked into a low wall, except for the gap I had just crawled through, where the track of handholds pocked the ground an arm-span in from the edge.

The sound of water – not just the low roar of the waterfall, but the sweeter trickle of—

There! There it was, a rivulet broken away from the main body of the Durma, just the way Sook-Sook had promised, streaming into a basin broad enough to hold my body.

I staggered to my feet, swaying on legs as wobbly as mounds of breakfast mash, tore off my pack, tottered over to the little pool.

Clear, beautiful water.

With a huge splash, I dropped into it face first, like an old tree falling.

I drank until I made myself sick, then drank again and pulled my pack over to the rim of the basin.

I plucked the black-beak, sitting there in the little pool and letting the feathers flow away with the water that spilled over the edge and found its way over the rock face back to its mother-stream.

Still without leaving the water, I ate as much of the brother-bird as my belly would hold, gnawing the tough, slimy meat from the bones, then breaking the bones and sucking the marrow.

Finally, after a long time – the sun was dipping toward nightfall – as the black-beak's strength rose in me, I began to take notice of things beyond eating and drinking: The small peeping sounds of life coming from the few gnarled bushes clustered back by the Wall. How tired I was. The riddle of why this place, this place clearly made by will and work was here. The fact that the end of the terrace led to a path just like the one below, a slim shelf that led upward and away from the Durma. The tiny fish, no longer than the space between one knuckle and the next, that nuzzled the hairs on my legs and tickled me. How filthy I was, how bloody.

I took off my head-wrap, tucked the feathers into my pack, and began to wash, first my clothes and then myself. After the long soaking, my body-wrap came away easily from my shoulder and the wound did not open. I scrubbed the blood out of the fabric, but the dark stains of it blotted the intricate patterns of Aunt Dokha's weaving. I scoured my hair, my face, all of me, using some of the grit at the bottom of the basin to rub away grime and old blood from my cuts and scrapes.

Clean at last, I braided my hair back up and spread my wraps to dry. The sun would bleach out some of the stains, but there was nothing I could do about the tears.

I lay down on the warm rock and slept.

I woke up shivering.

A wriggler as big as my thigh glared at me from the top of the stone rim of the terrace, pushing out his throat over and over again to tell me I was not welcome here. This was *his* place. The moon gave me enough light to see that he was not the kind you could eat, so I begged his pardon and rolled myself into my wrap, tying on the sun-shield, too, trying to get as much cover as I could against the chilly night wind, but I was still cold. I looked appraisingly at the little thicket of brush near the Wall.

The bushes were very old; you could tell that from their wind-sculpted limbs and knobby elbows, and the way their roots webbed across the stone like an old man's veins. Almost trees, though tiny. It would be wrong – disrespectful, short-sighted, greedy – for an upstart like me to hack and burn such venerable living wood, branches that had scratched a toe-hold for themselves here in this unfriendly place, sheltering all the smaller lives that depended on them. Wrong. Definitely wrong.

But I was so cold. The dirty wound in my shoulder was spreading its poison, carrying the knife-beak's intent to kill out to the rest of my body. The breeze-rustling of the bushes seemed to call me. I went to them.

I crushed one of the small leaves between my fingers and sniffed it. Oil-wood. It would burn so beautifully and its smoke would smell so sweet – the People prized its cones to burn at celebrations for their scent. It would not last long, of course, but it would be bright and hot while it burned. I could toast the black-beak's bones and eat what was left of its meat sizzling from the fire.

I dropped to my knees beside the oldest bush, to wrestle with myself, maybe, or to ask its Permission, but then I laughed. Cold and hunger had made me stupid.

I did not have to burn the living plants. The shallow trough in which they had rooted brimmed with many seasons' worth of dropped twigs and fallen leaves that had gathered there and crisped in the sun.

Giddy with joy, I raked out a pile, pulled the fire-stone out of my pack, and got to work.

Water. Food. Fire.

That night I sang thank-you songs to the spark-fly stars.

The next morning, I drank as much water as I could hold, deeply mourning the loss of my water-skin. A tiny pinch of go-strong leaf – just enough to get me moving without much altering my senses – pushed me onward, up the trail.

The walking was smooth here – not difficult, though uphill – with patches of rolling gravel to beware of. I kept my eyes sharp for movement, for cross-trails that might connect yesterday's prong-horn track to this new path, for *any* sign of people coming and going, but I never saw the Lonely One again. Brother Knife-Beak's rescue had been harsh, but thorough.

Around mid-morning, the shelf-path I was on ended at a sheer wall. A ladder of notches trailed up it, much like the one near the falls, though much shorter. This climb brought me to another smooth upswing of path sweeping back toward the Durma again and, in a few hours, I had a chance to drink once more at another terrace perched above her deep-cut banks, this one with a carved groove in the rock guiding her water into a shallow stone trough.

I drank and climbed again, beginning to feel some confidence that this kind path would bring me back to water if I just kept on.

And that was the way of it. I passed back and forth up the switch-backs of the trail, always coming back to the Durma.

The startling belief that I might make it began to dawn. I might actually win through onto the Plains of the Ancestors and come face to face with them. Perhaps my questions really would be answered. All I had to do was keep going.

At first, I thought the sound was a peck-bird going after its dinner. It had that same rhythm, clack-clack-clack, over and over again, with pauses between the clustered pecking.

But as I came nearer, the sound changed from a clack into a clang and from that into a sort of clink, like the sound my father's blade made when he was chopping through a tangle and accidentally hit rock. Sharp like that.

It was louder now, maybe just around the next bend. A ring-tail beating a rock on something, maybe? No, not this high. Not this far from the trees. Another Lonely One? No. No, please—

I eased around the curve, silent as a falling leaf, minding my feet against any telltale scrape of stone or roll of rock.

And there—

Squatting, face to the Wall, right on the path in front of me: arms and legs like a man, but with dusty, baggy hide, grey like dry dirt, the colour of no living flesh.

What *was* it?

And what was it doing? Tapping the stone with a chisel. Tapping the chisel with a hammer. Both tools shone fiery in the sun, like my father's blade.

With my hand on the hilt of Sook-Sook's knife, I stood stone-still and tried to make sense of the creature. It would place the chisel with care, then tap it delicately for a while, then run man-like fingers through the fallen bits of stone as if searching for something – sometimes finding it, picking up a tiny fragment and tucking it away into a drawstring bag. What was this thing?

No Lonely One from below – that was plain. None of the People had skin that hung and flapped like that, no matter how ill.

Could this be a Lonely One from above, cast out by the Ancestors, exiled down from the Plains just as the People exiled our own broken ones? Surely tapping so intently at a stone face was madman's work?

He was so fixed on the rock in front of his face that I took a step forward. The hammer and chisel covered the sound of my steps. The way was broad here; maybe I could get by him if I moved only when he was tapping.

Slow. Slow. Careful.

When I was only a few feet from him and barely breathing, I saw what he was doing: picking the blood-stones out of the rock just like I had done when I was small, just like every girl-child has done for her gathering bag. A crazy thing for a man to be doing. He was very, very confused.

I must have made some sound. The stranger sprang to his feet, spinning, brandishing the chisel in one hand and the hammer in the other as his head flew off.

But that thing that went tumbling over the edge into the empty air below – it was not his head at all, just a round of floppy hide that had covered his real head and hidden – I gasped – his night-black hair and coal-black eyes.

But in spite of that strangeness, this could only be a man. Taller than Aando, even, and strong-looking. What I had taken to be the baggy hide of starvation was nothing but some kind of wrap for each body-part separately, trunk and arms and legs. Underneath was muscle. And I was weak, sick from wound-poison and too little food. This man could overpower me easily.

But I had my father's knife.

I scuttled back down the trail, then stopped a few feet away, breathing hard. 'I mean you no harm,' I said. 'I just need to get by.'

The Garnet-Miner

The creature startled me so badly that I almost threw it off the Mine right then and there. It looked so crazy – gaunt battered face, huge staring eyes, and only a tattered blanket to cover its nakedness. My eyes pinched in on that long knife-sheath hanging at its waist and the scratched and scabby hand resting on it. I didn't see at first that it was a girl.

One of the Wildmen from below that haunt the Mine, had to be – those amber eyes, that voice croaking out meaningless sounds in a hoarse, breathless babble. Under the dust, I could make out the telltale blood-brown of Wildman hair. I tightened my grip on my chisel and mallet and braced myself for the first move.

It spoke again – still nonsense, but louder and more urgent – and pointed up the trail. This time, the voice nudged my attention to the creature's shape – even wiry with muscle, that wasn't a man's shape. A girl, then, but no less dangerous for that, especially out here where one tiny misstep can throw a man right off the Mine and into the next adventure. I didn't take my eyes off her.

She pointed at herself, and then up the path, making walking movements with two fingers as if they were little legs. She's telling me she wants to get by, I thought – probably a ruse, a way to get close enough to skewer me with that big chopper of hers.

171

She jabbered more insistently now, pointing up past me.

What could I do? I couldn't get back to the garnets with that girl ready to jump me as soon as my back was turned.

I told her to go away, stabbing my finger toward the downward path. Go away. This is *my* contract and you have no right to be here. I made brushing motions down the path. Away with you.

She didn't go, just stood there staring at me for a long moment, then took a step in my direction.

'Go away,' I insisted, raising my hammer.

She said something entreatingly and moved her hand away from her knife-hilt, cocking it up to show me her palm.

It could well be a trick. The Wildmen have killed a lot of canny Miners, men tougher and smarter than me. This could be—

She took another step toward me. 'Stop,' I warned again.

But the stranger didn't stop and I did what I would have done for any lady of the town.

I stepped out of her way.

She trudged past me with the dragging steps of a person about to drop from exhaustion, stiff and brittle-seeming when she turned her whole body back to look at me, instead of just looking over her shoulder. Dark streaks stained the ragged fabric she had wrapped around her – old blood?

No matter. 'Not my blood, not my problem,' my father used to say. I watched her until she was out of sight around a bend, then turned back to the vein I was working.

The picking here was easy. The brittle grey stone was spangled with gleaming flecks, like a cloudy night sky full of red stars. Most of the garnets were tiny, of course, good only for blood-sand. But where there's babies, there's mothers, and some of these stones were substantial, even bonus-worthy – maybe earn me a few days away in the city. My collection bag was already decently full.

I'd meant to pick a while longer before heading up to be off the Mine before night fell. But I couldn't settle back to the work. The thought of the girl kept me looking over my shoulder. My neck itched with the memory of that big knife – never drawn, but there – nearby, somewhere up the path.

People say the Wildmen eat Miners that venture too close to the heaving waves of jungle below. Maybe it was true; that girl looked hungry enough to keep me listening for the crunch of footsteps behind me. I couldn't keep my mind on what I was doing.

I gave up and packed up and started up. Better to be behind her than to have her behind me, hungry and crazy and armed.

Not too far along, I saw her up the trail in front of me. I breathed easier now that I could keep an eye on her. A small, rainbow-striped pack drooped from one shoulder. Then I noticed, just to the right of it, the tear in the yellow-and-orange cloth stretched across her back and the nasty wound that showed through it.

She must have heard me coming up behind her; she turned, said something fierce, then ploughed ahead.

'Wait,' I called. She looked back. 'You're hurt.' I pointed, but she kept walking. I hurried to catch up with her.

Coming closer, I could see the angry redness that streaked out from a ragged gash below her right shoulder. Infected. Badly infected – amazing that the girl was still upright.

I reached out to touch her – I'm not sure what I had in mind – and she whirled on me, gesturing that I should back away.

I let her put about five paces between us, then followed her, wondering how she would ever make it up the stiff haul to the top.

As we climbed, the girl's steps slowed. She wobbled sometimes on the steep places where you have to crawl up like a cockroach, hooking your toes and fingers into niches left by other garnet-pickers. I was afraid for her, tried to climb close enough behind her to catch her if she slipped, but she hissed at me and dropped her hand to her chopper so I backed off and let her do it on her own. It was slow going.

When we got to the third terrace from the top, I knew she had to rest or she would just fall over – over the edge – from exhaustion. She started across the flat space to the next line of toe-holds, but I stripped off my pack and threw my bones down on the rock, miming a yawn. 'Let's take a little break here, why don't we?' She stood there at the base of the ladder, looking back at me, swaying a little. Her big golden eyes were sunken, her lips, white-rimmed and cracking. 'You're dead on your feet, girl. There's still a long climb in front of us. Why don't you just sit down for a bit ...' I patted the rock beside me. She turned to the stone face and reached out a hand to climb.

'Wait,' I said. She turned to look at me.

I dug around in my pack and pulled out an orange left over from lunch. I held it out to her, along with my half-empty canteen, sloshing the water around so she could hear it. 'Here. Take it.'

She didn't move, didn't blink, didn't even seem to breathe – like she'd been turned into a statue. I kept my voice soft and low. 'Come on, girl. What choice do you have? Look me over good. Look me right in the eye – can't you *feel* that I'm a good guy, more or less? Yeah, there's men up there who would hurt you or turn you in or take you by force – I'm not arguing. I know some of them. But that's not me.'

It was like watching a starving stray dog when you offer it food – weighing its chances, watching your face. Watching for that one twitch that will make it turn tail and run. I stayed very still, the orange extended, the canteen swinging from its strap.

Then she dipped her chin. Her shoulders slumped. Her fingers fell away from the hand-hold. Steadying herself with one hand on the cliff-face, she stepped nearer and lowered herself carefully onto the ground beside me. Only then did she reach out for the orange and the water.

She drank and then ate with contained desperation, peeling the fruit, then sectioning it precisely. She didn't gobble it down, though she did go back and eat the peeling afterward. When she handed the canteen back, there was still some water chuckling in the bottom. She'd left some for me. Maybe that was why I wound up taking her under my wing. Or maybe it was just that sharing food and drink on a hard road turns people into buddies.

She shut her eyes for a few minutes then woke with a start and struggled to her feet. We climbed again.

Like I said, it was slow going. Not a bad thing, though; darkness can be a friend sometimes. It was well after sundown when we topped the rim. I don't usually do things like this, but the girl looked so forlorn, gaping this way and that, swaying there on the lip of the Mine, out on the edge of those great flat endless fields. So . . .

I motioned for her to follow me, not really thinking that she would, but by this time she was whipped, barely standing. The climb had taken the fight out of her.

I walked her past the checkpoint with no problem. The Watchman was snoring at his post, as usual, with his rickety chair tipped back and propped against the wall of the guard-shack.

About fifty yards beyond him, I made her sit down beside a row of dried-up fibre plants, making 'sit' and 'stay' gestures like you would for a dog. She seemed to understand; she waited quietly for me while I went back to the guard-shack, woke up Mr Reliable, signed out for the night, then came back to where she was dozing in a crumpled heap. Would I have to carry her? But no, she heaved herself to her feet and followed me toward town.

What could I possibly do with this girl? I couldn't leave her stumbling around alone on the road; somebody would get her for sure. But where could I take her?

The Contract-Miners' dormitory was no place for her. She'd wind up in somebody's menagerie for sure if I turned her in at the clinic; that sweet little body of hers and those exotic honey-coloured eyes would see to that. She'd clean up pretty, sure enough.

She did need doctoring, though, or something like it – she was empty-eyed and staggering by the time we made it into town. Every now and then she'd stop and look around her, then mumble a question. Always the same question, I think. I'd shrug: *I don't understand you.* Then she'd keep going, putting one foot in front of another like each single step was the only thing that mattered in the world.

I don't know if it was the right thing, but the girl had to go somewhere. I took her to the whorehouse.

THE FARM

Pyn-Poi

I walked the rows with the rest of them, these new clan-sisters of mine, pouring death out of the supple neck in my fist, poison running over my fingers where I squeezed the stopcock to make the spray fly out. And I vomited with my sisters, too, when we were all sick and dizzy afterward. Heaving up the too-little food in my belly and wasting it on the roots of a fibre-plant, I could taste that it was the poison making us sick. And not just *us*, here; all the faces and the deaths and the sad, stained leaves that I'd abandoned when I walked through that evil ghost-gate – they all came rushing down on me now like a horde of furious whizz-wings, stinging me with their accusations. Had I really done this thing, this killing thing? Had I really become *this*? What was I now? Surely no daughter of the People. Who was I? Had I really allowed thirst and wishful thinking to suck me into selling myself and everything I loved – all for a puddle of rice soup, a jug of stale water and the comfort of lying inside the bunkhouse walls?

The answer came, solid as my bones, after that first day. In the deep night, while coughing and retching barked in the darkness of the bunkhouse around me, while I pleaded forgiveness – from Gai-Gai, from my sister, from all the People – the trees came to me again, like a green flood washing everything away.

177

On the hard dead boards of the bunk-shelf, with Lakka's elbow poking into my ribs, the trees were suddenly with me again, limbs creaking, leaves stroking. Soft green light filled my eyes. Air that was moist and rich and fragrant with life wrapped me and held me. With snores and darkness all around me, amid sickness and strangeness, I was home.

The trees knew all about the dead fields, the one-plant-only obscenity beyond words. They knew it all: The poison. My hands holding the nozzle, aiming the spray, thumbing the stopcock. Of course they knew.

But they were not angry with me, not even disappointed. They had a temper, some of them and, back during my training days in the box, they could be sharp with me when I was lazy or let my mind wander. But this bigger thing – pouring out poison with my own two hands . . . Nothing. I had done as they directed; it had not been a wish-dream.

Seeds must be planted, they told me. You must go deep. You must carry the yellow weight on your back – and not just now, but later, again, when the caterpillars come, and then the brown-spot, and the grasshoppers.

But—

Seeds need humbling, they said. They need dirt and the darkness. They have to find what is at the bottom of things when all their pride and hardness are skinned away. What is at the bottom is what you stand on.

The trees began to come to me every night, harrying me with new lessons.

By this time, I was far from the newest on the Tract. Tanam and Ekabi had come after me, and another girl who didn't last. I was Number Forty-Five in the count now, but people called me by something like my name and I knew their names, too, only fifty-one of us now because the harvest had been hard and monsoon deaths had left the bunks less crowded.

Here in this place, when the rains came, there was no escape, nowhere to climb to, no well-drained refuge high above the floods. The sky opened. The water rose. The latrine overflowed. The rush of water under the floorboards sang its nightmare lullaby all night while we tried to sleep, wet against wet, under the roaring, leaking roof. How high would it rise?

Still, we worked – bedraggled, in the pounding rains, dragging out the brush that threatened to choke the ditches, shovelling mud into brown bags to wall off the bunkhouse from the worst of the flood, fighting the enemy trying to drown us all.

Nothing dried, ever. We worked wet, slept wet. Fevers came, coughs, belly-twisting diarrhoeas. And when the torrents tapered off and the flooded fields turned back to mud – and then to a hard-baked crust we had to chop open for the planting – well, a few missing faces just meant a little more space at night and maybe you didn't have to sleep with someone's toes under your chin.

Lakka, Pino, Korva, and I lay side by side on the top bunk on the right. The top shelf was our place because we were young, easier with the climb up onto the rough boards. Also, Pino didn't like being closed in – she had been punished once in the Managers' box – and on the top there was nothing pressing down on her.

That was our nest: four wet, hungry birds clustered close, keeping each other warm during the rains. Sometimes, we would rub each other's sore places. Sometimes, the other girls would tell stories and I would lie there trying to understand, trying to piece together a picture of the twisted world outside Tract Eleven. Sometimes, there would be giggles and the older women would shush us like tired mothers.

At night, the trees were with me always now. Pressed tight between Pino and Lakka, I would close my eyes and there they would be, waiting with directions for disciplining my Other body. But that was just the start of it.

Now the exercises were not just for making my Other body strong and purposeful. The lessons turned to improving my Other hearing, as well.

The People say that a person has big ears for this thing or that thing. My father had big ears for trees. My mother had big ears for her clan. My Aunt Dokha, for flowing water; Aunt Saggi, for the birds. Now I learned that this wasn't just a manner of speaking; hearing may be a talent, but it is also a skill that must be mastered with intention and hard practice.

And, oh, they did make me practise. First, to hear them not just as 'the trees', but to tease out their very particular voices, even when they were speaking together all at once. Tall, proud house-trees sound different from tangled-together forever-trees and they both sound very different from fruit-trees. So many trees. So many different voices.

And later, they turned my ears to the sighing of the fibre-plants. That was a sad song I thought I already knew well enough, as it was the background to every breath of every day, but they taught me that it, too, could be heard both as one voice and as many.

They made me open to it both ways – first to the whole, like the roar of a waterfall, and then to the one, like a single drip of water on stone.

Once I had managed to tease out the two, they made me change my hearing back and forth, from one to another, until I was dizzy and my Other ears hurt. They made me do it again and again, faster and faster, until it seemed I could hear both things, the single and the whole, together at one time.

If I worked well, the trees would nod. 'Rest now and send your roots home,' they would tell me. But if I was clumsy or inattentive, all they would say was, 'Again!'

At night, when the trees left me, I would dream of the Real. The boards of the bunk would become the springy strands that Uncle Dai had, so patiently, taught me how to twine together into a smooth, silky mesh. Lakka beside me would turn into my cousin Kimo, sharing my hammock as we had when we were giggling sprouts. The roof above us would become the branches of our house-tree, swaying and creaking with the pots and baskets and nets that held our kin's possessions. The endless abomination outside the bunkhouse walls would once again be a wholesome tangle, a weave of give-and-take, so many clans and kins of life that even my father could not name them all. I would be safe again, with the safety of one held in a many-corded net instead of dangling from a single strand of fibre.

That was my dream on the Tract. But the truth is that, back when I'd lived my every day wrapped in that safety, supported in that net, I hadn't noticed it much. It had just been *life*, the way things were, had always been. Would always be.

The thing we breathe – we don't see it, though it is all around us. Though without it we die.

When the ear-stabbing whistle yanked us back from sleep and into the crazy nightmare that people call 'waking', the shock of it was enough to bring tears to my eyes.

It was the second monsoon that taught me the next thing I needed to know.

The skies had broken open two days before. The fields were already flooded, ankle-deep mostly, some already knee-deep – deep enough at any rate that the Kennel-Managers kept their precious hounds locked up so they wouldn't be swept away.

Naina herded us out to wade the ditches. The water was rising too fast; we had to make sure the sluices off the fields weren't blocked or the bunkhouse itself would flood. Without the day-hounds to harry us, we could go out in small groups, so that we could cover more ground. We had to find and clear clogged places, anywhere tangles of debris and brush were slowing the Flow out to the river.

The pounding on my shoulders was as hard as a beating and wearing my gourd-helmet was like having my head inside a drum. Most of us were naked – we left our brown dresses back in the bunkhouse so that at night we could put on something less wet to sleep in. The rain stole our warmth, wracking us with shivering.

As we fought through the mud beside the roaring ditch, there it was again: the Stink.

It must have risen gradually, too gradually to catch my attention at first, like the way you don't really hear the night-song of the peepers and hoppers at home. But here it was, sharp and clawing.

Why? We hadn't sprayed, not for several weeks.

But the Stink *was* the spray, wasn't it? That and the poison powder they put on us at Hygiene Visits. Why did I smell it now? Why now, during the rains?

When I was a child and my kin was in rain-quarters, way up above the Real, sometimes just before the rains came, the night sky would blaze up all at once. Just for that moment, lightning like a night-time sun would show us *everything*: the shelf we lived on, our sheltering storm-tree, the awed faces around us, and the whole of the Real spread out below.

Like that, I suddenly understood, I suddenly *saw* – with big eyes riding moon-high above everything – not just these cursed plains and not just the Real down below, but both together in one piece:

I saw the poison sprayed out by a thousand hands, dripping down the fibre-stems, soaking into the dirt. And I saw the rains – harder and earlier these last few years – also soaking that dirt, flooding the fields, pushing out into the big ditches, and farther, into the river. I saw the tainted water rushing to escape this place: back toward the sunrise, back toward the Wall and the seven rivers that tumble down it.

I saw the rivers crashing over the rocks and the poison mist billowing up, smothering the Real and the People, filling our lungs, wetting our leaves, envenoming the roots of all things.

There was no question in my mind. These fields were the source. I saw, I saw – but what could I do with the seeing?

Knowing a thing is not enough. It is only a beginning, a first step on the climb.

By itself, knowing the path of the poison didn't change a thing. This was my second monsoon on the Tract – I understood what would happen next. The sky would fall on us and we would fight to keep the water flowing away. When we thought we could fight no more, and the river and the land became like one great sheet of water that spread from one edge of the sky to the other, then rains would finally begin to slow. Eventually the sun would come again, hard, and the mud would dry like fired clay. We would pound the ground with mattocks, break the crust, and plant again. Just the one seed, fibre, the same seed over and over. The tender feast would call the bugs that loved the crop, and of course they would come, and the brown-spot, and the droop. It would all happen again, and we would spray again, or starve.

To save my people back in the Real, there needed to be no spraying. But this was impossible. Even if some magic turned Naina's mind from spraying, our Tract was just one of the twelve that ran out from Administration like segments of an orange. And there were many Farms – I knew this from tract-sisters who'd had contracts on others. How many Farms? Were they all spraying? Surely they were, if they forced one-plant-only to stand there, massed like a great banquet for the bugs that fed on it. How could anyone be so stupid, so twisted in their understanding?

But I pulled myself back from that question. There were so many brutalities in this world – pain-causing games, punishments that took people to the edge of death, work that almost killed, objects with no other purpose than to hurt. The people here were crippled. They had lost their Other bodies, or were unable to send them out, and so any indecency was possible for them – no point in dwelling on the why of this. There was no wishing it away. Just take it as a fact, like the rain – not something to waste my time on, just something to consider as I made my plan.

But what *was* my plan? How could I stop the poison, not just on Tract Eleven but on all the Tracts on all the Farms above the Wall?

I didn't know enough yet. I just didn't know enough.

Should I run away? Could I? If I could get outside this big box we were all trapped in, maybe I could find out about the other Farms. Were they as bad as ours? Were the people there as crazy?

I sidled up to the idea, one night, talking with my sisters.

The waters had come up to the very threshold of the bunkhouse, flooding Cook-Mama's hearth so that there was no fire to cook hot meals. Instead, she would leave the rice to soak all day in her big pot. The soaking made it soft enough to eat – barely – but it also let it sour and bubble. Eating it was a bit like chewing on rice beer and made us all a little loose and tipsy.

We had to eat it in the bunkhouse, squatting on the floor or perching on our bunks. Pino, Korva, Lakka, and I had carried our bowls of the gritty soup up to our 'house', and were chomping fiercely at the rice. The soaking made the grains pasty on the outside, but with a hard core on the inside, and if we didn't grind them well with our teeth, our guts would grind them for us, painfully, later.

Maybe it was the beer-bubbles in the soup that loosened my tongue, that or the small feeling of privacy we had up there in the dark, with sounds of fifty wet and tired women eating and chatting around us. 'Has anyone ever run away?' I asked. 'I mean, escaped from the Farm? Before they finished their contract?'

Pino's fingers claw-clamped into my wrist. Her gourd bowl clattered to the floor, causing squawks of protest from the women below us. Lakka scrambled down after it. 'Shut up, Binpoy,' she hissed, retrieving the bowl, scraping the spilled mush from the floorboards, and handing it back to Pino. 'That's not something you ask.' Korva scooted aside to make a space for her to climb back up.

'Why not? I was just wondering—'

'Well, don't wonder about that.' Korva's voice, leaning in from where she sat cross-legged at the other end of the bunk. 'Not where anyone can hear you. If Naina finds out that you even *mentioned* running, you'll be on half rations till the sun shines through your ribs.'

'But why,' I persisted. 'Why can we not even *talk* about it? Talking can't hurt—'

Pino still clutched my wrist, spasm-strong. Now she shook it, beating it against her thigh. 'No, Binpoy, no. When the count comes and they find someone missing, they punish *everyone*. "Collective consequences". And then they zero out the Tract accounts. Years of credit, gone. No contract extensions, either; they let the whole Tract starve. People die. But not you. You, they put in the black box.' Her voice caught. 'They don't let you die in the box, you know. They keep you alive.' Pino was panting now. 'But there's no air,' she gasped. 'No air. And time doesn't—'

Lakka jumped down again, shouldered past me, and helped Pino down. Half-carried – Korva on one side and Lakka on the other – Pino staggered between the bunks as women pulled their knees aside to let them by. I trailed after and joined my three friends standing in the rain, calf-deep in the endless sheet of water outside the bunkhouse, Pino bent over with her hands on her knees, gasping for breath.

I could feel Lakka's hot breath by my ear. 'Give it up, Binpoy. Even if you *were* a heartless bitch who didn't care if she left her Tract to deal with the System's damned "collective consequences", there's just no way. This Farm has been around forever. Everything's been tried – trust me on that – and all the mouse-holes have been stopped. Across the fields? The hounds take care of that. The river? The crocodiles. Pretending to be dead? The Managers dump bodies in a pit at Administration, with a scoop of quicklime to help 'em rot. Out with the harvest, buried under the fibre? They prong every cart with sharpened pitchforks before it leaves the Farm. And bribes? Nobody *has* anything to offer. And even if you made it back out to the real world,' she whispered angrily, 'if you ever meet anyone, any living soul, wearing that half-moon on your cheek without the closing brand, they will lug you right back to claim the System's bounty. And then you go into the black box. It just can't be done and I won't help you try. You and Pino and Korva are the only family I have left. So drop it. I mean it. If you don't, I'll tell Naina myself. I'm serious about this; you hear me? Don't talk about this stuff, ever. Don't think about it. It'll make you crazy. And it's catching, like a fever – you can make other people crazy, too, make them do things that'll get us all slow-killed. So, just . . . don't.'

'But—'

'No "buts" this time. I know how you think, Bin; you think there's hope. You think that if you just push hard enough, you'll find it, some magic way out that no one's thought of before. But I'm telling you, the *only* way out is time. You're not a lifer. Just keep going, put one foot in front of another, stay alive. Don't do anything crazy, and one day they'll strap you down and sizzle that crescent on your cheek into a pretty little circle. You'll smell your skin crisping and squeal like a piglet, and then you'll be free. *There's* your hope. That's the only way.'

She looked me hard in the eyes until I nodded slowly. The idea of escape wasn't easy to give up, but Lakka knew things. She understood this place better than I ever would.

So.

'Collective consequences' – the System's 'or else'. Escape would hurt the clan, would destroy the 'credit' that came to us when we brought the harvest in. By this time, I understood 'credit', understood that our lives depended on it being greater than the 'rent' we sacrificed to the System. Credit meant food.

The women of the Tract were not my blood-kin. Anyone could see that by the look of me. Even dressed in the same filthy brown bag and stamped with the same amputation, labour and scars as the others, still I looked different. I talked different. I was not one of them.

But I *was*, my heart argued. Shared work, shared bed, shared food, shared stories – lives shared for almost two years – *this* makes you kin. I *was* one of them, kin and clan. We were melded like a forever-tree thicket – many trunks, only one tree.

I could not leave them if my leaving would take their food.

No escape.

In the nights, the trees pushed me deeper now, opening my ears to softer and softer whispers of things so small you cannot see them with the eyes of the flesh.

But in the days, I made Pino a little string doll, twisting some fibre scraps into a rough cord, then wrapping it over and over around four fingers to make a bundle for the body and then around three fingers to make a shorter bundle for the arms. I threaded the arms through the body and wrapped the whole, crisscrossed, to keep everything in place. Then I divided the body below the arms and wrapped each half to make the legs and wrapped each arm down to the wrist.

I gave the little thing to Pino and told her it was a charm that would open all closed things. She wore it until the sickness took her.

THE HAPPY PALACE

The Garnet-Miner

It was thick dark by the time I got the girl to the Happy Palace. The 'open for business' lamp was burning over the lintel. I tapped on the old tin door while the wild girl leaned against a post. She looked near dead.

We waited a while – busy night, I guess – before Boss Lady cracked the door open and sized us up. A wave of perfumed air rolled out. 'What's this you've brought us?' she rumbled, standing aside to let us in. 'A new girl?'

'Just someone who needs seeing to, Boss Lady – not for the trade. Found her out on the Mine, pretty beat up and not talking a bit of sense. Wildman blood, I'd guess by the look of her, but she hasn't tried anything on me. Well-behaved. She's hurt, though.'

'I can see that,' Boss Lady said, leading us along the unlit gallery around the courtyard. The girl stopped once, peered into Boss Lady's face, and said something very slowly and with great care; I think it was the same question she'd been asking me all along, but Boss Lady couldn't help her with it, either.

We passed an open door. I could make out the glitter of eyes and the outline of a woman's hips, but it was too dark to see much. Another door, this one closed, with the sounds of business going

189

on behind it. Then Boss Lady opened the door into her private 'sitting room'.

She settled us down on cushions around a brazier where tea was stewing and pulled aside the back of the wild girl's garment to inspect her shoulder, probing the skin around the wound with her fingertips, then touching it with the back of her hand like my mother used to feel our foreheads for fever. The girl stood this with surprising meekness; she hadn't ever let me touch her, not even to steady her when she stumbled.

'She needs some doctoring, I guess,' I went on, 'but I didn't want to take her to the clinic. You know . . .'

Boss Lady's lips tightened. 'Yeah. I do know. No clinic. But I don't run a hospital here.'

'But you know what to do,' I pressed. 'Better than the clinic doc, everyone says. Hurt or horny, they say, Boss Lady will take care of you.' She poured out tea into little cups that seemed too dainty for her size and too fancy for this tin-roofed rabbit-hutch. After taking another look at the girl's drawn face, she emptied four big spoonfuls of sugar into one of the cups and whitened it with cream before handing it to her.

'Slow down, girl – you'll sear that throat like a steak. As to doctoring – if neighbours have trouble, sure, I'll look them over, maybe give them some advice. But keep them here? Nurse them? No – my beds have paying purposes. Sick folks generally go on home and get seen to by their own people.'

'But what if they've got no people?'

'You think I'm running a charity here, boy? I've got expenses. Mouths to feed. Protection to pay. Pencil-pushers to bribe. I can't—'

'Look, Boss Lady,' I said, leaning toward her. 'I can give you something for her keep. Maybe for some medicine, too.'

'Has to be some medicine; that slash is infected bad and I can't afford a dead body without papers turning up at the Happy Palace.

But what's your interest in this pretty little lamb-chop? You hoping she'll rise up from her sickbed and make you a fine little golden-eyed Miner's wife? Or is this an investment toward selling her? Because I don't hold with that kind of thing.'

'No, the girl goes her own way as soon as she's well enough, not yours, not mine. Free. No strings, no contract.'

Boss Lady took a slow sip of her tea. 'Something for her keep, you said – how much did you have in mind?'

I wound up giving Boss Lady a garnet as big as a pea. Pretty stupid, I guess – everyone's heard the stories about what happened to light-fingered Miners. But I figured I could count on Boss Lady. A woman in her line of work needs to be discreet.

Boss Lady

Where was this mangy little kitten from? I wondered. Nowhere around here. Nowhere even close. Look at those eyes, as pale as weak tea.

I don't usually take in strays but, for some reason, this time I said yes.

The Miner (I couldn't remember his name, but no point in letting him know that) turned down my offer of a treat on the house – that garnet was worth a pile more than what it would cost me to keep the girl. He said he had to get to his Contract-Agent before the office closed for the night. True enough – a Contractor would not look kindly on a Miner who went off to sleep with a pocket full of garnets.

I said a friendly goodbye to the man – no matter what the business, you want to leave your clients feeling good when they walk out your door – and turned back toward my sitting room, hollering for anyone who wasn't with a customer. Bina's head peeked out.

'Put some clothes on,' I snapped, and sent her to Mr Ghilly's for some fever-powder and some medicine against infection.

'His shop'll be shuttered at this hour,' she protested. 'He'll be in bed.'

'Well, wake the man up then. Tell him it's for me. Have him put the stuff on my account,' I added, knowing better than to put cash money in Bina's hand, poor thing. 'Then you run right back here, quick as you can. No lingering on the way.'

The girl was there where I'd left her, slumped on the cushion, nodding off over the brazier. Better get her to bed before she fell over onto the floor.

I spoke to her and she looked up at me with those strange light eyes of hers. She said something back, a question, by the tone of her voice. What could I tell her? I just motioned for her to get up and come with me.

She followed me peaceably enough down the hall, stumbling a little in the dark, letting me lead her. I have to say that she didn't act very wild.

I pushed open the door to an empty room, lit the lamp, and stretched out the pallet the other girls had rolled up so neatly when Rashi left us to get married.

The girl let me skin her out of the torn fabric wrapped around her nakedness, but not the indigo scarf around her head; she clutched at that with a desperate fierceness that I had no intention of battling. I'd get it from her later, when she was asleep after I'd dosed her good and proper. All her clothing would have to be washed, maybe burned – lice can get a brothel a bad name quicker than the pox. She wrapped her arms around herself and shuddered with a chill. She'd need something to wear, something that wouldn't draw any more attention to her than necessary.

As she stood there, looking around the room in a bewildered sort of way, I held the lamp up to get a better look at her patchwork of bruises, cuts, and scrapes. That child looked like she'd been in your better class of bar-fight. 'Who did this to you?' I wondered aloud.

She answered me with gibberish.

She was feverish – I knew that from the shivering and the burning skin – but not so much to be delirious. I listened to her babble carefully, trying to make out some meaning.

My establishment caters to people from all over, not just local folks but all kinds of random contracts blown in from who-knows-where to work on the Mine or the roads. But this girl's jabber – well, I tried, but I couldn't make out any echo of any accent or rhythm I'd ever heard before. Not a single familiar shape. She really must be one of them, I thought, one of those wild people that live in down in that little strip of jungle between the Mine and the sea.

Pretty mild-mannered for a Wildman, though. When I pressed on the hot swelling near her wound, she jerked and caught her breath, but she didn't duck away from me. Hurt dogs are like that, too, sometimes. They may not understand what you're doing, but they can tell you're trying to help.

When Bina came back with the medicine, I sent her to bring my doctoring kit, another lamp, and the pot of leftover tea I'd left cooling by the brazier. That gash needed seeing to – cleaning, and probably packing, too. I might have to open it up to clear out the pus. I thought about waiting until morning – better light would help – but the red streaks spreading out down the girl's back made me decide that sooner was better. It usually is.

'You have to have a name if I'm going to boss you around.' The little stray's eyebrows scrunched; she was trying hard to understand me. The girl wasn't simple, not exactly – just couldn't talk, or not so it would help her, at any rate.

I pointed to myself and said, 'Boss Lady.' I said it again and she repeated it after me, giving an odd, drawn-out liquid sound to the l. But close enough. 'Good. Boss Lady. That's me. Now who are *you*?' I pointed at her and saw understanding rise in those strange tawny eyes.

'Binpoy,' she answered, pointing at her heart. 'Binpoy.'

I gestured for Binpoy to lie down on the pallet.

I had Bina stay with me in case I'd need someone to hold the girl – Binpoy – down, but it wasn't necessary. She took Mr Ghilly's pills willingly enough, but when I handed her the fever-powder, I could tell she'd never held a paper packet in her life. I showed her how to open the flanges of the little envelope and tip it up to pour the fine grains into the back of her throat. She grimaced at the bitter taste. I handed her a mug of sugared milk to wash it down.

She took a swallow, paused with the cheap ceramic rim still at her lips, and looked up at me with an odd expression, as if she could tell that I'd mixed some sleepy-drops into the drink. The moment seemed to stretch out as she searched in my eyes, and then she seemed to decide something, some choice I hadn't even known was on the table. She drank down the rest of the milk in long throbbing swallows and lay down on her stomach in front of me.

'Okay,' I said to Bina, 'hold her down.'

But Binpoy held her own self down – rigid and quivering but still while I scrubbed out the ragged flesh with tepid tea – just some twitching that she couldn't help.

By the time I'd packed the wound – far too late to stitch it up – and dressed it, Binpoy was whuffling with poppy snores. Good. She wouldn't remember much of this night's business.

I swabbed off her other hurts, the cut under her chin and the scrapes on her arms and legs, and painted them with salve. In the middle of it all, someone started pounding on the Happy Palace's door. Drunk, by the sound of it. I told Bina to go and tell them to wait. Nobody opens my door but me. That's the rule.

'Maybe blood poisoning won't carry you off after all,' I muttered as I threw a light blanket over her bare skin. In her sleep she was starting to shiver again. Another chill. Have to get this child some clothes, I reminded myself, as I stripped the blue scarf from around her head to let her brain cool from the fever. A long braid plopped onto the pillow, red-brown like no hair I'd ever seen.

As I turned to the door, shaking out the indigo fabric, a rain of feathers fluttered to the floor: scarlet, yellow, blue, green. One had the sheen of peacock's tail-eyes. One was brown, dull as dirt. I gathered them up again – they must have been important to the girl, hidden away like that in her turban – and laid them on her pack by the foot of her bed, seven, in all.

I went to let my waiting customer in.

Binpoy was up before the rest of us in the morning. Could have killed us all in our sleep; evidently the Wildman world keeps early hours. Earlier, at least, than my girls, all rolled up on their pallets until noon, like caterpillars waiting for the rains.

I found her wandering around the place with her blanket wrapped around her like a bath towel and her little pack slung over her good shoulder. I think she was trying to find a way out. Good thing I key-lock the front door. Mr Ghilly's medicine had done the trick;

the girl's fever had broken during the night and she might have wandered off down the street wrapped up like a bite of man-bait.

Damn that Miner. What had he gotten me into? 'She goes her own way,' he'd insisted. Easy enough to say, but this girl was a baby, a baby with the body of a juicy half-grown woman. If I let her walk out into the hungry world outside the Palace's walls, she'd be in someone's clutches before an hour passed, sellers or Guards, maybe, who'd hand her on up the line as a novelty, to end up in a menagerie somewhere. That was no life. Not for anyone.

But I couldn't keep her locked up forever. If I'd wanted to be a jailer, I would have chosen a different line of work. Sure, I keep my door locked and my windows shuttered with nice strong slats. But that's to *protect* my girls. They understand the reasons. If they want out, all they have to do is ask. Just tell me where they're going and when they'll be back. It's a rough town and I don't want anyone wandering off alone where something might happen.

But that's different. My girls are smart, mostly. They know how to handle themselves out there and how to back away from trouble. This girl . . .

I got Binpoy out of the blanket and into an old dress from the trunk Rashi had left behind. I should never have let that Miner – whatever *was* his name, anyway? – foist her onto me. Worse than taking in a stray cat.

Pyn-Poi

The Ancestor's wrap frightened me. When the big, night-eyed Ancestor-woman – Bazleti – pulled my hands through the cloth tunnels, I thought maybe it had been a mistake to give her my name. Then, when the cloth slid down over my head and closed around my neck like a snare around a tree-hen, I panicked a little and tried to tear the thing off. She stopped me and showed me the ties that held it on me and how to undo them. Then I felt better.

The thing was made of impossible cloth, as if someone had taken a hundred lifetimes to undo a hundred hundred spiderwebs and then weave them up again into a fabric as light as lace-wings fluttering against your skin.

And it was like a skin itself, formed to my form in a way no weaver could ever weave, wide where my hips and chest were wide, but narrow around my waist and neck. A long sweep of it swished to the floor when I turned, like reeds and rushes stirring around my legs.

Bazleti wore the same kind of impossible dress, though hers was in swirls of red and orange. Mine was in a colour that does not exist in the Real, somewhere between sky-blue and indigo, dark and bright at the same time.

I let the dress stay on me because Bazleti wanted me to and because she was a healer-woman, but its softness made me uneasy.

It was very strange, the place where the Ancestor women lived. The house-tree was a lonely one-legged pucker-fruit tree in the middle of an empty square, boxed off on every side with a roofed walkway. Caves like enormous boxes, very square, hung off this, each with a solid gate taller than I am. The Ancestors lived behind these gates.

None of this, none, was supported by the frail, frightened house-tree. Instead, you could see the bones of dead trees, unnaturally straight and stiff, spanning the ceiling and holding up the cave walls. How was this respectful? Perhaps dead trees were the way of things on the Plains of the Ancestors? But why would anyone build their houses from the dead? Perhaps here, where it is so dry that your nose crackles and dust rides the air around the pucker-tree, dead trees do not rot like they do down in the Real. And the Ancestors themselves are dead, are they not? So maybe dead things are more respectable here.

The healer-woman, Bazleti, does not seem very dead, though. Her hands are strong and heavy with life, like my mother's. Hot with life. Pulsing with it.

Very confusing.

Boss Lady

With the help of the medicine Mr Ghilly sent us, over the next two days Binpoy did well. The sunken wells around her eyes filled out and she moved better – never letting go of that pack of hers or the feathers, though I'd taken her big knife and locked it away. She delighted Cook-Mama with her gobbling appetite. I knew, though, that she had to keep taking the pills against infection until the swollen redness went out of her shoulder and a few days after that, so I kept her behind the locked door of the Happy Palace. Anyway, she couldn't go wandering the streets, looking like she did and knowing nothing at all about anything. We had to show her how to use the toilet and how to wash herself with a sponge and a bathing bucket. She was very taken with the sponge – could have played with it for hours if I'd let her.

The other girls treated her like a pet, teaching her tricks and giving her sweets when she did them. Things like sweeping, washing dishes. Table manners. I didn't object. It was good schooling for her. She couldn't stay with us forever.

Not that I wouldn't have liked to bring her on – she had that kind of trim, well-muscled girl-body that makes some men tingle and her honey-coloured eyes were just odd enough to make her a star. Her hair, too – needed washing, needed cutting, but what an amazing colour. A shame about the scars but, even with them, she could have had a real career. In the city, even.

But I'm a woman of my word. I'd made a deal with that Miner – no trade for the girl. I locked her in her room at night – didn't want a customer to get confused on her – and let the girls play with her during the day. Somehow Binpoy was going to have to learn to act like one of us, and their little games weren't a bad place to start.

Pyn-Poi

This Ancestor place that I had come to was a household, a whole household, of sex-witches. Women of great power. Their healing was strong, although their house-tree was sad and weak; the knife-beak's slash didn't fester and my fever was gone. They spoke to each other in secret words I did not understand and they taught me how to say their names: Bina, Faria, Laly, Medira, Khukmama, and Bazleti.

They taught me their secret words if I pointed at things – rice, water, broom – but there were too many words you cannot point at: Stink. Poison. Death. Why. Nobody had told me that the Ancestors would not know the words I knew. Where did their language go when they died? How could I ask them about the Stink if I did not know their words?

Boss Lady

Every week, I take my girls to the baths. They all get dressed up decent in their town clothes, veils pulled sweetly across their faces. Good practice for them; they won't work for me forever. Then we all trail down together like a family of ducks to the little town square.

The town square. It would barely count as a crossroad, most

199

places, but out here, well – it's what we've got. What passes for a market is clotted up against one edge of the lopsided triangle that everyone calls the square. As you face the dusty stalls, on your left hand you'll see the splendour of our Justice Hall, people milling in and out of the shabby portico and loafing on the steps leading up to it. Children stalk the cracked tiles, hawking slices of fruit and thimbles of tea, watching for a chance to slip those sweet little fingers of theirs into somebody's unwatched pocket and get locked up in one of the handy jail-cells underneath the building.

On the third side of the 'square' stands the hotel, such as it is, and, below it, the town baths. I pay Rigam to close them off for us once a week so that my girls can go in and not have to rub elbows with the ladies of the town. That would be awkward for everyone.

What would I do with Binpoy on bath-day? I couldn't leave her alone and unwatched at the Happy Palace – even Cook-Mama comes with us on our bath outings. And the little stray had been coming along nicely, learning to talk a little, how to use a spoon, things like that. She deserved a treat, and it might be a good idea to see how she handled herself outside the walls of the Happy Palace.

I worried about the Bath-Attendants, though. Akuny and Nivrop are shameless gossips, no other way to put it. No one on the streets would be the wiser about Binpoy's wounds and foreign looks if we covered her up in long sleeves and skirts and veils. But in the baths, everything comes off.

You go down the old stone steps and swing open the door to the dark little anteroom where Rigam takes your coins before you step through into the baths proper, men to the left, women to the right. Akuny and Nivrop are waiting there to hustle everyone out of their clothing. Dresses and veils are hung from the row of iron knobs that runs down the wall under the low vaulted ceiling. Then they follow us into the tub-room, where some of the girls splash and play in the deep tiled pool in the middle of the room while others wash each other's hair at the spigots around the wall. Akuny and Nivrop see to the soap and towels and pumice-stones and scrub-brushes. They'd dearly love to see to the oils and massage, as well, but I'm not a rich woman. Clean is good enough for us. Let the wives pay for scented oils. My girls have other assets.

Even if they didn't already resent missing out on tips for sand-scrubs and oil-baths and foot-massages and such, I still wouldn't trust Akuny and Nivrop with any secrets. What they see in the baths, the whole town sees – a fist-bruise on a breast, a new baby-swell on a belly, the first grey hairs on a woman's head. What the bath attendants know, the town knows. I'd have to do a little something about Binpoy's hair before bath-day.

Pyn-Poi

I think this world of the Ancestors may be broken. The dirt here is as dry as morning ashes after you have let the fire die. The air, too, is dry and wanders restlessly, moving the dirt around as if it were looking for something, so that a fine grit gets everywhere, even into your eyes. The sex-witches fight back against the dirt, the 'dust', with brooms and rags and feather-weapons with which they cleanse their sanctuary every day.

How can a place be so dry and yet live? These Ancestors seem very much like living people, and yet their house-tree is not well and they do nothing for it except for sloshing basins of water on its roots after they bathe the floors. It is pathetically grateful for these sips of dirty grey water, but it does not thrive. I spend time with it every day, doing my best, but it is lonely, starved, and dry. Among the People, if any house-tree drooped and straggled like that, something would be done.

And that is why I am here. Our house-trees are drooping and I am the thing that is being done. But *what* am I supposed to do? I have no words to ask and I have not smelled anything that speaks to me of the Stink, though there are many strange smells here, especially when the sex-witches anoint themselves for their rituals. But though their soaps and oils and creams are strange, they are not alien, just flower-waters and the oils of barks and leaves.

I thought the hard part would be to climb the Wall. I was wrong. That was just the beginning. The hard part is this, finding what to do now that I am here.

Boss Lady

On market day, Cook-Mama needed a half-peck of dried apricots. To signal that I was a serious shopper and Adimar should settle in for a stint of bargaining, I bent to set down my basket in front of the worn plank that serves as her counter. As I stood up, I slid my eyes over the bins of nuts at my feet: cashew pods, almonds, pistachios in the shell, butternuts. And there they were: walnuts. A whole bushel basket of walnuts still in their spotty green husks.

After we settled on a price for the apricots, I slapped my own cheek at my forgetfulness. 'And some walnuts,' I added.

'How many you need?'

'I'll take them all. Cook-Mama is making a sweet for Faria's birthday, and that girl is a pig for walnuts.'

Walnuts.

We made a party of it that afternoon, all the girls who weren't busy with customers, out under the scrawny lime-tree in the courtyard, whacking the walnuts with rocks, picking out the nut-meats, and –

more to the point – setting aside the bumpy green husks in an old basket beside the pump. Hatheer tuned up her zither, a good thing if any of the nuts were actually to get to the kitchen, because the girls couldn't nibble while singing. Binpoy, not knowing that all this carrying-on was about her, worked along with the rest, cracking shells. An industrious little thing. She'd be a good—

No. Woman of my word, and so forth.

What did she make of all this? Of us? What was it like to wind up someplace where you couldn't know what was happening around you? Not one single thing, not a whisper of a clue about what people were saying? Faria told a story, something ridiculous about a customer – Binpoy's eyes were riveted on her, intent and hungry. Then when everyone burst out laughing, she jumped and looked around at the others, just hurting to know what the joke was.

The girls, kind souls that they are, mostly, noticed that Binpoy tried to sing along on the O-la-la-la part of 'Lover-Boy's Lament', and they started to teach her the chorus, even miming out the action for her. The nut-cracking fell apart as the actors acted and the audience collapsed in typhoons of giggles. Eventually, they pulled themselves back together, gasping.

Laly held up her hands. 'Look at my fingernails – black as a tractee's!' she complained. 'And my palms! How am I ever going to get the stain out?'

I want my girls to be educated, to have know-how that can make a woman's life easier, even after the blush of beauty gets blown away by the years. So I gathered them around me and explained the plan.

'You've all noticed how our Binpoy doesn't look like people from around here?' They had. Women in our line of work notice how people look.

'And you know there's folks out there, outside the walls of the Happy Palace – pimps and sellers and such – that grab onto people who look ... well, *special*. People will pay a goodly price for *special* and won't study too hard on how they come by it. Or how they treat it, either.' They nodded, big-eyed and serious. This was something they really did know about, some of them first-hand. A few of them had wound up with me just exactly because some vulture had come after them, trying to own them, trying to lock them down. It's a dangerous thing to be a pretty girl in this world. Especially a pretty girl alone. My girls aren't alone anymore. They stick up for each other and, between all of us, we can pretty much handle any man – customer, Guard, or pimp – who gets high-handed.

I went on. 'Well, Binpoy looks special and doesn't know her way around yet, so we have to keep her safe from the carrion-scum that might grab her for a quick profit.' More nods. They were listening close now. Nobody was cracking shells.

'So here's what we're going to do. Cook-Mama is going to stew down these walnut husks, boil them until there's nothing but a black sludge in the bottom of the pot.' Cook-Mama grinned her snaggle-toothed grin. She likes games like this, plots and schemes and trickery of any kind. 'Then we're going to take care of Binpoy's hair. I mean *stain* it, like that stain on your fingers, Laly, dark enough so the bath-ladies don't chatter in the town about this strange brown-haired girl, new at the Happy Palace.'

'But what about her eyes?' Bina wanted to know. 'Nobody has eyes like that.'

'Nothing to be done about her eyes,' I answered. 'But with a veil—'

'Maybe we could cut her hair,' Bina said, 'you know, so it hangs down in front and hides her eyes a little. Like a fringe.' She looked at Binpoy appraisingly. 'A *long* fringe.'

That actually wasn't a bad idea. Sometimes I think Bina isn't nearly as silly as she looks.

Binpoy watched alertly. She could tell that something was in the air.

The next morning, back under the lime-tree, I did my best to explain to Binpoy what we were trying to do. I pointed to the tarry black ink at the bottom of Cook-Mama's stew-pot and to our palms still stained from husking the walnuts. Then I held up Binpoy's red-brown braid next to Laly's black one. I think she understood. She let us – Bina and me, with the others looking on – comb out her hair, divide it up, and paint every inch of it black, from the roots to the wispy ends. Then she sat there under the lime-tree, stiff and still, with her shiny black hair-snakes spread out on a board while the walnut stain dried.

We rinsed the stuff off just before lunch, sluicing her head down with buckets right by the well so the stain wouldn't get loose in the house.

Then there she stood, one of us, or nearly – hair black, like nature intended. The girls clapped and congratulated her, rubbing her hair between their fingers as if the colour might come off. 'If it won't come off your hands,' I snapped, 'why's it going to come off Binpoy?' I was actually a little taken aback by how normal she looked now, all except her eyes. Well, what can't be changed must be hidden. A fringe of hair across her face like a veil, I thought; Bina's notion would do the trick.

'The rice is getting cold,' Cook-Mama bawled from the kitchen and I chased them all in to lunch.

Pyn-Poi

I look like them now. Bazleti is pleased. Why?

Does having hair as dark as night-tree branches make you an Ancestor? I do not feel dead. I do not feel different at all. Just darker.

Boss Lady

Dyeing Binpoy's hair went smoothly. Cutting it did not.

I didn't want hair all over the floor of my room and the light there's no good anyway, so I brought the shears out into the court-yard. Binpoy was sitting on the bench where I'd put her, gazing up into the branches of the lime-tree. I showed her the shears, and she brushed a cautious fingertip against the shiny metal with a startled look of wonder in her eyes. She said something under her breath. What do these scissors mean to you, girl? What does any of this mean?

I mimed cutting her hair, scissoring my fingers across her eye-brows. She looked up at me trustfully and sat quiet while I undid her braid and combed out her hair so that it hung down in front of her eyes like a brown satin curtain. A shame to cut it, really. But . . . I slid the blade in, right at her temple, just a little above the ear and took the first snip.

Things fell apart.

A deafening shriek – fury? Fear? Pain? What—? Had I cut the girl?

And then the pain's all mine. A claw-like vice digs into the tender strings of my wrist. The handles of the scissors wrench my fingers in directions they were never meant to bend. Let 'em go, fool! Let the damn things go.

A crash as the bench goes over. The shears tear loose from my hand. Squeals as the watching girls throw themselves out of the way as our Binpoy, our patient, compliant Binpoy, whirls on me, shouting, clutching the side of her head like she's been stabbed. My eyes lock onto that metal point, held low, aimed at my belly, weaving from side to side. She hisses something – words – and then everything goes very quiet.

In the silence, the tiny splats of blood dropping from my hand onto the flagstones sound eerily loud. Binpoy's narrowed eyes dart to the ground, then to my bloody hand.

The shears clatter from her fist. She stares, stricken, pointing at my torn hand with a wavering finger, babbling.

'It's okay,' I said, making little patting gestures, keeping my voice low like you would with a drunk. 'It's just a little cut. Nothing broken.' I waggled my fingers to show her no harm done – or not much, at any rate – and another drop of blood fell to the ground. She gasped, like someone who'd never seen red before. The girls stayed quiet and still, bless them.

'Let's just take a little breather here, why don't we?' I scooted the fallen shears away with my toe. Laly scooped them up. 'Laly, why don't you take the bad scissors away and put them in the chest in my room. Okay now, Binpoy?' I was breathing hard from the scuffle. 'No haircut. No problem.'

She was still gaping at my hand like she'd seen a ghost. Cook-Mama flipped me the dishcloth she keeps tucked in her belt and I wrapped my hand, hiding the blood, pressing on the ripped skin at the base of my thumb. 'See, everything's fine.'

But now her eyes were riveted on the bright drops on the floor at my feet. 'Faria, get a rag. Wipe that up. Let's see if we can calm things down a little.'

Pyn-Poi

Red.

Bazleti's Flow is red.

But that cannot be, can it?

But it is. Red like mine. Red like the living People.

But she is an Ancestor.

But she cannot be an Ancestor. Her Flow is—

Who *is* this woman? *What* is she? What are any of them? If not Ancestors, then—

Is there another breed of person for this place? Did the Mother give birth to another kind of children? Or are the dark-eyed ones children of some other mother? No. That is not possible. The Mother is the Mother.

But who *are* these people?

Just people. No Ancestors of mine.

I climbed the Wall. I did. I pulled myself up over the stone lip onto the Plains of the Ancestors. This is not dream. But Bazleti . . .? These people . . .?

Where are the Ancestors?

If they are not here, if they are truly elsewhere and everything I have ever known was wrong, then who is poisoning the People?

Someone is. Maybe this makes more sense: If these beings are neither kin nor clan of ours, perhaps they—

Bazleti betrayed me. Tricked me, and I do not understand why. I have not understood much since I came to this place, but I thought I understood Bazleti. Her touch is tender, her eyes soft, her voice firm with the ring of truth-telling. I thought she wished me well. And she is the Mother of the sex-witches.

I have been so wrong. Maybe this was the reason.

These are no Ancestors. Their Flow oozes out, wet and bright, red as mine – but they are not People, either. I do not know what they are, but I let them seduce me, lure me like a fish into a weir-net with their fine clothing, fabrics softer than water, brighter than blossoms, finer than any hand could weave. Their skin-paints that make your eyes big and your lips bloody. Their strange and wonderful purifications. Their rich meals, mounds of grain and spicy meat. Their sweets – oh, I love their sweets, so many shapes and textures and colours and flavours, all sweeter than honey and flower-water and much more interesting. And sleeping late every day, no real work to do.

No.

That is not right.

I *have* work – I just have not been doing it. It is as if they drugged me. Like that first night, with Bazleti's bitter milk. I have fallen asleep to the work I came to do.

As I gather up the strands of me that Bazleti amputated, I see a memory-ghost of Aunt Saggi gentling a ground-hen right before she cut its throat: her touch tender, her eyes soft, and her voice solemn with truth-telling as she thanked it for going into our stew-pot.

And then her knife.

I have to leave this place. I have to get out.

Boss Lady

Things settled down. Binpoy was quiet enough, though she seemed more skittish than before, watchful and on edge. I was watchful and on edge, too. If I didn't understand what set her off, how could I keep it from happening again?

After three days without bloodshed, I decided to go ahead with the plan to bring Binpoy with us to the baths. I don't regret much in this life, but if I could take that back, that one decision ...

Bath-day came. At first I thought the business was going well. Binpoy did try to pilfer a citron from a seller's stall as we walked along the front of the market, but Hatheer saw her and made her put it back before there was any fuss. Also, there was a little difficulty getting her down the stairs to the baths; the stairway frightened her for some reason. The girls gathered in close and shielded the scene from prying eyes while Bina coaxed her down one step at a time. We had a hard time getting her to leave that old, torn-up bag of hers on the hook, but when she saw the rest of the girls leaving their clothes there, she gave in. Once we were down in the baths themselves, Akuny did ask about the healing wound on her shoulder, but Faria jumped in with a stirring tale about a wild-dog attack that would have ended badly if it weren't for the handsome young road-builder who fought off the beast with his bare hands. I almost believed her myself.

As to why the girl didn't speak our language, we told the bath-ladies she was a foreigner – true enough. 'You can see that from her eyes,' Faria added. 'That's the look of Dollface Island, where she comes from, way out in the Eastern Sea.' That girl's talent for lying worries me sometimes.

It was something to see, Binpoy in the baths. Big-eyed and jumpy at first, she watched the others splash into the big bright-tiled central tub and beckon her to join them. She crept up to the edge, as timid as I'd ever seen her, crouched, and swept her fingertips back and forth across the steaming surface as if to reassure herself that it was, in fact, water. With some encouragement from the girls, she sat on the side, dangled her feet in the pool, and eventually eased her body in. But once she got in, once she relaxed a little, she played like a river-rat, diving and splashing and sometimes staying under so long it scared me.

Through it all, I must say, Binpoy's new hair colour did us proud. The real test, though, was the towels. Black dye would scream out loud on one of those big rectangles of bleached, rough-woven fibre. But not a smudge – the colour held true.

It was after the baths, on the way back to the Happy Palace, that trouble hit us.

Pyn-Poi

Angry squawks. Men yelling. Heavy feet pounding after me. Chasing me? *Why?*

Does not matter. Run, run, run.

A tight ravine. Too tight. Too many people, too crowded, too narrow to escape. I dodge around an old woman, a flock of children, a tall basket full of something. People everywhere, jabbering and pointing, and the shouts still behind me. Where, where—?

A talon clamps onto my arm, hooking my forward speed into a flying spin. My legs twist under me, tangling, tripping. My cheek smashes down into stinking water and wet stone. Night flaps one wing over my eyes.

Then: Leaves and peels in a runnel of water in front of my nose. What—? Giant feet, armoured in leather, stomping around me. My head yanked back – my neck! – all my weight hanging – my braid in someone's hand. I writhe, clawing for the man's eyes, his throat, his ears, but stone fists close on my arms and then they have me.

One of the shouters brings his face close to mine, spitting and rabid. I ram my knee upward into his soft parts and he goes down, curling around himself. I burn like an oil-wood brand, but then come the fists, and after that the kicks, and after that I don't remember.

THE BOX

Boss Lady

Damn, damn, damn. Careless, stupid and careless. I *told* the girls to watch her. I can't do everything myself. That child swiped an orange from Bathera's fruit-stand. An *orange*. And it had to be Bathera, that resentful little prig, always looking for ways to make life hard for us, as if it were *our* fault that her sour, straight-laced ways don't bring her husband to her bed anymore. That woman nurses her grudges better than her children. So, instead of just hollering at me to get back her property, Bathera sicced the Guards on Binpoy. The girl ran, of course – who knew what she thought when those oafs came after her, shouting and waving their night-sticks around like idiots. Now I'm going to have to dress up all respectable and go down to Justice Hall and spend a pile of money on bailing the little stray out of jail, money I had other plans for. Well, this comes out of her keep, believe you me, and it will be a nice big bite, too; garnets don't fetch all that much around here, trading under the table. And when I get her home, Binpoy's going to learn a thing or two about keeping her pretty little fingers off other people's property.

213

The Trees

'They have buried her.'
  'I know. That is what they do to seeds.'

Pyn-Poi

I knew I was under the ground. I could feel the press of earth on every side, leaning in on me, squeezing the air from my lungs. It was cold and there was nothing to do. My pack was gone. Nothing happened, except when leather-shelled feet came and pushed food under the door. The dull glow through that square hole up high in the wall faded and rose again, but all I could do was wait.

I did not understand the waiting. Why would they leave me here in this stone box? There had to be a reason. Was this a punishment? Some kind of twisted not-Ancestors-not-People vengeance? I ran from that gang, yes, but anyone would, surely? And when they cornered me in that canyon of house-boxes, I did try to hurt them. But they grabbed me first, snatching the half-eaten orange I had taken from someone's hospitality-table, waving it in my face, barking at me like carrion-dogs in words I could not understand. Anyone would fight back, surely? And they had clubs. Three men with clubs. I only had myself. Then Bazleti got there and she was barking, too, maybe at me, maybe at the gang-men who had me, I could not tell, and I was kicking and biting at them. I hurt one of them, I know – a well-swung knee to his tender parts and some bloody bites on the arm he tried to get around my neck – but then I woke up there on the cold, hard floor with a bad head and a lump over my ear.

Once I could sit up without sickness, I looked around me in the dim light. Another box, square, like the ones at Happy Palace. But the sex-witches' boxes were airy and filled with things: Incense. Bright images. Cushions and filmy fabrics. Clothing and little pots of paint and potions. This place was empty, no things at all, nothing but a wide shelf hanging from one of the walls and a filthy, stinking bucket.

I beat on the dead-wood door, shouting for someone to let me out, and threw myself against stone-hard walls that did not even shiver at my passion. I did this for a very long while.

I had never known this thing, that people could be boxed up like rice in a grain-barrel or food-animals in a pen. No, not like food-animals – they at least can see the trees and breathe the living air. They can talk to each other, and to us. This was just a death place.

This was a thing of the not-Ancestors-not-People – it could not happen back in the Real. Never down under the earth like this. If anyone tried to dig a people-box into the ground, the waters would seep in and melt their work to mud. Mother Durma would see to it. People do not bury People.

Would they ever let me out again? Had they forgotten me here? I exhausted myself against their walls, so then I dug at the door with my fingernails, tried to gnaw at it with my teeth, but the dead boards only crushed my lips. All the while, I kept shouting, howling for the box-keepers to come and face me. 'Explain yourselves,' I bellowed. 'Let me hear your reasons. Let me hear your excuses.' I shouted myself hoarse, rested, then shouted some more. Voices yelled at me every now and then through the door. I learned their word for 'Quiet!'.

I was not quiet.

Bazleti came the second day. She clutched me close, like real blood-kin, then held me away from her so she could look me over. She touched the broken place on my head. Her eyes were worried; her voice was sharp. She was angry. At me? I understood nothing. Nothing.

She brought me a basket of real food. I said 'thank you' and named the food-things for her, the words I knew, just like I had done back in her sanctuary. She softened and told me the words for the things I did not know, not just the foods but the parts of my box as well: Window. Bunk. Blanket. Bucket. Bars.

Bazleti's face told me that she did not want me to be here. Good. We would leave together. When she stood to go, I tried to walk out with her when the box-man opened the door, but she told me to stay. She looked sad and said many words and used many gestures and pointings. I explained to her that I could not stay in that place, that there was nothing alive there. I said it as clearly as I could, using simple and strong words, and then tried to follow her out the door, but the box-man hit me behind the knees with his club. I fell down with the pain of it, and he pulled her out, kicking away my hand where I clutched at her leg. But before he slammed the door behind her, I caught one glimpse of tears smudging the paint around Bazleti's eyes.

Tears. I thought about that all the long day, trying to understand, and this is what I came to: I had done something to cause this box-ing-in. Something to do with the orange. But there had been a whole mound of them on an altar by the path. Clearly a hospitality-offering. And I had taken one. I was thirsty for fruit – the sex-witches ate meat and grain and thrilling little mouth-candies delicious beyond belief, but not much that was fresh from the trees. So I had taken an orange. And now that taking meant I had to go under the ground. Was this burial some kind of purification? Had the fruit been somehow tainted? Or was this some kind of an initiation? Whatever it was,

Bazleti was sad; she did not want this for me. I had fallen into the hands of someone or something more powerful than she.

More powerful than the kin-Mother of a household of sex-witches?

Be careful, Pyn-Poi. Think. Listen. Understand.

I had to learn their words.

Boss Lady

Someone should strangle that Bathera. This is worse than I thought. Much worse. Not just theft of one measly little fruit, oh no, and not just walking the streets without papers, as if that wouldn't be bad enough. But when they got her to the lock-up and took her pack away from her (and *that* must have been a pretty scene – *I'd* never been able to pry it loose), they found that she was carrying a stash of fire-weed, pure and uncut. And that's a carelessness that I can't blame on anyone but myself. That child doesn't look like a fire-eater, but still, I should have checked the pack more closely. When I searched her things on that first night, I was really just looking for weapons – I didn't want the wild-child cutting our throats on us while we slept – and I didn't open that harmless-looking little packet. Me. I should know better. But I missed it.

Spilt beer – no use crying over it. But the Guards take a nasty view of anyone dealing fire-weed without cutting them in for their share. I tried to explain to the jowly old Justice Clerk that the girl wasn't selling, but nothing doing – evidently Binpoy was holding enough to make us all rich.

I probably could have sorted all that out with the proper application of some big, juicy payoffs *if* Binpoy hadn't, perfectly understandably in my opinion, kicked the boss of the Watch in the nuts. Men just don't forgive that kind of thing, and they tend to hang together about it. The Justice Clerk wouldn't let her out for any amount of grease, even when I threatened to ban him from the Happy Palace for life.

He did let me see her, though. I don't know what good it did either of us – tore me up inside, just tore me up.

I've visited other girls in lock-up – part of my job – but seeing Binpoy in a cell was *wrong*, so wrong, like it couldn't be real. Like seeing a candle held under water, a candle that keeps burning somehow. There was still fight in those wild golden eyes of hers, but there was desperation, too. I looked her over pretty good. It didn't seem like she was damaged too badly, just a big goose-egg over one ear where that Guard-lout whacked her. It must have hurt like ten toothaches.

I did my best to tell her to be good, to obey the nice men with sticks because they could hurt her. I'll come back, I told her. I'll bring you food. I'll find you a law-man.

Those golden eyes studied me furiously, trying to understand.

Pyn-Poi

There were no leaves in that place, no branches, no roots. Walls of stone. Floor like stone, but smoother – no cracks for tiny things to grow in. The ceiling and the door were made of sliced-up trees long dead – just bones. Only a little barred window up above my head kept the box from black darkness. I starved for green and for the rustling of living things. I starved for work, because there was nothing in that box to tend or train. So why should I eat the ugly mush the boots pushed in under the door? I pushed the bowls back out again, still full.

I think it was the fifth or sixth time that night came in through the bars when the trees gave me a talking-to. 'You are wasting time,' they said, and told me that yes, there *was* something living inside that box, something that required tending and training.

If I withered, they said, then who would deal with the Stink? I was the one, the only one, who had been sent. They reminded me that making bridges was not hurry-work. What would happen to the People if I just dropped my flesh against the wall and let it go? Marak would say, 'Lazy, lazy,' and the trees would shake their heads.

I was indignant. 'Look at the walls around me,' I demanded. 'Look at the floor that is not earth. Look at the dead-wood door. They have put me in a death-box and I cannot get out.'

'You cannot get out? Are you your father's daughter?'

'But the door,' I whined. 'I have tried. Look at the bruises on my shoulders. It will not open. Only when Bazleti comes with her basket. And then there is always the club-man. He hurts me when I try to leave. Look at the bruises on my legs. I have tried. If I had Sook-Sook's knife, then maybe. But what can I do? They have taken everything.'

'They took more from your father when he walked away from his house-tree to learn his craft. He came to us naked. Younger than you are now. No food, no bow, no fish-hook. Nothing in his hands when he reached out to us for teaching.'

'But I cannot get to you.' I kicked the door again. Were they being deliberately stupid? 'I'm *boxed up*.'

And that is when they showed me, all at once and completely, the spider-silk roots that ran from my toes, the vines and tendrils like snakes of light that twined from my fingertips, the blood and heart of *being-with* that pumped through me, even in that dark death-box. And once seen, this being-with can never be not-seen, never taken back or undone. They showed me that, of course, I was with them. I was with the trees. I still am.

When I had caught my breath, I apologised for my bone-headedness and they accepted my apology and offered me my apprenticeship, right there in that grey-floored box. I said yes with all my heart.

So the next morning, I woke into the box only enough to push my bucket out to the leather-clad feet waiting for it. Only enough to eat the tasteless mush that came in through the flap. To slide the bowl back through the hatch when the boots returned. To stretch my joints and work my muscles so that my limbs would not go dry and brittle. Pacing back and forth – three strides, then turn, three strides, then turn – my bones were slender stems of living wood, like air-roots swinging in the wind, and my words were leaves. I learned from the trees (as I would learn again and again) not to die, and turned my face to the tiny window's dull grey light.

Then, after the tending was done, the training began. I lay down on the thin bed-mat and pulled the tattered blanket over me so that my flesh body would not cool too much while I did my exercises. And the trees put me to work.

For my training, they made me start back at the beginning. I protested: My father had taught me long ago how to lift my Other hands and I had already once stepped all the way out of my flesh, that day on the Wall when it was dying in the sun. But no— 'There is an order to things,' they insisted, 'a Flow.' So, the beginning.

The beginning was very like the games that Sook-Sook used to play with me back when I was a child. They took a lot of concentration, those games, keeping my Other body whole and clear while I followed the trees' directions. At first, the tasks were simple and silly: Wiggle your Other toes. Raise your Other arms while keeping you flesh arms still. Grow your Other hair so that it is a hand-span longer.

But as the morning went on, the exercises got more complicated: Raise your Other right arm but leave your Other left arm on the bed while raising your left flesh arm and keeping your right flesh arm still. Slow your Other heart-drum. Now speed it up, while keeping your flesh heart-drum steady. Again. Again.

And so on, for hours, until I lay there on the hard, flat bunk panting and quivering with effort. The trees knew instantly if my attention wavered and would scold me about wasting my valuable time in this deep sanctuary without distractions. One of them, a forever-tree I think, was very gentle but always nudged me to do just a little bit more, a little bit longer, a little bit better. Another, a mud-stander, was stern and sarcastic when I complained a bit about being tired. 'Learn it now or regret it later.' Its voice reminded me of Marak.

Every morning, when my water and food slid in under the door, I would make words at the boot-man. The trees insisted that I learn my keepers' speech, very different from the sex-witches'. The first words I got from them were for water and the mealy mush they doled out in the morning. Also, the word for piss-bucket. This makes me smile a little, because what was my life about, if not what we need and what we must get rid of?

The first words I ever picked up from Bazleti were 'Thank you'. Whenever something slid through the flap at the bottom of the door, I said these words because it is the People's way to be grateful for water and for food, but also because I was so hungry for even the tiniest give-and-take with a living person. I have said them so often over the years that I would have worn them out if they were not such sturdy words.

I also said the greeting words to the food-bringers, although I could not see their eyes. Bazleti said these greeting words when she brought my basket. I was almost certain that they meant 'how are you?' because, after she said this, she always looked at me with question-eyes and waited for me to answer. 'How are you?' is a very powerful thing to say, and I said it to the boots each morning when they came. Sometimes there was no answer. Sometimes there was. Sometimes the answer would have a few words I could understand and I would catch my breath with wonder.

I lay on the bunk all morning, gripped with concentration, until a rattle at the door called me back. I excused myself and sat up, a little light-headed from the work, to greet Bazleti.

That day, a stranger was with her, a man: tall, knife-nosed, and dark-eyed like all the people in this place. When Bazleti settled on my bed-shelf, he stood stiff by the door and refused to share the fried vegetable dumplings I offered from Bazleti's big basket.

This man talked at me, as if he had never heard that I had different words. I tried to be polite, looking at him when he spoke and repeating the last thing he had said. (This had often pleased the sex-witches when they were trying to teach me, but the stranger did not point at things, so I never learned what his words meant.)

After he had finished, I asked Bazleti how the other witches were, saying each name with a shrug and a question-lift in my voice: Bina. Faria. Laly. Medira. Khukmama. She told me stories about them, and sometimes I caught a word or two. Something about Bina's wrap. Something about Khukmama's sandals. Something about Laly and one of the worshippers. It did not matter, I was so glad to be with a person after a whole day with nothing but trees for company. But soon there was the rattle at the door and Bazleti stood up to go and I stood up, too, but remembered that I could not go with her; there was the door, and the boot-man, and the club. I started to cry a little, and Bazleti started to cry and hugged me until we were both crying very hard. The stranger-man pulled her away from me.

I held myself back from following. The door closed behind them.

I lay down on the bunk and gave myself up to darkness for a while, ignoring the trees, but they became very pointed and so I went back to work.

Boss Lady

The law-man nodded slowly. 'I think you're right. That child is not broken-brained. But nonetheless, that might be her best defence – say she's simple and didn't know what she was doing. We could get a witness – a School-Manager, maybe – pay them to say the girl's backward. That could explain, too, why she wasn't carrying papers when they caught her.'

'Because she'd lost them?'

'Or because she wasn't trusted with them. Either way, of course, you're going to have to, shall we say, *obtain* papers for her.'

'I've already set that in motion.' Another expense I hadn't planned on, and the forger was charging double, too, for the rush job.

He went on. 'But you have to remember that, even though a plea of incompetence of mind might get her out of jail and save her from a hard-labour contract, she would still wind up in the System and spend the rest of her life making buttons in some administrative "school" somewhere. At least a stint on a penal-farm has an end to it. Being sent off for incompetence – that's a life sentence.'

'What? They wouldn't just put her into my charge? I don't want her locked up at all, not on a prison-farm and not in any of those so-called "schools". I think it would kill her. You saw her just now – you think she could survive something like that? No, Binpoy has to stay with me.' Hearing myself say it shocked me a little – I'd never meant to become fond of the girl, never meant to adopt her. But there it was: If she wasn't my responsibility, she was nobody's.

'Admirable sentiments, indeed. But the fact is that you, dear lady, serve your community in a profession that is not deemed suitable for guardianship. Are you prepared to lay down everything you've built in this town and take up a respectable life just in order to take in this young woman, who, I might remind you, has no claim on you – none at all.'

I opened my mouth. Shut it. Quit the life? And leave my girls, my other girls, out on the streets with no one to look after them? Impossible. But to see my Binpoy locked away, maybe forever?

Just as impossible.

Pyn-Poi

The next morning, the trees made me start back at the beginning as usual, but today they stretched out the time so that I could get further before Bazleti interrupted with food and the company of my own kind.

The work was still very hard but things were getting more inter- esting. The trees began to have me sit up out of my flesh and walk about in my Other body. It was like being a baby again, tottering around, having to learn where my feet were and how my toes should grip and push off and how my knees should bend and straighten. Too many details. I cried in frustration after the fourth time I came apart and went rushing back into my flesh with a thump.

I argued with them: It had been so easy, that morning on the Wall, just to float up into the air, without all this work of remembering to plant my feet and swing my arms. Much simpler. Walking was just too hard; why not fly?

But the trees insisted that the footsteps were important. They told me that just spewing myself up into the sky, like I had done when I was dying, was dangerous. Forgetting my flesh was dangerous. Also, travelling too far was dangerous. Too easy to get uprooted, they said, too easy to get spread out on the Other wind. There was risk, they said, to letting your bodies go in two directions, and not just the risk that your flesh would cool and slow and start to dissolve, but that your Other body, too, could scatter and melt away like a sprinkle of salt in water. No, they said, I had to take one step at a time, planting each foot with care and attention and lifting it up again with the same.

So: Beginners must only be in one place at a time.

So: Footsteps.

It was exhausting.

How long?

I got confused about the days. How long did they keep me in that box? More time than I could keep lined up in my mind. I did not know to count the days, like we did later on the Tract, with little hatch-marks scratched onto bunks or walls.

How many wakings? How many baskets, brought at first only by Bazleti, but later by the other sex-witches so that I got to see more faces, hear more voices from outside? More stories, words mixed with acting out: Khukmama dropping a pot of stew. Bazleti chasing some drunken worshipper away with her big stick. It was good to know that the world had not melted away. It was still there. Only I was not.

Tapping the tip of each finger like a child learning to count, I asked Bazleti how long I had been in that dark no-place, but she just shrugged. Either she did not understand what I was asking, or she did not want to tell me. Or maybe she thought I was asking how long I would have to stay there and *that* was what she could not answer.

The trees were no help at all with keeping track. They stretched and shrank time as it pleased them so that sometimes when my basket came it was as if many days had passed. I did not much like how rubbery they made the time – I felt like I was in a river that was too strong for me, almost drowning and then bobbing to the top to snatch a breath before being pulled back under into the rushing dark. Not knowing whether I would ever see the sky again. Not knowing anything.

Sometimes I cried. If Bazleti or one of the others came and saw a tear-face, they hugged me or patted me and made sorry sounds, but the trees were not very sympathetic at all. Once, when I was having a tantrum at the door, bruising my shoulder against the unyielding boards and making my throat raw from shouting, the trees stopped me and made me look at my memories: Gai-Gai with a handful of her wrap clutched to her nose, trying to keep out the Stink. The slick, limp body of my dead sister. The brown leaves that should have been green.

My tears turned cold then. Alright, I said. Alright. And I went back to work, back to my Other body, setting one foot in front of another, bargaining with the dead tree that barred the door to let my bits flow through his spaces and let his bits flow through mine. The trees made me practise this over and over again before I was allowed to go further. My Other body could not be locked away from my flesh and bones, they said. I understood this. This was important.

So I would do it again, stepping across the threshold, the wood like a short burst of wind blowing through me, making me shiver at the chill of it.

Then I was on the outside, in the long, narrow tunnel with many doors. Good, they would say. Now, do it again.

I would whisk back through the door.

Again.

Again.

One night, I walked through one of the other doors, just to see something different. But it was not different. The same piss-bucket and the same empty bowl. The same bed-shelf. And a person, too, a scraggly-bearded man curled on his bunk, bumping his forehead against the wall over and over again. I reached out to lay my hand on his shoulder, to let him know he was not alone, but the trees stopped me, forbade me to make myself known to him.

'But why?' I pressed, pushing against their woody resistance. 'Why shouldn't I touch him? Can't you see how hopeless he feels? How lonely? How *bored*?'

They broke into many voices then, and reasons spattered at my feet: 'Too soon . . .' 'Not ready . . .' 'Not your business . . .' 'Distrac-tion . . .' 'Too much.' And other things that I could not make out. I argued, but trees can be unbending.

I walked on, that day and later, too, when the trees let me step into the other boxes and witness other sufferings that were not mine to mend. I obeyed and did not greet the buried ones around me. But I saw.

Even though the trees would not let me speak to the men and women in the other boxes, still I went to them. Every night, I would step past their doors and study their despair, or rage, or terror. I would tell myself stories about who they might have been before coming to this place and wonder why they had been put here and what would happen next for them.

I think the trees, being naturally social themselves, understood that seeing the faces of my own kind was needful to me. It swelled my Flow, even though with sadness, and made me less brittle. They allowed it.

So after my other work was done, I watched the box-people and saw that, even with their incomprehensible language, strange ways, and night-black eyes, they were not that different from me. Some of them howled and beat against the doors like I had done. Many paced their boxes, either to keep their bodies strong or just to give vent to the fires inside them. Some lay in their bunks, sleeping day and night, maybe freed from that place by dreams.

I recognised one of these sleepers. It was like a splash of cold water in my face, seeing him again, that tall, strong man whose blanket did not cover him and whose feet hung forlornly off the end of his bunk.

He was snoring, a gentle, homey sound that shot me back like an arrow to nights in my own house-tree, with my kin's sleep-sounds all around me.

I took one step closer, to see his face better, and the trees did not stop me. Yes, it was him, the rock-pecker from the wall, the big man who had given me his water and his orange. He had seen me to the top of the Wall. Shown me the way into town. Taken me to Bazleti for healing.

The first kindnesses of this world had all come to me from this man. And now, here he was, in a box. Why?

I took another step toward him – still the trees said nothing – and saw that his face was bruised and swollen. Had he fallen? He stirred restlessly, grimacing in his sleep. Without thinking, I bent and smoothed his tangled hair. He quieted, like a child, and I sat down beside him, perching on the edge of his too-small bunk.

He rolled toward me and I lay my hand on his chest, to pat it like I had seen my mother pat wakeful babies. But my hand, being Other, slipped through the weave of his shirt. Skin, muscle and hard, shielding bone made way for my hand like warm mists, and my fingers settled around his heart until I could feel the throb of his Flow.

The trees did not say a word.

The Garnet-Miner

The night after the Judge handed me that fifteen-year contract, I dreamed strange dreams. Not the sort you'd expect after the day when your life got flushed down the sewer: gentle dreams of a dim, green place with air full of life and as steamy as the baths. A tangled place, everything connected. A jungle place, though for all its strangeness I felt calm and at home there. There seemed to be voices all around me, though I didn't understand their speaking.

Maybe it was the dream of some forgotten story from childhood, some fairy-tale place with friendly animals and talking trees. But it wasn't childish – I don't mean that. It wasn't simple at all. It was very, very complicated.

Like I said, I felt at home there. Safe. Comforted.

Waking back into those cold stone walls – putting on the System's burlap for the long walk – was hard.

Boss Lady

At last. The Justice Clerk finally let us have a date for Binpoy's hearing, after I slipped him a sweetener big enough to choke a mule, half in cash, half on account at the Happy Palace, which the girls won't like at all – I've known stray dogs that bathe more often than Shadan. But that's the price of being part of the Happy Palace. We do what it takes to look after each other.

The high-priced law-man said things could go either way. 'It all depends on how the honourable Judge is feeling that day,' he explained.

'What am I paying you for, then?' I snapped.

'To make the best out of a bad argument: That a girl who was out on the streets without papers, had them. That a girl who was carrying a double handful of prime, uncut fire-weed, wasn't. That a girl who assaulted an officer of the Watch, didn't. That's what you pay me for, my dear, and you know there's nobody better than I to make the case that up is down. But the Judge is getting ever more, er, shall we say *arbitrary* in his findings, now that he is so troubled by bad digestion. Once my case is made, I'm afraid that much hangs on whether or not His Honour has heartburn on the day of the trial.'

'Then you make sure he doesn't. Make that sure he has a good night's sleep before the trial and that his wife is sweet to him that morning. Cook his breakfast for him if you have to. Remind him that he has a daughter that looks like Binpoy. Just ...' – I looked him hard in the eye – '... just do what it takes.'

Pyn-Poi

The next night, the tall rock-pecker was gone. I whisked in and out of all of the boxes, in case the boot-men had moved him, but I found only strangers. I never saw him again.

Boss Lady

I took Binpoy the most respectable dress we had in the Palace, a prim old thing that Laly wore that night she first turned up at my door all mottled purple from her husband's fists. It was heavy fibre, not silk – nothing that draped and clung and flattered. No fringes, either – nothing to sway with the hips. Plain as possible. Childlike. Innocent.

I gave some thought to what I should do about covering her head. Before, I'd been trying to hide how she looked, to protect her from pimps and sellers trawling for exotics. But veils and head-scarves are seductive, mysterious – not to be trusted. Maybe it would be best if she wore no head-covering at all, like a little girl. Maybe letting her strangeness out into the open would make her seem more vulnerable. Someone to be pitied. To be returned to her family.

The courtroom smelled bad, like a drunk lying in his own soilings. A fly kept landing on me – my cheek, then my hand, then my forehead – and finally settled peacefully on the furry lip of the old woman snoring on the bench beside me. I was thinking that I'd best boil my matron-costume when I got back to the Happy Palace – didn't want to bring home any lice to my girls – when they finally pulled Binpoy, wearing that muddy blue sack of a dress, into the wooden box in front of the Judge.

Good – her eyes weren't defiant, just curious, casting around the room, lingering on the high windows that hung open to catch any hope of air. Taking in the benches, the ragtag watchers waiting for the next case, or the one after that. Landing at last on me.

Her face changed when she saw me, like sunshine lighting up a room when the curtain's thrown open. Such a pretty girl when she smiles.

She turned to come toward me, and put a hand on the swinging door of the dock. I shook my head violently and motioned for her to stay put before the Bailiff could bring his night-stick up. The world is a dangerous place for someone with no clue about anything.

She understood, stepped back, and settled, gazing at me with an expression I can't describe until the Bailiff, young Shrey, pushed her around to face the Judge.

Binpoy looked once over her shoulder at me and I nodded at her, trying to look more confident than I felt. Good girl. Behave yourself and we'll get you out of this mess.

The whole thing didn't take long. The old prune-faced Judge asked Binpoy questions she didn't answer. My law-man oozed respect as he told the tale of an impoverished traveller – a simple-minded girl, almost a mute, too stupid to be held responsible for her own mis- takes – fallen into bad company who used her to carry contraband fire-weed until she finally fetched up under the protection of a local business-woman with a heart for taking in stray girls. I snorted at that, but under my breath.

The law-man told a pretty story, I'll give him that. I almost believed him myself. But one of the jailers stepped up to testify that the girl was no mute – she spoke to the Guards every day, saying 'here's my bowl' and 'thank you' at breakfast and even asking them how they were when they made their rounds. Damn the girls for teaching Binpoy to speak. And damn me for not thinking of the jailers when I was ploughing money into every pocket involved in this pig-show. And then the head of the Watch, a nasty vindictive man, didn't stay bribed. He spoke against Binpoy, looking me right in the eye all the while, saying that nobody with a broke brain could fight like this girl had, holding her own against three strong men with batons. There were snickers around the courtroom at this.

The Judge scowled. I knew it was all over when I saw him empty a packet of white powder into his water-glass and slug the fizzing mixture down.

It took less than ten minutes.

A six-year contract. For stealing an orange.

Pyn-Poi

The boot-men pulled me away from the big box with windows without letting me go to Bazleti. I'd learned to notice that first small movement of their hands toward the club that hung from their belts like an extra penis. I watched for that telltale twitch and would stop whatever I was doing before they struck.

I let them take me back along the narrow cave with many doors. I knew by then that those doors opened onto other boxes just like mine, with people in them just like me. Some had been there a lot longer than I had. As I trailed back toward my box, boots clomping in front of me and behind, I could smell misery leaking out like a heavy smoke.

Before shutting me away again, one of the boot-men handed me two rope-soled sandals and a bundle of scratchy, rough-woven cloth the colour of a tanned hide, the colour of the sick, pale dirt here in this land. He made me understand that I was to take off Bazleti's blue dress and put on these different clothes. 'Tomorrow,' he said – a word I knew from the goodbyes after each of my basket-visits. 'Tomorrow, you go.'

Boss Lady

The law-man sat across his big desk from me, bland and unfazed as I yelled out my anger at him, at the Judge, and at the stupid, stupid System. When I paused for breath, he interrupted me.

'Your frustration is perfectly understandable, dear lady, and perfectly acceptable to express in the privacy of this office. But I have every confidence that a woman with such wisdom and worldly experience will not be uttering such disaffection outside these walls. A little emotional release, a little venting of feelings, is fine, of course, but—'

'I don't want to vent my feelings! What I *want* is to get that child out of jail. Six years on a prison-farm? It'll kill her. It's murder pure and simple. There has to be something we can do. A re-trial. I'll go back to that wretched Guard and find a way to shut him up so he stays shut. Or the Judge. Judges are expensive, but . . .'

'Judges are *dangerous*. You'll do nothing of the sort. You know the penalty for attempting to suborn a Judge as well as I do. If you are even *considering* such a thing, tell me now and you and I will part ways right here. I can't be involved in such—'

'I know, I know. You're right. It was just a thought. But we have to do *something*.'

'I'm afraid there's not much we *can* do, legally speaking. There's no appeal in cases involving assault of officers of the Watch. And I would urge you in the strongest possible terms *not* to consider extra-legal actions.'

'You mean, like helping her escape?'

'As you say. Such a course could endanger your own freedom. What, after all, do you owe this girl?'

What, indeed? The price of a stolen garnet? My word given to a Miner whose name I couldn't even remember? The trust in those golden eyes peering at me over the top of a mug of milk mixed with poppy-juice? What did I really owe the little stray with the handful of feathers that were even now tucked away in the torn pack beside my chair?

'She won't need this, where she's going,' the Bailiff had chuckled when he handed it over to me.

I came very near to slapping him.

Pyn-Poi

The next morning, everything happened as usual – the bucket, the water-jug, the bowl – except for, this time, the boots called out for the dress. I knew the word well because sex-witches in this place think and talk a lot about their clothing.

I rolled the blue fabric up into a tight bundle and pushed it out through the flap with regret – it was so much softer and more comfortable than the rough, itchy, colourless sack I was wearing now. I told the door that the dress belonged to Bazleti. I hope he understood me. I hope he gets the pretty thing back to her.

When I stepped back under the sky again, tears blinded me, tears and the low morning sun that stabs like a knife in this land unsheltered by trees. So long, so long I had been in that box that my eyes had forgotten light. I shielded my face from it behind my pinioned wrists, hiding from it at the same time that I wanted to drink it in. I heard rough laughter around me.

One of the boot-men knocked my hands away from my eyes and spun me back toward the blazing glare. He pointed at the sun and made loud words that oozed with mockery, then laughed.

Light. Air. Walking.

Walking again was beautiful to me. Walking without walls to turn you every few steps. It was a song – to my legs, to my lungs – even with my hands trapped in those strange double-bracelets that kept

235

my arms from swinging free. The sun struck glints from the sandy ground, like tiny daylight stars.

I walked behind two of the boot-men. Two more strode behind me.

We walked together down a path between the house-boxes of the town and people looked up as we passed. Looked up and fell silent. Behind my back, I could hear their conversations start up again, but I could not catch any words that I knew.

Three heavy cleanup-birds flapped across the road in front of us. I watched longingly as they rose into the sky.

This was not the ravine of the Happy Palace. There was nothing and no one here that I knew.

The spaces between the house-boxes grew. Squares of emptiness, patchy with sickly grass. Land-hens pecking at dirt. Scrawny square-eyes bleating for food. Snuffle-pigs. Sad, lost pucker-fruit trees, leaf-poor oil-trees covered with dust. How flat the land was here, how colourless. But no, not colourless everywhere—

There, up in front of us. I saw them, all of them, dressed in their finest, most power-filled shimmering swaths of colour, faces painted so that their eyes were enormous like ring-tail's, lips stained as if they'd just eaten blood-fruit. Even little Khukmama glowed with colour, her wrinkled mouth fire-orange.

They all stood quietly while Bazleti, in shining gold and green with tinkling fringes hanging down like leaf-coloured hair, talked words at the oldest boot-man and pressed a big food-basket into his hand, along with something small that he pocketed. Then, at a word from him, the sex-witches were all over me, pressing me from every side, patting me, talking too many and too fast for me, kissing my cheeks. Khukmama put something sweet and chewy in my mouth. Bina stroked my hair.

I saw tears all around me. Do not cry! – I did not want them to streak the power colours on their faces – but I could not stop them and then I caught their tears and could not stop myself. Bazleti took

me in her arms, squeezing hard, whispering words I did not understand, until the grizzled boot-man barked at her and she let me go.

The four men boxed me up between them again and the sex-
witches stepped back, wailing like mourners when the birds come.
'Walk,' one of the men snapped at me. Laly crumpled against Hatheer
and I began to be afraid. This place I was going . . . It could not be
worse than the walled-up buried place where I'd been so long. But
everyone was crying, crying, crying. Crying for me.

I looked over my shoulder, back at the garden-bright women
against the mud-coloured town. Bazleti stood in front of them,
holding up something in each hand. I turned to get a better look.

A crack of pain shot up my thigh from a blow by a boot-man's
club. I cried out and staggered forward, into the laughing men in
front of me, then on, down the lane and out of the town.

But I had seen what Bazleti held up to the sky for me: A handful
of feathers. And my father's knife.

THE FARM

Pyn-Poi

I wanted to argue with Lakka, to insist that escape was possible – we just hadn't found the way.

But she was right; I could never abandon my tract-sisters to the System's vicious 'collective consequences'. So what *could* I do? The feathers were still the feathers, even if they were out of my hands, somewhere back in the box-village with Bazleti. How could I be faithful to the Mothers' charge?

At home, there was always a clear path, ancient step-stones set among the roots of trees. The People's feet polished them, kept the moss from overgrowing them and hiding the way. But here, on the Tract, I could see nothing but a spider's web of dry lanes between the endless fields.

One seed more, just one. Drop it in. Stab the next hole. The next seed. Drop it in. Like a fire-chant, drowning out every other thought.

Each day passed in a sort of bent-backed trance, and then it would be night again and so many rows had been planted but I had done nothing, nothing, nothing toward the saving of my People. My other

239

people. All my strength and will was going into the dirt with the seeds. By the time the rains came again, would I even remember my real name?

I stopped dreaming of home, of the riotous, many-voiced tangle of life as it is meant to be. Now, anytime the trees weren't with me, my dreams were filled with crumbly, grey-brown dirt. Dirt gripping around my ankles so I couldn't run, pressing on my chest so I couldn't breathe, filling my mouth so I couldn't speak. Monsoon water rising around me and no place to go. Sometimes the flood was a solid sheet of hungry, sharp-jawed bugs covering the fields, burying us all, stripping the flesh from the bones of my sisters. Skeletons. We were all nothing but skeletons. I dreamed of a black box, a door swinging shut.

The trees still came at night, though. I would wake in the morning, confused about where I was, with a dim sense that my teachers had been with me. But the knowing would be like a bird in a tree, fluttering from branch to branch, hidden by leaves. You know the bird is there but after a while, you begin to wonder. During the day, I no longer remembered the lessons, the exercises that they set for me at night.

I'd changed in my body, as well. I was still strong – I was one of the ones Naina called on now when there was a fight or someone went crazy from the sun. But I was no longer sleek. My arms were ropy from field-work. My ribs and hip bones stuck out. If I were home, no one would want to marry their son to such a skinny girl. But that wouldn't even be a question – I'd stopped bleeding. Everyone did, after a few months on the Tract. Our bodies were wise, knowing not to waste Flow in a world with too little food to make babies.

I suppose this shouldn't have mattered to me – the only men we dealt with were in Administration and they didn't see us as women at all, or even as people. I think they saw their dogs more than they saw us; to them we were just tools, like shovels and rakes, just something to be kept track of as long as it was useful. But still, I grieved becoming a crone before I ever had a chance to be a mother.

After the second year's planting, a new girl came. It was always an excitement when someone arrived from the outside. It meant news, for the others, of the world they knew, and sometimes a new talent – maybe a singer, maybe a storyteller. Also, a whole new personality to fit into the clan.

I helped to bathe this girl on her first night. She looked so fat and pretty, I thought as I scrubbed the streaks of dog-shit from her full, smooth cheeks. We put her to bed between Mareery and Taivo. Their gentleness would calm her, help her know that this thing, this being on the Farm, was something she could survive.

But the next morning, when the whistle blew, the girl was feverish and whiny. We put it down to her being new. Coming to the Farm was like being born – suddenly you were helpless again, like a baby, and everything was hard and sharp. You had to learn the most basic things: how to talk the language of Tract Eleven, how to line up for counts, how to run and work without wasting your strength – the ways of the place. So we just pulled the new girl along with us and tried to show her how to thin the young plants so that they would be lined up right for the picking.

But when the sun got high, I heard chattering from a few rows over. I stood up to see what was happening and take a moment to rub my back. The new one – I never learned her name – was sprawled in the dirt. She'd fainted across the row. 'Crushing the new growth,' was my first thought. 'Better get her up before Naina sees.'

Mareery was kneeling beside the girl and had her head in her lap. She sprinkled water on her face, and patted her cheeks, trying to get her to wake up. I started to step across the row toward them, but just then I heard Sibba's shout that Doc would take care things and the rest of us should get back to work. I bent to pull another green shoot and throw it aside.

Doc looked the new one over, saw the scattering of bumps on her nose and cheeks, and dashed across the field to speak with Naina.

I was one of the group they sent to carry the girl back to the bunk-house. We squatted along each side of her body and I wriggled my hands underneath to grip Nepaka's wrists. I remember thinking how fleshy the girl's haunches were, not yet shrunken away by hunger and hard work. Then we were lifting her, Lakka beside me sharing the shoulders' weight with Chirun, Pino at the back, supporting the head, Chombly and Sibba leading, holding the legs. We walked this way, slowly, awkwardly, back to the bunkhouse, surrounded by ten or twelve others Naina sent back with us to fend off the dogs.

We lay her in the special bunk at the back – the bunk where people died – and left her there with Doc trying to force the neck of a water-gourd between her lips while the girl fought, knocking it away, flinging her head from side to side.

Within three days, the new girl was dead and most of the Tract was sick.

That was the beginning of the bad time.

I was one of the few who didn't get sick at all. Naina, too, and some of the other old women who'd had the spotted fever when they were children.

Some, a few – again mostly the old ones – just took a light case. A few days of hot cheeks and hard coughing, and they were done.

But for most, the sickness was a terrible thing. A fever that drove them to mad waking dreams or bone-shaking convulsions, and a thickness of the lungs that turned the bunkhouse into an echoing hall of wheezing, racking gasps.

Those first days, Doc tried to fight it off, to keep the sick separated from the well – at first, with the sick in the back of the bunkhouse, away from everyone else in the front. Later, when there were too many, she kept the sick inside and the few who were still well slept in the dirt under the eaves. But every morning, some who lay down well woke up sick.

Doc told the Managers that the doctor from Administration should come. She told them that we needed medicine. We could pay, Naina said – there was credit in our account. But after one look in the door of the bunkhouse, the Managers rode away on their mules and didn't come back, not to bring the medicine, not to bring the doctor. They didn't bring our tools in the mornings. They didn't come to count us. They didn't even come to take away the bodies.

After the third death, when the Managers still hadn't come, Naina damned them all and said that we couldn't wait for them to bring the cart that took corpses away so that they could be accounted for. 'If they want to count them, they can dig them up,' she growled and told me and Varna to sink a big hole.

We buried them inside the precincts of the bunkhouse so that the dogs wouldn't dig them up. The holes we dug got shallower as the days passed and there were more to bury and fewer to dig. It sickened me to lay my sisters under the dirt, where the birds couldn't get at them, but Naina said it needed to be done and I no longer argued with Naina.

Goban

'Damn the luck.' Kai's mule felt her agitation and sidestepped under her as she pulled herself into the saddle. Kai flailed for balance, then whacked its flanks with the butt of her dog-lasher. It settled, uneasily. 'This had to happen now? Right at the beginning of second season?'

She was pretty rattled. Kai doesn't rattle easy, but this was her first time seeing sickness take a Tract. 'Well, you see how filthy they are. What'd you expect? We just have to keep it contained, is all – make sure it doesn't jump to the other Tracts.'

'Make sure it doesn't jump to *us*.'

I snorted. 'It won't. We'll leave 'em alone till it burns itself out. And anyway, this kind of thing, well . . . The tractees are different from you and me, you know, not healthy stock. Not strong. That's why they wind up here. They can't really make it on their own, out there, outside the Farm. And sometimes, not inside, either. We'll see what happens.'

'But our bonuses . . . I was going to buy a—'

'Well, as far as any harvest-bonus this year, you can kiss it good-bye. But, in the long run, this could work out for the best. Might be time to thin out this lot, get rid of some of the useless eaters. And if they do *all* go down, then Administration will get us a whole new set, fresh muscle, not like these skin-and-bone types that can barely drag a bag at harvest.'

'But that'll take some time, won't it?'

'Not too long.' I kicked Blue-Boy's flanks and we headed back toward Administration. Jagath would want to know about this as soon as possible. 'There's always people out there just begging for a stint on the Farm.' Kai snorted. 'The Administrator just passes a word to the Judges to step things up a bit, and we're back in business in no time, brim-full with eager new tractees. Of course, the Judges get a little off the top the first year, but still . . .'

'Have to teach 'em to work, though,' Kai said thoughtfully.

'Well, we know how to do that, don't we?' I slapped the dog-lasher on my hip. Blue-Boy skipped forward at the sound.

Naina

Dying. They are all dying and I can't stop it. One by one, they get sick and fade and rattle and go.

Get a hold of yourself, Naina. They aren't all dying. Shano's getting stronger, and Chirun here looks like she might pull through, too. As for the rest – they need you. They need you not to fall apart.

But the Managers have stopped coming, and we're almost out of rice.

Don't think about that. We're not out yet. Just do the thing that needs doing. One step after another. Keep your eyes on what's in front of you and don't think. Do not think. Just keep moving. Put food in their mouths. Bring them water. Lift Chirun's head up from these damned hard boards, too hard to hold these sick and bony bodies. If only they had a little—

Stop that. They don't – they only have you, you and the handful of others that are still strong enough to do what you tell them to. But *you've* got to tell them: Pump the water. Boil the rice. Feed and clean the sick ones, and move the bodies outside once it's finished.

They're good girls, the ones still on their feet. They're doing what they can. I should be nicer to them.

Don't be an idiot, woman. They don't need you to be nice. They need you to be strong. Hold this thing together.

But what happens if the Managers don't bring us more rice? Can we brave the dogs and walk to Administration? But if they won't send the oxcart, my girls aren't strong enough to carry the rice sacks back with us. And who would tend the sick ones if we left them?

No. The Managers will bring the rice. They have to.

Pyn-Poi

Naina was a Mother's Mother during that time, organising the few of us still standing to bring water and food to the sick and try to keep them clean. At the very beginning, she sent some of us into the fields to do what could be done with the crop, but soon that group was too small to make the dogs leave us alone and Naina kept us all at the bunkhouse. I saw her many times, sitting beside some woman with one foot here and one foot already where she needed to go, chewing up morsels of rice and putting them into the sick one's mouth like a mother weaning a baby from the breast. And Naina did wean some away from death with an angry ferocity that was frightening. Death was her personal enemy, a cackling thief that insulted her and mocked her at every turn.

I never knew how long Naina's contract was for. I never asked – I was afraid to. But however many years it was, Naina would spend them fighting Death any way she could, whether it was cleaning the runny wastes from a bunk full of women too weak to get to the latrine ditch, or taking over the cook-pot when illness stripped the kitchen of workers. If Naina could have met her enemy in a fair fight with a weapon in her hand, Death would have died bloody.

Marak would have liked Naina. Or maybe they would have fought like hunter-cats. One or the other. But there would have been respect. There would have been knowing. Mothers know Mothers, they say. Like those two, there are none.

Without Naina, the Tract would have burned itself out in the bad time like a cook-fire when all the fuel is gone. Without Naina,

I wouldn't have known, really known, in my belly and bones, that it was possible for a woman to save her people.

We lost Doc to the sickness. Of my three friends, only Lakka lived, much changed by the fever. And by the grief.

When it was done, thirty-one of us were left on the sky-side of the ground, and most of these so weakened by the illness that they could not do one hour in the field without falling over. Work once shared by all had to be done now by whoever could do it. Water had to be pumped and doled out. Food had to be seen to. And the fields . . .

I was too busy to think or be afraid. The lines on Naina's face cut deeper, grimmer, fiercer.

After the worst of the sickness had passed, Naina took us out to walk the fields, to take stock, she said. She'd said we should talk about what to do now, but her silence deepened as we paced the chewed-up rows until it seemed that any word spoken would sink into the dirt and be swallowed.

That night, the Council met like they used to, sitting on the dirt outside the door of the bunkhouse, sipping from gourd cups of cat's-tooth tea. Repjim, still gaunt and shaky on her feet, took her place with them. She might be too weak to walk, she said, but she wasn't too weak to think. They talked for a long time. We fell asleep to the soft rustle of their voices, our Council still (even if Doc was no longer with them) thinking, arguing, deciding. Taking care of us.

The next morning, Naina spoke to us all together, inside the shadowy bunkhouse so that even those still abed could listen.

'The fields have gone to shit,' she said. 'We did the best we could, but that's the way of it. And when the bugs come back, well, even if they hold off until we're on our feet – which they won't – we can't spray fast enough to fight them back with this few people. So this is what we're going to do. We're going to give up the three big fields closest to the river as a lost cause. Just forget about them this year, pour everything we have into the nearer fields, get the most we can out of those. We can't handle any more, not with the hands we have. But we've also got fewer mouths to feed now and I think, if we get the weeds under control, that maybe we can make it. So work hard, help someone else get stronger, and we may be able to see out another year.'

She shut her mouth. That was it, all Naina had to say. Work hard. Help someone else – and then the trees kicked me.

Maybe kicked isn't the right word. Trees don't have feet. Maybe they slapped me. Maybe they picked me up by the scruff of the neck and shook me like a puppy. Or maybe they threw water on me like Marak used to do when she thought I was lying too long in my hammock. It's hard, in words, to say exact things about how the trees talk and teach. The only language for it is the language of 'as if' – and it was truly as if the trees had done all these things at once.

I worked through the day in a haze and then lay down that night beside Lakka on our too-roomy top bunk with my head buzzing like a hive. I didn't know how to do this thing the trees proposed, but . . .

That night, the trees talked to me in a way they hadn't for a very long time – in a way that I could hold in my mind even when the sun came up on a new day.

The next morning, I asked Naina for one of the fields we were abandoning.

I would have liked to ask her for all three fields, but I wasn't sure I could deal with more than one. A single success, though, would maybe prove it could be done – if one season was enough to bring back the friendly bug-eaters and if I could really manage to bring in a harvest without poison. And maybe having the two fallow fields on each side would serve as a sort of shield between my crops and all the spraying.

I asked. Naina said no.

She listened, though; I'd earned that much of her regard, at least. She didn't turn away or brush my words aside as I promised her that I would only tend the field at night, after my day-work was done. What about the dogs, she said – I'd have to take people with me to keep the night-hounds off, people who should be sleeping, resting, saving their strength to do the work of seventy with thirty pairs of hands. We couldn't split the forces of the group – we were too small now. That was the whole point of letting the three farthest fields go. 'We have to put all our fruit in one bowl, Binpoy,' she said, 'and guard that bowl!'

I didn't have an answer for this. Trying to tell Naina about people far away, my People, dying because the Stink came down on them from the fields with the rains – this would just be a fire-story to her, nothing real, nothing that mattered. Everyone on the Tract knew, of course, that the poison made us sick – fast, with the vomiting and trembling and spots in our vision right after spraying, but slow, too, with the rashes and lumps that grew under people's skin and ate them away to nothing. But immediate hunger was always more real to Naina. Her eyes were on getting us through today and tomorrow, on the close-up problem of survival, not on the long-view problem of the poison. She said no. I opened my mouth to argue—

Then shut it again—

Could the work be done in my Other body?

Was it even possible? The trees had sternly warned me against taking my Other body too far from my flesh body, or staying away too long. Those early trips beyond the door of my dark training box in the town had been very short and they had supervised every step, constantly nagging at me to pay attention: 'Mind where you put your feet. Bring your arms with you. Don't forget your hands. Now where are the limits of your skin? Where are they now? And now?'

The trees did not want me to dissolve and I didn't want this, either, not really, though on hard days it might be tempting to let my shape go and allow myself to be blown away by the wind. I might be blown homeward and tumble over the Wall like one of the rivers. But no. I had this thing to do first.

So, could I do it? Could I hold my Other body together across the long walk to the fields and through the night as I did the work that must be done? Would my flesh body be waiting for me when I returned? Would it still be warm and breathing?

Could I do it? I asked the trees, and they said, 'Do it.'

Those first nights, the work was just to listen.

I would walk barefoot down the rows of fibre, the sandy soil gritty between my Other toes, and grow my ears big. Big as my head, big as my whole body, big as the sky. I would turn my enormous ears this way and that, listening like I had never listened before.

Loudest, of course, was the steady, all-the-same mewling of the fibre plants. They were starving, poor things – we had not yet fed them their grow-big tea before the bad time came. Having known hunger myself, I grieve for all hungry things, but Naina had decided to let this field go and none of the Tract's credit would be spent on the nourishing tea this year.

As I listened deeper to the soughing whine of the fibre, I could begin to hear – as if from far away, from far beyond the line where the chubby moon was setting – the voices of the sister-plants, the hopeful greens that we usually hacked to pieces with our hoes or pulled up by the roots to keep them from crowding the precious fibre. Their song, when I first found it, reminded me of the fire-circle singing of the People where the women sing one tune and the men another. The boys and girls, too, each have their own tunes, as do the old men and women and the middle-people. We each have our own parts and they are different, but they fit together like strands of a hammock, yielding and united – one whole.

That was how the song of the sister-plants sounded to me, many voices, many tunes, braiding, weaving, twining. Voices of tiny sprouts and sprigs fighting their way up between the fibre plants, vigorous and hopeful like kicking babies, each bringing their gifts and needs into the light. I had to listen carefully – the sound-weaving was beautiful, but it was very soft, much softer than the song of the trees. Oh, how I listened, turning sometimes to the ditches and the lanes between the fields where there were older plants, plants more settled in their personalities. These voices were clearer and we could speak more intelligently.

And, although it is very hard to listen to dirt, I began to get a sense of the ground itself, of the Flow of it, the way the fibre ate up the living juice of the land, the way the knobby-rooted twine-vine tried to replenish it. Like work and sleep, I thought, as I walked back toward my bunk through the watchful hounds. Passing through them in my

Other body made them uneasy. They would look around, hackles high, and rumble quietly under their breath, as if they didn't want their fellows to hear them growling at something that wasn't there.

'Do it.' A new leaf budded on my life.

I still worked all day in the dirt with the others, harder than I ever had before, because now I was one of the strongest ones, with Chirun still as wobbly on her feet as a new kitten and Chombly gone under the ground.

The Managers came back, which meant the idiotic whistles and count-lines again – precious time wasted – but it also meant that they brought us our tools again, the hoes and mattocks we needed and 'rented' from Administration for a share of the harvest.

The days were exhausting. The Tract wasn't yet working at strength, but most of the survivors were in the fields again for at least half the day. Those of us who could work until sunset did so, coming back near dark and throwing ourselves down under the eaves to lean against the bunkhouse wall until dinner. Grenda, the new Cook-Mama, would shoo everyone else away from the swept patch of dirt we called the kitchen and gather her helpers. While we waited for food, the rest of us would just sit and breathe for a while. Doing nothing, maybe, or stitching together worn places in our bag-dresses. Fixing our sandals, which were always coming apart. Devising straps and belts to carry our water-gourds more comfortably. Talking.

That time of day was when we told stories about the ones who were gone. They left us so quickly that there'd been no time to honour their living. While the rice-pot boiled and the sharp smell of the onion-breath tickled our noses and made our bellies growl like night-hounds, someone might tell how Doc always said that onion-breath would help us fight off sickness. And everyone who heard would be quiet for a moment, because nothing at all had helped Doc fight off the spotted fever. But in that memory, Doc was still with us, the way the old Cook-Mama was still with us when Grenda tried to do things the same way as before the bad time. And many things were told that I'd never heard before, about the small heroisms of people's lives on the Tract and about what people had done that caused the System to put them there. I listened carefully to every hint about this System of theirs, what kind of creature it might be. I was beginning to understand that someday I must have dealings with the System.

Someday. If I survived this place.

I often stayed up late because the Council, with Doc gone, began to invite some of us younger women to come and listen – not talk – during the meetings they held after dinner, in the dark, with their tea. Many nights, I came close to falling asleep as they argued what to do next with a certain field or a certain person or a certain problem, but listening to them was how I began to learn how Mothers think, how they measure what is needed against what is possible and then weave the plans for their people.

When I was a child, I loved my father very much. I loved being with him. I loved learning from him. I honoured his big eyes and ears and touch for trees more than any other talent.

My mother, I mostly just endured. She criticised me and controlled my life, like she controlled the lives of everyone I knew. Every minute with her was about jobs I was supposed to do, things I was supposed to learn. The things that I wanted to do and learn were just a 'waste of time' to her and the things she did, I was blind to. Her work – planning for, organising, running our family, kin, and clan – wasn't something I noticed or understood or even saw. My eyes just didn't work that way. I did, of course, feel the power and intelligence in her – you would have to be dead and carried away not to – but I just did not see the net of strands her power and intelligence engaged with. Blind to that complexity, I'm ashamed to admit that I thought her talents were mostly wasted.

Those nights sitting on the hard dead dirt with the Council, listening to them argue how to discipline, how to spend our credit, how to feed us, how to keep us alive, I thought a lot about Marak. Would I ever see her again? Would I ever get to look at her with my bigger eyes, to perhaps speak a word of appreciation for her gifts?

But after all the evening things were done, the resting and eating and listening to the Council, I would clamber up onto our sleeping-shelf, curl up into Lakka's back, and return to the gifts of my father. I would send this flesh body of mine down into the dark waters of sleep while my Other body strode out across the fields under the moonlight.

Over time, it got easier to move about at night in my Other form. Less of me had to focus on things like keeping my legs attached to my body and my head floating above my shoulders and more of me could attend to my ears.

After many long nights of patient, probing listening, it came to me that the first thing I should do was persuade a few of the little castor-plants to grow tall as fast as they could. I approached them delicately, with just the tip of my Other forefinger flowing in to join them, and we talked.

At first, they said no to the idea of height. They said that they would much rather be bushy than tall. I explained that the field needed perches, places for birds to sit and survey the rows of fibre. High places from which they could launch themselves to swoop down and pluck bugs from the plants and from the air.

The castor-plants didn't care about the birds. They preferred to be bushy, to send their forces out into many small branches and leaves to catch the sun. Ah, I said – but if they were tall, then the sun would get to them first, before even touching the other sister-plants. (I was trying to appeal to their pride, you see.)

But still they said 'bushy'; it was better to be thick and bushy. So I threatened them. I told them that, unless a few of them – just a few, five or six, no more – agreed to be tall, people would come back again with hoes and poison.

Hearing this, they turned and whispered to each other for a long time. I waited, scratching patterns in the dirt with my toe, until they spoke to me again. They'd chosen a few of their kin, they said – one at each corner of the field and an upstart in the middle – to send all their juices into making their central stalks tall and strong. I couldn't expect more than that.

So, soon we would have some perches to invite the birds back to eat the boll-worms and the caterpillars and the cutter-bugs. With the field so close to the river, it wouldn't take the feathered kins long to find us again.

It turned out that the taller castor-plants did well with the exchange. The perching birds dropped their wastes around them, enlivening the soil, and everyone was happy.

You might think I would wake up tired after spending those nights in the field. I didn't, though – for the first time in two years, I woke up strong and rested, as if maybe I had taken a sip of some grow-strong tea that made me well. Happy, even.

The thing was still small when I found it, no bigger than the tip of my little finger. A pebble that had somehow burrowed into me and lodged itself in the fold of skin between my armpit and what little was left of my breast after more than two years of starving.

It wasn't tender like a boil, or hot, or red. It wasn't anything. Maybe it was one of those parasites that mothers tell their children about to make sure they go to the bathing place every day – horrid creatures that tunnel into you when they are tiny things, then feed on you and grow until they are big enough to break out and crawl away.

But the thing under my arm never broke out. It only grew.

So.

Now there's the lump to consider. Time is rising around me like a monsoon flood. And this System of theirs – how do I get to it?

One night, after a long day of hoeing, Chirun was telling a story about back before she came to the Farm, when she worked at one of the System's factories. (A factory is where many people make one thing over and over, whether they need it or not.) This gave me an opening to ask something that had been much on my mind: 'Where does the System actually live?'

Everyone laughed at the question. 'Oh, you sweet little cherry,' Grenda said, pinching my nose. 'The System is *everywhere*, its claws deep in every town and city and mine and farm, every single one of them. There's nowhere you can go where the System isn't.'

I started to argue, to tell them that I knew of one place where it wasn't: over the Wall and under the trees.

But then I closed my mouth. The poison spilling down onto the Real – that was their System, invading. It was coming after the People and it wanted to turn our leafy Real as barren and deathly as the Farm.

It had to be stopped. I had to find it. To explain. To persuade. But how do you find a being who is 'everywhere'? And even if I could find it, how would I ever convince it that poison wasn't the only way to squeeze out this fibre that it craved so badly? I had to show it, to show them all.

My field.

It had to succeed.

Time.

What would speed the healing of my field?

While the castors worked on becoming tall, one night I called a circle of the other sister-plants. I told them that they were now free – no, more than just free, they were welcome, they were *invited* – to move in among the fibre, around the bases of the plants but also out in the naked dirt between the rows.

There was a certain amount of doubtful rustling at this announcement. 'Are you sure about this?' They reminded me of how we'd always hacked at them and cursed them and uprooted them in the past when they tried to befriend the fibre.

I assured them I was serious. 'Too much of one thing, all together in one place, summons the eaters of that thing. We all know that,' I said. 'The eaters fill their bellies, and then they breed like on a drunken festival night. Too many baby eaters are born, and they too stuff themselves until there is no more food left.

'But if you move in,' I went on, 'you will make the field a mix again, the way it should be, a healed thing. Then, maybe, yes, a few cutter-bugs will come, a few boll-worms, but not a flood that will drown the whole. So now, today, come and be welcome again. Stand between the fibre plants and let everyone grow and be eaten in the way the Mother intends. Let there be something Real here, a small Real, a clan of mixed kins.'

I let my voice get a little grand as I finished up this speech. Would my appeal seem ridiculous to them? But either because of my words or because it was in their nature and they'd been eyeing that empty soil anyway, the sister-plants soon began to move in. Roots, runners, seeds, and tendrils found their way into the empty spaces of the field. Green things happened.

This made me very happy. The twine-vine would give good Flow to the soil. The richer soil would make the fibre-plants stronger, more able to stand against brown-spot and to bear a little loss of leaves to the cutter-bugs. Healthier plants would yield up fatter bolls, heavier bags at picking time – more credit from the Weighmaster. Also – and this made my Other mouth water – the twine-vine, allowed to grow, would yield fat pods of fine green peas for Grenda's rice-pot.

But even the other plants, the ones that give nothing back to the soil, made me very happy. For one thing, the star-flowers were even more appetising to most bugs than the fibre was; they would draw off some of the pests when they came.

And of course they would come. Nothing would prevent that. Even if my fibre was mixed in with rows of thriving sister-plants, the obscene fields were too nearby, the ones we'd battered into hosting only the one tortured crop. These would sing out to the hungry swarms of eaters and my field was too close to be ignored.

What would I do when that time came? How would I shield my fibre and make all this work worthwhile?

As my night expeditions found my field working together ever more smoothly, my thoughts turned more toward the mysterious System. How was I ever going to find this thing, to face it? How would I tell it my story? What words did I need to learn first?

With new urgency, I listened hungrily to the Thought Hygienist on our monthly visits to Administration. I'd always more or less ignored her, concentrating mostly on not falling asleep during the endless recitations from those rustling white leaves of hers. If you dozed, a sharp crack of her lasher across your back would jerk you awake, so we cultivated an open-eyed trance that let us rest our bodies without attracting her attention.

But that waterfall of words we sat under for hours and hours – the *Principles of Productivity* the Hygienist always spoke from – was supposed to come straight from the System itself. Could it give me clues? Help me understand what kind of being it was? Could it show me the creature's thoughts, so that when we finally met, I would know its mind and its powers?

But even though I had learned to understand much of the speaking of this place by then, the Hygiene incantations were full of strange language that was never used in the daily life of the Tract. The System had its own words, it seemed – not surprising for a being of such power.

It turned out that the meanings were not secret. Not exactly. That season, I made a habit of memorising some of these words of power every month and asking Lakka about them as we trotted back to the bunkhouse. The sounds had a certain beguiling rhythm to them – 'opportunity', 'loyalty', 'prosperity' – a power to fascinate – 'property', 'responsibility', 'wealth' – so I was very careful with them.

Lakka claimed to know what they meant, but did she really? She could never point at things to show me what they were and she had a hard time finding other words to tell me.

Even after she'd 'explained them', these power-words remained riddles and conjurations. None of them gave me any clues about where the System lived or how to sway it. And, worse, the twisted web of meaninglessness began to raise a new question: Was the System itself some kind of abomination, as twisted and reasonless as its deathly Farm?

259

I rolled the lump between my fingertips. Was it bigger? There was no pain, but still I touched the thing very delicately, very gently – I didn't want to wake up whatever lay sleeping just under my skin. I didn't want to crack its shell and let it out. I only touched it at night, in the dark, after everyone was asleep.

The change was very gradual, so it was hard to tell for sure. I tried to let it go a whole month, moon to moon, without touching it at all so that I could feel if it was growing.

But it was impossible to keep my fingers off it at night, this stranger riding in my flesh. I wished that I could talk to Doc about it. I wished that I could talk to my mother.

Bats.

The field wanted bats.

Back in the Real, each kin of the People had a kin of leather-wings, too. Every year, their dwellings would be washed away by the rains, just like ours. Every year, during Drying-Out, we would replace their houses even before we re-did our own, hauling the big closed baskets up to the sunny top of the house-trees, where the bats would stand their guard over us, plucking the nibblers out of the air and making our homes healthy for another season.

We had no real trees on the Farm, but could the newly inspired castor-plants support the weight of small bat-houses? Like everyone in the Real, I knew how to turn reeds into baskets, but there were no reeds here, except by the river where the big-jaws waited. But the stems of the fibre plants in the abandoned fields – couldn't they be woven into some sort of suitable bat-house? But how would I keep such a thing secret? And how would I get it to the night-field?

Slowly, steadily, the birds came back to my field. Spiders – a few at first, and then a lot. Even some lizards. And all through that long season of reclamation, while my secret fibre grew, the thing under my skin grew also. It didn't hurt, not with actual pain, not the pain of the flesh. A different kind of pain: As steadily as the thing grew, grew also the realisation of what it meant. Slowly, like the way light changes at the end of the day, leaving everything in shadow.

I was becoming – had become – one of them, one of the accursed, spotted, bumpy women that had so frightened and bewildered me when I first came to the Tract. The same plague that had fallen on them had fallen on me. I'd become a lump-woman.

Not all of the lump-women died. Some lived on for a time, growing more and more bumps on their skin or labouring under weighty tumours that swelled an eyelid, a jaw line, a breast. Some lived for years. Some went quickly.

We didn't talk about the lumps on the Tract. There was a sort of shame about them, a surface shame that covered the fear at our core. No one got up in the morning and announced, 'It's happened. It's happened to me.' So I had no way of knowing how much time usually passed between when your own fingers found the stranger in your body and when others could see it in you. And when you—

How long would I have?

My life became a race, a desperate dash run at caterpillar-speed:

To bring a harvest in from the field by the river. To show that it could be done.

To find this System of theirs and make it stop. To show that it could be done.

To live long enough to do these things.

The cutter-bugs came early that year.

The fibre wasn't much more than knee-high in the fields. A shout went up from the end of a row and some of the women ran to show Naina the orange beetles in their hands. There was no panic. Maybe it was because everyone knew that, with fewer mouths to feed, we had some credit on last year's harvest if we needed to buy spray. (It was *next* season that would kill us, if we emptied our account.) Or maybe it was just that after all the sickness and death people's hearts were numb, too used-up to be much afraid.

Whatever the reason, there was a sort of clenched-jawed calm as everyone dropped their hoes and tried to fight off the creatures by hand. We searched the plants – every inch of them, every branch and leaf – and picked the bugs off one by one. We picked and crushed and picked and crushed until our hands were sticky with their guts, and it seemed like we were winning the battle. Maybe we could do it without the spray. It wasn't impossible – it happened sometimes. Why not one good thing in this terrible year? I wasn't the only one who hated the poison and how sick it made us.

But the next morning, it was as if all the work we'd done the day before had never happened, as if a hard rain had fallen with every drop a flame-orange beetle. The next time the Managers lined us up for counting, Naina asked to buy the poison.

That night, in my Other body, I walked the rows of my beautiful, tangled, many-voiced field.

The cutter-bugs had found the fibre, even hidden as it was between rows of other plants. There weren't as many as in the single-crop fields, but they were here. I stooped to inspect the damage by the light of the pale stars.

The castor-plants were completely unharmed, of course – not surprising, because they're deadly poison – and the tooth-bushes, also, were untouched. The big, sticky leaves of the green-glue were covered, solid orange with beetles that had landed on them and been trapped in their viscous sweat. The other sister-plants were stricken or not depending on the taste the cutter-bugs had for their foliage. The creatures had gorged on the star-flowers as I'd expected, and this did protect the fibre some, but not enough – the young leaves of the crop were tattered around the edges, as shaggy as the dress I wore, and the meal had just begun.

What was I going to do? Give up the whole thing as a failure? Go back to the meaningless labour of surviving so that there could be another season of the meaningless labour of surviving? Or fight for my field, for my hope that fibre could feed people without killing people – *both* my peoples. But how could I fight? What weapons did I have? What allies?

I did not know what to do.

So I asked.

Consider a rope. You can look at each thin fibre of it, how long each is, how strong, how fat, where it falls within the whole, how it coils along the length, and what it would take to break it.

Or you can look at the rope as a single braided thing, with the twists of the gathered fibres holding them all together to support their shared strength.

It is like that when you ask questions in your Other body. Two ways. Very different. This is not something 1 learned from my father. Maybe he didn't know it. Or maybe it was what he did that time he 'took a little sleep' in front of the invading all-one-kind vine that tried to eat the Real when I was a child. Maybe if he had stayed . . .

But it was only the first way that he taught me, the conversation with one single strand, leaning in with my Other ear against the trunk of one tree – always a single tree, with its own story and personality – and listening to the Flow of it until that soft hum began to shimmer into distinct sounds, words that I could understand and respond to.

Or, he showed me, I could dip my Other hands deep into a tree – a single tree – and feel that one Flow as it mingled with my own. Then I knew what the tree knew and it knew what I knew. This was a good way, but it was harder. When you're flowing with a tree, you can't always remember the questions you wanted to ask, and then later it's hard to remember the answers, because the knowing doesn't come in words.

But my father never taught me this business of letting yourself come apart and be scattered like a handful of ground spice-bark caught on a puff of air so that you can swirl through a whole net of kins and clans, letting yourself be sucked up from the ground by a hundred stems and breathed out by a thousand leaves and rained back down by a thousand thousand raindrops.

Coming apart this way was something I learned from my own life, from the trees that were my teachers, and from the field itself as I eased it back from abomination into health. And I think, maybe, the field had learned, a little bit, to talk to me, too.

So, that same night, I brought the question of the cutter-bugs to the field itself. And the field answered me.

It doesn't hurt, not really, to crumble and be mixed into the Flow of something whole and many-voiced. (Unless you try to cling, of course. If you try to hold on to yourself. Then it hurts.)

It is confusing, though. You forget which way is up and how to be a person in a place. The intelligence of a field is very different from the intelligence of one being. I don't know how to describe this well. You will experience it one day, maybe, and then you will know.

It is, I suppose, most like turning into water, or maybe into wind, and joining with another Flow that has its own push and liveliness. You join its journey while it thumps into blockages and shoulders its way through narrows, splitting into separate streams and gathering again, circling back on itself so that push adds to push in great standing waves and whirlpools that hold their shapes and places, stable though they are not still.

That night, I rode this Flow, not separate from it, clutching my question hard so that it would not get ripped away from me in the rush: What should I do to save the fibre?

But no matter how tightly I held it, I could feel the question unravelling in my hands, strands loosening like a braid come undone in a high wind. What should I do to save the fibre, the field, the family?

The question itself turned to Flow.

What should I do to save the water, the wind, the world?

It streamed away from me and I sank below the surface of ordinary knowing, down into the dark waters where the roots of all things reach deep into black, cool mud.

The night-sounds of the bunkhouse whispered around me, told me I was a person in a place again. Hard boards under me pressed against the limits of my flesh body, with Lakka sleep-breathing in my ear and my heart pounding like a hammer-beak. It was very dark but an image filled my eyes, an Other image, huge and glowing: A certain toy from my childhood. A spinner.

I don't remember getting my first spinner, but I'm sure – I watched my father playing with my young cousins as I grew up – that it was Sook-Sook who gave it to me. I do remember when he taught me to make them, though.

He took me down to the bathing place and helped me gather the long, flat rustling reeds we used for mats and baskets. Then he showed me how to fold them to make little cups at the bend. When you arranged them in the same direction and pinned them onto a cane wand with a stabber-thorn, they went round and round if you blew on them. Blow hard and steady, and they would spin so fast that they turned invisible to the eye, though you could hear them whir.

That is the image I came back with from my conversation with the field: a spinner, madly whirling in one direction, so fast that you couldn't even see it go. And I understood perfectly.

Things were spinning in the wrong direction, each push adding itself to the wrongness. The spin must be reversed.

I rolled over on the hard boards of the bunk and let myself begin to know what I knew.

It was hard to come back from a night like that night. Hard to stumble out to the big earthen hearth and hold out my gourd for food, as if nothing had happened. Hard to pull a yellow sprayer from the mound in front of the bunkhouse and strap it on while pictures from my Other life flickered in front of my eyes like the shadows of moving leaves, or the arms of a spinner moving too fast to see, or a whirlpool chasing itself around in circles. The tall wheels of the ox-cart that held the big black barrel of poison caught my eye – they turned, too. The wrong direction. I had to push them backward, make them roll the other way.

I let myself be pulled along by the press of women lining up to fill their sprayers at the well, but someone bumped into me and the floppy, empty bulk of the tank on my back pulled me off balance.

'Hey!' Lakka caught my arm and steadied me. 'Where are you this morning?'

Where was I? The wheels had to turn in the opposite direction. The eaters must be eaten. The soil must be fed. The birds . . . Bats . . .

I shrugged stupidly. 'Just thinking,' I said.

'Thinking, huh?' Lakka looked at me as if her Other eyes were studying my face. 'Dreams again?'

Lakka and I had never talked about the Other life. She knew that I'd come from another place, just as I knew she had. I'd told her about my family, about my father who trained trees and taught me that skill, but we'd never talked about time outside the flesh. The People don't, usually. Just with our teachers, or with our families. But there were moments when it felt to me like Lakka must know more than I'd told her in words.

'Yes. Dreams.'

'Well, wake yourself up, little sister. There's work to do and Naina will slap your face off if you're sloppy with this damned spray.'

I dipped my head in a sort of rueful nod and stepped forward to have the snaky black hose pushed into the top of my shoulder-sprayer. I set my feet against the swelling weight. Just water.

Then we joined the line at the cart. Manager Goban and her little scoop. The powder that turns water into poison.

I stepped forward, turned my back, bowed my head to make it easy for her. I could feel stray bits of the powder, gritty on my neck, mixing with my sweat, leaching through my skin, making me one with the Stink.

Then I walked out into the field with the others and, with them, I fought the orange beetles the only way they knew how.

I sprayed with my tract-sisters, but I walked my row seeing two worlds.

One view showed the wings of the spinner all turning toward wrongness: A single plant, alone and dense, screamed out for the eaters of that plant. And the eaters came. The first turn of the spin. So we poisoned things – everything, the whole field – killing the birds and bugs and crawlers that should have eaten the eaters and killing, too, the sister-plants that should have thinned out the eaters' drunken banquet. The next turn. Without the sister-plants to enrich it, the soil grew poor and the fibre starved, too puny to resist the eaters. Another turn. As the fibre languished, the eaters grew stronger every year, with our sprays killing off the weak ones and leaving only the strong to breed. Turn, turn, turn – all in the wrong direction.

But with my other eye I saw, a wisp at a time, puffs of breath that would nudge the spin back in the direction of life.

Little things, already happening, that could build over time: We needed even more star-flowers along the edges of the field, to lure the cutter-bugs and other eaters away from the fibre. More green-glue, too, to trap the bugs on its sticky leaves. And bats – we needed bat-houses to invite them.

But also big things, new things, that had to happen right away: Tooth-bush – its seeds, ground, soaked, sprayed. And something else – I didn't fully understand this part yet – about collecting the cutter-bugs that dangled upside down under the leaves, using them like poison, using them to make the others sick and confused.

Spinning. Spinning back: The two visions jostled each other, made me unsteady on my feet. I staggered and almost fell, but caught myself and was single-minded again.

My hand clenched around the nozzle. My friends, off on either side of me. The smell I hated above all things, filling the air with death. A distant bark – the hounds had drawn off well away from the spraying.

How could I do these good, healing things that I'd learned in the night? I could ask the star-flowers to grow, and the green-glue, too, at night in Otherness. But soaking and spraying the tooth-bush seeds? Gathering the crazy, upside-down hanging bugs? Building and hanging a bat-house or two? I looked down at my flesh hands: Dirty. Broken nails. Calluses. Scars.

The work would need *these* hands, not the Other's. And a sprayer. And time.

I puzzled on the problem all day, while I tramped up and down under the hammer sun with the others, doing the one thing I hated most in all the world. How, how, how? To start with, I simply could not see a way to get past the night-hounds.

I was afraid of the day-hounds. They harried us when we straggled behind the others, and more than one of my tract-sisters had died a slow death when a bite on the ankle festered and streaked and burned to a fever. But the beasts were trained to let us work, to herd us in a tight group as we moved through the fields to plant or harrow or harvest. The night-hounds were different.

The night-hounds didn't care about groups or work. They had just one purpose: to keep anyone from leaving the bunkhouse precincts at night. They wouldn't harm us on the clean-swept patch of dirt in front of the door, nor in the tangled gourd-vines that grew around the back of the building, or on the short walk to the latrine – there was a magic line that they wouldn't cross, marked off by a few stubby, knee-high stakes in the ground. But if we stepped over that line ...

Once, in my first season on the Tract, a girl had gone crazy and done it. She crossed the line. She had been a sweet girl – quiet, never any trouble to anyone. But then she'd found a hard lump on one of her ribs, and went silent and strange-eyed, knowing what was coming.

Vela. Funny that I remember her name when I forgot so many others.

Vela didn't get far, but the noise of her death didn't wake us. Surely there must have been a scream, at least one scream, and some racket from the dogs, but tractees sleep hard and we didn't know anything until the Managers whipped us out to where she'd died, just twenty or thirty paces beyond the latrine. Later, we all said Vela must have gone crazy, but I don't know. Maybe she'd just got tired. Maybe she just needed to make an end, and out on the Tract there was no easy way.

The Managers made us gather what was left of her and roll it in a stained rice-bag for them to take away. They wanted to make sure that terror kept us in our place, and it did. When I thought about walking across the fields at night, my guts turned to water.

That evening, the hour before dinner was quieter than usual, with everyone feeling sick and dizzy from the day's spraying.

I was sitting in our regular place by the wall with my dress off, trying to repair a rip where one sleeve had been partly torn away as I slid the straps of the heavy sprayer down my arm. Back in the Real, we never would have sat naked in public like that, not after we were three or four, but on the Tract we were all well past body-modesty. My dress was torn and I had no other and it was too dark inside the bunkhouse to sew.

I'd twisted some old fibre-fluff into a sort of a thread and was working it back and forth through the coarse weave with a folded-over stem. Back in the Real, if I'd stayed, I would have inherited my mother's kit of delicate bone needles, things of great beauty, in every size a family might need to stitch leaves or bands or leathers into usefulness. Some of the needles – you could tell by their silky smoothness and mellowed colour – were very old. My granny's grannies' hands had held them, going back, maybe, to Those Days. If the Stink hadn't come—

But it came, Pyn-Poi, it came. And here you sit in what's left of the daylight, naked in the dust, stitching with a twig.

Lakka dropped down beside me. I scooted over to make room.

'Naina's in a—' She caught her breath. I looked up to see her eyes on my armpit, just at the crease where breast and arm meet.

The lump showed like the tip of some horror's thumb poking up through my skin. I jerked the dress up, to shield the thing from her seeing. 'It's nothing,' I said, using all my strength to let the dress fall, to begin sewing again. 'Maybe it's nothing.'

Lakka touched the thing lightly, with two fingertips. I didn't flinch. She dipped her head – a quick heavy nod – and murmured, 'Nothing at all.'

The next day, while my thinking still spun in circles – *must* get to my field, *can't* get to my field – our poison war against the cutter-bugs dragged on. My fingers cramping around the nozzle. The nozzle spurting. Poison from my hand. The stench so bad that it didn't seem outside me anymore; it was a part of me, in my blood and meat. The sun doing what it always did, adding its stone weight to the tank dragging down from my shoulders. Every step I took stirred up orange bugs that whirred around me in frantic swirls, driving into my skin like dry rain.

I heard a commotion off to my right, and saw Maja and Jui on either side of me turning to look. Oh. Over there. Near the end of our line. A knot of women clustered around a body twitching on the ground: Esk, having a seizure.

This happened every now and then, almost always when we were spraying, although sometimes the sun by itself was enough to send someone into the hard jerking spasms of a body crying out, 'No more.'

There wasn't much we could do when this happened. Doc always used to clear the space around the person, pull away any farm tool or other hard thing that they might bash themselves against, and then we would all stand around uneasily and watch until the jerking was over. Then Doc would have a group of us carry the sufferer, stunned and dopey like a sleepy drunk, back to the bunkhouse to rest out of the sun.

Doc was gone now, but strong arms would still be needed to haul Esk out of the field. Naina would hate it – it would take twelve or thirteen of us to walk through the dogs without harm, and losing the work of that many hands right now would send her into a stiff-lipped fury.

I started across the field toward Esk, and Lakka joined me, wading through the orange-dotted fibre plants that snagged and tugged at our dresses.

In the dimness of the bunkhouse and the small confusion of wrestling a limp Esk onto her middle shelf, I slipped off the tank on my back and kicked it under the bunk behind Esk's. No one saw.

Then I volunteered to stay with her. Omna glared at me for shirking the nastiness of the spraying and declared that Naina wouldn't like it. 'Everyone's supposed to take a hand,' she growled. 'Share and share alike, food *and* work. There's few enough of us left.'

'Doc wouldn't have left Esk alone, not so soon after a fit. What if she has another one?'

'That's right,' Lakka chimed in. 'I'll stay, too. We should clean her up a little.' Esk had soiled herself when the seizure took her.

'I can take care of that. You go on back with the others.' Let me concentrate on the problem of where to hide my secret sprayer and how to get to my field at night.

But Lakka went on. 'And the two of us will get the fire going and pump up the water for supper. Naina won't mind if we get some work done here.' Omna shook her head balefully and turned on her heel.

I watched from the door as my sisters trudged back down the lane between the fields that had once seemed so monstrous and bizarre to me. Now those same fields seemed almost normal to my eyes, and those brown-clad women, once strangers, were my clan, more real and present to me than my dim and distant People – and both were being destroyed by the vileness in the half-empty tank hidden under the bunk.

Lakka and I did our best for Esk, laying her on her side like Doc had shown us so she couldn't choke on her spit. With a gourdful of water and a handful of fibre, we bathed her, to cool her and to scrub away any spilled poison on her skin. We rinsed her dress, wrung it out, and hung it from the eaves, covering her with an old rice-sack. She slept through all of this like a person drugged.

After we had done all we could for her, we stepped away from her

273

bunk. I had to get the sprayer hidden before the rest of the Tract came back for dinner. But Lakka . . .?

'I'll watch her a while,' I said. 'Why don't you go out and start work on supper – show Naina that we weren't just dodging work?'

In the shadows, her eyes seemed to rest on me strangely, for a little too long.

'Alright,' she said.

I waited. Let Lakka get her mind on what she's doing. Then I'll slip out.

The *only* possible place to hide something as big as the sprayer in a world as naked as ours was underneath the bunkhouse, behind the thicket of gourd-vines that sprouted there. It was still fairly early in the season – I should be able to push through the tangle without breaking the long stems and leaving a trace. All I had to do was wait until Lakka was looking away from the doorway, then slip out and around the corner of the building – and be very, very quiet about it.

Esk was snoring, still on her side. I retrieved the sprayer and stepped to the threshold.

Lakka was on her knees in front of the hearth, arranging dried dog-turds and bundles of fibre over the ashy mound from breakfast. Her back was to me. Perfect. I stepped out, quietly, quietly.

Without turning, as if she could see through the back of her skull, she said, 'And now you are going to tell me exactly what is going on.'

Among the People, it is a delicate, private thing to talk about our Other lives. Oh, at breakfast, of course, fresh from our dreams – of course we talk then. Every kin does. I'm pretty sure every kin does.

My father spoke about how things were with the trees. Aunt Dokha spoke for the water, Aunt Saggi for the birds, Aando for things with fur and teeth, and so forth. How could our Mothers make good decisions, if they didn't hear from the Other lives of their kin?

When a new husband came into our house-tree, he would be bashful about this for a few days, blushing and stuttering over the morning porridge as we shared our night-dreams and coached each other in searching out how our Other life connected with this one. And we children would tease the newcomer until Marak put an end to it.

The shyness about sharing our Other lives was strong, though sometimes the littlest children might forget and brag to their play-mates about something they'd done while out of their flesh. They learned soon enough, though, from people's uncomfortable looking-away.

So, when I made that heart-beat decision to ask for Lakka's help and tell her everything about why I had to get to the abandoned field, I was swimming against a whole life's worth of habit. I was also pushing against one of my life's long stupidities: I always think that there is just one way to understand things and I am always wrong.

Back then, I was absolutely certain – so certain that it never entered my mind to question it – that Lakka, too, had an Other body but simply didn't talk about it, in the same way that I didn't talk about mine.

I *had* wondered about the Managers about whether *they* might have some disorder of their Other bodies that kept them from touching, kept them from feeling the Flow in any beings outside themselves. But Lakka? It had never even occurred to me to consider whether or not she had an Other body. Of course she did. Everyone did.

So I didn't have any idea, really, of the act of belief I was asking. I'd been in this twisted world for almost three years and, though I'd seen the insanity of the planted fields, I hadn't really taken in, hadn't *understood*, that this was just the eye showing above the water – below the surface, there was a dark lurking body of difference. Difference in how we walked in the world. Difference in how we walked in our bodies. That day in the bunkhouse, I was just at the first step of understanding that difference. But I hadn't even reached that first step of understanding that, if these people were odd and crazy to me, I was also odd and crazy to them. I didn't appreciate that what I was telling Lakka would be like a fire-story to her.

Not the fact that I'd climbed the Wall, up from the green Real – no, that was not the difficulty. Lakka had always known that I was from somewhere else. Even though I'd learned the language of her world and the monthly head-shaving kept down the oddness of my brown hair, I was still obviously different. It seemed that there was some history of raiders climbing down the Wall to steal People and of Garnet-Miners falling to Lonely Ones from the Real. Lakka had no trouble believing that I was from that place.

What she didn't understand, and what I had trouble understanding that she didn't understand, were the most basic facts of how People – *my* people, at least – carry our existence. So, when it came time to explain to my best friend why exactly I had been restless at night and distracted during the day, there was a lot of talking to do, a lot to explain. A lot of marvelling, on my part, at how anyone could walk around in a flesh body without being awake to an Other one.

Lakka

That day, alone in the hot bunkhouse, Binpoy told me about a world that couldn't exist, a world of trees growing so close together that the sun didn't touch the ground. The 'Real', she called it, a world without contracts. A world where families took care of each other. A world where food was everywhere: hanging from branches, rustling in the undergrowth, flashing through the streams, springing up from small gardens delicately folded into the jungle. A fairy-tale world.

It was the kind of story your mother tells you at bedtime to give you sweet sleep. But Binpoy had never looked more awake. Urgent. Intense. She really wanted me to *believe* her. I tried to reason with her, to ask questions to help her see that this was all just a wish-dream. Those happened all the time on the Tract – nights full of eating all you could hold or being wrapped in the arms of a person that loved you. Oh, those dreams – sweet while they lasted, soul-destroying when you woke up. Dangerous. Those dreams took your eyes off surviving in the here and now.

But for every question I asked, trying to shake her awake, Binpoy had an answer – not a sane answer, maybe, but an answer. Why live up in the trees? Because you were safer from hunting animals there. Why not use wood to build houses? Because dead wood rots in the wet and living trees do not. How did she get from that place to this one? By climbing a mighty cliff. And why did she come here? To stop the 'Ancestors' from poisoning her people. The details grew and came together with a sort of crazy logic all of their own. Oh, Binpoy . . .

Some kind of plague had fallen on her dreamland, she said, and it had something to do with the stuff we sprayed on the fibre to kill the bugs. She believed that when the rains came, all that poison got washed off the leaves, into the soil and then into the river. How many Farms were there, she wanted to know.

'Many,' I told her. She nodded grimly.

Binpoy loved that world she'd made up, more than I ever loved anything, way more than I'd loved the little store Midun and I had tended together; that place meant nothing to me except for a way to feed ourselves and keep a roof over the children we thought we'd have someday. I wondered what it would be like to love a place, even a made-up place, so much that you'd be willing to climb right up out of it and leave behind everything and everyone you knew to protect it.

Because that was what Binpoy was doing every single morning when she heaved herself up off the planks of our bunk and blinked up at the vicious sun. She was pulling herself, one more time, up and out of that soft green dream to join us here and try to rip one more day's survival out of this damned and dusty dirt.

'So we have to get to the field by the river,' Binpoy finished up. 'We have to gather these sick bugs. And we have to do it in our flesh bodies.'

We had to get to the field, the one we *weren't* cultivating, to gather sick bugs that hung upside-down from the edges of the young fibre leaves? My heart twisted inside me.

It wasn't all that unusual. On the Tract, people just went crazy sometimes. They looked at gourd bowls that held a handful of rice and saw porcelain plates brimming over with meat and sweets and bread and vegetables. They turned their tools against other tractees, or sometimes the Managers. Or maybe they became so afraid that they couldn't walk out of the bunkhouse. Some talked to people that weren't there, or stopped talking altogether and stopped eating so that they thinned away to nothing, and then they were gone.

Binpoy had always seemed so sturdy, though. Strange, maybe, but strong. She'd been one of the ones who kept us going when the sickness hit – kept *me* going when first Pino and then Korva went. But now this.

No. I was not going to lose Bin, too, not now.

But could I take care of her, crazy like this?

Sometimes people got better. You gave them a little extra to eat and maybe a little less work and then they got to be themselves again. But sometimes they didn't.

Oh, Binpoy . . .

Pyn-Poi

Lakka didn't believe me. Of course she didn't. The sun. The poison. People's minds broke sometimes. They saw things that weren't there, or suddenly began to scream, or cried and couldn't be comforted. No surprise that Lakka thought I was one of those.

What did surprise me was how much I cared, how much I hungered for just one person in this mad place who I could speak with about what was real. Not just real in the flesh body and the bunkhouse and in the twisted fields, but real in the bigger way.

And so, when Lakka patted my cheek and murmured soothingly, 'It's been a hard season, Binpoy – sometimes your brain can play tricks . . . ', I snapped like a vine taking too much weight.

I grabbed hard at her hand on my face and pressed it to me, letting my Other hand sink past her sun-leathered skin to feel her bones and the Flow of her. I let our Flows mingle, not in the dizzying way I had joined with the field, but in the easy way of two friends, old friends well beyond modesty, when they meet each other naked at the bathing place.

THE ROAD

Pyn-Poi

At first, the joy of leaving that dark underground box behind – stepping into sunshine and air and the scrubby brush around us – lightened my fears about what lay at the end of this broad, unbending path.

Little winged creatures lifted from the bushes on either side of us as we passed: small dun-coloured birds, hoppers, nibblers, buzzing things heavy with the powder of hidden blooms. The smell of greenness shielded from drying by aromatic waxy coats. Small lives rustling in dry leaf-litter. My heart began to open again after being clenched so long that it was sore.

The Plains of the Ancestors, or whoever these people were, were very flat. Easy walking, in a way, but as the sun clambered into the sky it got very hot. Without hills and hollows, without grandmother and grandfather trees shielding us, there was no shade. Where would the water go here, if it ever rained?

The boot-men carried leather bags of water slung over their shoulders on straps and drank as they went along, but they did not offer me any and I did not ask. I got very thirsty – not to death, like I had been on the Wall, but dry-mouthed and drooping. Luckily, the men were not fast walkers so, even with my hands bound and the weakness of my imprisonment just beginning to lift, I was able to keep pace with them easily. I tried not to think of water, of the stone well under the tired tree in Bazleti's courtyard, nor of the clear brown waters of our bathing place on the Durma. These men would give me water when it pleased them. Or maybe they would not. (But surely they would not march me this far to watch me die of thirst.)

Finally, near the blaze of noon, the big grey-haired one called a stop near a cluster of scrawny trees no taller than I. The men settled under the patchy half-shade to rest. I leaned against one of the little trunks and let myself slide down it to the ground, closing my eyes, breathing in the spicy scent of the plants here and letting my body rest.

The smell of food brought me back. The men had opened the basket Bazleti had given them and pulled out two big rounds of bread and some leaf-wraps full of bean mash. A pile of orange fruit.

Seeing the food, smelling it, caused the soft flesh under my tongue to pucker with readiness and the men laughed at my hungry eyes while they ate, every now and then waving dripping morsels my way and then popping them into their own mouths, smacking and humming with pleasure at Khukmama's cooking.

I wondered about these men. They each bore sticks swinging from their belts, but not heavy-headed clubs like hunters would carry. These were lighter – longer and more springy – and they whirred in the air like the dart of a hum-bird just before coming down on my legs or back with a crack of pain like fire. Not for killing – for hurting.

And this, this little torture of waving food in front of a hungry person, what was this about? Was this some little-pain initiation to make me strong, to toughen me for some mystery to come? Or was it some punishment for something that I had done, some wrong I had committed without knowing? I wondered, too, if these men could instead be angry at me (back in the Real, anger and punishment are kept separate). But they did not seem angry. They seemed jolly as they waved Bazleti's food under my nose and then gobbled it themselves, cheerful as they watched me swallow back the juices that jumped into my mouth.

Finally, I stopped watching them, turned my eyes up to the sky through the thin small-leafed canopy, and reached out to the trees until the thud of an orange hitting my ribs made me jump. The men laughed at this, and someone threw a crust of bread at my head. I caught it in my cupped hands.

'Thank you,' I said, and ate.

The path we walked on was straight as a hunting spear. Straight as an arrow's flight. Straighter than any natural thing. And why should it not be, I reasoned, in a land unshaped by rivers and slopes and boulders, why *not* travel in straight lines? But it unsettled me to move across the land without the swoops and loops and switchbacks of the trails I was used to.

The sun sank behind our backs as the afternoon wore on. I could feel the skin on my neck burning like meat on a griddle, but I had no head-wrap. Bazleti would keep that for me. I would go back, of course, to recover the Mothers' feathers and my father's precious knife, and on that day, I would re-wrap my head in the complex blue-and-white cloth Marak had woven for me. But meanwhile, I reached up to tug at the base of my braid, to try to loosen it a bit so it would cover more of my neck, but was not able to do much with my wrists bound and my fingers swollen and clumsy from the binding.

Every now and then, we met people on the road, poorer people than in Bazleti's village – dirtier, skinnier. Hungrier. People dressed in faded rags that barely covered them. Some carried bulging sacks on their backs, some, towering baskets on their heads, baskets near-overflowing with bales of some pallid, unformed thing.

I watched as these people drew near us. Saw them take in the boot-men, then me, barelegged in the dirt-coloured dress. Saw them notice the tight double bangles that held my wrists. Saw their eyes slide away from me as if from something dead beside the path. Some of them spoke a respectful greeting to the boot-men, but most of them just stood aside from us and studied the ground or the strange far-off line where the land bent up to the sky.

Sometimes we overtook giant beasts, hoofed and horned, dragging rolling sledges: massive things, huge open box-trays on spinning rounds, as if someone had sliced a tree-trunk and threaded the slices on spindles. The creatures pulled along dispiritedly, heads hanging low, clomping one great foot in front of another, kicking up dust that painted their people as white as ash-dancers.

The second time we passed one of these carts, I noticed that the rider carried a long slender switch to move the big animals forward, just like the boot-men and their sticks moved me along the road. But the pulling-beasts were huge, standing as tall as I at the head – strange to think that such a slender cane could make them obey.

What was in the shell of these carts, I wondered, but got no view or clue of their freight. Not the ones going in our direction, that is – some of the ones coming back toward the town were open and I could see great masses of bone-white, shapeless stuff, sheaves of drying leaves, or mounds of cut grass – mysteries.

Bazleti's orange damped my thirst for a while, but not long. The sun, not veiled by treetops or clouds like at home, sucked away my juices. Pride went with them. Finally, I stopped walking.

Bent over, hands on my knees, panting, I looked up at the men. 'Please water please. Please.' Then I threw in 'thank you' for good measure. 'Please water thank you.'

I pushed myself back upright in time to see the grey-haired boot-man make a sign to the others, like someone brushing away a nibbler. The little runty one uncapped his water-skin and held it up. I reached out to take it from him, but he squeezed it hard, making a jet of water spurt out and hit me in the eye. I ducked, still reaching for the bag so that the precious water would not be wasted, but he backed away from me, making little spits of water jump from the bag to wet my hair, my dress, my face. A little ran into my mouth and I turned toward it to catch more, but the stream lowered, rolling down my neck and between my breasts.

The men laughed and yelled as I dropped to my knees to catch the water in my mouth, cupping my hands under my chin. There it was, more beautiful than light and air and food, filling my mouth and I swallowed passionately but I was losing it again – lower now and I had to bend down to catch it, falling forward onto my elbows, crouching like a dog, head arched back to offer my mouth to the slim waterfall.

Two of the other boot-men pulled out their own bags and began to waste them against my flank and rump, making the rough cloth of my dress cling to me, but I didn't care – I drank.

Then the old one shouted at them to stop. Someone grabbed my braid and yanked me to my feet.

We walked on.

Late afternoon, now, and maybe my head was hanging down like the pulling-beasts'. The trees had made me do my best to stay strong in the long grey time in the box – pulling up to the window to keep my climbing arms strong, squatting for my legs, curling for my middle – but in spite of working my body hard twice a day, much of my strength had melted out of me.

I was tired in a way that a mere day's walking would never have tired me at home. Maybe it was the naked sun beating against my shoulders like one of the boot-men's sticks. Or maybe it was just that my kind are not meant to walk in treeless places and even the little man-high tree-dwarfs we had passed in the morning were gone now. Here, on either side of us, for as far as I could see, there was nothing but a flat table of land covered with floppy grass, bushes, and dense, low brambles. Nibblers began to plague us as the sun drooped low.

Or maybe this weariness came from being among people who were neither kin nor friend. Had I ever done this before, walked like this with people who did not wish me well? No, never. Sometimes, when I was little, scrambling up a tree-trunk behind Aando and the older cousins, they would tease me and say mean words to drive me away. But even when they shook the branch I was on or threw twigs and seed-pods to make me go, I had known with a knowing as deep and strong as the tree-roots themselves that Aando would never really let me fall and, if a hunter-cat found us, he would always put me behind him and his bow.

These men I walked with now, though, were different – happy to watch another grovel at their feet for a mouthful of water, happy to chivvy me along with lashes across my buttocks. Really *happy* – they laughed when I yelped like a kicked fur-friend. Were these men broken? Had their Other bodies floated away and escaped them, leaving them without the means to touch the pains and wisdoms of any creature outside themselves? Had they offended some person of power and been cursed, left alive but severed from the Other as a punishment?

Questions without answers weighed me down like a heavy pack, so finally I put them aside and used all my mind only to move my feet, one in front of the other, one step at a time.

Something on the path ahead. What was it? The men saw it, too, and I could hear the satisfaction in their voices as their pace quickened and the little one swiped at my legs to make me keep up.

What was it? Twin posts, like a ghost-door, straddled the broad path and supported a lintel-beam with odd, faded markings that gave me the chilly feel of magic. A gateway? But not a gateway – there was nothing behind them, nothing on either side, no walls, no fence, nothing for a gate to enter or exit. Nothing but more flat and empty land.

When we passed through this gateway into nothing, with its long shadow stretching out in front of us, the old boot-man turned back to me and pointed up at the cross-beam and its symbol-markings. He said words. His teeth showed when he grinned.

Somewhere up ahead of us I heard a yapping howl. It was answered by others.

THE FARM

Pyn-Poi

I let go of Lakka's hand. My Other fingers merged back into the bones and sinews and skin of my flesh, still pressing her palm to my face. No time had passed.

What had I done?

'Are you okay?' I whispered. Usually only healers . . . And married people . . . Was it too much? I'd never done such a thing before.

Her palm lifted from my cheek as slowly as a petal opening. 'I know,' she said. Her eyes were big and wet. 'I know everything now.'

Lakka barely spoke to me for the rest of that evening – just what needed to be said as we pumped up fresh water for the rice-pot and woke the fire. Later, after the rest of the Tract got back, she ate dinner beside me as usual and I caught her gazing at me every now and then, but she said nothing. Had I gone too far? Had I ruined things between us? But hadn't her eyes been warm with wonder after we touched? Hadn't she said she knew everything now?

Could everything be too much?

That night, just before I stepped outside for the Council circle, I whispered, 'Are you alright? Are we?'

I felt her palm, light and dry, rest on my shoulder and her thumb run across my collarbone.

'Give me time,' she said. 'You can't expect a person to digest an entire extra lifetime all in one sitting.' She turned and climbed up into our bunk.

Naina

Chirun stepped away from the meeting to vomit. The whole Tract felt pretty sick after two long days of spraying. Well, they'd feel sicker after they heard what we had to say after reviewing the accounts. I looked around at the little circle, shadows in a dark place, with only glints showing that their eyes were all on me.

Chirun rejoined us wordlessly, wiping her mouth. Another bellyful of rice wasted. The Council waited, waited for me to say something, to pull out one more miracle to save us.

But the accounts ... Numbers are numbers. There's no arguing with them. The Tract owed ... oh, there was no bottom to what we owed. Rent on the land, even for the ones who had died in the sickness, even for the fields we'd already given up on. Rent on the tools, even for those long weeks that the Managers didn't even bring them because they were afraid of catching the sickness. Hygiene services – those useless, time-wasting monthly visits to Administration. Purchase of food, and seed, and of the damned, damned sprays that we were going to need again and again through the season, in increasing amounts and ever more complicated combinations.

Weariness suddenly crushed me like a physical weight. Too tired to say the words, I let Sibba say them: To keep the Tract eating, we would have to take out a contract extension.

Pyn-Poi

I woke up the next morning to find Lakka's eyes on my face.

The two of us would never have privacy for a long discussion of what I'd shared with her or what it meant – tractees' lives weren't like that. And even in the few moments we found, she didn't ask me about it. She never, ever questioned what I'd showed her, never backed away from what she knew. That wasn't Lakka. But that first morning after it happened, in the hustle to get to our places in the count-line, she did squeeze my hand and breathe, 'I'm remembering your father now. Riding on his back, listening to a story, tugging at his hair.' As we jogged to the field, I heard her whisper, 'I'm remembering your mother and how tall she seemed.' Once, across a row of fibre, she asked me if I could teach her to be Other, too. I told her I did not know.

That night, in our bunk, a tickle on my earlobe dragged me up from dreams. I reached up to brush away whatever was crawling there, but Lakka's strong fingers wrapped around my wrist and I felt her breathing by my neck, her lips by my ear. I came fully awake.

This was our privacy: the black-dark bunkhouse, everyone else asleep. This was our time for secrets.

'I've been thinking,' she whispered. 'This thing you're considering – this idea of bringing in some fibre from the fields we gave up on? It may not be as stupid as it sounds. I mean, the planting's done, right? Seed's already in the ground – seed's going to do something, whether you hoe it or not. And with the help of those tricks of yours—'

'Not mine – the field's.'

'Right. The field's.' Lakka's eyes turned inward, as if she was consulting a memory. 'I'm not sure I understand it all. I mean, the tooth-bush seeds, maybe. It's like they are some kind of poison, right?'

'Poison to the bugs, but not to us.'

'Okay. I get that. But the thing about the upside-down bugs . . .? Remember, your word-thoughts aren't in my language; I got impressions, images, but I sort of have to translate before I can really think about them. And the whole thing with the field, when you were with the field, that wasn't . . .'

'Wasn't in any words at all. I know. A different kind of teaching. It's hard, taking wisdom from one branch and grafting it onto another.'

'But you've been doing it all your life. I'm just now . . .' She fell silent.

'The way I understand it is that those upside-down bugs are sick. They're dying. If we gather them and soak them, then spray the water on the crop, the bugs that come to eat it will catch their sickness, too. They'll die, as if they'd been poisoned. Only—'

'Only no poison.' Lakka's teeth showed ghostly in the dark; she was grinning. 'I like it. And even if all this tomfoolery doesn't protect the crop all the way, something is better than nothing, I figure. People have harvested overgrown fields before, you know. A few years ago – before your time – a bunch of us got tapped for a work crew to go pick some fields where the whole Tract had gotten killed off. It was a mess – weeds totally out of control, half the bolls rotten with worms. It took forever to pick and we got maybe less than a third of what you'd get from a tended field, but still, it was something. It *was* something. And *something* could keep us alive, maybe, without knuckling under to this contract extension that's going to turn us all into lifers. Naina might even like the plan.'

There was a long silence. Neither of us had to say it aloud: What, exactly, *was* the plan?

How could we gather the tooth-bush seeds and the drunken, upside-down bugs?

We turned the question over for a while, but fell asleep without an answer.

Lakka

That night. That unbelievable night that couldn't have happened, but did – that was only the beginning.

I'd never spent much time in school, barely learned to read, never sat still while some expert person taught me important things. Never wanted it. Never missed it.

But this was different. Binpoy became my school. One teacher. One student: me.

She taught me with her eyes, making me see what she saw in the fields, making me notice what she noticed. 'Look where I'm looking. Open your eyes. It's right in front of you. If it were a crocodile, it would have eaten you.' The texture of the dirt. The runnels where the rain flowed off the fields. The weeds in the ditches. The direction of the winds.

She taught me to see strands of connection, not just here and now, but across time: This causes that, which leads to this other thing. Circles of connection, with causes joining, looping back, feeding each other. Invisible things, you might say, but real and solid once Binpoy had her way with your eyes.

She taught by asking questions: What if ...? How ...? She made me imagine things that didn't exactly exist, not in the usual way, not yet.

Sometimes when the morning whistle cracked the day open, I would jerk up out of a green wild-woven place and know that Binpoy had been with me again, teaching me in my dreams. I didn't always remember these night-lessons, not exactly, not like you remember a recipe, but they changed me, changed what I paid attention to, how I thought, and how I treated things. Something like politeness was born in me, saying 'please' and 'thank you' to dirt, asking plants' permission, apologising for stepping on things.

Binpoy – Pyn Poi – taught me through stories, too, stories told piecemeal – whispered while we stood in line to be counted, gasped while we were running. I could almost remember her father's voice in the dark, telling them around fading coals, under a tall, tall tree.

Pyn-Poi

Upside-down bugs and tooth-bush seeds. This was what the field had asked for.

The cutter-bugs were everywhere now. I'd picked two out of my rice at breakfast. In spite of three days of spraying, anyone with eyes could see the orange tinge that stained the fields. All our work had barely diluted it – bad in one way, good in another: Lakka and I could gather the sick bugs from anywhere, at any time. The tooth-bush seeds, we could get from any of the ditches that ran along the edges of the fields. So, we didn't have to get our flesh bodies to the field by the river to gather the medicine it wanted; we only had to get there to apply it.

But how?

Urgent whispers in bed, before the others woke: Could one of us get away during the work-day? Or would we need to go to our field at night?

Suggestions breathed to each other at the latrine ditch: a staged seizure? A faked errand to Administration?

Objections embedded in talk about other things: How could we keep things secret with eyes all around us?

But always: What about the dogs? We had no weapon. Our thoughts circled around and around the problem of the dogs.

The next morning, as usual, the Managers snapped their dog-lashers to make us run, but the gurgling tanks on our backs slowed us to the pace of tired old women. Lakka and I were able to steal a few words as we panted along. 'I'll handle the crazy bugs,' she said. 'You get the tooth-bush seeds.'

Get the seeds.

As we jogged along, I watched the ditches on either side of us. The tooth-bushes were everywhere, bushy with bright green new growth but also dangling with dried-up black pods filled with last year's seeds. Those pods were what I needed; the seeds had something bad for the bugs. Not just cutter-bugs, but boll-worms, too, and the flying grasshoppers that sometimes darkened the skies. Was it the same thing that kept our mouths from going foul when we chewed on twigs of it to clean our teeth? I remembered Doc, always urging us to gather it from the ditches, to bring it back . . .

And then it came to me. I could get a whole bush of it, drag it to the bunkhouse, right under the noses of the Managers, the dogs, and the whole Tract.

That evening, when the Managers whistled us in from the field, I lined up in my usual place for the count, but as soon as we started our run, I veered toward the outer edge of the group, running alongside the ditch.

I watched the circling dogs closely. Those tearing teeth – if they bit you . . . Even if the Managers saw fit to pull them off you before they killed you outright, we had no good way to care for wounds on the Tract and people often died later from bite-fever.

Sometimes the pack spread out all around us; sometimes they clustered together. I watched for a moment when most of the animals were clumped on the other side of the running tractees.

Day-hounds wouldn't crash through a tight group of workers – they would go around. That would give me my chance. The timing had to be perfect, but the plan *could* work, if I could be patient until just the right moment.

I watched them and waited.

Finally, almost back at the bunkhouse, I saw my opening. I let myself stumble and fall.

The bulk of the near-empty sprayer on my back made it hard to control the direction of my tumble, but I steered myself toward the ditch and half-rolled, half-slid into the stinking water. I heard the baying of the dogs, immediate and closing fast. Hurry. Hurry. Hurry.

No time to ask Permission. I wrapped my fingers around the base of one of the smaller tooth-bushes – low down, right where its roots sank into the muck – and yanked hard. It didn't come loose.

Above me, my tract-sisters were shouting, trying to gather close around me to muddle the dogs' sense that one of us had broken from the group. I yanked again, with both hands this time, sinking my feet deeper in the mud as I jerked against them. Hoof-beats pounded near. I could feel the roots begin to loosen.

And suddenly I was on my backside in the fetid water, clutching the base of the tooth-bush while my tract-sisters yelled and snarling dogs splashed toward me.

I floundered out of the water. Hands reached down to heave me up the bank. A Manager barked an order. A dog-lasher cracked – at us or at the dogs, it didn't matter which. I had my tooth-bush.

A mule forced its way into the tight knot of women around me. People fell back to avoid being trampled. I scrambled to my feet, dripping. The dogs yapped sulkily as they backed off. No meat today.

Kai glared down at me. 'Is there a problem here?'

Naina stepped forward. 'No problem, Manager Kai. None at all. Someone just stumbled, slid into the ditch. But we've pulled her out now, and all is correct.'

'Correct? Who are you to say . . .?' And she went off on a long rant about Naina's arrogance and misplaced sense of superiority. A part of me wanted to shrivel away to nothing for pulling the Manager's attention down on Naina, who just stood there and took the abuse, but another part of me was dancing with delight. I had my seeds. The little bush I'd uprooted lay there at my feet, ready to snatch up when we ran again.

They lined us up there, facing the setting sun, for another count, then did it again because they knew we were famished, and then again, just from pure meanness. But when they finally snapped their dog-lashers to get us moving, I was dragging our tooth-bush at my side.

It didn't take Naina long. People made room for her as she swerved and threaded her way through the jogging crowd until she was running by my side, anger wisping off her like steam off a cook-pot. I didn't wait for her to ask.

'We needed it,' I panted.

'Why?'

'Doc said.' Conversation on our runs to and from the fields was all short words and long pauses for breath. 'We have to take care . . .' – another pause – '. . . of our teeth.'

I kept my eyes on the bunkhouse up ahead, but I could feel Naina's gaze on me.

'Our teeth . . .' she repeated.

'Since Doc died . . .'

'Ah,' she said. 'Yes. We've been neglecting . . .'

'We need—'

'What the Tract needs is *my* business.' We ran along for a while in silence. 'Next time you have an idea like this, Binpoy ... You tell me first.'

We got to the bunkhouse. The empty sprayers clattered down into a pile by the well. The wagon would come again tomorrow, with more powder. We'd mix it with water and head back out into the fields. We'd—

Naina's hand locked around my upper arm. 'You tell me first, Binpoy.' Her fingers dug in like talk-bird claws. 'You know I hate surprises.'

After dinner, while everyone was still sitting around with their bowls in their laps, I handed out twigs from the tooth-bush and reminded people how Doc had taught us to chip off the bark and chew on the woody stem until it got all bristly, then use it to brush the scum off our teeth and gums. The branches that were too big for this, and the pods, went onto the fire-pile with the dried dog-turds and bundled stems from last season's harvest.

I would see to those pods later, after everyone went to sleep.

That night, after we hauled ourselves up to our bunk, Lakka showed me how she'd tied a handful of the crazy upside-down bugs into a corner of her hem. In deep shadows of the bunkhouse, the cutter-bugs' orange had turned to black – black angular dots against the rough fabric of Lakka's improvised pouch. Dots that didn't move.

I touched them with one fingertip; they were dead, their wings tucked chastely against their sides, not flopped wide open, like when the sprays got them. Whatever had made them dangle so oddly from the edges of the fibre-leaves, that was what had killed them. It would kill the bugs in my field, too. I took them from her and folded them into the hem of my dress, then bent the roll of fabric together and tied a knot to hold them there.

I didn't have anything to show Lakka. 'Tonight,' I whispered. 'While they're sleeping.' I jutted my chin at the door and the fire-pile outside it where the precious tooth-bush pods waited.

'It has to be tonight,' she said against my ear. 'Otherwise . . .' I nodded. Otherwise, the pods would go onto the fire in the morning, when Cook-Mama's crew made breakfast. 'You want me to help you?'

'Better not. Less noise with only one.'

Back in the Real, where no one worked more than half a day at anything and hunger was just your body's gentle reminder to eat, I wouldn't have hesitated to lie down that night and nap while I could. It would have been enough to tell myself, 'You have to wake up at moonrise to deal with the pods. Moonrise.' I would have closed my eyes, confident and relaxed, and opened them again, alert and rested, at exactly the right time.

But that confidence, that self-mastery, belonged to another me, a sleek, well-fed, well-loved child who didn't have to work from first light until sunset every day on too little food. It belonged to Pyn-Poi, daughter of Marak, not to Binpoy the tractee. This skinny, exhausted bone-woman couldn't be trusted to wake up before the morning whistle splintered her sleep. What would my mother say if she knew?

I had to keep myself awake. I had to lie still in the dark and keep my drooping eyes open until everyone around was asleep and the moon cast enough light for me to open the pods and collect the seeds.

I fought sleep with everything I had. I pulled my lids up with my fingers. I pinched the tender skin on the inside of my elbows. I bit my tongue. I bit my lip. I sent lightning-flashes of wakefulness through my body by remembering scary stories Sook-Sook used to tell around the fire to make us squeal. But the thing that really worked best to keep my eyes open was true fear, wave after wave of it washing over my body when I let myself ask the questions about home that I'd pushed away for so long: How far had the browning of the trees gone? And the People? How many had sickened? How many had died? Was my mother still alive? Almost three years had gone by since I'd seen her. If she was dead, could the kin survive? Could the clan? Aando's wife hadn't been raised and taught by Marak like I had; would Pariat be strong enough to lead when her turn came? Had I been wrong to leave them? Was I truly where I needed to be? When I climbed the Wall, had I abandoned everybody on a useless whim?

Finally, after what seemed like years of anxious fretting, a dim rectangle of lesser-darkness showed at the door. Moonrise.

Everything was quiet. Nothing but sleep-sounds: a snort, a cough, a rustle as someone turned restlessly, trying to find comfort on the hard boards. I wriggled out from under Lakka's protective arm and sat up.

Lakka snuffled softly, deep in sleep. I scooted down the bunk to the end near to the wall – I didn't want to put a foot in Omna's face as I climbed down.

Dropping my legs over the side, I took care not to let my heels thump against the bunk below, then rolled my hips in that long-practised move that takes you from sitting on the side of the top bunk to facing it as you jump down. No jumping tonight, though; I supported my upper body on my arms and waist as I reached down with my toes until I felt the worn, splintered edge of the bottom bunk.

A creak as I lowered my weight onto the floor. I froze – waited – but no one woke. Everybody was too tired and sick from the day's spraying. I made for the door's dim light, feeling my way through the darkness. Almost to the door, a stupid misstep rammed my right foot into the stanchion of the last bunk. I gasped at the sudden pain in my toe and reached out to steady myself after an ungainly hop to catch my balance again.

I stood rock-still, listening.

No one stirred.

I stepped out through the door and onto the gritty ground.

The moon was slim but bright enough, with its spark-fly stars glittering all around it. The memory of Sook-Sook's moon-story took my mind back to him. Was he still out prowling the wild trees alone, or was his bad knee keeping him near the house-trees now? Who would look after him as he got older? I shook off the question. There was nothing I could do for him from here; or rather, there was: The thing I could do for my father was to teach these people how to raise their precious fibre without poisoning the trees he loves.

I squatted by the fire-pile and began to gather the black tooth-bush pods into the lap of my dress.

Getting the seeds out was harder than I expected. The heavy pods were as solid as wood. I broke a few, just with the strength of my hands, but that only freed the seeds right where the tough shell had snapped – I needed the whole thing to open longways, like a clam-shell. Worse, the loud snaps had attracted the attention of the dogs. They knew someone was outside the bunkhouse and they gathered along the line that marked our safe space and stood there watching me, eyes gleaming a bloody red in the moonlight. They didn't bark or howl; that unnerved me the worst. They just stood there watching, so different from the day-hounds, so intent. So hungry.

Ignore them, Pyn-Poi. The seeds – get the seeds.

But to get at the seeds, I needed a tool. A rock to smash the pods – but there were no rocks in the pale, sandy ground here. A knife to pry them apart – but I had no knife.

I carried my lapful of pods to the post that supported the roof over what we called the kitchen. That was where Cook-Mama kept our cooking things, big gourds from the vines behind the bunkhouse and old pieces of broken hoes and mattocks used to stir the pot and poke the fire. I tried the blades of the tools, one after another, but none of them had an edge sharp enough to fit into—

'What are you up to, Binpoy?'

Naina's voice shocked a gasp out of me.

What was I up to? What could I possibly say?

'Oh, Naina – you scared me. I thought everyone was asleep.'

'Everyone *was* asleep, until a big, lumbering river-cow staggered into our bunk. And then I hear what sounds like someone snapping crabs open to get at the meat, and here I find you poking around in the kitchen in the middle of the night. You're not after food, are you, Pyn-Poi? Because you know the—'

'No, no.' I fumbled for words, ideas, anything at all that could save my seeds.

The truth?

Maybe.

'I was just . . . I was trying to get these tooth-bush seeds out of their pods.' I held up the evidence of a broken pod. 'Nobody needs them. Tomorrow they'll just go onto the fire.'

'Getting tooth-bush seeds?' Naina snorted. 'And you just happen to be right by the rice-gourds?'

'But I need them. I do.' Naina's eyes glittered, bright as the hounds'. 'My people use them for medicine.'

'For medicine. I see.' She didn't believe me. 'And why do you need medicine, Binpoy, a nice strong girl like you? You're probably the healthiest—'

'I . . .' And then the words rushed out of me like birds startled from a tree. The truth: 'I have a lump.'

Time spun out, like a silken thread from a spider. Then Naina said, 'Show me.'

Feeling an odd reluctance – was it shame? – I tugged the neck of my dress down over my shoulder to expose my armpit. Even in the pale moonlight, the protrusion could be seen. I heard a short, sharp suck of breath.

Naina reached out to touch the place, but her fingers stopped, hovered in the air, and drew back. She was silent a moment, then turned to the door.

Over her shoulder, she remarked, 'If you put those pods on the ashes of the fire, the heat of the coals will pop them open.' She vanished into the dark of the bunkhouse.

I sat there, turned to stone, staring at the empty doorway for a long moment. Then I did what Naina said. We always did what Naina said.

The Tract cared for its fire as tenderly as a mother cares for a breast-baby. There were no trees on the Tract, nothing with branches stout and springy enough to make a fire-bow. There were no rocks to strike sparks with. If we let our fire go out, we had to pay our Managers to start it again for us. This 'service' was expensive, but we had to pay it several times a year, after the invincible wetness of the monsoons and any time someone got careless about banking the fire. One of Cook-Mama's most important duties was to see that the embers got raked together after breakfast and dinner and then buried under ashes that would keep their glow alive. It was on top of this hot, dusty pile that I laid the pods side by side and waited.

Nothing happened. They neither opened nor went up in flames. The dogs' eyes watched, unblinking in the moonlight.

I fidgeted a while, then decided to use the time to retrieve the sprayer I'd hidden underneath the floor in the back of the bunkhouse and fill it with water from the trough. The field had told me that the seeds and the crazy bugs should be soaked for at least a day. While I waited for the pods to heat, I could get the water ready.

The night-hounds followed me around the corner of the bunkhouse. There seemed to be more of them now, as if even without howling the pack could communicate: 'Here's one, outside and alone. She's going to wander. She's going to step over the line any minute now, and then she's *ours*.' Turning my back on them made the skin at my neck prickle.

I waded into the vines, stepping over and around the snaky stems, moving as quietly as I could, placing my feet carefully. At the wall of the bunkhouse, I dropped to my knees and reached under to pull the near-empty sprayer out from behind the support-beam where I'd hidden it. As I hauled on the strap and guided the bulky thing out, the poison dregs sloshed and gurgled.

Was it the Tract's habit of thrift – that poison cost us a lot of credit – that made me look around for something to do with it, somewhere to store it while I used the sprayer for other things? Or was it that I didn't want to stain the soil with the vile stuff near where we cooked and ate and slept?

Whichever it was, as I stood up with the tank slung over one shoulder, my eyes searched our sparse little world for options: The shelter around the kitchen, in deep moon-shadow. The big gourds dangling from the overhanging roof, hung there to dry and become the only things we owned. Beyond, the bare ground where we lined up and were counted, morning and night, day in and day out. Off to the side, the pump where we got our water. Lying by the pump, the mound of bulbous sprayers, waiting for tomorrow, their unwholesome yellow faded to bone-white by the pale moonlight.

The sprayers. The unused poison could go into one of the sprayers that would be refilled tomorrow and used on our fields – nothing wasted, nothing spilled.

The watching red eyes followed me back along the wall to the pile of sprayers, silently, the way a hunter's arrow tracks a moving prong-horn just before it flies off the bowstring. I shivered in the night, but all at once, as if a moonbeam had broken through, I saw how the impossible thing could be done. All at once, I understood how I could get past the night-hounds, and not just in my Other body – how I could, in my flesh, take the strange brew we were preparing to my field.

I almost laughed. It was so obvious. I had been thinking wrong.

I had been thinking that tract-women had no weapons against the dogs, nothing at all that could keep them off us once we stepped away from the boundaries of the bunkhouse. How stupid, when we all knew that the dogs kept away when we were spraying. If that burning stink stung *our* noses, *our* throats, I couldn't even imagine how it would torture the dogs' much keener sense of smell – but it made me wickedly cheerful to try.

So I had a weapon, then, better than any knife because I wouldn't need to be close with my enemy – the poison could jump several paces from the end of the sprayer when you squeezed the hand-pump hard. And the weapon would be ready and waiting; whenever the fibre was besieged by pests, the Managers left the sprayers with us overnight, so they wouldn't have to collect them and hand them out again the next morning.

The tanks weren't always completely empty at the end of the day. Dregs sloshed around in the bottom, a finger's-breadth or two of poison.

Dregs could be powerful. Dregs – added together – could be enough.

I checked the pods on the ashes. One was beginning to twist and split, enough for me to get one of Cook-Mama's old hoe-blades into the crack. I left the others to heat a while longer and went back to the stack of sprayers and began – very carefully, because the empty tanks were as resonant as drums, to pour all the left-over poison together into one, the weapon that would get me through the dogs.

'Just wait,' I whispered to the watching blood-stone eyes. 'Just you wait.'

The gathered poison sloshed noisily as I pushed the sprayer, now heavier and more awkward than before, back under the bunkhouse, through the vines and into its hiding place behind the post. My weapon.

The dregs in all the sprayers didn't add up to more than a quarter of a full one. Would it be enough? How hard-headed would the dogs be? Would I have to keep spraying the whole way to the field, or would one good snout-full do? I'd learn the answers when I made my assault tomorrow night. Meanwhile, I needed to let my allies – Lakka's bugs and my seeds – soak so that their power would go out into water that we could spray onto our field – like spraying poison, almost, but something that would not kill the land.

I looked at the gourds hanging from the roof-beams like heavy fruit, waiting to be turned into hats, bowls, water-jugs, ladles, and – the largest ones – storage vessels for our rice rations. Before they could become useful, we had to dry them – up off the ground so that they didn't rot when the monsoon came – and then scrape the seeds out, either with our hands or, for the smaller ones, with old, stiff fibre stems. Then, the ones that would hold food or water needed to be soaked a long time to coax out the bitter taste of the gourd-rind.

At first, I dismissed the little ones, thinking they were too small to hold the amount it would take to spray our field. But then I realised that was not a problem. All I had to do tonight was to soak the seeds. Tomorrow, I could thin out the strong broth with more water, like watering down a too-thick soup.

I picked a gourd – a well-formed one with a long goose-neck – pulled it down, emptied out the foul soaking-water and rinsed it. Then I split the heated tooth-bush pods, popped out the seeds, and let them stream, along with Lakka's bugs, from my cupped hand down the slim neck into my chosen vessel. Then I refilled it with fresh water from the trough and hung it back in the same place I'd found it.

The empty husks of the tooth-bush pods went back onto the fire-pile. I looked around me to make sure I'd left no trace of the night's work. The moon was low now. Dawn wasn't far off. There wouldn't be much sleep for me tonight. I slipped silently into the bunkhouse.

As I edged past Naina's bunk, I thought I saw the gleam of two eye-shines, but when I whipped my head around to look, they were gone.

I crawled up into the dark and nestled into Lakka.

Sleep.

Rest.

The next day in the field was hard. Not enough sleep. My steps were heavy and the sprayer was heavy and the sun was heaviest of all. I barely made it through the day without toppling over.

I stumbled on the run back to the bunkhouse that evening and bloodied my knee. Lakka and Emmi helped me up and we ran on.

I dozed a little in the shade while we waited for our supper, my head lolling back against the wall of the bunkhouse. It helped a little, but still, lying down on the hard boards of our bunk that night was welcome. Too welcome – it would be so easy to sleep through until morning. But tonight was the night. I would see my field in the flesh.

Lakka told me to sleep for a while. She would wake me later.

'Moonrise,' I said.

'Moonrise,' she whispered.

'I'm going with you,' Lakka hissed like a snake in my ear.

'No. You're not. This will be—'

'This thing you've done – you don't want me to see it? You don't want me to know it with my own eyes? You're as crazy as one of your damned upside-down bugs if you think—'

'Hush, Lakka, you'll wake the others. Naina already—'

'Let 'em wake, then. I don't care. You can explain the whole scheme to them . . . or just take me along with you . . .'

'Lakka, dear heart, sister, love – no. The dogs—'

'Better with two. Back to back. Four eyes watching.'

'No.' I could feel her eyes on me in the deep black of the bunk-house. I was wavering, and she knew it – knew that I was afraid, that I wanted her with me. 'No.'

'Then how will you manage? Two sprayers, you said, right? One for the dogs and one for the field. How will you even carry them? You'll make a noise like a banging drum. Wake Naina and she'll never believe you aren't trying to escape. She'll turn you in to the Managers herself. She'll do it, you know – anything to protect the Tract. And then you'll go into that black box back at Administration, and, and, and . . . It has to be both of us. You know it as well as I do. Both. Together.'

I shut my mouth. I felt Lakka's breath on my cheek as she started to say more. But she was right. I hated to drag her along, out past the safe-line and into the night, but I did need her help.

I shrugged. Truly, I would be glad to have her with me.

Lakka would see my field.

Lakka and I stood side by side in the moonlight. The hounds strained across the safe-line, ready, rocking from side to side, snapping at each other and jostling to get close to us. We could hear their low under-the-breath whines of eagerness, see the gleam of their spit in the moonlight, smell their musky fury. They smelled us, too, our fear and maybe a hint of our resolve.

Lakka squeezed my hand and then let go so I could work the nozzle on the sprayer – I carried the tank with the poison, while she had the heavier one, filled to the top with the brew we'd retrieved from the gourd and mixed with water from the trough.

I pumped up the force inside the tank until it was tight. When I was new to the Tract, that first time I'd sprayed, the never-ending squeezing of that grip to keep the poison coming had been agony until my hands got strong. Now I didn't even feel it, but still, I used both hands on the last few pumps so the stream would jump hard and far at the dogs, not let them come anywhere near us. Tonight, poison, for once, be my friend. Help me. Keep the hounds away.

'Ready, Lakka?'

'Do it,' she said.

Hard and far, I told the stream and raked the thin line of poison back and forth across the hounds' faces. They yelped and spun and raced away.

As simple as that.

Lakka and I stepped over the safe-line and walked into the moonlight.

It had been years since I'd paced free under the stars. And to be side by side with my friend, without dozens of others pressing near – as sweet as honey, as intoxicating as palm-wine. Maybe I can be excused for relaxing too much? But it almost cost us everything.

As we got close to my field – our field, now – I heard a frail high cheeping in the night. Peepers. Tears sprang to my eyes. Could it be? Frogs already? It had been so long since I'd heard their voices. Was that all it took to bring them back – just a few months without the poison? Could things truly heal so fast? My heart sang and I cheeped back to them, one more voice in the night.

Lakka looked at me. 'Now? Out here? You've picked *this* night to finally go crazy?' She was trudging heavily, weighed down by the full sprayer on her back. It was a long way to the fields by the river.

I cheeped again. 'Don't you hear them, Lakka? The frogs? They eat bugs – any bugs. All bugs. Cutter-bugs, Lakka, cutter—'

And that's when the hound hit her.

It came from behind us, some loner without a pack to warn it about these dangerous poison-spitting walkers. It launched like a diving knife-beak, like an arrow leaving the bow, a killing thing aimed straight at Lakka's neck.

The beast hit the tank on her back and knocked her sprawling. Shrieks, snarls, and the sound of flailing thumps filled the night, dirt flying, spattering like rain. Too fast, too fast.

Or was it I that was too slow? – my hand with the nozzle coming up like something pushing through deep mud. Squeezing. The spray flying through the air, dowsing the beast.

It didn't even notice. As if I had sprinkled it with water.

The poison had landed on its back, not its face, like with the others. Not its eyes, not its nose.

Now it had something in its mouth – Lakka? – and was flinging its head from side to side like a rattle.

Lakka!

No time for thought, just Sook-Sook's words, repeated so often they were woven into me: 'Eyes, ears, balls, little sprig. The tender places. If the worst ever happens: eyes, ears, balls.'

I leaped onto the thing's rank, poison-soaked back. My father's hands guided mine to its long, hanging ears. I grabbed, I clamped on, I yanked with all the strength in my body.

The dog yelped. Its head reared up, straining to face me, but I controlled it, hauling back, holding on with fingers like claws, like talons. Hold, hold, hold!

Together, we rolled away from Lakka. I dropped my whole weight onto the beast's hindquarters. Crush it. Keep it from twisting. Keep those claws and jaws from turning. 'Neck,' I gasped. 'Lakka! The neck!'

I wrenched my two fistfuls of ear back even further, forcing the head back, arching the neck. The yelp rose to a full-throated scream.

Lakka's fingers, beautiful in the moonlight, dug into the fur under

311

the snapping chin and closed around the thing's neck. Lakka has very strong hands.

The dog thrashed longer that you would think, sharp-nailed paws tearing at the dirt while I rode it. Forever. We held on.

And then it was quiet. 'Don't let go,' I panted. 'Make sure.'

We lay there, the hound and I with Lakka crouching over us, until we were very sure. Then we dragged him to the ditch and tumbled him in. Let the cleanup-birds carry him where he needs to go. He was brave and he never gave up.

The heavy sprayer on Lakka's back saved her life, shielded her from the worst of the attack. What had so terrified me, that furious side-to-side head shake meant to break the neck of the hunter's prey – that hadn't been Lakka in its teeth, but the tube from the sprayer. The dog had treated it like it might treat any snake, whipping it back and forth until it went limp and dead.

But was our sprayer-snake dead? Had all our preparations been for nothing?

The tube had come unhitched from the little neck that anchored it at the top of the tank. With trembling fingers, I twisted it back into place and pumped up the force. At least the pump and the nozzle hadn't been crushed.

'Does it still work?' Lakka's voice was shaky now as her fierceness ebbed. I looked up at her and squeezed the nozzle.

The thing worked, more or less. Fluid came out the tubing, not in a straight, high stream but in a low, drooping arch. The dog's fangs had pierced the tube in a few places and the brew leaked out there, bleeding away the force inside. I slapped my palm over the punctures and clenched my fist. The stream strengthened, length-ened. We would be able to spray.

The night-hound's kicking feet had raked Lakka's legs badly, but the dark scratches weren't deadly deep. They weren't bleeding freely. But on the Tract, any skin-break could fester. I wished I had clean water to bathe them. I wished I had more tooth-bush seeds and a way to grind them, to make a poultice like Marak had taught me.

'Let's go,' Lakka said. 'We're wasting moonlight.' And she was right. We walked on in the dark.

Just before we got to the field, I heard the low call of a night-singer and the whir of wings above our heads.

'Listen,' I said.

Another work of power. Another sign.

Along the path, every so often, a length of massive tube, like a hollow log, had been laid in the ditches and buried under hard-packed dirt to make a sort of earth-bridge into the fields. How many times during the monsoon had we stood there neck-deep in the floodwaters, wrestling away debris that threatened to choke off the flow: mats of old fibre stems and other things, too, twigs and branches and dead things from some faraway land that still bore life.

But now, of course, during the growing season, the water was low in the ditches. Lakka and I crossed dry-footed over the water-tunnel and entered our field.

She stopped, clutching her hand over her mouth. 'Oh, Binpoy!'

'Oh', indeed. Now the field was full of life. I'd known this from my night-visits in my Other body, but to know it in the flesh, to smell it, to *feel* it, was very different.

The fibre plants sprawled everywhere, thick and disorderly, as none of us had come to thin the seedlings into straight lines. The darkness veiled any damage done by the cutter-bugs. The castor-plants had shot up tall, as agreed; soon we would be calling them trees. Young vines snaked into the bare rows we would have ordinarily weeded to annihilation. This field wouldn't just give us fibre, it would give us food – greens, berries, maybe even squash.

'Oh, Binpoy,' Lakka said again. She sounded dismayed, not excited by the thriving fullness around us. 'All that work, and now . . . this. The fibre, gone. I'm so, so sorry!' She stopped at the edge of the mass of growing things. 'It's all turned into a jungle.'

This was not a word I knew.

'What does "jungle" mean, Lakka – alive, not dead? Then yes, jungle. Big breathing, growing jungle. And the fibre is still there in the middle of it all, Lakka – it *is*. The strong plants are thriving. The weak ones are going into the ground. The twine-vine – see there, between the rows – that's making the dirt rich and strong, without us having to pay for the grow-big food from Administration. The sister-plants are distracting the cutter-bugs and . . . Oh, Lakka, don't you see? This is how a garden should be. Don't you remember? From when we touched . . .?'

'Maybe, yes, maybe I do remember a little, Binpoy. But it was all so strange, so far away, and it's fading now. But—'

'You'll see, though. We'll just give things a little help with this good medicine.' I slapped the tank on her back.

She dipped her chin slowly in that way that means 'I think you are wrong, but I'll go along', and straightened her back under the weight of the tank. 'So let's get on with it, then. There's a lot of field here and not much time. I don't want to be strolling up to the bunkhouse at breakfast and have to explain . . .' We both shuddered at the same time, and then grinned at each other.

I kept the tank of poison on my back, not to use it on our beautiful jungle-field, but to guard us against any more surprises from the night-hounds.

Spraying was awkward work now that the sister-plants had moved in between the rows. Stepping over the vines – I insisted she be careful of them – Lakka had to keep one hand pressed tight over the punctured places in the tube, which only left her one hand to work the pump and the nozzle – she couldn't switch back and forth when her muscles cramped up from squeezing like we ordinarily did. So, after a while, we traded off, with me spraying and Lakka watching over us, not just for the hounds, but for big-jaws, too, now that we were so close to the river – the young ones sometimes crawled up into the fields at this season and could tear off your foot before you could take a breath to scream. Would spraying poison in a big-jaw's face turn it away? I didn't know and I didn't find out.

We ran out of the seed-and-bug brew before we got to the river – maybe we'd sprayed too generously back closer to the ditch – and turned back toward the bunkhouse.

The moon had set a long while ago. The stars did the best they could, but it was very dark. Out on either side, packs of night-hounds moved with us, never coming close, but not ignoring us, either.

We got back to the bunkhouse before people were stirring, but just barely.

Which of the two sprayers should I keep and which to put back on the pile by the pump? I didn't want to have to deal with the punctured tube while we were doing our night-time ministrations to the secret field. But if we kept the good one and put the damaged one back, one of our tract-sisters would pick it up in the morning. She would see that it was leaking. Would report it to Sibba, who would report it to Naina, who would report it to the Managers to get a replacement.

'How did this happen?' the Managers would demand. How did this tubing come to have what are obviously, *obviously*, bite-marks.

No. No questions about a chewed-up sprayer. Sadly, I motioned for Lakka to take the good one over to the pile. I poked my head under the bunkhouse, pushing the damaged one in front of me.

As I was backing out again on hands and knees, something clamped onto my ankles and yanked me back, jerking me onto my belly. I clenched my teeth against the shocked yell that tried to escape me and kicked and struggled as something hauled me back into the starlight and flopped me over on my back.

Then my feet were free. I scrambled to get up, but something – a hard, heavy foot – drove into my belly and stayed there, pinning me to the ground.

I gasped for breath and thrashed to get up. 'Stay down.' The voice hissed like a snake.

Naina.

Naina

'Binpoy.' I let my voice do that thing that scares people. 'And Lakka, too, is it? I believe I've mentioned before that I don't like surprises.'

I stood over her for few long breaths, letting the silence gather weight and leaning hard on the foot I had in her middle. Why do they try this, even the level-headed ones like Lakka and Binpoy? Could kill us all if the Managers catch them, the Tract's credit gone in one swift flush of selfish stupidity. And they know it, too, know all about the System's 'collective responsibility' crap. Now I'm going to have to . . . Damn. But better one or two of my girls go into the black box than lose the whole lot of them to starvation.

Why do they put me in this position? People, the rest of them, have to know, have to *see* that I will not tolerate this kind of foolishness.

But what kind of foolishness were we talking about? What were these two up to? They'd walked away – but then they came back. How did that make sense?

I lifted my foot off Binpoy's stomach and resisted a strong urge to give her a good kick in the behind while she scrambled to her feet. 'Okay,' I said. 'Let's hear it.'

Pyn-Poi

Naina's fingers ground into my upper arm like jaws as she dragged me over to where Lakka stood rigid by the pile of sprayers.

'Talk,' she said.

What to tell her?

I didn't lie – *nobody* lied to Naina – but I didn't tell her everything, either. I didn't tell her about the trees, or the People, or the Real, or how I'd blended my Flow with the field, and with Lakka.

I *did* tell her that there was a field by the river – one of the ones we'd planted but then abandoned – that I'd been tending at night.

'We'll get some fibre out of it at the end of the season. I'm not sure how much, but something. Maybe it will help . . .' Naina's bright, hooded eyes studied me in the washy light. Dawn was near. Inside the bunkhouse, someone was stirring.

'Uh-huh,' she said. The morning whistle shrilled. 'We'll talk about this later. Meanwhile, you spend a little time remembering just what a lock-out feels like.'

That night, hideous nightmares of home:

My father, pale with heart-pain, pulling his hands away from a mighty trunk. 'The tree says Yes.' People around him gasp and shuffle. 'And if it is to be done,' he continues, 'then I will do it.'

The kin stand big-eyed and silent as he lifts his pruning axe and drives it into the flesh – Sook-Sook, STOP! – of our own house-tree.

Wake me up. Please, wake me up.

But the sharp wedge of knapped stone crashes against the living wood, over and over again. A low moan escapes the watchers. Escapes me.

Pariat, big-bellied with child, reaches out to Aando. Their hands meet. Saggi scrubs away tears. Aiu whimpers and is hushed.

Why can't I wake up?

My father's hands, hacking harder, faster now. He doesn't want the tree to suffer. He wants this thing to be quick.

But it is not quick, though he chops and chops, grunting with each blow as if the axe-head is cutting into his own flanks. But the tree, though it somehow understands and blesses this, does not give up its matter easily. The wound in its bark opens like a slow, sad smile as chips of wood rain down on its roots.

Sook-Sook's breathing comes harder now, more like sobs than breath. Tears and sweat smear his face. His axe-blows fall slower and bite less deep.

Then Peng lays a hand on Sook-Sook's shoulder, stops him mid-stroke, takes the axe from his fingers, steps into his place, and goes on.

Naina didn't say anything the next morning, nor later, though I could feel her eyes on us in the dark, as we slipped past her bunk each time we eased out of the bunkhouse to do our work.

We didn't have to visit the field often, not in the flesh. I would check on it in my Other body, but the sister-plants were handling things better than Lakka and I could have arranged it if we'd thought hard about it all season. Also, it was very tiring to work all day and then work again through the night. I made suggestions where I could, but mostly I just left the plants alone to do their work.

Then the grasshoppers arrived. Just a few at first, but everyone on the Tract knew what was coming. There was panic in the fields, both the day-fields and our night-field. Naina bargained with Administration for poison. Lakka and I had to get more tooth-bush seeds; for this plague, there would be no helpful dying bugs to make the others sick. Only the seeds.

This time, we simply told Naina that the Tract needed more tooth-bush. 'For our mouths,' I said. 'To keep our teeth healthy.'

She looked at me hard, and said, 'We'll see.'

That evening, she stopped our jog home from the fields, stopped it long enough for Lakka and me to snatch some plants from the bank of the ditch. The Managers shouted at us; Naina stepped up to argue with them. I didn't hear what she said – I was busy yanking at a tough young stem – but it gave us precious moments – all the time we needed.

Then Chirun was bellowing at us to get moving. But it had been enough. Lakka and I and, surprisingly, several others finished the run dragging clumps of tooth-bush behind us.

Lakka

It wasn't just the water from tooth-bush seeds that we sprayed. When the milk-flies came, the field told Binpoy that we had to soak onion-breath root and hot-berries for spraying. That brew would sting if you got any in your eyes. Binpoy said it made the leaves taste bad to the bugs.

And when the boll-worm came, we had to spray blackwater from the latrine. That was nasty, but Bin said it left some kind of bump-iness on the stems and leaves that the 'eaters' didn't like.

And it wasn't just spraying that protected our crop – lucky, because that sprayer was *heavy* and it was a long way to our night-field.

Some of the weeds, what Binpoy called 'the sister-plants', were more delicious to the insects than our precious fibre. They could help us by luring pests away. It would be better if those tasty favourites would grow at the edges of the field, not in the middle of our crop. So Binpoy said that we had to 'help them learn to grow that way'.

What she *meant* was that we had to weed. Not hacking everything up with hoes, like we did in the day-fields, but carefully, asking 'permission', pulling up and moving the plants that would 'do better elsewhere'.

So on clear nights, the moon would find the two of us – and then, later, me and the others that Naina sent to help and learn – out there crouching in the dirt, digging up young star-flowers with nothing but our fingernails, replanting green-glue plants to spread evenly through our field, and stepping over and around the twine-vine like it was precious crystal, because Binpoy said it fed the soil and strengthened the crop.

It took a lot of time, this kind of weeding. That first season, I didn't get much sleep on moonlit nights. Trust made me do it, trust in Binpoy and in the fading, blurry memory of that day she touched me and I stepped for a moment into the Real, a world of flows and strands all woven together into a lovely green lace. Gradually, I was learning to feel for that world myself, maybe not like Binpoy, but like me.

All that spring and summer, Binpoy shrivelled and shrank, as if the life in her was leaching out into the dirt and the swelling bolls of our fibre. Still she watched our field at night in that strange 'other' way of hers, keeping an eye on things, especially when bugs attacked the day-fields and slopped over onto ours.

When they came, when she saw that the hungry insects lured in by the 'all-one-kind' fields were overwhelming our frogs and birds and lizards, then it was time to spray again. We would pretend to sleep, then fill up the hidden sprayer and sneak out across the fields. The dogs didn't bother us anymore. They'd learned.

But the night work exhausted Binpoy. The sprayer weighed her down. She moved slower and slower. One night, she fell asleep so soundly that she didn't wake up when I slipped out of the bunk, so I just went alone. I sprinkled the hem of my dress with the bad stuff – just enough for the smell to remind the night-hounds' noses of the nasty dowsings they'd gotten from us in the past – shouldered the sprayer with the tooth-bush solution and handled things myself.

Bin was mad at me the next morning, said it was too dangerous – what if some new night-hound that wasn't broken in . . .

We argued about it. She tattled to Naina, who put her foot down and said someone had to go with me. So that's the way we did it from them on: Binpoy would care for the field in her 'other' body, I would go in the flesh with Chirun or, later, one of the handful of others Naina let in on our secret.

Pyn-Poi

Terrifying dreams every night now, dreams like leeches that won't let go: My family. An axe-head shattering against our house-tree, spraying shards of stone in all directions. Blood trickling down Peng's cheek where one knife-edged chip cut deep.

Now Aando chops, now Biang, then Peng again, then Jhur. A second axe breaks, then a third. Without a word, Doblang offers the smaller hatchet she uses to split fallen limbs and size them for the cook-fire.

Marak takes it.

NO!

My mother steps up to the wound in the mighty trunk that has lifted her family above the world's dangers since the Beginning, raises the axe, and strikes.

Somewhere, out toward the river, a dog yelps in pain. Shouts and furious barking rise on every side.

Heavy footfalls crash through the trees. Shrieking ululations stab through the night. Masked bodies flash into the firelight, knocking over smoking-racks, crushing traps. The kin huddles together around the wounded tree-trunk. Marak shouts at the invaders to stop, but they do not stop, these strangers who are no longer our people.

Someone kicks the fire apart. Someone scoops up the hearthstones and scatters them. Knives slash at our storage nets, dropping precious food onto the dirt to be trampled. Axes chop at our beer-gourds. The hands of people who were once our friends smash our pots and bowls.

And then they are gone. Aando shouts for the men to get their bows, but Marak calls them back. 'Let them go. What did you think? That we could become tree-killers and our neighbours would have nothing to say? Let them be. They are desperate and afraid. The old ways are all they have left.'

'Our neighbours …' I can hear the tears in Pariat's voice, and I ache to wrap my arms around her. 'But we asked them to come with us. We explained. We invited. If they stay here, they will die.'

'They can come with us, certainly, and welcome,' Marak says. 'So we will not make them enemies tonight. Here, daughter – help me with these hearthstones.'

I wake gasping.

Lakka

The night-field was ready for harvesting long before the other fields were. Maybe the sprays themselves slow down the growing. Maybe the soil by the river was better from the yearly floods that drop their rich mud onto the land. Maybe the fibre likes being near water. Or maybe it was love.

I remember, when I was a child, how my mother used to talk to the flowers she had in pots by the doors and windows of our house. Not to the vegetables that fed us, only to the flowers.

'Oh, poor baby – you need a little sip of water. There. Is that better? And you … What's the matter? You want me to take off those nasty old withered leaves? This won't hurt. See? You look better already.'

She talked to them more tenderly than she ever did to us and her flowers were the wonder of our neighbourhood. People brought sick plants to her like to a doctor. And they always bloomed under her touch. (I wonder what would have become of her children if she'd loved us as much as she loved those damned flowers?)

Binpoy loved that field the same way my mother loved her flowers, and the field loved her back. The fibre bolls popped open for her, spilling their creamy white fur, long before the other fields were anywhere near ready.

Time to talk to Naina. Harvesting the field wasn't something we could do in secret. We would need daylight and other hands to pick the tangled plants clean. We would need bags. We would need the oxcart to carry the load to the Weighmaster. Yes, there was that much fibre waiting for us.

That night, we cornered Naina out by the latrine and explained the problem. She looked ..., well, she looked like Naina always looks with a problem to chew on: Grim. Not optimistic.

'So. Do we have a story?' she snapped. 'What's our story?'

Binpoy and I looked at each other. *Our* story. Naina was with us. But what could we tell the Managers? What possible reason would make them let us go to the night field – without revealing that tractees had been traipsing around the fields in the dark? Binpoy's bony shoulders clenched into a shrug.

'Well,' I started. 'We just say we want to glean the fibre ...'

'Go on,' Naina said.

'We had to abandon the field, see, because of the sickness – too few hands ...'

'That much is true,' Naina said. 'Always good to sprinkle as much truth into your lies as possible. Makes them taste better. Go on.'

'So, we gave up on that field, but now we're scared that the harvest won't be good enough to get us through next year ...'

'Also true.'

'So we just want to take a day, just one day, to go down and glean the plants, get what we can from them before the real harvest comes in. The other fields aren't ready, anyway, so why not?'

'So we ask for bags. You think one day will do it?'

'Picking will be a lot slower, with the jungle growing between the rows,' Binpoy put in.

'But with the whole Tract working together ...'

'We can do it,' Binpoy said.

I don't know how Naina managed the Managers, but she did. They hadn't been happy about the blow their shares took when the sickness hit the Tract. I guess they saw the 'gleaning' as a way to make up some of their losses, to squeeze a little more out of us.

At any rate, one morning, after the count, they turned our run toward the river. A murmur of confusion and dissatisfaction rustled through the group – were we being taken to work some other Tract's fields? We hadn't done anything to deserve a punishment detail. Not fair. Not right. (As if anything on the Farm was ever fair or right.) Naina would never allow ... Surely not.

The run slowed; the Managers cracked some people at the rear with their dog-lashers and got it moving again, faster than before. I took Binpoy's arm and we ran together. She grinned at me, already panting, too breathless to talk.

Finally, we saw the gear-cart standing there, the ox's head drooping as if it were too heavy to hold up anymore. The back of the cart held nothing but a mound of brown harvest bags.

The run jumbled to a stop. Sibba shouted for quiet.

Naina raised her voice. 'Listen,' she said. 'It's been a bad year. Real bad. We had to pull together, dig in, really pour all that we had into just a few fields with the people we had left after ...' The women nodded.

'But our Managers have graciously allowed us to come back to this acreage we planted in the spring, to see if we can get anything out of it. So that's what we're going to do.' People were looking doubtfully at the tangled mass of green in front of them. 'I know, I know. It looks a little ... shaggy. But there's fibre in there, sure enough, and we're going to get it out. It's going to feed us, stave off a contract extension, maybe let us buy some beans, who knows? So we're going to do this just like we always do, put one foot in front of the other, and pick some fibre. Ignore everything else, unless it's good to eat. In which case, either eat it or bring it back for the pot. Looks like there might be a lot of ... *salad* out there.'

There was a ripple, not quite a cheer, at this.

'So, what are you waiting for? Step up. Get a bag. Get moving.'

Well, Binpoy was right. We could do it. We *did* do it. In spite of the vines and the weeds and Binpoy following people around, nagging at them not to step on the sister-plants and Garima getting scared out of her skin by a harmless little green snake, we did it. We brought the harvest in.

That evening, when we heaved the bags back up to Goban on the cart, they were bulging and heavy. Maybe not so full as at other times, but not bad. Not bad at all.

Even the Managers were cheerful as the cart rumbled off to the Swindlemaster. We wouldn't know how much credit we'd get for the load until Naina checked our account on our next Hygiene Visit. But it would be something. But no matter how you cut it, something is better than nothing. Especially something that didn't have any debt hanging over it for sprays or fertilisers or even tool rental.

The run back to the bunkhouse that evening was slow and easy – the Managers' good feelings, I guess, plus our own light-heartedness from having pulled our little something from nothing.

I jogged along beside Binpoy, my head swirling with thoughts about how this new way of bringing in the harvest could change things. Surely Naina would let us try again, maybe with two fields this time, or three. And it wouldn't have to be secret, so the others could learn how to do it, too. No spraying. No poisons.

'Next season,' I started. 'This will change everything.'

Binpoy wasn't smiling. I would have thought she would be smiling. But she just rested her hand on my shoulder and we ran for a while like that, connected, touching.

Pyn-Poi

Dreams of agony: I am the house-tree, fallen, divided, split open like a fruit, my branches amputated. Burning.

Slow, deep fires all along the length of me turning my heart to coal.

Then they come to me, my People, asking for something once again, with tears in their asking.

Yes, I tell them once more. Make me hollow, make me light.

So they hack and scrape away my core until there is nothing left of me but the shell that can carry them, and I say Yes.

Lakka

During that long, hot time just before the monsoon, our runs out to the fields slowed a bit, as they always did when someone was failing, until the Managers got annoyed and Naina assigned Domasa and me to 'help' Binpoy along – our arms around her waist, her arms over our shoulders, her feet barely touching the ground.

And then one morning, when the harvest from the day-fields was nearly in, Naina told the Managers that the count in the field would be down by one that day. Someone would stay in the bunkhouse. A contractee too sick to work.

I wanted to argue: No, Binpoy was fine. We'd help her. She wasn't that sick. The lump had grown – they always grow – but it hadn't broken out into the kind of ugly, seeping wound you see sometimes, raw flesh that stinks and attracts flies. That wasn't Binpoy. Binpoy

327

was strong. I wanted to shake Naina and make her understand: Binpoy would be alright.

But.

How kind would that be, insisting that my poor, tired Binpoy had to work, had to lug a heavy bag out there under the sun, just because I was too much of a coward to admit that she was leaving us? Leaving *me*.

It wasn't fair, not after everything she'd done to keep us alive, to show us the way.

Women who came in on new contracts – someday they might not have to spray, might never have the poison sting their eyes and roll down their arms. They might never get the lumps or the rashes, the patches of sick pale skin without pigment. Someday, because of Binpoy.

And Binpoy was dying. How was that fair? How was that right?

Stupid question. Stupid. Nothing in the System is fair, nothing is right – I'd been around long enough to know that. A better question might be how would I ever, ever be able to keep getting up each morning, lining up for rice, putting one foot in front of another, day after day, all without – no, that was a stupid question, too. People died. That's what we did here. People died and the Managers took them away and that was that. You went on. You just went on.

Pyn-Poi

'Big eyes,' someone said.

'One leaf is small.'

'Have big eyes for the future.'

Those voices. Familiar. Who?

Was it the trees? No, I forgot – no trees here. I dropped my head back onto the plank of the bunk and let my eyes fall shut again.

But I could still hear the voices. The trees, or the humming of the fibre, maybe, or the sweet harmonies of the sister-plants. I couldn't tell – everything was so meshed together at the root, forever-trees and fibre and twine-vine all woven into one, tight as a basket.

I cleared my throat, tried to talk to whoever was there. 'They – my kin – my mother . . . They need to know. You can reach them, root to root. Talk to my father. Please tell him. They need to know I failed. Tell him. Tell Marak I'm sorry. The System . . . I failed them all.'

'Failed? You talk like someone with feet, not roots. Nobody has failed here. You have done your part. You know what happens to seeds. If a seed never breaks open, breaks down, *breaks* – then it is not a seed, it is a stone. You are not a stone. Your father—'

But just then, Lakka broke in, her lips shushing in my ear. Told me everything was alright. Told me to rest.

Lakka

As Binpoy got sicker, she got more and more obsessed with the System. She wanted to know all about it. How old was it? Where did its powers come from? Where did it live? They had to meet; how would she find it?

How to find the System? How do you find the air you breathe?

I didn't know what to say, but I had to tell Bin something or she would twist and fidget, keep trying to get up, muttering in the strange sing-song language that none of us could understand. I would push her back, wipe the sweat from her forehead, but nothing would distract her.

So I told her about the System: About its mines, where people like us tunnel for gold or coal, or peck the cliffs for garnets and diamonds. About its factories, where people like us stand in lines all their lives to twist one screw or pound one rivet over and over again until they die. About its road-crews that flatten forests and mountains so that its goods can be carried from here to there.

Stories about the System aren't sweet or easy, not what I would choose for the deathbed of someone I love. But they satisfied her somehow, like she was finally learning something important about the world, something she needed to know. I would start, and she would lie back and close her eyes, as if to listen better. As I talked and stroked her bristly skull, that look of furious concentration would soften and she would finally rest.

Pyn-Poi

I was too slow. Is it all too late?

Does anyone still walk beneath that whispering green? Or are the forever-trees bare now, the People gone? That world below looks very far away from here, not real; our lives there small, like tiny dolls seen from some high place.

Those memories melt and mist like dreams. But that place was Real, all and only, the true and entire reason for everything I've done.

There's still so much work to do here. But Lakka will take care of it. Our field. Our fields. And she will teach the others. They can do that part now without me. But the System . . .

This body is too weak now to ever climb back down the Wall. I will never in the flesh walk back into the wild and branchy Real. I will never go home.

But sometimes, when I'm tired, wishing shakes me like a fever. If I could only make it back to the Wall, maybe, and stand there again, looking down over the edge onto that far-off boil of green.

But the System . . .

If I did stand there, I might lean out, just a little, and if I leaned, I might fall.

If I fell, I would be safe. The trees would catch me and break this flesh open. The cleanup-birds would carry me where I need to go.

But there is this still this System to deal with.

Only a dream, but still . . .

Aando standing in the shallows, clutching the rim of the great hollowed log that bobs restlessly on the Flow. Pariat is already in, balancing elegantly behind a crosswise bench packed with our children. Her feet already recognise this floating thing as home. With the long pole in her hands, she pries against the river bottom to keep the log steady while Aando helps me climb in. I settle onto a bench between Marak, with a baby on her lap, and Gai-Gai. Another woman sits on the far side of Gai-Gai; I can't really see her face, although I think I know her. She looks strong and hale but I can tell that she is very old.

Other people clamber in and find places on the benches behind us. Other logs are already out in the river, crowded with our kin and some of our neighbours who decided to flee with us after all. I even see some outclan faces I remember from River Crossings gone by. The floating thing sways and strains as if it is eager to carry us away from this poisoned place, down the Durma and into the Swamps. Where no one lives.

Where we will live.

We will live. My people will live. We will find solid ground somewhere. Or not. Maybe we will be able to fish again, once we are away from the Stink. Maybe we will invent a whole new way of being, living in these . . . things.

Don't call it a 'thing', Pyn-Poi – this is still your house-tree, the same that has sheltered your kin since the Beginning. Do not treat it like a stranger. It has simply changed its form.

What once stood tall and straight in the wind now lies flat and dances like a leaf dropped in a pool. What once was one, now is four – its trunk divided, split, and hollowed – vessels to contain my people and all we need to survive.

With a shove outward into the Flow, Aando throws himself awkwardly into the vessel, and the children laugh at his sprawling.

Lakka

She was fighting so hard, trying not to die. Stubborn. Stubborn as always.

'Binpoy, dear one, you can let go now. We'll be okay.' The words choked me, but her fingers were like little bird-bones in my hand. 'We've finished the bat-boxes, you know. They're beautiful, like bee-hives. As soon as the rains stop, we'll put them out. You've taught us what to do. Everything we need. We know how to manage this crazy weed-bird-bug thing. We can do it. No more spraying. We can bring the fibre in. And it'll work, Binpoy. I'll make it work, even without ... Maybe not perfectly, not all the time, but when you count what we'll save by not buying their damned poisons, well, we'll make out. Even when you're gone. We'll be fine. You'll see. Don't worry about us. I'll miss you ... So much you can't imagine, you know I will, but your body ... You're so tired, little sister. It's time to let go.'

'Can't.' Her breath came in gasps, ragged with effort. 'Work to do ... Feathers. The Mothers' feathers ... The System – opposite of Mother. I have to find it, make it ...' She tried to get a grip on the bunk above, to pull herself up. She was still trying to get out of bed, to get back those damned feathers of hers and get at the System.

'Oh, Binpoy – we've talked about this before. Don't you remember? You can't *find* the System. It's everywhere; it's not a person, not like you and me. It's just . . . the way things are. We call it "the System" because you've got to call it *something*, this, this . . . *thing* that owns us and bosses every minute of our lives, the contracts and Administration and the Managers and laws and courts and *everything*. It's all too big to talk about or even think about, if it doesn't have a name: this big, unbeatable power that runs everything. But it's just an idea. It isn't real, not a real person with a flesh body and a heart. It's something else.'

'Something Other?'

'That's right. Something other.'

And for some reason, this was enough for her. She settled back onto the bunk and closed her eyes with a little smile of . . . what? Satisfaction? As if she finally understood what she had to do and knew that she could do it.

Pyn-Poi

Something altogether Other. A being without flesh, ruling these people who are only flesh, without Otherness themselves.

I understand now.

I finally understand.

Lakka

She's lying on the bunk where people die. The rain is pounding on the roof like a furious child, trying to get at us, but Binpoy is quiet now. No more struggle.

Naina lets me stay with her during the day, instead of going out with the others to keep the ditches clear. 'Sisters', was all she said. But there isn't much for me to do. I keep the flies off and give her water sometimes, though I shouldn't; it just makes things take longer, Doc always said, and Binpoy is ready to go. She's ready to break out of this place and move on to wherever her people go when they die. But she's strong and stubborn. It's taking her a long time.

She begged us not to let them have her body. She wants us to lay her out in the field and let the buzzards come. I promised, and it seemed to soothe her, though I think she knew I lied. When she's done here, the Managers will just take her, like they take everyone, and plant her in a mucky hole with a shovelful of quicklime so she'll rot fast.

Pyn-Poi

Breath.

Breath.

Breath.

How did this chest get so heavy? Each lift – so much hard work.

The bathing place. My father. Teaching me how to hide underwater. So Marak cannot find us. Hold tight to this root, little twig. Take this hollow stem of float-flower. Suck air from above.

But the stem is getting longer now, Sook-Sook. Too long. Too narrow. The air too thick.

Breath.

Breath.

Breath.

I can feel the trees nearby. They know nothing useful about doing this. For once, they are silent.

Just beyond them. Others waiting. I can't see their faces yet.

Somewhere nearby, a fur-friend barks.

Aiu?

Lakka is asleep beside me. Here on the bunk where people die.

She's tired, poor thing. I start to stroke her cheek. But I forgot how heavy my arms have grown. It's okay. I can lie still here beside her. Lakka knows. Lakka will take care of them. The fields and the people, both. She knows what to do.

And so do I.

It has taken me a long time. Lakka has been trying to tell me all along. The System's many limbs, many eyes, hungry belly – these are not things of a flesh body. Not like this poor husk here that is working so hard to stay alive. Lakka always said it: Just an 'idea'. An unfleshed spider-thing stalking the Plains of the Ancestors, throwing death like an invisible web over the land and the people and the plants. 'The System can't be killed,' Lakka said.

I understand now. You cannot fight a power like that, or even *find* it, while you wear a flesh body. No. To face the System, these withered muscles and bones will have to stay behind. Here on these hard boards. The bunk where people die. I will have to lift myself up out of this worn-out flesh, stretch out my Other arms and legs. The System is waiting for me in the Other world and *that* is where we will meet.

Soon.

Or maybe now?

I am coming for you, old Long-Legs. How afraid you must be – Marak's daughter is coming.

Breath.

I sit up, feeling my Other hair streaming down my shoulders, unbound, long again and whole, my Other arms sleek and strong, my Other breasts full and unmarred. Is it time?

Breath.

I settle my Other feet on the floor and gaze down at myself. At the sight of that skeletal head pillowed there on Lakka's bony arm, a wave of tenderness wells up and floods my eyes with Other tears. Is this what it feels like to be a Mother?

Breath. One last—

I lean down to kiss my flesh body on the forehead, then lay one finger lightly across those lips. Hush, now. Be still. The work to be done now is no longer yours to do.

Rest.

The First Bridging

In Those Days, First Tree-Woman gazed at the great rivers the Ancestors sent down and saw how they sliced up the Real and divided the clans. How lonely the People are, she thought, cut off from each other by the roiling waters. She felt sorry for them, so close to each other and yet not able to trade or talk or fight or marry.

So First Tree-Woman walked among the trees, touching them and mingling with them, asking favour of their trunks and branches. And the trees consented, and arched their trunks across the rivers and twined their branches alongside these arches so the People would not slip on the moss and tumble into the dangers below.

And so the People dared to cross the waters.

And so the clans were joined and the world made whole.

THE HAPPY PALACE

Lakka

For years, back on the Tract, I dreamed about this day. I would get out, become a fine lady, then go back home with a fancy husband, rich and well dressed. I'd strut it all, right under their noses. Revenge.

Today is nothing at all like that. Those old dreams never included my feet sore and blistered from the long walk in these stiff new shoes they give you when you go. They never included the burning round scar on my cheek or this other burning, this hot, bright purpose in my chest – work to do, and the strength and know-how to do it. This is very different from any dream. This is real.

The long road from the Farm brought me here at last, to this pathetic little city, down these dry packed-dirt lanes twisting deep into this shabby, dark-side-of-town neighbourhood. Many turnings in the narrow passageways. Many stops to ask for directions. But finally I found the alley I was searching for. A coffin-maker's wares lean against a wall. An open butcher shop across the way stinks of blood and meat. People, free to come and go as they choose, squat and chatter in front of living spaces with curtains to close them off for privacy.

And here it is. Binpoy's door.

Today something is beginning.

Not that the work back on the Farm is done, of course –

Administration is always pushing for more: bigger harvests, more fields planted. Always squeezing to get just one more drop of blood out of the tractees. But the people I left behind – ours and Tallman's, too – they know what they're doing. I made sure of that.

Binpoy's way isn't simple and it never turned tract labour into an easy life. Nothing softens the blows of the sun or lightens the drag of the bags at picking time. But once Administration took notice that profits were higher without the sprays, once they made us teach the other Tracts – even the men – how to manage . . .

No more vomiting and shaking and skull-crushing headaches on spraying days. Fewer and fewer lumps and rashes and wounds that won't heal. The wasting-sickness, mostly gone now, though the old hands still fall victim from time to time. Leftovers from before Binpoy.

And more food, too – the seeds of the star-flowers that bait the pests away from the fibre. The thumb-sized yellow ground-cherries that sprawl across the rows and help keep scurvy away. The leafy green 'sister-plants' that Grenda adds to the rice-pot now, along with eggs stolen from the birds' nests – taking just one from each clutch doesn't hurt anything now that the birds are well and truly back, along with lizards and spiders and the bat-houses Bin never lived to see. I taught them everything Binpoy taught me, and some new things, too, that I figured out on my own over the years. Now it's time for the next thing.

An unlit lamp hangs over the entrance, with the words 'The Happy Palace' arching over it in frilly red script. Nothing frilly about the lock on this ancient tin door, though. Nobody's breaking into this 'palace' without some serious noise and effort.

It's a whorehouse, no question about it. Binpoy never mentioned that. Did she even know? Oh, little sister – for all your hard-headedness, so innocent, from beginning to end. Did you even understand the idea of selling yourself for money?

At one point in my life, I wouldn't have let my shadow fall across a doorstep where 'that sort' of women ply their trade. That Lakka would have fled in disgust and fear that her own precious little reputation might be soiled.

I pound on the flaking metal door.

The old Lakka is gone, long gone, tamped into the dirt with quick-lime years ago beside Pino and Korva and Binpoy and so many others. This is a new Lakka standing here at this shabby threshold, in the undyed fibre dress they put you in when you leave the Farm, with this freshly closed circle brand still raw on my cheek – half wound, half scar – showing the world exactly what sort of woman I am.

Odd that there's a kind of freedom to that. There's no door I can't step through now. No reputation to worry about. Nothing at all to lose.

He'll survive, Tallman will – I still think of him that way, like I did when they first sent Chirun and me across the Farm to teach the men: that tall man who seemed to understand things before I ever explained them, as if he had seen Bin's field in a dream or another life. Tallman's tough; he'll make it through – just two more years on his contract. He will walk away from that evil place. One by one, they all will: Chirun, Grenda, Lilon, and the rest. And when they do, I'll be waiting for them just outside the gate. What started on the Farm will not end there.

The hinges creak open. A big, fleshy woman jingling with beads stands in the shadowed hall, just a shape against the brightness behind her. Over her shoulder, I can make out a sunny courtyard with a well in the centre and a lime-tree off to the side. Someday we'll have a house with a little courtyard, too, and if it doesn't have a tree, I will plant one.

'I'm here for Binpoy's feathers,' I say. 'I understand there's a knife as well.'

And, although there is no wind, I see the leaves on the lime-tree shiver.

ACKNOWLEDGEMENTS

Uncounted millions of non-fictional people are dealing with the same enemy that Pyn-Poi grapples with in this book. I learned about the issue from one specific group of heroes in a little community called Punukula, in Andhra Pradesh, India, which found, and now helps other villages find, the same sort of freedom that Lakka and Pyn-Poi fought for. If you want to learn what this story looks like in what we laughingly refer to as 'The Real World', look up Punukula (http://www.gerrymarten.com/publicatons/pesticide-Addiction.html) and see what humans working together can accomplish. I am so grateful to Dr Gerald Marten of the Ecotippingpoints Project for connecting me with the people of that amazing village, enabling me to visit them on a Fulbright Senior Environmental Leadership Fellowship, and teaching Pyn-Poi about ecology. Gerry and Ann Marten read early versions of this novel and their contributions and encouragement were precious to me.

I regard laying down hours of your life to read a friend's wobbling early drafts as something akin to donating a kidney – generous beyond belief. Steve Brooks, another Ecotippingpoints brother; Linda Falcao; Katherine Potter Thompson; Lee Isaacson; Karen Lacey, of The Uncommon Octopus; Lynn Morgan Rosser, of The Complete Caregiver; master naturalist Scott Dean, of WNC, Naturally; Harvey Stern, of the Louisiana Purchase Cypress Legacy Project; Scott T. Barnes, of New Myths; and Susan Sachs all offered me this kindness Their sensitive questions and feedback were invaluable in helping to draw the book to its next level. My old bestie from junior high school, Kathy Panks, listened to parts of the rawest discovery drafts of this book over the phone, often on the same day they were written. (And that's *raw*, folks.) She also, over years when I often came close to abandoning ship, kept prodding me about how that rainforest girl was doing, and insisting that I had to get her out of that camp.

On the other end of the process stand the folks who put the final polish on the rough-cut manuscript. Some editors possess a sort of supernatural power to sense the shape of another person's dream and then utter the magic words that invite it onto the written page. Jo Fletcher is such a shaman and I am heart-shakingly grateful to her and to my agent, Richard Curtis, who got me to her. Then the amazing Ian Critchley juggled two worlds with two languages, along with a main character whose voice changes across time, as he delicately wreaked consistency and order on this manuscript. After Ian wrought his magic, Kay Gale's sharp proofreading eye put the final sheen on the text.

Patrick Carpenter, Keith Bambury, and Emma Embank gave us a book-cover that made me cry. Nick May produced the lovely leaf motif that orients the reading eye to scene changes in the text, and the beautiful typesetting was handled by Ian Binnie.

Ajebowale Roberts' and Mahvesh Murad's sensitive reading and feedback were invaluable. The efforts and expertise of Giuliana Caranante and Rachael Hum of Mobius ensured that Pyn-Poi's story got to American audiences; Emma Thawley's ushered it out into the wider world. Tania Wilde at Quercus held the many moving pieces together. Anne C. Perry's sure hand on the helm guided the last part of the voyage and gracefully brought the book home

For time to write without the distractions and demands of ordinary life, I owe a great debt of gratitude to the Trelex Poetry Garret, Jentel, Hambidge, Arteles, Zvona i Nari, Stiwdio Maelor, the Fulbright Foundation, and Kunstnarhuset Messen. People who want to support art and artists can do it beautifully by supporting the funding of such nurseries of creativity.

The Night Field is, in part, a memorial for two dear friends who allowed me to walk with them as cancer came into, and then took, their lives. My friends' names are Karen Ashley Greenstone and Nina Anmahian Lantis. Each reader of this book holds other beloved names in memory. I hope *The Night Field* invites you to remember absent friends and consider – and maybe reconsider – the decisions our culture is making that invite cancer into our world.

The initial inspiration for Pyn-Poi came in one of those odd random micro-videos that drift across your screen, a snippet about the tree-bridges of the Khasi people in Meghalaya, India. If you'd like to see what this brilliant architecture looks like in the real world, take a look at https://youtu.be/JoNTkprRPAo.

Everything I write owes its existence to what I learned about language from Frank Parker, what I learned about story and voice from Patricia Lee Gauch, what I learned about fantasy and science fiction from Jeanne Cavelos, what I learned about humanity from Patricia Dunbar, and what I learned about dreams from Jeremy Taylor. Jeremy's fingerprints are particularly bright on this book, as he helped me to understand that I was writing about a major trauma in human history, the moment when people stopped merely taking what the Great Mother offered and began to live out a kind of daily agricultural rape.

My farm-girl mother, Dortha Meade Williams, and my large-animal veterinarian father, Dr Donald L. Williams, not only passed on their interest in agriculture, but also their love of story and language to me. My grandmother, Nell Dowd Williams, and my great-aunt, Naomi Dowd Jameson, shared their memories of picking cotton with me; this book would never have been written without them.

Ron and Cathy Arps shared their knowledge and love of living soil with me on their beloved farm. Richard Carriere gave me the eagle, along with countless long days in swamps, marshes, and forests of Louisiana, learning to be a creature. John Slater gave me 'one hand for the tree'. Jeff Gottlieb helped me imagine just how people without metal tools could chop down a really big tree. Laurey-Faye Dean showed, and still shows me on every hike, how a person with big eyes can teach that gift to others.

A thousand thanks to fairy-godmothers Daniele Gair, Susan McGraw Keber, and Margret Avery for the secret gifts only they could give, and to Kij Johnson for telling me so firmly that this was a *big* story that would need more than one hero to carry it. The Gauchos have blessed this book with support every step of the way: Lisze Bechtold, Tara Carson, Susan McGraw Keber, Sarah McGuire, Stella Michel, Elysha O'Brien, and Joni Sensel. Weaving friends over the years have helped me understand the central place of fibre in culture, especially Susan Morgan Levielle, Cassie Dixon, Neal Howard, and Emily Burt-Hedrick. Deep thanks to the Exquisite Living circle that has been my kin and clan during The Big Weird: Connie Hanna, Julianna Padgett, Neal Howard, Diane Casteel, and Emily Burt-Hedrick.

Ultimately, though, all honour goes to the Mystery from which we all take dictation, known by many names, Source of All Story. Thank you!